The Take Charge Series
Book 1: Charlotte Lucas Takes Charge
A Pride & Prejudice Variation

By Shana Granderson, A Lady

CONTENTS

DEDICATION

This book, like all that I write, is dedicated to the love of life, the holder of my heart. You are my one and only and you complete me. You make it all worthwhile and my world revolves around you. Until we reconnected I had stopped believing in miracles, now I do, you are my miracle.

ACKNOWLEDGEMENT

First and foremost, thank you E.C.S. for standing by me while I dedicate many hours to my craft. You are my shining light and my one and only.

I want to thank my Alpha, Will Jamison and my Betas Caroline Piediscalzi Lippert and Kimbelle Pease. A special thanks to Kimbelle for her forthright and on point editing. To both Gayle Serrette and Carol M. for taking on the roles of proof-readers and additional editing, a huge thank you to both of you. All of you who have assisted me please know that your assistance is most appreciated.

My undying love and appreciation to Jane Austen for her incredible literary masterpieces is more than can be expressed adequately here. I also thank all of the JAFF readers who make writing these stories a pleasure.

Thank you to Veronica Martinez Medellin who was commissioned to create the artwork used for the cover.

INTRODUCTION

<u>The Series</u>:

The Take Charge series are all stand-alone books. There will be at least four books in the series and as they are not sequels or not connected one to the other, you may read them in any order you choose. None of the books in this series are just about the title character, but how their taking charge affects those around them.

The series tells a Pride & Prejudice Variation/Vagary tale in which one of the characters we know and love from canon takes charge and assert themselves. We see how the actions of that particular character affects the others and the trajectory of each individual tale, both known from canon and some non-canon characters.

We know Elizabeth Bennet and Fitzwilliam (William) Darcy well and how they are depicted in the original, they will not have a book in their names, but will, as it should be, feature very heavily in each of the stories where someone else takes charge.

<u>Book 1: Charlotte Lucas Takes Charge</u>:

Fanny Bennet dies of an apoplexy two years prior to the start of this story.

As in canon, the Bingleys, Hursts, and Darcy arrive in the area residing in the leased Netherfield Park. Up until the Reverend William Collins arrival, things are not far from canon. Collins is the sycophant we all love to hate and sets his sights on Jane. Bennet tells him in no uncertain terms he will not consent to such a man marrying **ANY** of his daughters.

Charlotte Lucas overhears Collins ranting to himself about how he will evict the Bennets from Longbourn the day Bennet passes. He then tried to woo Charlotte soon after and she too rejects him. He is derisive when she rejects him out of hand, he tells her that no man would ever offer for one on the shelf, without fortune, and as homely as her.

Collins then proposes to Matilda Dudley, Lizzy's friend and Longbourn's widowed parson's daughter. Matilda accepts him much to Elizabeth and Charlotte's surprise.

Collins's words to her spur Charlotte to take charge, the story tells the tale of what she does and how it affects the lives of not a few people. The book examines how Charlotte actions change the trajectories of some of our favourite (to love and hate) characters.

PROLOGUE

Bennet and his five daughters were in mourning for his wife, Fanny. His oldest was Jane, twenty, followed by Elizabeth, eighteen, Mary, seventeen, Catherine, called Kitty, fifteen, and the baby of the family, Lydia, thirteen.

After Lydia, Mrs. Bennet did not fall with child again. For years, Bennet had made sport of his wife's worry over being thrown into the hedgerows as soon as he died because she failed to deliver a son. With each successive daughter, rather than make accommodations for the future, Bennet withdrew into his bookroom and became more and more indolent.

Longbourn suffered from an entail to heirs male. Ned Collins, his illiterate and mean distant cousin, had left the mortal world, but his son was the current heir presumptive. If the son was anything at all like the father, Bennet had no desire to meet him.

That morning, when Fanny had not joined the family at breakfast, waving her lace square and bemoaning her fate, Bennet had sent Mrs. Hill up to her chambers. He was not overly concerned as sometimes his wife slept later than most.

Mrs. Hill returned, white-faced, and requested the master follow her. Fanny was cold, and her face was contorted. Mr. Hill, who served as his valet, manservant, and butler, was sent to request Mr. Jones attend him at Longbourn with all speed.

The Bennet girls knew something had happened, but Bennet was not ready to talk to them until Mr. Jones completed an examination of his wife's corpse. "I believe your wife was struck by a massive apoplexy, Mr. Bennet; it was likely over in an instant," Mr. Jones opined.

In Bennet's mind, the worry finally became too much for her, engendering feelings of guilt for making sport of her when he should have soothed her. He and Fanny were not compatible—something he only discovered after he had married Miss Francine Gardiner. Her vivaciousness and beauty had blinded him to her lack of intelligence and mean understanding.

In Bennet's mind, the fact they did not have a loving marriage did not excuse the way he used to behave toward his wife, or for that matter his daughters. Jane, always demure and serene, and Elizabeth, his favourite, were very different from his three younger daughters, who he termed the silliest girls in England. That said, he did nothing to help them correct their faults.

Elizabeth had inherited her father's love of the written word and had an insatiable thirst for knowledge. Jane was everything that a proper lady should be, and was a beauty without equal, or so her mother had often told her. Jane disliked conflict intensely, so she always tried to see only the good in any person or situation and ignored the bad. She and Elizabeth, Lizzy to the family, were the closest of sisters and friends.

Mary, the middle child, had taken to quoting scripture, most especially the drivel from Fordyce's sermons to garner attention, as she was lost in the middle of five Bennet daughters. Bennet decided it was time to start working with her, to see if he could redirect her reading preferences and put an end to her moralistic quotes.

Even though Kitty was two years older, she followed her brash sister Lydia around, and would do anything the younger decided they were to do. Lydia had been thoroughly spoiled by her mother and her behaviour reflected her belief she could get away with anything, for all she had had to do in the past was run to her mama and his wife would decide things for her no matter how wrong Lydia was.

Bennet tried to put off the delivery of the earth-shattering news longer; he had to tell his daughters, but he decided before he informed his daughters, he would summon his late wife's sister, Hattie Phillips, and her husband Frank, the town's solicitor. He also sent an express to her brother, Edward Gardiner, who lived on Gracechurch Street near Cheapside. Once the note and the express were completed, there were no more excuses for procrastination. Bennet had Mrs. Hill summon his daughters to the drawing room.

"Papa, what has happened? I saw Mr. Jones leaving, looking grim." Elizabeth asked. Bennet should have known with her perspicacity Lizzy would miss nothing. "Why have we not seen Mama today?" Elizabeth voiced the question all her sisters had.

"Please sit, girls," Bennet requested. Once they had complied, Bennet took the time to look at each of his daughters and then performed his sad duty. "I am sorry to tell you your Mama has been called home to God," Bennet stated evenly, as much as he could be calm on such a day.

The older girls hugged one another and began to sob, even Elizabeth, who had been derided and ill-treated l by his wife; nevertheless, she had been her mother. The younger two looked around, not understanding what their father had said.

"What do you mean, Papa? La, can you not talk plainly and tell me why my sisters are crying?" Lydia asked, demonstrating her lack of caring for any but herself, and that she had inherited her mother's mean understanding.

"Lyddie, Mama is dead!" Elizabeth told her between her tears.

As soon as Lydia began to wail, Kitty joined in, for she had waited to see Lydia's reaction before she showed her own. She had suspected what it was their father was telling her, but she did not want to say anything to upset or show Lydia up.

Bennet then hid in his study, with his head in his hands, his port left untouched as he heard his girls crying. As he sat in his study with the sounds of his five daughters lamenting their mother's death, he felt crushing guilt for his inaction and his decision not to alleviate Fanny's fears. He berated himself for his cowardice in not being able to face his daughters' anguish, for with each new wail his feelings of guilt increased. It was in this aspect his brother Phillips found him some minutes later.

"You have my condolences, Bennet," Phillips stated. "Hattie is with your daughters."

Bennet was not sure how much comfort his wife's sister would be. It was likely they would need more comforting than she was able to give. Hattie Phillips was like her late younger sister in many ways—mean of understanding with an insatiable love of gossip.

The Phillipses had not been blessed with children, so Hattie doted on her nieces and nephews, including the Gardiners two daughters and two sons. Bennet had always enjoyed his brother Phillips' company. They were both intelligent men who preferred more serious pursuits, although Phillips did not share Bennet's penchant for making sport of one and all.

"Have you sent a notice to our brother Gardiner?" Phillips asked.

"I posted an express to the Gardiners just before the note I wrote to you. What do I do now? I have five daughters and no wife to help look after them!" Bennet wondered with not a little self-pity.

"This is no time to wallow in your grief. You must take charge of your family, there is no choice. I do not want to speak ill of your wife, but you and I both know that she never checked your youngest. Lydia is a brash, flirtatious, uncouth girl who will ruin herself and her sisters if you do not exert yourself, Bennet. Where Lydia goes, so goes Kitty." Phillips did not sugar-coat his speech. Although he did not say it, Bennet knew Phillips meant he was as much, if not more, to blame than his late wife.

As much as Bennet wanted to refute what his brother said, he could not. But knowing what needed to be done and the doing of it were, unfortunately, two vastly different things.

~~~~~~~/~~~~~~~

The Lucas family were the closest friends the Bennets had near Meryton. Lady Sarah Lucas had grown up with the former Miss Fanny Gardiner and they had always been friends, while at the same time rivals. The then Miss Sarah Warrington had also set her cap for the son of one of the principal land-owners in the area, only to watch her friend capture Thomas Bennet and walk up the aisle with him at St. Alfred's Church in Meryton.

The two, along with Hattie Phillips, were the principal gossips in the area. Sarah Warrington had settled for William Lucas, the owner of the general store in Meryton. She had hated how Fanny had lorded over her because she married to a landed gentleman while Sarah married a tradesman.

About twenty years ago, when their oldest son, Franklin, was seven, Charlotte five, and John two, Sarah was with child, resulting in the birth of Nick some six months later. Her husband then held the largely ceremonial title of Mayor of Meryton. King George III and Queen Charlotte had stopped in the town. Mayor Lucas had addressed the monarchs, and, for some inexplicable reason, the King knighted William Lucas.

Suddenly, they were Sir William and Lady Lucas, something her friend and rival had never lived down. Sir William was enamoured with his new title, especially after his investiture at St. James Palace, which is a tale he recounted as many times as he could to any who would listen.

Because of his new rank, Sir William decided he should not be a tradesman any longer. He sold his business and house in Meryton and purchased a small estate adjacent to Long-bourn, which he renamed Lucas Lodge. Although he was worse off financially, he cared not, for he was a landed gentleman and a knight!

The last Lucas to arrive was Mariah, who was not yet fourteen, right between Kitty and Lydia Bennet in age and a close friend to both. Charlotte, who was five and twenty, was the intimate friend of the oldest two Bennet daughters but was somewhat closer to Elizabeth.

The Lucas family had just broken their fast when a groom from Longbourn delivered a black-edged notice from the Bennets. All thoughts of rivalry were forgot in an instant when Lady Sarah Lucas read about the passing of her friend Fanny Bennet.

Not long after, notices were delivered to the Goulding and Long families, both close to the Bennets. Once the notices had been delivered it was not long before all the neighbourhood was aware Mrs. Francine Bennet was no longer among the living.

As soon as Charlotte prepared herself, she made for Longbourn as fast as her legs could carry her to go condole with her friends. At five and twenty, Charlotte, unlike the Bennet sisters, was not romantic and knew she was considered *on the shelf*. With an almost non-existent dowry, she was aware her chances of marriage were slim to none. She had resigned herself to that fact and planned to make the best of her life as a spinster. She would find a way not to be a burden to her family even if that meant taking the position of a governess or companion.

~~~~~~~/~~~~~~~

The Gardiners arrived before sundown, for they had departed Gracechurch Street within an hour of Bennet's express. Edward Gardiner was the youngest of the three Gardiner siblings, and the opposite of his sisters in temperament and intelligence.

After Oxford, rather than take over his father's law practice in Meryton, the one his brother Phillips now ran, Edward sought employment with an import-export company in London. The owner, who had no children or relations, retired, and sold the business to Gardiner at a price he could afford—which was a fraction of the actual value of the company. Edward renamed the business Gardiner and Associates to honour the original owner. Within five years he had built a thriving business with a healthy income.

Gardiner had tried to convince his brother Bennet to

allow him to invest Longbourn's profits and his sister's five-thousand-pound dowry, but up to that point Bennet had done nothing—it was too much trouble and the effort would have taken him away from his beloved books. After a few years of wasting his breath, better conserved to cool his porridge, Gardiner dropped the issue.

Some eight years ago, Gardiner had married Madeline Lambert. Her father was the rector of the church in Lambton, Derbyshire. They were blessed with four children, two sons bracketed by two daughters. For this trip, the children remained home with their governess and nursemaids, as it was a sombre occasion.

When Aunt Maddie entered the drawing room, her two oldest nieces fell into her arms. She had always been closest to Jane and Elizabeth, who she treated as surrogate daughters before her own oldest, Lilly, had been born.

Charlotte Lucas looked on as her two friends cried on their aunt's shoulder. She wished there was more she could do for her friends, but she knew just being there and supporting them was healing for Jane and Eliza. Charlotte and her family were the only ones who called Elizabeth Eliza rather than Lizzy.

As it was becoming warmer, it was decided the funeral would be on the morrow. Charlotte and the three oldest Bennet girls helped write notices to the members of the local community announcing the date and time of the funeral service, which would be held at Longbourn's church, with the interment in the family plot directly following.

~~~~~~~/~~~~~~~

"Charlotte, I feel guilty for all the times I participated in making sport of my mother with my father. Now I will never be able to beg her forgiveness," Elizabeth moaned as she sat with her friend while the men were at the church for the funeral and interment.

"Eliza, reproaching yourself will change nothing. Besides, you told me it was only done in the privacy of your father's study. Unlike him, you never showed disrespect for your mother publicly," Charlotte pointed out.

"I suppose that is true," Elizabeth allowed, through a watery smile.

"You loved your mother as I know she loved you, even if she had a hard time showing her love at times. I know it is but two days since your mother passed, Eliza, but what is it you are always telling the rest of us?" Charlotte asked her eyebrows raised.

"Only think about the past as the remembrance gives you pleasure?" Elizabeth returned.

"Now is the time for mourning, but life has to carry on. Once you have mourned your mother as she deserves to be mourned, you will live by that credo once again," Charlotte assured her grieving friend.

"It is hard to see moving past this now, Charlotte, but I dare say you have the right of it—in time," Elizabeth allowed.

"Who will push you and Jane to get married now?" Charlotte tried to raise her friend's spirits.

"I am sure Aunt Phillips will take up that particular mantle," Elizabeth smiled, although it did not get close to reaching her eyes.

"Has anyone written bad poetry for Jane lately?" Charlotte asked, trying to get Eliza's mind off her grief, even if for a short while.

"Not since Mama, may she rest in peace, ran Mr. Jeffries off; there has not been another. It is just as well, as Jane felt no inclination toward the hapless man," Elizabeth remembered. Their mother had pushed Jane out at fifteen, reasoning her security would be assured if she got her daughters married well as soon as might be.

The Jeffries had leased Netherfield Park, and the son had been chosen by Fanny Bennet as Jane's future husband. At first, he had been interested and had written Jane some of the worst poetry either Jane or Elizabeth had ever read. His parents were disgusted at the relentless campaign waged by Mrs. Bennet and left the area, son in tow. Mrs. Bennet had complained they used Jane ill. No one ever told her the real reason the Jeffries abandoned the neighbourhood was her and her vulgar behaviour.

As Elizabeth and Charlotte remembered the occurrence, Elizabeth acknowledged her mother had been a singular character. Luckily, even if Aunt Phillips tried to fill the office of matchmaker for her nieces, she did not live at Longbourn.

~~~~~~~/~~~~~~~

Two days later, Gardiner and Phillips were meeting with Bennet in his study. "Will you at long last allow me to help build up some capital for my nieces' future?" Gardiner asked.

"Take the five thousand pounds from Fanny's dowry and do what you will with it," Bennet waved his wrist in his brother Gardiner's direction. "If there are profits, I will send them to you also."

Gardiner was sure Bennet would forget his resolution as soon as he and his wife departed Longbourn, but at least he had his late sister's dowry to work with. Unknown to Bennet, his two brothers had decided they would add principal as well so their nieces would have something when needed. It would not be an enormous amount, but it would be better than the one thousand pounds they each had now.

"What will you do about the girls' education?" Phillips asked.

"The same as we do now. They are free to learn that which interests them," Bennet waved the question off.

His brothers knew talk of him stepping up had been just that, talk. They were sure he would closet himself in his book room and the work of running the house and caring for his younger daughters would fall to his two oldest. They did not push Bennet. They would revisit the subject after allowing him time to mourn his wife in peace.

As much as his wife and her attacks of nerves had often disturbed his peace in the house, Bennet admitted to himself that the house was too quiet now. He accepted the truth; he did not know what he had until it was gone.

The following day, the Gardiners returned to London and their children, leaving the six Bennets alone in the house to mourn. Many of their neighbours and friends visited to condole with them, but the one constant was the almost daily presence of Miss Charlotte Lucas, much to her friends' pleasure.

CHAPTER 1

October 1810

It had been a little more than two years since Mrs. Bennet's demise, and life had indeed gone on. Unfortunately, Bennet's resolve to assert himself over his younger daughters did not last long, and the two youngest, now seventeen and fifteen, were as badly behaved and vulgar as they had ever been, with nothing but redcoats on their minds. Jane and Elizabeth had tried to curb Lydia, knowing full well success with her meant Kitty would fall in line as well, but without their father's support, nothing changed.

The one change Bennet had been able to make was with Mary. At Elizabeth's suggestion, he had started to pay her attention and work with her. She had blossomed under his direction, revealing he had three intelligent daughters. It had been almost two years since Fordyce's sermons had been opened or any moralistic quote had crossed Mary's lips.

Netherfield Park had been let at last in September, after standing empty for some years. The new tenant was the wealthy son of a tradesman who was following his late father's charge to ascend to the ranks of the gentry. His name was Mr. Charles Bingley. He was accompanied by his two sisters, Miss Caroline Bingley, who would act as his hostess, and Mrs. Louisa Hurst, his older sister. Louisa's husband, Mr. Harold Hurst, and Bingley's friend, Mr. Fitzwilliam Darcy, made up the balance of the Netherfield Park party.

The day the Bingley party arrived to take up residence, there was a quarterly assembly in Meryton. Mr. Darcy was proud, aloof, and haughty the whole night, refusing to be introduced to any of the locals; then, he insulted Elizabeth Bennet within her hearing.

His friend had tried to convince the taciturn man to dance and suggested Elizabeth as a partner. She was sitting out a set to allow others their chance to dance. Mr. Darcy barely looked at her and pronounced she was 'not handsome enough to tempt' him and added that 'he would not give consequence to women slighted by others.' From that instant, the name Darcy had been disliked by all in the neighbourhood.

After that, Elizabeth Bennet hated the very sight of Mr. Bingley's friend, even before Mr. Wickham, a handsome and charming gentleman of the Derbyshire Militia, shared his tale of the perfidy of Mr. Darcy. The tale Mr. Wickham's related to her in September, just after Darcy's insult at the assembly, reinforced her already negative opinion of Mr. Darcy.

Charlotte had pointed out the impropriety of the lieutenant's disclosures to Elizabeth after such a short acquaintance, and the many contradictions and inconsistencies in his tale of woe, but Elizabeth was not open to logic. She accepted his story as the truth, as it fit the narrative in her mind about the dastardly Mr. Darcy. How could it not be so, with such a pleasant countenance as Mr. Wickham had?

The Netherfield party attended a few events in the neighbourhood, the last one at Lucas Lodge where Elizabeth had noticed Mr. Darcy always stood near her or stared at her. She was certain he looked to find fault, while Charlotte believed her friend was wrong about the reason Mr. Darcy always looked at her. That night Elizabeth refused to dance with the proud, disagreeable man. It was also the night she noticed, for some unfathomable reason, Miss Bingley took a decidedly negative view of her and would use any opportunity she had to denigrate the second Bennet daughter.

~~~~~~~/~~~~~~~

The only thing of interest besides the Netherfield party and all the Redcoats was the receipt of a most *interesting* letter from the heir presumptive of Longbourn, Mr. William Collins.

Bennet called Elizabeth into his study and read it to her:

8 October 1810

Hunsford Parsonage
Near Rosings Park, Westerham, Kent

Dear Sir,
I offer my condolences on the passing of your esteemed wife. I still suffer from the loss of my dear parents.

The disagreement subsisting between yourself, and my late honoured father always gave me much uneasiness, and since I have had the misfortune to lose him, I have frequently wished to heal the breach. For some time, however, I was kept back by my own doubts, fearing lest it might seem disrespectful to his memory for me to be on good terms with anyone with whom it had always pleased him to be at variance.

"Who writes in such a fashion; he must be insensible!" Elizabeth opined. Her father nodded, much diverted by the letter.

My mind, however, is now made up on the subject, for having received ordination at Easter, I have been so fortunate as to be distinguished by the patronage of the Right Honourable Lady Catherine de Bourgh, widow of Sir Lewis de Bourgh, whose bounty and beneficence has preferred me to the valuable rectory of this parish, where it shall be my earnest endeavour to demean myself with grateful respect towards her ladyship, and be ever ready to perform those rites and ceremonies which are instituted by the Church of England.

As a clergyman, moreover, I feel it my duty to promote and establish the blessing of peace in all families within the reach of my influence, and on these grounds, I flatter myself that my present overtures are highly commendable, and that the circumstance of my being next in the entail of Longbourn estate will be kindly overlooked on your side, and not lead you to reject the offered olive-branch.

"Olive branch! Papa, please tell me this man does not

think he is to marry one of us!" Elizabeth was horrified at the thought.

"I will not allow that, I promise you, Lizzy," Bennet soothed his daughter.

I cannot be otherwise than concerned at being the means of injuring your amiable daughters and beg leave to apologise for it, as well as to assure you of my readiness to make them every possible amends—but of this hereafter. If you should have no objection to receive me into your house, I propose myself the satisfaction of waiting on you and your family, Thursday 25 October, by four o'clock, and shall probably trespass on your hospitality till the Friday sennight following, which I can do without any inconvenience, as Lady Catherine is far from objecting to my occasional absence on a Sunday, provided that some other clergyman is engaged to do the duty of the day.

I remain, dear Sir, with respectful compliments to your daughters, your well-wisher and friend,

William Collins, Reverend by the beneficence of Lady Catherine de Bourgh

"Papa, I know you want to laugh at him, but please promise you will protect us and not leave him alone with us!" Elizabeth sought reassurance.

"I will have my sport, but he will not be allowed to be alone with any of you, and I will send him to Mr. Dudley as much as I am able. I am sure he will enjoy the company of a fellow parson," Bennet averred.

~~~~~~~/~~~~~~~

The Monday after receipt of Mr. Collins' letter, Jane, who had been asked to dance twice at the assembly and then again at Lucas Lodge by the amiable but puppy-like Mr. Bingley, had been invited to have dinner with Miss Bingley and Mrs. Hurst. Elizabeth had dubbed them 'the *supercilious sisters*' because they thought themselves superior to all in neighbourhood, conveniently forgetting they were from trade.

The carriage horses were being used on the farm. Jane

almost cancelled due to the oncoming storm, but instead she rode Nelly to Netherfield, hoping to arrive before the rain. She had been caught in a prodigious downpour and had taken ill; a note advising them of her condition had been sent to Longbourn that night.

The next morning, Elizabeth walked the three miles to Netherfield Park, with no care for how much mud was on her petticoats; all she wanted was to make sure her Jane was well. Since their mother's death, all of them, including Lydia, were worried when any of them succumbed to illness.

To her chagrin, when she arrived at Netherfield, the first person she saw was the proud, disagreeable Mr. Darcy. "Please show me to my sister," Elizabeth asked curtly, and without preamble.

"Follow me, please," Mr. Darcy set off towards the manor house.

Unfortunately, on hearing voices from the breakfast parlour, Elizabeth could not be so rude as to ignore Mr. Bingley and his sisters, entering the parlour to greet them quickly.

"Welcome, Miss Elizabeth," the ever-affable Mr. Bingley greeted Elizabeth.

"I apologise if I am disturbing your meal; I am merely here to check on my sister. Ever since our mother passed away, we are extremely careful when any of us fall ill," Elizabeth explained.

As much as she wanted to, even Miss Bingley could not make a caustic comment at that. Mr. Darcy, having lost both his parents, easily understood the sentiments expressed. The housekeeper was summoned, and Elizabeth Bennet was shown to her sister's room.

As soon as she was out of the breakfast parlour, Miss Bingley gave full vent to her vitriol against Miss Elizabeth, snickering with her sister about Miss Eliza's petticoats. "You would not allow your sister to walk three miles to attend Miss Bennet, would you Mr. Darcy," Miss Bingley cooed.

"No, I would not allow her to walk that distance to visit

Miss Bennet," Darcy replied leaving the woman confused as to his meaning.

"I am sure her eyes do not look so fine to you any longer," Miss Bingley gave her sister a conspiratorial look.

"Actually, they showed an uncommon brightness from the exercise, and the sisterly affection she displayed is to be commended. It is a pity more ladies do not do such for others without guile," Darcy replied.

As they usually did, Miss Bingley's caustic comments ended up hurting none but herself.

~~~~~~~/~~~~~~~

Elizabeth found Jane was better than she had feared. While she did have a fever, it was not overly high. Mr. Jones had been and gone and had left some draughts for the patient. It was heartening to see her dearest sister was not as ill as she had been when suffering with colds in the past.

"I should not have ridden, Lizzy, but I had accepted the invitation and did not want to cancel. I hope Mr. Bingley does not think I contrived this to see him after he and the gentlemen returned from dinner with the officers," Jane coughed after her long speech, and Elizabeth brought a glass to her lips to allow her sister to drink to lubricate her dry scratchy throat.

"You could have cancelled, Jane, but it is not who you are. And there is naught to do about it now, so get better and I will see you on the morrow," Elizabeth gave her sister a kiss on the forehead.

"Lizzy, please do not leave me," Jane begged.

Elizabeth could never deny her sister anything, even though the man she detested was in residence. She was about to go find Mr. Bingley to convey her sister's request when the man obliged her by knocking on the door. After making sure Jane was adequately covered, Elizabeth allowed Mr. Bingley entry.

As soon as he heard Jane's request, Mr. Bingley extended an invitation to Miss Elizabeth without delay. When he relayed the information to his sister, Miss Bingley was most ungracious in receiving the news, though a groom was quickly dispatched to Longbourn to have a trunk for each sister sent.

After eating her dinner on the tray which had been sent up, Elizabeth made her way to the library once she was assured Jane was asleep. She found a book and was about to leave, when none other than Mr. Darcy walked in. While she was cursing her bad luck, he was admiring her pleasing face and figure. Elizabeth gave a quick curtsy and took off before he could react or speak.

Darcy was further impressed. Rather than try and take advantage of them being alone, Miss Elizabeth had immediately left to preserve propriety. He was certain had it—heaven forbid—been Miss Bingley, she would have screamed compromise to the skies, not that it would have helped her.

Elizabeth escaped as fast as her feet would carry her as she could not countenance spending any more time in the company of the dastardly Mr. Darcy than she was forced to do. She thanked her lucky stars she found a book before the man entered the library.

Jane was more than well enough to return home by Wednesday and denied Mr. Bingley's entreaty to remain another day. Even Jane, who chose to ignore someone's faults, could not overlook the duplicitous side of Miss Bingley, and realised she was no friend. She was also aware of Elizabeth's distaste of being in Mr. Darcy's company, so she was unwilling to subject her dearest sister to suffering him further.

A note was sent to Longbourn requesting their father send the carriage, and three hours later, it was waiting for the sisters in front of the manor house. The Netherfield party were all present to see them off, even Mr. Darcy. Elizabeth knew Miss Bingley was happy to see the back of them, and she was reasonably sure the same was true for Mr. Darcy, who never ceased looking at her to find fault.

She had done everything in her power the night before not to give him a set down when the proud man had mocked her when he had listed extensive reading as a requirement for an accomplished woman. Insufferable man!

~~~~~~~/~~~~~~~

Even Kitty and Lydia were in front of the house to welcome the returning sisters home. It was good to be home and away from the objectionable people at Netherfield Park.

Charlotte visited that afternoon, and Elizbeth was not happy when her best friend told her that in her opinion she was wrong, Mr. Darcy had not mocked her, and men did not look at a woman to find fault. If he thought something along those lines, he would not look at her at all. Charlotte posited it was the opposite reason he stared at Elizabeth.

"Are you foxed, Charlotte? What nonsensical drivel! Mr. Darcy admires me? I would sooner call Miss Bingley a wit!" Elizabeth tried to claim.

"Normally you like to consider all sides of an argument, so why is it you refuse to do that with Mr. Darcy? Remove his insult and the residual resentment you refuse to release, and then tell me honestly, would you see things the same way? You pride yourself on honesty, Eliza, so be honest now," Charlotte challenged her friend.

Elizabeth, at some level, knew Charlotte was correct. Her ego had been bruised by Mr. Darcy's comment, and if she allowed herself to acknowledge it, she would have to admit she went out of her way to discover any information which reinforced her bad opinion of the man.

A seed of doubt started to creep into her mind as far as Mr. Darcy was concerned. As much as she disliked being proven wrong, she was starting to see the possibility of it; she continued to fight against the inclination to admit she was wrong—yet.

"Mayhap Mr. Wickham's disclosures were not appropriate, but does that mean they were not true?" Elizabeth asked, trying more to convince herself than Charlotte.

"Eliza, you are too intelligent to ask such a question. All you have is one side of the story. Neither you nor I have any idea about the truth of Mr. Wickham's assertions, but you, my friend, accepted them as gospel because you wanted to! Until you have heard Mr. Darcy's side, you simply do not know," Charlotte asserted.

"You always were the sensible one among us, Charlotte," Elizabeth admitted.

~~~~~~~/~~~~~~~

While the two friends were talking, Bingley reached a decision. "We will hold a ball to thank our neighbours for welcoming us to the neighbourhood so graciously," Bingley stated.

"You cannot be serious, Charles!" Miss Bingley screeched. "You would invite a bunch of country bumpkins with no fashion and who are far below us to our house?"

"I say, Darcy, since when are landed gentlemen and women below tradesmen's children? I must have missed that lesson at Oxford," Hurst drawled.

Miss Bingley went purple and was seething with rage, now directed at her brother-in-law. Normally, the drunken lout was asleep, but he just happened to be awake and not only pointed out their damnable ties to trade, but in front of Mr. Darcy no less.

"Things have not changed, Hurst. Landed gentlefolk are definitely above those from trade," Darcy replied evenly. He was too polite to highlight Miss Bingley's pretentions directly to her. In this case he was only answering a question put to him, it would have been rude not to answer, after all.

"As I said, we will plan a ball for a fortnight hence. I am sure there will be enough white soup by then," Bingley decided.

"But Charles, you know some of our guests may not enjoy a ball," Miss Bingley looked at Darcy as her colour started to return to her normal pasty pallor.

"If you mean Darcy, he may stay in his bedchamber if he does not want to participate," Bingley waved his sister's concern away. "You are always talking about your skills as a hostess; is this not the perfect time to show one and all that you are, in fact, a good hostess?"

Miss Bingley decided she would put on the best ball ever

seen, and then Mr. Darcy would finally see she was the ideal person to be the mistress of Pemberley and Darcy House. "Yes, I suppose it would be good to show these country mushrooms how a real hostess puts on a ball. Come Louisa, let us go make our plans," Miss Bingley preened.

After the ladies departed, the men retired to the billiards room and enjoyed their brandy as they challenged each other.

~~~~~~~/~~~~~~~

George Wickham was thankful he had chosen not to attend the dinner with the gentlemen of the neighbourhood, as Darcy had attended. So far, he had seen his nemesis a few times, but had not been seen.

How he had enjoyed plying Miss Elizabeth Bennet with his tale about Darcy; whatever the prig had done made her susceptible to his story, he neither knew nor cared. It had not taken him long to see she was far too intelligent to be seduced, but her flirtatious younger sisters were another story.

Wickham was sure he would be able to bed the youngest Bennet, and her sister who followed her like a lamb, without too much trouble. Miss Lydia would believe anything he told her, which he suspected meant so would Miss Kitty. His tried and true 'if you love me, you will not make me wait until after the wedding' line had worked on many a young, impressionable maiden.

As they were gentleman's daughters, he would have to be careful. From what he could tell, the Bennets were well respected in the neighbourhood. They would be ones to pluck just before he left, which would be once there were demands for payment of his debts, already high.

If only Darcy had not arrived in Ramsgate early, he would have plucked mousy Georgiana Darcy and had her fortune of thirty thousand pounds. Damn Darcy for spoiling his plans yet again! Rather than turn him over to his cousin, Darcy had sent him on his way with a flea in his ear, warning him never to speak of Miss Darcy again. Darcy had added some nonsense about both he and his cousin the colonel having to approve ahead of time the release of his sister's dowry.

The cousin was a man Wickham truly feared. He was more than frightened of Colonel Richard Fitzwilliam, as he knew that the Colonel would run him through without hesitation. Luckily, Richard Fitzwilliam was in the Dragoons, so he was on the Continent; Wickham was safe here in England to do as he pleased.

CHAPTER 2

On Thursday at exactly four, a hired gig pulled up under the portico in front of Longbourn. Elizabeth had gone for a walk an hour earlier and saw the same gig parked in the lane. She had mentioned seeing it to her father, who looked at her, sporting a huge grin; she gave him a half nod and tried to keep her composure as.

"William Collins at your service, Cousin Bennet." The man bowed low, and his hand made a flourish with his hat revealing a balding crown. What hairs were present were extremely greasy.

He was about Bennet's height but had a portly midsection bordering on corpulent. If the odour emanating from the man was any indication, he did not bathe daily. There was no missing how he leered at the five Bennet daughters, especially the oldest one. He had never seen a woman to match her beauty.

"Welcome to Longbourn, Mr. Collins," Bennet welcomed the unwelcome visitor.

"Would you introduce my fair cousins to me?" Collins asked, displaying his want of manners and lack of knowledge of protocol.

"My oldest, Miss Jane Bennet." Collins tried to plant a slobbering kiss on the lady's hand, but she withdrew it before he was able to. "Miss Elizabeth," Elizabeth made sure her hands were behind her, as did the other three, "Miss Mary, Miss Kitty, and Miss Lydia," Bennet named his daughters.

"What elegance and beauty in one place..." Bennet cut his loquacious cousin off.

"I am sure you are tired from your travels, Mr. Collins, and are in want of a *bath*. We will meet in the drawing room at half past five." Bennet shepherded his daughters into the house before the man could close his jaw, which was hanging open.

Once the spluttering man was led upstairs by Hill, to the guest chamber farthest from his cousins, Elizabeth followed her father into his study. "Papa, that ridiculous man was waiting in the lane so he would arrive at the time he said! What did he think would happen if he arrived early? Was he worried it would cause Armageddon and the world would come to an end?" Elizabeth was stupefied by the man who had presented himself at their door.

"From his letter, he venerates his patroness as if she were equal to God Himself. I am sure we will find out in due course that she impressed the need for punctuality on the man, as I expect she will be a large part of any of his conversation."

"Will we have to put up with him for a full sennight, Papa?" Elizabeth asked.

"Unfortunately, as we accepted him as a guest, it would not be good form to expel him early unless he does something which warrants such an action," Bennet explained. "Please convey to your sisters my desire that none of them are ever to be alone with him. I would prefer three of you together with him and, if possible, with a servant present."

"I will make sure my sisters are aware of your wishes. Do you think he would try to compromise one of us otherwise?" Elizabeth asked, not wanting to believe a man of the cloth would resort to such behaviour.

"Did you not see the way the man drooled when he looked on all of you and for far too long, especially our Jane? With the look I spied, I would rather not leave things to chance, Lizzy," Bennet clarified for his daughter. "I do not know the man well enough to know if he has any vicious propensities. Given his mix of pomposity and sycophantic behaviour, I fear he thinks his status as a parson and the beneficiary of Lady Catherine de Bourgh's largess makes him above the rules which apply to the rest of us. It may be necessary to point out to him the fact that a parson is below a landed gentleman and that of a gentleman's daughter, as he seems to revere rank."

"Papa, you remember I told you about Mr. Wickham's disclosure to me, and you urged me to think critically?" Elizabeth changed the subject.

"I do, my child. Have you reconsidered your strongly-held opinions, biases perhaps?" Bennet asked. As much as he loved his second daughter, he was not blind to the fact she became very stubborn, especially when one slighted her as Mr. Darcy had done at the assembly.

"Charlotte pointed out the impropriety of Mr. Wickham's disclosure to me, and the fact I only have one side of the tale. It is possible I was prejudiced against Mr. Darcy and allowed it to colour my opinions—a little," Elizabeth owned.

"I knew there was a reason I always liked Miss Lucas; she has a good head on her shoulders, that one! I am happy she was able to get you to look at your opinions and re-evaluate them," Bennet told his daughter.

"It has not changed the fact I dislike the man and think him proud and disagreeable, but I am willing to own I may not know the full story," Elizabeth admitted.

~~~~~~~/~~~~~~~

"Mrs. Nichols has informed me we will have more than enough white soup by the end of the month, so I have decided the ball will be on Thursday coming, the first day of November," Bingley informed the Netherfield party.

"I still say this is casting pearls before swine! How will a group of country nobodies so far..." Miss Bingley checked herself to avoid that lout Hurst reminding her, and more importantly Mr. Darcy, of her actual status again. "I mean, all my efforts for those who do not have the class to appreciate it."

"As long as I get to dance with Miss Bennet, I do not care about anything else. She is an angel," Bingley opined. "I have never before beheld such beauty."

"You cannot be serious, Charles! Did you hear nothing of what Louisa and I told you of her connections! One uncle a country solicitor and the other a *tradesman* who lives in Cheapside," Miss Bingley whined.

"I would not care had she enough relations to fill Cheapside!" Bingley insisted.

"What your sister is trying to say is the family's connections materially lessen the chances of the Miss Bennets making a good match," Darcy added, trying his best to push the image of a pleasing figure and fine eyes out of his mind. This would not do; how could he, a Darcy of Pemberley, and a scion of earls, be infatuated with a country miss?

"You see, Charles, Mr. Darcy agrees with me," Miss Bingley preened. She looked at Darcy like a cat who caught a canary. "When you marry, you need to marry someone of the rank of say—dearest Georgiana, who will raise the status of our family."

Darcy just stopped himself from giving the shrew a set down. It was not the first time she had tried to intimate her brother would marry his baby sister, who was still a few years from being out! Not only that, but the woman also ignored the fact that her brother's marriage would do nothing to raise *her*. Only her own marriage would do that, if, in fact, someone was willing to marry her. It would never be him; he had told Bingley that even if she compromised him, he would not offer for the woman.

"I will deliver the Bennets' invitation personally on the morrow!" Bingley asserted. He and Darcy left the drawing room and made for the study.

"She smiles too much; you know that Bingley, do you not?" Darcy told his friend as they seated themselves in the study. Darcy was appreciative Bingley was cognizant of the fact his friend disliked spending time with Mrs. Hurst and Miss Bingley, particularly the latter.

"Who smiles too much?" Bingley asked.

"Miss Bennet. She is a beautiful woman; I will not deny that, but your sister, as much as I hate to agree with anything she says, is correct that she does not have the connections to help raise you up," Darcy pushed.

"I care not; she is an angel!" Bingley stated.

Bingley always followed the advice his older friend gave him. Darcy decided he would observe the woman closely, so if he noticed anything of concern to his friend, he would direct the biddable Bingley in a different direction.

~~~~~~~/~~~~~~~

Dinner was an interesting meal at Longbourn. Throughout the meal, Mr. Collins constantly praised his patroness to the sky, whether his mouth was full or not. Unfortunately for the Bennets and Miss Lucas, the man had not used the bath which had been prepared for him. Due to his odour and uncouth mannerisms, the meal was spoilt for all except the man himself. Elizabeth had invited Charlotte to come witness the man for herself, as she was sure her friend would think her exaggerating otherwise.

"To which of my dear cousins am I to thank for this splendid meal. It is to their credit they are so skilled at cooking. As my patroness always says..." Bennet cut the fool off before he could launch into another soliloquy about his revered patroness.

"We have a full complement of servants at Longbourn, Mr. Collins, including a cook!" Bennet retorted with evident frustration. Bennet had quickly realised the entertainment value did not come close to outweighing the annoyance factor his cousin caused.

Collins placed his hand over his mouth, as they all wished he would when his mouth was full of food to hinder his spraying it around liberally as he talked. "I did not mean to offend, Cousin," Collins stated contritely.

Thankfully the meal was over, so the females were able to abandon the dining parlour and their father with all speed. They needed to escape both the odour and the idiotic man's ridiculous pronouncements. Even Mary, who had been predisposed to like the man as he was a clergyman, could not bear to be in his company.

"Eliza, it is good that you invited me. Had I not witnessed

it for myself, I would never have believed anyone could behave as this man does. I would have been sure you were exaggerating for your own entertainment! I pity whoever the lady is who ends up tied to that man," Charlotte stated in wonder.

Jane and Eliza, who wished to marry only for the deepest love, would never be able to accept Mr. Collins. Charlotte Lucas would settle for a comfortable home and a respectable man, but even she, a woman willing to accept a marriage of convenience, would never be able to accept Mr. Collins. Eliza had done Charlotte a great service, allowing her to see the man in all of his glory for herself.

"He is not all that bad," Jane opined, allowing her desire to see the best in one and all override her good sense.

"*Jane!*" her four sisters and Miss Lucas chorused.

"Even you cannot make him less ridiculous than he is, Janey. His repellent odour would be enough, but have you listened to him? He makes a fool seem a genius! Ask Charlotte what she thinks; you know she is the most level-headed person we know," Elizabeth suggested.

Jane looked at Charlotte questioningly. "Jane, I know you want to see the best in everyone, but you can place rouge on a pig, and it will still be a pig. You know my opinion of matrimony differs markedly from yours and Eliza's, do you not?" Jane nodded. "What does it tell you that no matter how good the man's situation, and even though one day he will inherit this estate, I would not marry him under *any* circumstances?" Charlotte asked.

"Then I would have to allow that I *may* be wrong in this case," Jane owned.

"Have you ever smelled anything as bad as that man?" Lydia asked, her brashness unchecked, as usual.

Before the discussion of the man's odour could proceed, the drawing room door opened, and Bennet and Collins entered. It was easy to see the parson's frustration at the way the ladies were seated. He could not sit near any of them, and he had intended to sit near the blond, blue-eyed beauty to further his suit, which he had no doubt would be successful.

"I will read from Fordyce's *Sermons to Young Women*," Collins said without being invited to read to those in the drawing room.

"NO—thank you Mr. Collins, after dinner is a time for other pursuits at Longbourn," Bennet stated firmly.

His daughters and Miss Lucas all relaxed, as they would not have to hear the odious man read to them. Mr. Collins looked put out, but no one paid him any mind. For her part, Mary was most thankful she had re-evaluated her reading material.

"Do you not think your daughters would benefit from some of Fordyce's wisdom, Cousin?" Collins asked petulantly.

"Let me ask you, Cousin, when you are a guest in Lady Catherine's drawing room, do you dictate what the entertainment should be?" Bennet asked pointedly.

"I would never dare dictate anything to Lady Catherine in her house," Mr. Collins puffed up with affront on behalf of his patroness.

"Then why do you think you have the right to do so here, Mr. Collins?" Bennet challenged. Confused, Mr. Collins stared back at him as if his brain were about to overload.

"But I am the heir here!" Collins returned, presuming it was all that needed to be said.

"You are the heir *presumptive*, nothing more. Until the day I leave this mortal coil and there is no heir with a greater claim, you have no right to demand, dictate, or anything else at Longbourn!" Bennet told the spluttering man. "Just as you are a guest in your patroness' house, so you are in *my* house. Do we understand one another, Mr. Collins?"

"I think I will retire for the night," Collins told no one in particular. He then turned on his heel and left the drawing room in a huff. No one repined his departure.

"This is going to be a long seven days," Elizabeth voiced the thought all were having. She turned to her friend. "It pleases me you will sleep here tonight, Charlotte. At least we were able to provide you with entertainment."

"It is good Charlotte is here to see what an odious man our cousin is," Lydia stated. "Mariah would have thought I was prevaricating otherwise."

"I would have confirmed the truth, Lyddie," Kitty added.

"Even being here myself, I can scarce believe such a man is a clergyman. I feel sorry for his parishioners; I am sure anything said in confidence by them reaches the ears of his patroness," Charlotte opined.

"Surely not!" Jane was horrified at the idea a clergyman would behave in such a way.

"I must agree with Miss Lucas," Bennet added. "The way he adores and extols Lady Catherine, as if she were all powerful and wise, I believe he would do exactly that. If you prompt him, I am sure he will admit it with pride to prove how valuable he is to his patroness."

"If he does so, he could be defrocked! It is against church law!" Mary stated seriously.

"I would wager our Mary knows more about the Bible and church law than Mr. Collins does," Elizabeth opined. Mary beamed; for it was so seldom she received any praise for her former pursuit of biblical learning.

"Papa, may we walk into Meryton in the morning?" Lydia asked. "Kitty and I would like to go see the," about to say officers, Lydia checked herself, "the new ribbons at the haberdashery."

"If some of your sisters walk with you, then you and Kitty may, Lydia," Bennet agreed.

Lydia looked at Jane and Elizabeth hopefully, knowing Mary would not want to walk to Meryton to look at fripperies *or* officers. Jane looked at Elizabeth and Charlotte and both nodded. "Charlotte, Elizabeth, and I will accompany them Papa," Jane told her father.

"Do you think we should ask Matti if she would like to walk with us on the morrow?" Elizabeth asked.

"Unless Jane objects, I see no reason not to include Matti

on our walk. I am sure she will enjoy seeing what new wares have arrived in shops in the town," Charlotte agreed.

"Of course, I do not object. It is not late; why do we not make the short walk to the parsonage and invite her now in case she decides on other plans for the morning?" Jane suggested. "Papa, you do not object if we walk out to the parsonage, do you?"

Bennet waved them away as he made for his study, leaving Mary reading and his youngest two tearing a bonnet apart so they could remake it.

~~~~~~~/~~~~~~~

Matilda was the only daughter of Mr. Dudley, Longbourn's rector. He had lost his wife some five years previously. Matilda was not the most intelligent young lady; she could be quite vapid at times, but she was basically a good person and had been friends with, Jane, Charlotte, and Elizabeth since her father was appointed to his living fifteen years ago. Matilda was of similar height to Elizabeth, but walking was not something she did if she did not need to, so she was on the portly side.

She was not a comely young lady, and at four and twenty she was younger than Charlotte but had no more prospects of marriage than Miss Lucas. Her father was a pleasant man who would sit and play chess with his patron when he was not busy with parish business. His one true weakness was his daughter; he could deny her nothing that was in his power to grant her.

Mr. Dudley's housekeeper showed the three young ladies into the parsonage's sitting room. "Welcome, you three, to what do I owe this honour?" Matilda welcomed her friends.

Jane explained the purpose of their call and their plans for the morrow and extended the invitation to join the group walking into Meryton.

"May I join them, Papa?" Matilda asked. Although she preferred not to walk the mile into the town, she wanted to spend time with her friends.

"I see no reason why not, Matti," Mr. Dudley replied jovially. If one were asked who the more jovial man was, Sir William Lucas or Mr. Dudley, one would be hard pressed to decide.

"It is decided then. What time should I be at the manor house?" Matilda asked.

"We will depart at eleven," Jane replied.

With Matilda's acceptance, the two Bennet sisters and Miss Lucas wished the Dudleys a good night and made the short walk back to the manor house.

CHAPTER 3

"Come, Darcy, if you ride with me, you will not be left with Caroline, unless you would prefer that," Bingley sported with his friend.

As much as Darcy was trying to avoid Miss Elizabeth, who was invading not only his nightly dreams but his waking thoughts as well, spending time in Miss Bingley's company was even more abhorrent, so he agreed to join his friend.

"You know you are giving the Bennets much consequence by delivering the invitation personally instead of it being received from your footmen like everyone else in Meryton," Darcy tried one more time to discourage Bingley.

"Darce, why would I care? Please explain to me how the son of a tradesman can give consequence to a landed gentleman, or are you as confused about social order as my sister?" Bingley asked. "I am not my sisters; I know what my roots are."

Darcy had no answer. Bingley was correct about the social order. If he were honest with himself, he would admit part of his desire to steer Bingley away from the Bennets had naught to do with their connections but his own feelings for the second Bennet daughter. "You are correct, Bingley. Give me a half hour to change into riding attire and I will meet you in the entrance hall," Darcy agreed.

As he departed the drawing room, Darcy was thankful he had allowed his friend to talk him into accompanying him, as Miss Bingley glided in as he walked out. He cared not about the pinched look on Miss Bingley's face as he escaped her company.

~~~~~~~/~~~~~~~

Lieutenant George Wickham was feeling good about himself. He had established credit at every merchant in this little nowhere town, and he had so far bedded two trades-men's daughters—both under the age of fifteen. Both chits had thought he would marry them!

He threatened to tell their fathers and the whole town they had gifted him their virtues if they told anyone or men-tioned him marrying them again. It had worked in the past to keep things quiet—at least until after he escaped the loca-tion, which was always before any consequences of his actions would be visible.

Best of all, Darcy's name was mud in Meryton. He had slighted the Miss Bennet who had been so ready to listen to his story of how Darcy had cheated him out of the living in Kymp-ton. Now, Wickham understood why Miss Elizabeth had been so keen to hear the prig's name being blackened.

Wickham knew he would have to hold back telling his story to the rest of the population until Darcy left the area. So far, he had not come to the man's notice, and in the back of his mind he was aware even if Richard Fitzwilliam was out of the country, he would return. He needed to be circumspect for now, as the thought of Darcy's cousin made him sweat.

In the meantime, he would build up his wardrobe and acquire as much as he could so when he finally wore out his welcome in the town, he would leave with far more than he arrived.

He realised he would have to gamble less. His debts of honour were mounting fast, and it would not be long before his fellow officers would ask to collect what they were owed. He needed to keep on Denny's good side. To that aim he was on his way to meet his *friend* and join him for a promenade down the main street in Meryton.

~~~~~~~/~~~~~~~

Mr. Bennet's daughters and their friend Miss Lucas had managed to avoid the odoriferous parson so far. They had broken their fasts early and then returned to their chambers until it was time to meet Matilda and leave for Meryton.

Collins was frustrated. So far, each attempt to spend time

with his chosen Bennet daughter had come to naught. When he broke his fast, he had been alone. After he was done, eating almost everything that remained on the sideboard, he sought out his cousin in his study.

"Will you not summon your daughters to the drawing room, Cousin?" Collins asked hopefully.

"I am sorry, Mr. Collins, but they set their own schedules," Bennet returned impatiently. He did not like being disturbed when reading, especially not by this man whose foul odour filled the study.

"They need to learn to pay deference to their betters; a man needs to take a strong hand..." Collins started to pontificate when there was a knock on the door, something he had omitted to do when he disturbed his cousin.

Jane Bennet opened the door and knew who was within with her father by the smell before she had fully opened it. "Papa, we are going to await Matilda in the drive, and then we will be off to Meryton."

"Go ahead, Jane," Bennet waved her away.

"Cousin Jane," the greasy parson called.

Jane, having no polite way to do anything else, turned toward him. "Yes Mr. Collins?" she replied.

"As I have not seen the town, other than when I traversed it briefly on my way to my—your home, I will join you on your walk," Collins stated.

Jane was caught between preference and being polite, even though he invited himself to join them. She could not refuse him without being most ungracious, something she could not bring herself to do. If only she had asked Lizzy to inform their father, for her sister would have refused the man without blinking.

"We leave from the drive at eleven, Mr. Collins," Jane informed the man as she turned and made her way toward the front door before the man could offer his arm. As Jane joined her sisters and Charlotte, they all cringed when they heard Mr. Collins calling.

"There you are my dear cousins; I will wait with you to protect you," he stated as he puffed himself up with self-importance.

"Mr. Collins, we are standing on the drive in front of our house. What fearsome creatures do you suspect roam here from which you need to protect us?" Elizabeth challenged.

"It is not right for females to be without the protection of a male. As I will one day be head of this family…" Collins began to explain when Elizabeth interjected.

"If and when you inherit our home, you will have the estate, but never will you be the head of *our* family. You are a distant relation, and we have two uncles who will be designated our guardians, Mr. Collins. We walk to and from Meryton and have done so for many years, and never have we been beset or needed the protection of anyone," Elizabeth stated with steel in her voice.

Collins was about to retort when Matilda and her father arrived. Mr. Dudley was to meet with Mr. Bennet. The introductions distracted Mr. Collins. He was about to deliver a set down to his impertinent cousin when his attention was redirected. Before he could recover, the object of his ardour had linked her arm with the plain Lucas woman on one side and the impertinent miss on the other.

The two younger Miss Bennets walked together, their inane chatter discouraging Collins from seeking to walk with them, so he was left to offer his arm to Miss Dudley. Although not the object of his 'affection,' she seemed to be all that was proper, and to her advantage, her father was a fellow clergyman.

After walking a little while, Mr. Collins mopped his brow furiously as the sweat poured off him due to the exertion it took to catch up to the three women leading the fast pace towards Meryton.

"Miss Bennet, Cousin Jane, will you not walk with me?" Collins demanded.

"I am quite content walking with Charlotte and Lizzy.

35

Thank you for your kind offer, Mr. Collins," Jane demurred.

"As you are to be my betrothed, I think it is entirely proper you obey me and walk with me!" Collins managed between trying to catch his breath.

The three ladies stopped, and Elizabeth turned toward Mr. Collins with anger flashing in her green eyes. "Mr. Collins, have you received permission from my father to make such a claim?" Elizabeth asked pointedly.

"I did not address you, Miss Elizabeth. I am sure my cousin will be only too happy to have me as a son," Collins avowed staunchly.

"Then, sir, before you make any further declarations, speak to our father. I am sure your patroness would agree with me on the order these things are supposed to take," Elizabeth wielded Lady Catherine's name like a rapier.

As Mr. Collins realised his patroness would not countenance him not following acceptable protocol, he re-joined Miss Dudley. For the rest of the walk into town, the surly parson hardly spoke as he brooded on how he would take pleasure disciplining the Bennet sisters once their father was no longer alive.

As the group from Longbourn turned onto the main street, Lydia, always on the lookout for anything in a scarlet coat, saw Lieutenants Denny and Wickham across the street. "Yoo-hoo, Denny, Wickham," the brash girl called out at the top of her lungs.

Charlotte and Lydia's older sisters cringed at the lack of propriety she continued to display at every turn. Lydia had the body of a woman, but she was still very much a young girl, both childish and selfish. Her father did not spoil her as her late mother was wont to do, but Lydia had quickly learnt all she had to do was disturb his peace to gain what she desired.

Kitty had come out at seventeen and Lydia demanded to come out as well as she refused to be the only one not out even though she was but fifteen. At first her father refused, but all she did was caterwaul and burst into his study as often as she could, shrieking about how unfair he was to her. After a day of her tactics, much to his two eldest daughters' chagrin, he had given in and allowed Lydia out.

Something their late mother had mentioned to Kitty and Lydia about a Colonel Millar's regiment, which had visited Meryton before Fanny married, and how well the officers looked in their scarlet jackets left the two youngest Bennets obsessed with officers.

The two officers crossed the street and bowed to the ladies with a flourish. Miss Bennet introduced the two to Mr. Collins, who did his best to try and puff himself up to look good next to the tall and handsome officers.

Denny's and Wickham's backs were to the street when Mr. Bingley and Mr. Darcy rode towards the group. "Look, there is Miss Bennet," Bingley spurred his horse forward and jumped off his mount's back, handing the reins to a boy who was gifted a shilling to hold the horse.

When he joined the group, Miss Bennet did the honours. Mr. Collins became even more surly than he had been as he saw the way Mr. Bingley looked at his *betrothed*, and the smiles and blushes she returned. He vowed to talk to her father to inform him of the honour he planned to bestow on Miss Jane Bennet as soon as they returned to Longbourn.

"Darcy and I were riding to Longbourn to invite you to the ball we are holding this coming Thursday," Bingley handed the invitation to Miss Bennet, who received it with pleasure.

Elizabeth and Charlotte were watching Mr. Wickham when Mr. Bingley mentioned the name Darcy. Lieutenant Wickham blanched and turned white as he turned and saw his nemesis sitting on his black stallion scowling at him. Mr. Darcy was red with anger while the other man was fearful in the extreme.

When he realised Mr. Darcy was not about to dismount and engage with him, Wickham's colour returned and gave the man an insolent salute. Darcy wheeled his mount and turned back toward Netherfield Park.

When Bingley noticed the officers, he turned to Mr. Denny, "Please inform your colonel he and all of his officers are invited to the ball," Bingley offered.

"It seems your friend has departed," Collins informed Bingley, intending to have his competition leave. It had the desired effect, except for the fact the man kissed *his betrothed's* hand.

"I must away," Bingley doffed his beaver to the rest of the party and mounted his horse and made to follow his friend.

Wickham tried to cover his reaction when he saw Darcy. "I am sure you saw the manner of our greeting," he pointed out. To his chagrin Miss Elizabeth did not take the bait.

"Will you attend the ball, Mr. Wickham?" Elizabeth asked interested to hear his response.

"If Darcy does not wish to see me, it is he who must leave, I will not be cowed by the likes of him," Wickham said as he puffed himself up.

The officers excused themselves and the group made for the haberdashery, where Collins waited out front, talking to Miss Dudley while the rest of the party was inside looking at ribbons.

Charlotte pulled Elizabeth aside. "What did you see in the meeting between your favourite and the man you hate?" she asked.

"Mr. Wickham is not my favourite. I saw two men who cannot bear to be in company one with the other," Elizabeth stated stubbornly, even though she knew her depiction was not accurate.

"Eliza! Are you trying to tell me you no longer have any perspicacity? Wickham was afraid and Darcy angry! If what Mr. Wickham told you had more than a kernel of truth to it, would not he have looked angry and Mr. Darcy ashamed? I will make a prediction now. Mr. Wickham will not attend the ball, and he will have some excuse for which will completely contradict what he just told you," Charlotte opined.

Elizabeth made no response as she had a feeling her

friend had the right of it, but she was not ready to allow herself to admit that much just yet.

~~~~~~~/~~~~~~~

Bingley caught up with his friend on the outskirts of the town. "Darcy, why did you take off without a word?" he asked.

"Do you remember I told you about the son of my late father's steward?" Darcy reminded his friend.

"Yes, George Wickham, the one who was at Cambridge," Bingley confirmed.

"The same. He was one of the lieutenants talking to the Bennet ladies and their friends," Darcy shared. "I could not be in his company. I had an urge to vault off Zeus and pummel the man into a bloody pulp! If I did not leave, I would have done so, and you know how much I hate to make a spectacle of myself!"

Darcy had told Bingley much, but nothing of Georgiana's near ruin at Ramsgate. Besides Richard, he had only shared the truth of the event with his aunt and uncle, the Earl and Countess of Matlock, and his older cousin, Viscount Hilldale. Heaven forbid his other aunt, Lady Catherine de Bourgh, should hear of the almost disaster, she would use it as leverage to force him to marry his cousin Anne—something he would never do.

"I understand, Darce. Were it me, I would have pounded him!" It was one of the many differences between the friends. Bingley was impulsive where Darcy was contemplative; Bingley was easily led where Darcy was a leader. Ever since Darcy saved Bingley from being beaten by some lordlings at Cambridge who did not appreciate a tradesman's son among them, the two had been friends.

"Please do not mention anything about my relationship with Wickham to your sisters. I do not want to sound impolitic, but you know Miss Bingley's penchant for malicious gossip," Darcy requested.

"Say no more, Darce. Even though I dislike confrontation, I am not blind to my sister's faults." The two men rode the rest of the way back to Netherfield Park in companionable silence. When they reached the fields, they gave their horses their heads as they streaked towards Netherfield Park.

~~~~~~~/~~~~~~~

Wickham knew it was inevitable Darcy would discover his presence; he was just not ready to see him on this day. And worse, Miss Elizabeth and Miss Lucas had seen his fear when he saw Darcy. In his mind he had recovered well and had a little story ready to explain his reaction.

He would not go to the ball; he quickly forgot his words to the ladies regarding not allowing Darcy to chase him away and started working on a tale that would paint Darcy in a bad light to explain his absence.

His one worry was whether Darcy would warn Meryton's shopkeepers not to extend credit to him. Wickham doubted this, as he was sure Darcy would do nothing overt to anger him with the story he could tell of the prig's mousy sister.

In the end, Wickham decided if he avoided being in company with Darcy, he would be able to carry on unimpeded.

CHAPTER 4

As soon as he gained the house, Collins made a beeline for his cousin's study and threw the door open without knocking. "Mr. Collins, is this what you call acceptable behaviour? To barge into my private study without knocking, and without an invitation? Whether it is acceptable to you or not, it is not to me, and if you cannot regulate your behaviour, I will have you removed from my estate." Seeing Collins was about to bluster, Bennet pre-empted him. "Do I make myself clear?"

"Please excuse my agitation, Cousin, but I find I must talk to you about a matter most urgent. After seeing the wanton and unacceptable behaviour of your daughters, not to mention the impertinence of Cousin Elizabeth, I find I must speak now and help you rescue your family from ignominy," Collins decided to show a little contrition, even if he felt none as the estate was essentially his, after all, as he needed this man's permission to obtain his heart's desire.

"What is this *wanton* behaviour you intend to save my family from, Mr. Collins?" Bennet asked acerbically.

"First, your youngest daughter hails officers and then openly flirts with them!" Bennet cringed internally, though he would not allow Collins to see his reaction. Mayhap it was time to exert himself with Lydia, and by extension Kitty. "Then some strange man talked to your daughter, Cousin Jane, and worse, kissed her hand when he departed! A man by the name of Bingley," Collins complained.

"Mr. Bingley is well known to me; he is the master of the neighbouring estate of Netherfield Park, and from what I have seen, he is unofficially courting Jane. They have known one another for some months now, and if Jane did not object to his manner of leave-taking, it can be nothing to you," Bennet stated as he leaned back in his chair, observing the outrage on his cousin's face. He had been sure he would have more time before he had to have the hard conversation he was currently having.

"What is it to ME?" Collins's voice reached a high pitch as he looked incredulously at cousin, unable to fathom his being so blind after he had clearly stated his intentions in his letter when he explained his reasons for condescending to visit the Bennets. "I have decided to take Cousin Jane as my wife, so she will the future mistress of this estate. As I will be head of this family and owner of this estate, it is very much my concern!"

"Have you asked Jane if she will accept you?" Bennet asked evenly.

"What kind of question is that? Of course she will accept me! I am to be master of this estate!" Collins asserted. "I deserve such a bride with my position in life."

"Enough! As much as I enjoy this *witty* banter, I must inform *you* of something, Mr. Collins. Firstly, you will *never* be head of my family! You know you need my consent to marry any of my daughters, do you not?" Bennet looked at the parson.

Mr. Collins looked as if he had been slapped. Had he not made his intentions plain? Was he not doing this man a great service by deigning to marry one of his daughters? His cousin's consent was but a foregone conclusion. He had no choice, otherwise his daughters would be thrown into the hedgerows the very day of his demise.

"We both know you would not dare refuse me anything I ask for, but if you would like to go through with this charade, I intend to take your eldest daughter as my bride," Collins stated.

"Mr. Collins, let me be rightly understood! I will not now, nor will I *ever* allow any of my girls to marry you! Do you think I would ever permit my daughters to be tied to a senseless man who is naught but a sycophant? A clergyman who seems to revere his patroness above God Almighty! No Sir, you are very wrong. There is nothing you could offer to induce me to allow you to marry any of my girls." Bennet held his hand up as the spluttering man was about to interject. "If you importune any of my daughters on the subject, you will be evicted from my home immediately and will not be permitted to return until and *if* you inherit this estate."

"I have never been thusly insulted in my life!" Collins retorted indignantly. "My patroness charged me with returning a married man, or at the very least betrothed man, and to marry one of my cousins. I will make another mistress of this estate, as I am sure once I explain the behaviour of your daughters to the beneficent Lady Catherine de Bourgh, she will understand my not wanting to marry one of my cousins!"

"I wish you good luck, Mr. Collins. As long as it is not one of my daughters, I will wish you happy when you find the future Mrs. Collins," Bennet said sarcastically.

Collins said not another word as he turned on his heel and stalked out of the study, slamming the door behind him like a petulant child.

~~~~~~~/~~~~~~~

Charlotte wished her friends farewell, picked up her valise, and started her walk back to Lucas Lodge. Cutting across Longbourn's park, it was about a twenty-minute walk, or as Eliza would call it, a short stroll.

As Charlotte approached the large oak with a swing suspended from an upper branch, she saw Mr. Bennet's cousin Collins sitting on the bench with his back turned to her. She knew she should not listen, but the man was talking to himself, and none too quietly.

"...not allow me to marry any of his daughters! I will show him! The very day he dies I will throw his daughters out of my home. As the head of the family, I will confiscate their dowries as well.

"Lady Catherine will laud me for not marrying one of these uncouth hoydens! Now I need to see on whom I will bestow the honour of my proposals. I know: the plain one! Miss Lucas is no Cousin Jane, but how it will smart when I throw them out and their friend becomes mistress of their home. I will show my smug cousin..." Charlotte backed away, for she had heard more than enough.

What a petty, vindictive man. If he thought she would ever marry him, he was insane! Just as she started to walk, she stepped on a twig making a loud crack. The parson turned and noticed her as she tried to make her escape.

"Miss Lucas," he greeted her as he approached her with a lecherous grin. "Are you returning to your home?"

"I am, Mr. Collins. Good day Sir," Charlotte tried to leave.

"Miss Lucas, I cannot in good conscience watch a lady of your quality walk home alone. Even if the Bennets are not attentive to such things, you will find, like my beneficent patroness, I am," Collins preened, thinking he was making a good impression on the lady.

"If you choose to walk the same direction as me, I cannot stop you, Sir, although I have made this walk since I became an *intimate* friend of the Bennet sisters, and do not require an escort," Charlotte hoped the horrid man would take the hint. She could have said she did not want him to walk with her, but her good manners overrode the desire.

"You know I will be master of this estate one day soon," Collins began to woo Miss Lucas.

"Really, Sir. Is there something you know about Mr. Bennet's health we do not? He looks hale and healthy to me," Charlotte averred.

"Well yes," Collins did not bother to address her point which was nothing but the truth. "I also hold the living at Hunsford in Westerham, which boasts an income of more than five hundred pounds per annum. That pales in comparison to the condescension I receive from the eminently wise Lady Catherine de Bourgh. Do you know she is so intelligent she advised me to place shelves in my closets?" Collins related with pride. "That is the reason I need to marry now, for Lady Catherine told me I need to set the example to my parishioners by being married. And when I bring you home to Hunsford, Lady Catherine will do you the great honour of waiting on you, my dear Miss Lucas," Collins preened, sure that this time he was about to attain a wife.

"Firstly, sir, when did I permit you to use any endearments when addressing me?" Charlotte demanded. "Secondly, why would I be at Hunsford and have your patroness wait on me?" Charlotte was pleased they were in sight of Lucas Lodge already.

"I am to marry you, Miss Lucas. I have selected you as the fortunate lady who will have the honour of gaining my hand," Collins explained. Mayhap Miss Lucas was not as intelligent as he thought if she could not understand he was saving her from spinsterhood.

"Of what do you prattle on about, Mr. Collins?" Charlotte asked, flabbergasted at the presumption of the man and barely able to keep from gagging at his odour.

"Believe me, my dear Miss Lucas, your modesty, so far from doing you any disservice, rather adds to your other perfections. You would have been less amiable in my eyes had there *not* been this little unwillingness. Allow me to assure you your parents will approve of this address. You can hardly doubt the purpose of my discourse; however your natural delicacy may lead you to dissemble. My attentions are now too marked to be mistaken. Almost as soon as I saw you," Charlotte had to force herself not to laugh, "I singled you out as the companion of my future life. You are eminently more suited than my wild and misbehaving cousins! But before I am run away with my feelings on this subject, perhaps it would be advisable for me to state my reasons for marrying—and, moreover for coming into Hertfordshire with the design of selecting a wife, as I certainly did."

The idea of Mr. Collins, with all his solemn idea of wooing a woman, being run away with his feelings almost caused Charlotte to lose her composure. And still he did not pause, but charged ahead with his ridiculous speech, not allowing her any attempt to stop him.

"My reasons for marrying are, first, that I think it a right thing for every clergyman in easy circumstances—like myself—to set the example of matrimony in his parish; secondly, I am convinced it will add very greatly to my happiness; and thirdly—which I have mentioned earlier, it is the particular advice and recommendation of the very noble lady, whom I have the honour of calling 'patroness.' Twice has she condescended to give me her opinion—unasked for too—on this subject; and it was but the very Saturday night before I left Hunsford—between our pools at quadrille, while Mrs. Jenkinson was arranging Miss de Bourgh's footstool, that she said, 'Mr. Collins, you must marry. A clergyman like you must marry. Choose properly. Choose a gentlewoman for *my* sake and for your *own*; let her be an active, useful sort of person, not brought up high, but able to make a small income go a good way. This is my advice. Find such a woman as soon as you can, bring her to Hunsford, and I will visit her.'

"Allow me, by the way, to observe, my fair Miss Lucas, I do not reckon the notice and kindness of Lady Catherine de Bourgh as among the least of the advantages in my power to offer. You will find her manners beyond anything I can describe; and your intelligence, I think, must be acceptable to her, especially when tempered with the silence and respect which her rank will inevitably excite. Thus, much for my general intention in favour of matrimony; it remains to be told why my views were directed towards Meryton instead of my own neighbourhood, where I can assure you there are many amiable young women. But the fact is, being as I am to inherit the Bennets' estate after the death of my cousin, I could not satisfy myself without resolving to choose a wife from among his daughters," Realising what he said, Collins paused to try and recover from his gaffe. "Err, as I said, my cousins are unsuitable to be an exalted parson's wife, hence the honour has fallen to you, Miss Lucas. As the Miss Bennets misbehave so, I will not keep them under my roof once we become master and mistress of the estate."

It was necessary to interrupt him now. "You are too hasty, sir," she cried. "You forget that I have made no answer. Let me do it without further loss of time. Accept my thanks for the compliment you are paying me. I am very sensible of the honour of your proposals, but it is impossible for me to do otherwise than to decline them," Charlotte retorted. As much as she wanted to give the awful man a set down, her good manners prevented her.

Mr. Collins replied with a formal wave of the hand, "Am I am now to learn that it is usual with young ladies to reject the addresses of the man whom they secretly mean to accept, when he first applies for their favour; and that sometimes the refusal is repeated a second, or even a third time? I am, therefore, by no means discouraged by what you have just said and shall hope to lead you to the altar ere long."

"Upon my word, sir," averred Charlotte, "your hope is a rather extraordinary one after my declaration. I do assure you that I am not one of those young ladies—if such young ladies there are—who are so daring as to risk their happiness on the chance of being asked a second time. I am perfectly serious in my refusal. You could not make *me* happy, and I am convinced that I am the last woman in the world who desires to make you so. Nay, were your friend Lady Catherine to know me, I am persuaded she would find me in every respect ill qualified for the situation."

"Were it certain Lady Catherine would think so," said Mr. Collins very gravely, "but I cannot imagine that her ladyship would at all disapprove of you. And you may be certain when I have the honour of seeing her again, I shall speak in the very highest terms of your modesty, economy, and other amiable qualifications."

Charlotte could see the man would not understand good manners. "Had I not had the displeasure of your company at Longbourn and understood exactly what kind of man you are, Mr. Collins, I may have entertained a proposal from you. Thankfully, my friends invited me to come see for myself what sort of creature you are. Even though you never actually asked, I will not now, nor will I *ever* marry you, Mr. Collins. If you were the last man in England, I *still* would not marry you!" Charlotte exclaimed.

Seemingly not to hear her, Collins spewed forth a yet more incomprehensible statement. "When I do myself the honour of speaking to you next on the subject, I shall hope to receive a more favourable answer than you have now given me; though I am far from accusing you of cruelty at present, because I know it to be the established custom of your sex to reject a man on the first application, and perhaps you have even now said as much to encourage my suit as would be consistent with the true delicacy of the female character."

"Mr. Collins, I had not known you five minutes before I knew you were the last man in the *world* I could ever be prevailed upon to marry! Do you think I could ever align myself with one who plans to hurt my dearest friends? You stand here telling me how you will throw your cousins from their ancestral home with glee! Do you think I do not know about Mr. Bennet refusing his permission to marry any of his daughters? No, Mr. Collins, I am not trying to increase anything in you with regards to myself except that I am in earnest, Sir, for I will not marry you—ever!" Charlotte stated as plainly as she could.

Collins was flummoxed. How could one with excellent prospects such as he be turned down, by first his cousins and then this plain spinster? "You senseless woman! No man would ever offer for one as homely as you. I was doing you a great service to condescend to offer for you." Collins tried to intimidate Charlotte by leaning in close to her.

She recoiled, not in fear but from the sickening odour emanating from the man. Her brothers, Franklin and John, having seen Charlotte talking to a man neither knew, had come out of the house in time to see the man try to stand too close to their sister.

"You dare stand so close to my sister?" Franklin growled. Collins, as he was a coward, shrunk back in fear.

"Frank, John, I thank you, truly, but Mr. Collins was just leaving. Were you not, *Mr.* Collins?" Charlotte demanded; her seething words too marked to be mistaken.

Collins turned and scurried away as fast as his legs could carry him, leaving a noxious trail behind him. As he put distance between himself and his tormentors, Collins thanked the heavens he had not struck the chit as he had been about to do, for he was sure her brothers would not have allowed him to live had he done so.

"Charlotte, are you well?" John Lucas asked as he and his older brother escorted their sister into the house.

"I am well, John. Thank you and Frank for assisting me. Are mother and father in the sitting room?" Charlotte asked and Franklin nodded. "Let us go see them so I may tell this story only once."

Once Charlotte told all, neither of her parents disagreed with her decision not to accept the man. Her brothers wanted to go after Collins to punish him for his words to their sister and his intentions toward hurting their closest friends, the Bennets.

"There is no need; I think there is a better way to teach that man a lesson," Charlotte stated, for an idea started to form in her mind about how she could take charge of the situation and teach the horrible man a good lesson at the same time. "I need to think; please allow me some solitude to do so." Her father told her to take as much time as she needed, his eyes gleaming with the expectation of being able to assist his friend and champion his daughter at the same time.

~~~~~~~/~~~~~~~

William Collins did not know how first his cousin and now Miss Lucas had the temerity to throw his condescension back at him in such a disrespectful manner. Not only was he a clergyman, but he was the beneficiary of the infinitely wise counsel of Lady Catherine de Bourgh, which only elevated him

SHANA GRANDERSON A LADY

further.

He could have explained the reason he did not return married or betrothed to one of his cousins, but with Miss Lucas's refusal, he was in danger of returning and facing Lady Catherine's wrath for disobeying her edict.

As he was wandering in Longbourn's park, trying to divine a solution to his quandary, he noticed Miss Dudley and her father walking towards the parsonage next to Longbourn's church. The lady was not comely like his cousin, but she seemed much more pliable than Miss Lucas had been.

Why did he not think of her before? She was ideal, the daughter of a fellow man of the cloth. Who would know how to be a proper parson's wife better than the daughter of one? Collins turned to follow the Dudleys to their home.

~~~~~~~/~~~~~~~

Although Matilda Dudley was not nearly as intelligent as her friends, Charlotte and Elizabeth, she was not bereft of wit. She knew that at four and twenty she was considered on the shelf. She had long held a tendre for Franklin Lucas but did not think he was interested in her. Her dearest father would never ask her to leave his home, but she had long dreamed of her own situation.

The problem was, she had to compete with the older Bennet daughters for local men as they were both younger and far comelier than herself. Matilda was not unaware of the fact when Jane and Elizabeth were in a room with her, no one looked her way. Even Charlotte Lucas, who was considered plain, was more pleasing to look at than herself.

Her father had entered the house, and Matilda was sitting on a bench in the parsonage's small garden. As she was sitting, she smelt Mr. Collins before she saw him. "Good day, Miss Dudley. I would like to speak to you on a particular subject, if I may," Collins bowed low to her and then reached for her hand, intending to gift her a kiss. It was not a good beginning for his third attempt to find a bride as the lady withdrew her hand.

"I am not averse to hearing what you have to say, Mr.

Collins, but I am about to join my father for dinner. I would be happy to receive you in two hours *after* your bath which I am sure you take before dinner each day," Matilda batted her eyelids, trying her best not to insult the man too much.

"Yes, of course Miss Dudley, I will see you and your father two hours hence," Collins bowed again. He would bathe, for he did not want any impediment to his third suit that day, though he could not understand why all these people were obsessed with bathing. Had his honoured father not told him it was not healthy to bathe above once in ten days?

~~~~~~~~/~~~~~~~~

Dinner at Longbourn was pleasant for two reasons that day, and both were associated with Mr. Collins. He did not stink, and he said not a word. His eating habits were as they had been since his arrival, but given the other two advantageous things, which were very agreeable to the six Bennets, his manner of eating was less bothersome than was usually the case. As soon as dinner was over, William Collins quickly wished his cousins a good evening and was off like a shot towards the parsonage.

CHAPTER 5

The next day, Charlotte Lucas took a long look at herself in the mirror. She had made some decisions, but did she have enough gumption to carry her plan forward?

She thought back to the insulting words Mr. Collins had flung at her the previous day, which were combined with his desire to punish the Bennets for not wanting an alliance with him beyond that of distant cousin. The more she considered, the more she resolved to carry through with her plan.

She would leave Lucas Lodge after breakfast, and if she was able to convince the master of Longbourn of the merit of her plans, she would take charge of her future and it would take a turn in a different direction than any of the paths currently available to her. Charlotte very much hoped, successful or not, once Jane and Elizabeth were informed of what she had suggested, she would not lose them as friends. It was a risk she *had* to take! Regardless of their understanding now or not, what she was trying to achieve was as much for them as it was for her. Perhaps even more so.

~~~~~~~/~~~~~~~

Much to the residents of Longbourn's pleasure, no one saw Mr. Collins when they broke their fasts, though it was unlike the corpulent man to miss a meal. As they could not repine his absence, no one felt anything about his absence other than relief.

As it was only three days until the ball, the five Bennet sisters decided to walk into Meryton. Before they left, Jane and Elizabeth urged their father to talk to his two youngest daughters. If he did not check them, they would be fixed as the most determined flirts ever to make their family ridiculous.

Bennet loved his peace, but he recognised the fact that if both of his older daughters felt he needed to step in—this was not the first time they asked—it was not an anomaly and he needed to act. He had Hill summon Kitty and Lydia to his study.

The two girls thought it was providence they were being called to the book room as they had spent all their pin money and needed to ask their father for more coin to purchase fripperies.

"Sit," Bennet ordered firmly after Kitty closed the door. The two looked at one another, neither liking their father's expression, for they had never seen him look at them so severely before. "Lydia, if it comes to my notice one more time that you screeched for officers or have any contact with officers without either Jane or Elizabeth with you, I will put you back in and send you directly to the schoolroom! The same goes for you, Catherine! I know you follow what your sister does, but that will not excuse you if you contravene any of my rules. And before you ask, if you waste your pin money—on whatever it is you spend your funds on—you will not receive a ha'penny from me until the next month's pin money is distributed." Bennet held up his hand, giving both shell-shocked girls a stern, quelling look.

"I have told all three of your sisters to not lend you more money. In fact, I have asked them to tell me how much each of you owe. Half of your pin money will be used to repay them until you have discharged your debts." Bennet stated with purpose.

"But, Papa, why should we pay them back?" Lydia whined, though he was gratified that at least Kitty had the decency to look embarrassed.

"Borrowing is not a gift, Lydia. Every penny you *borrowed* from your three sisters will be paid back from both of your monthly allowances!" Bennet averred.

"My sisters are just jealous the officers like me better than them!" Lydia pouted like the young girl she was.

"Believe what you will, but my orders stand, unless you want to be back in!" Bennet threatened, unamused when he saw Lydia forcing tears out of her eyes. "I am immune to your crocodile tears! If you think to start caterwauling, you will be going to the nursery and not to Meryton!"

As much as she hated seeing it there, Lydia saw the resolve in her father's look and shut her mouth with a clack. "May we go with our sisters now, Papa?" Kitty asked quietly and received a nod of dismissal from her father.

"We must find a way to see the officers!" Lydia hissed once they were out of the study.

"*NO*, Lydia!" Kitty insisted. "If you want to return to the nursery, it will be without me!"

"You are no fun anymore, Kitty," Lydia complained.

Some fifteen minutes later, the sisters departed Longbourn after the eldest three received revised and clear orders from their father.

~~~~~~~/~~~~~~~

Ever since seeing Wickham in the town, Darcy had been in the darkest of moods. As much as he would have liked to warn the people of Meryton of Wickham's propensities, he could not take the chance his private family business would be exposed, especially not as it pertained to his sister Gigi—Miss Georgiana Darcy. He felt badly for the locals, but he could not chance word of his sister's *faux pas* being known abroad.

Other than during his long morning rides, Darcy felt like a prisoner at Netherfield Park. Thankfully, Miss Bingley kept Town hours, so he did not see her at breakfast, but there was no escaping the woman at dinner, and then there was the time he was forced to spend in the drawing room until supper was called.

As much as he had commanded himself to not think of the country miss any longer, neither his heart nor his head seemed inclined to heed his intentions. Miss Elizabeth Bennet invaded his thoughts, no matter whether he was awake or asleep. The erotic dreams had started just after she and her sister departed for their home from Netherfield Park, and no matter what he told himself about her unsuitability, the dreams and thoughts persisted, despite it being almost a week since he had seen her.

During the day, unless he had an occupation to think on, his mind would betray him, and before he knew it he was again thinking about Miss Elizabeth Bennet. He told himself part of it was their shared experience of losing their mothers, but he had to admit the lie of that being the main reason.

Darcy was sitting in the library, such as it was, trying to think of anything but Miss Elizabeth when Bingley entered the room. "Is my sister so bad you need to hide away for most of the day?" Bingley asked. Seeing Darcy's quelling look, Bingley raised his hands in surrender. "I admit I know what my sister is, I just do not like to have confrontations with her. You have been spared one of her epic tantrums so far."

"Bingley, my friend, my patience with her is wearing thin. If you are not able to take her in hand, I am afraid she will end up ruining herself and your family along with her. I will repeat what I have already told you. I will *never* offer for your sister. If she tries to compromise me, she will only compromise herself," Darcy reiterated. He had told Bingley the same on several occasions but was sure his friend did not think him serious.

"I will try and talk to her," a despondent Bingley stated.

"Buck up, Bingley, you will soon be dancing with your latest angel in three days," Darcy reminded his friend.

"That is true," Bingley perked up right away. "Miss Bennet may be the most beautiful woman I have beheld," Bingley shared. "I cannot wait to dance with her at the ball!"

Darcy was happy his friend, at least, was so easy to distract. If only the same could be said for himself.

~~~~~~~/~~~~~~~

"Miss Charlotte Lucas to see you master," Hill informed Bennet.

"Please let Miss Lucas know the girls have all walked into Meryton. She may find them there, or they will be home in three hours or less," Bennet waved his man away.

"Miss Lucas said you might say that Mr. Bennet and asked me to explain she is here to see you," Hill informed his master.

"Show her in, Hill," Bennet frowned in confusion. He had no idea what his friend's daughter wanted to see him about, but she was a sensible lady and he had been grateful for her presence on the many occasions as she had helped him with his daughters. Miss Lucas entered the study and before Bennet was able to instruct Hill to leave the door open, closed it quietly herself.

"Do not be alarmed, Sir, I am not about to compromise you. But there are things of a delicate nature I need to discuss with you, and it would be better not to have a servant hear any part of what I have to say and jump to the wrong conclusion.

Until she had mentioned the word compromise, it was the last thing on Bennet's mind, and he dismissed the worry as quickly as it had formed. Charlotte Lucas was both intelligent and honourable. And, if he was honest, he had never viewed her as a young woman of her own standing with her own wishes and desires until she said the word compromise. After she said it, he looked at her differently than he had before. But she had said she would not affect a compromise, so she would not, and Bennet scoffed at the idea that a young lady like Miss Lucas would be interested in a man in his late forties.

"May I speak candidly, Mr. Bennet?" Charlotte requested. Bennet nodded, pointing to the seat directly across his big oak desk. "As I see it, you and your family have a problem in the form of the nonsensical entail, and one Mr. William Collins. And I believe I have a solution."

"You have piqued my interest, Miss Lucas; please carry on." Bennet owned to being intrigued.

"If my information is correct, you denied Mr. Collins any path to propose to one of your daughters yesterday. Is that correct?" Bennet allowed it was so. "From your study, he took himself to rant in the park, just as I was about to walk home. I know it is impolite to eavesdrop, but I will not apologise for doing so. I overheard him state what he planned to do to your daughters in the unfortunate event, which he seems to wish for, of your demise..." Charlotte went on to tell Bennet all, from the ranting she could not help but hear, to his proposal to her after following her home to Lucas Lodge.

She shared his words to her, as well as hers to him. Bennet was not happy at the attempt to intimidate Charlotte, but he smiled as he thought about his cousin cowering when Franklin and John confronted him. He had already pegged his cousin as a cowardly bully, and Miss Lucas had just confirmed it.

Bennet sat back in his chair, considering both what he had been told and the reason why. He agreed that Collins was a problem, but what solution could Miss Lucas be intending to offer? Then it hit him, the true way to thwart Collins was to remarry and sire a son, something he had not seriously considered until that moment.

But he would need a woman young enough to be able to bear children! He saw Miss Lucas was watching him cogitate with a mysterious smile on her face. '*She is offering herself as a solution! Surely not!*' Bennet scoffed, watching her watch him as his emotions played over his face, yet not saying a word.

"Miss Lucas, am I to understand your solution for me is to marry and sire a son?" Bennet asked carefully.

"Yes, Mr. Bennet, it is the one true answer to all concerns," Charlotte replied evenly.

"And do you have one in mind who would marry me, Miss Lucas?" Bennet enquired.

"I do," Charlotte averred simply.

"We can continue to beat around the bush, and you to answer my questions narrowly, or we can be candid with one another. Please inform me who the lady is, and how you know she will be amenable to an offer from me?" Bennet asked directly.

~~~~~~~/~~~~~~~

At the same time Miss Lucas was meeting with Bennet,

the subject of their musings had requested a private interview with Miss Matilda Dudley. His request had been granted by Mr. Dudley. The man was certainly not Mr. Dudley's first choice for his daughter, but she had communicated her willingness to hear his offer to her father, so as always, he granted her wish.

Matilda listened patiently while Collins gave a speech; she was not aware it was the same one he made to Charlotte Lucas only yesterday. At least he remembered to substitute Miss Dudley's name for Miss Lucas'. At some level, she was concerned he did not intend to allow the Bennets to remain at Longbourn if any of them were unmarried, but as much as she sympathised with their future plight, it was her future she was securing at that moment. If only Franklin Lucas has been interested in her.

After he had exhausted hyperbole, unlike his first two forays into the world of selecting a bride, Collins was accepted on condition he bathed every day, to which he agreed. He applied to Mr. Dudley, who, after he confirmed his daughter genuinely wanted the match, consented. Collins asked if Miss Dudley was willing to marry by common licence the Friday after the ball, to which she consented.

Collins was happy his third attempt had borne fruit. At least he could return to Lady Catherine with his head held high and a wife on his arm, and he had secured the next mistress of Longbourn. As he thought about the pleasure he would derive from taking his cousin's dowries and then turning the Bennet sisters out of his house, he almost salivated with anticipated revenge.

Had Collins been aware of the happenings at Longbourn, he would have had an apoplexy.

~~~~~~~/~~~~~~~

"Come, Mr. Bennet, you are far too intelligent not to know exactly what it is I am suggesting," Charlotte responded.

"I think I do grasp what it is, but if it is all the same to you, I would like to hear it from you in your own words," Bennet returned.

"Based on that man's words to me, I have as much interest

as you in seeing him never inherit this estate. I will not lie; my suggestion is driven partly by revenge for the words he flung at me. That is the smallest part of my reasoning. We are both intelligent people.

"I am no longer a young woman, and I think we both seek companionship. If, from our union, one or more sons result, so much the better. For me, the most important part is I sincerely believe we are compatible on many levels. I know I am about twenty years younger than you are, but that is not and should not be a consideration," Charlotte explained her philosophy.

"The age is not an issue for me, but you are very good friends with my two eldest daughters, and what about love?" Bennet asked, truly needing to know her thoughts on these matters before he would allow himself to entertain the thought in truth.

"Both Jane and Eliza are intelligent women. When *we* explain *our* reasoning, I am sure they will understand. You may or may not know this, but I am not a romantic. I do not need to be in love with my husband, but I do require mutual respect. And you should know, unlike the previous Mrs. Bennet, I will not be made sport of unless it is just the two of us. That being said, given we both enjoy the written word and are both debate partners for Eliza, I believe we will attain a level of felicity in the union, if you offer for me. You did not enjoy your first marriage, but a second one with me, I trust, would be more palatable to you. I do have one or two conditions, however," Charlotte informed Bennet.

"And what would those be, Miss Lucas?" Bennet asked carefully.

"Nothing unreasonable, I believe. I would want responsibility for taking Kitty and Lydia in hand and I expect your full support regardless of my mandates," Charlotte enumerated.

"I believe that will be an easy thing for me to grant," Bennet allowed.

"Secondly, I would expect you not to be in your bookroom all the day long. I know from talking to Eliza, this estate could reach three thousand pounds per annum with but a minimum of effort from you. I would ask you expend the needed energy to attain such," Charlotte concluded.

Bennet cogitated again, going over the pros and cons in his mind. Pros there were plenty, cons almost none. He stood and walked around the front of the desk to sit in the chair next to Miss Lucas. "As much as you may want me on one knee, it would be too hard to stand up again," Bennet stated dryly. "Miss Charlotte Lucas, will you marry me?" Bennet asked simply.

"Yes, Mr. Bennet, Thomas, I will marry you," Charlotte averred in the affirmative.

"If you agree, Charlotte, I will talk to my oldest three daughters when they return from Meryton. Once I explain it to them, I will go see your father on the morrow in the morning," Bennet informed his betrothed.

"May I make a suggestion, Thomas?" Bennet nodded. "I should be with you when you talk to Jane, Eliza, and Mary. That way, and together, we should be able to address any questions or concerns they may have," Charlotte recommended.

"I think your suggestion has merit." Yes, it would be very different having an intelligent spouse, and suddenly he had hope he had not felt in almost fifteen years.

CHAPTER 6

I t had not been easy to keep the two younger Bennets away from the officers, especially Lydia, but they had done so by raising the spectre of going back in for Lydia. She had been most displeased, but she had complied—to their knowledge. She was determined to have her fun and had decided she would have to wait until her boring sisters were not keeping such a close watch on her.

Their father had allowed each girl to acquire one new gown so they were at their final fittings at the dressmaker. Without respect to Lydia's demands for a dress unfit for a maiden, with too low a neckline and an abundance of Belgian lace, the seamstress followed instructions from Mr. Bennet, which he conveyed to her after canvassing Miss Lucas's opinion. As he was the parent and the one who would pay, she would not disobey his orders.

The Bennets walked past Wickham and Denny with a curtsy and nothing else, which left the two men scratching their heads. Even if the older Bennets behaved more circumspectly, the younger two usually flirted freely, but not today.

Wickham worried the truth about him would be spread abroad before he could acquire all that he needed. He could not have that yet. He was about to try and charm Miss Elizabeth to determine the cause of their curt greetings, but before he could speak, they were gone.

The five Bennets arrived home just before the time father expected them to return. Lydia was the only sullen one, and no one doubted the cause was having to pass the officers without having received the attention she believed she deserved. Was that not how her late mother taught her to behave? It was, in

Lydia's mind, expected and correct.

Since she behaved correctly, why did her older sisters always tell her she would ruin herself and the family? Even worse, now her father was starting to assert himself. Things were definitely not going the way Lydia wanted, and she was used to getting her own way. She would have to increase the number of her secret meetings with the man she loved.

"Lydia and Kitty, please go to your room until you are called; Sarah is waiting upstairs to assist you," Bennet instructed his youngest. "The rest of my girls, please join me in my study." Bennet knew Lydia, like her mother before her, had a propensity to listen at his study door when she was being excluded. To prevent that, Hill was positioned in the hall just outside. It was a well-considered ploy, as Miss Lydia appeared not a minute after the door closed, scowled mightily, and stamped up the stairs when she saw she would not be gratified in her quest.

After entering the book room, the three older Bennet daughters stopped short when they found Charlotte sitting inside. "Charlotte?" Elizabeth asked, questioningly.

"Hello Eliza, Jane, and Mary. Your father will explain all," Charlotte greeted them in return.

"Please sit, girls," Bennet indicated the settee. "I am sure there are going to be many questions, so I ask you three to wait until *we* have finished sharing our *intentions* with my three most intelligent daughters." None of his daughters missed the 'we' intonation but acceded to his request they wait to ask their questions.

For her part, Mary was beaming as he included her in the group of intelligent daughters. The attention Bennet had given Mary since her mother passed away, had paid off in many ways for Mary. Giving her confidence in herself and redirecting her away from the book of sermons she once parroted were two of the main benefits of her father's attention.

"While you were in Meryton today, I asked Charlotte to marry me, and she has agreed to be my wife," Bennet related the main point first. Three mouths hung open and he could see all three wanted to pepper them with questions, but they caught themselves by remembering their promise to ask questions at the end. "Charlotte will start by telling you what transpired yesterday, and then I will add some information. After that, you may ask any questions your heart's desire.

Charlotte related everything, from hearing Collins's rant until his ill-judged proposal. She repeated the words he had spoken to her verbatim, and the more she spoke, the more outraged her friends became, almost forgetting the surprising impact of the lead statement—that their father and Charlotte Lucas were betrothed.

Once Charlotte told her portion of the tale, both she and Bennet related everything they spoke of from the time Charlotte arrived at Longbourn—their betrothal, the decision to tell the older sisters together, and everything in-between. "Now," Bennet allowed, "if you have any questions, please let us try to answer them."

"This is what you both truly want?" Jane asked first.

"It is, Jane. You know I have never been romantic, and I will not lie to you by telling you that I love your father for I do not, but I do esteem and respect him, and I believe it is the same for him," Charlotte shared. "Our feelings today do not preclude the possibility we may develop tender feelings for one another in the future."

"Charlotte is absolutely correct. I have tried my best, especially with you, Mary. To my chagrin, only in the last two years have I tried to teach you to think critically as I did for Jane and Lizzy. If you look at the facts—our likes, dislikes, intelligence, and all other factors—Charlotte and I are far more compatible than your late mother and I were." Bennet saw the hurt looks his three daughters wore. "Do not misunderstand me; I am not sorry I married your mother because she gave me five daughters who I love dearly, even if two are on the silly side."

"Charlotte, you cannot expect us to call you Mother," Elizabeth injected some humour.

"Noted, Eliza. You are exempted from calling me Mother," Charlotte smiled widely.

"Why were our other two sisters not included in this meeting, Papa?" Mary asked.

"Excellent question, Mary. You know how poorly your younger sisters are able to keep a secret, do you not?" Bennet asked. Mary and her sisters nodded, as that was a well-lamented fact in their family. "First, I have not gone to Sir William for his consent and blessing. Good lord, he will be my father-in-law!" Bennet grinned as he considered the implications for the first time. "Second, we do not want to make any announcement until after Collins leaves the area. I am not afraid of him, but I would rather avoid unpleasant scenes in public with the upcoming ball."

"I understand, Papa. Is it going to be just like when Mama was alive?" Jane asked with trepidation, hoping she would not offend her father. "Will you be in here all day long, and Charlotte managing everything, including the girls?"

Before Bennet could answer, Elizabeth interjected. "Will there finally be rules for our younger two, especially Lydia? I truly scrutinized the way she looked at the officers today—and the way they look at her. It made me sick to see the way grown men looked at a child! She may be physically mature for her age, but she is still a child who should never have been out in the first place, Papa!" Elizabeth had never censured her father before, and here she was doing so before her sisters and his betrothed. "I am sorry..." Bennet held up his hand to interrupt her apology.

"No, Lizzy, let me for once in my life feel how much I am to blame. I am not afraid of being overpowered by the impression. And I will not allow it to pass! Charlotte and I have discussed this. Lydia will be back in after the ball; until then she will be carefully watched. Kitty will be out in Meryton only, unless we see she is not able to comport herself properly. If needed, they will both be sent to school, separate schools!" Bennet stated with purpose.

"I still feel badly..." Elizabeth tried finish her intended apology until Charlotte placed her hand on her friend's arm.

"Eliza, your father and I discussed this very topic, and I said much the same as you. Mr. Bennet, Thomas, agrees and sees the error of his ways. None of us are perfect; we all have and will continue to make mistakes. The important thing is to learn from them," Charlotte reminded her, looking directly at Elizabeth as she spoke.

Hearing in her friend's words, especially what had not been spoken, Elizabeth admitted she had much re-evaluating to do. What she had seen of Mr. Wickham in Meryton, and the way he leered at her fifteen-year-old sister, went a long way to forcing her to admit she may have been wrong about both Mr. Darcy and Mr. Wickham.

"There is no guarantee you will have a son and thwart that man," Mary pointed out.

"As we all know, the gender of a baby is in God's hands. But do not forget, I come from a family of three brothers and only one sister," Charlotte averred. "It does not guarantee anything, but I believe in my heart we will be able to keep the estate in the hands of a Bennet!"

"The good thing is the entail ends with the next heir. If Charlotte and I are blessed with a son, there will be no more entail when he reaches his eighteenth year," Bennet informed his daughters.

"It will be strange to have you as our stepmother, but welcome to the family, Charlotte," Elizabeth stood and hugged her friend. She was followed by Jane and Mary, who welcomed Charlotte as a member of the family without reservation.

"For the most part, I expect you will act towards me as you always have, with a few necessary changes. The biggest changes will be for Kitty and Lydia," Charlotte told the three sisters.

"When will you two marry?" Jane asked.

"After the Netherfield Ball. Collins will have returned to Hunsford by then. We will acquire a common license," Bennet explained. He still had to face Sir William! Charlotte was of age, but she preferred having her father's blessing.

~~~~~~~/~~~~~~~

When the Bennets ate dinner, Collins was again conspicuous by his absence, which no one repined. At the end of dinner, instead of making for his study as had been his wont, Bennet accompanied his daughters to the drawing room.

"There are going to be some changes around here," Bennet announced once everyone was seated. "Lydia, if you are thinking of climbing out of your window at night to go flirt with officers, know that I have hired extra footmen to be on duty. If you even make an attempt, you will be back in the nursery, and you can forget the Netherfield Ball," he held up a hand to stop her protest, "or any other opportunity to dance for many years!"

"Kitty, you tattletale!" Lydia screeched and made a move to get to her sister to scratch her, but Bennet stood between the two before she could reach Kitty. She sat back down in a huff.

"Lydia, how could I have told? I have been with you since you told me. We walked down to dinner together," Kitty proclaimed her innocence.

"Lydia, Kitty said nothing, but you just did. Your choice: try your reckless plan, which will ruin you and you *sisters* if you succeed, or dance at the ball," Bennet said calmly.

Lydia stamped her foot in frustration. She really wanted to dance at the ball, so her plans would have to be put on hold, but *only* on hold. "I will not attempt to leave the house!" Lydia exclaimed petulantly, proving again how young she was.

Just then the door opened, and Collins was shown in, accompanied by Mr. Dudley and his daughter. "Dudley, were we supposed to meet?" Bennet asked in confusion.

"As they are to be my family, I invited them, Cousin," Collins announced.

"Mr. Collins, when you are a guest in your patroness's house, what would she say if you invited another without her permission?" Bennet asked calmly.

"I-I-I would never. I am to inherit..." Collins spluttered, and Bennet cut him off.

"Until the day I leave the mortal world and you are notified you are *indeed* the heir, you have *no* rights here. I would ask you to leave tonight, but as there are only two days left before you depart, I will not have you thrown out of *my* house!" Bennet stated. The steel in his voice was unmistakable.

"Bennet, I apologise, I tried to inform my future son-in-law it was not done, but he insisted," Dudley stated contritely.

The statement was met by silence from all the Bennets in the drawing room, until Lydia burst into unrestrained laughter, soon joined by Kitty. "Miss Dudley, you accepted him?" Lydia managed between laughs.

This was not the reaction either Dudley expected. "Y-yes, Miss Lydia, Mr. Collins requested my hand and I have accepted him," Matilda confirmed.

"Lydia and Kitty," Bennet commanded, as you are not able to behave as ladies, go up to your bedchamber!" Seeing Lydia was about to protest, Bennet added and emphatic "Now!" His two youngest daughters decided not to test his resolve as he had just threatened one of them with not going to the upcoming ball.

"When I am head of this family..." Collins began his familiar rant once again.

"Mr. Collins did not both myself and my daughter Elizabeth explain to you that regardless of the eventual disposition of the estate after my death, you will *never* be the head of the Bennet family? There is only one who can make that determination, me! My will is very specific; however, I will be amending it on the morrow so there is no ambiguity. In it I will state you are disqualified from guardianship of any of my daughters who are not of age or not married when I go to my final reward. *If* you inherit Longbourn, that will be the *only* thing you will have control over." Bennet stared at the man who soon had to look away.

"What do you mean *if*, Cousin?" Collins asked, having

finally heard that word.

"You never know what will happen between now and then, and, with the vagaries of life and death, there is no guarantee you will survive me. As I understand it, that is knowledge to which only God on High is privy," Bennet replied dryly.

It irked Collins to find out the impertinent one had been correct. He would not have any control over them, and worse, he would not be able to touch their dowries. As his cousin's words sank in, he realised for the first time he could predecease the man, and then he would never inherit. He reassured himself with the knowledge that God would never allow such an injustice to occur.

Matilda seated herself with Jane and Elizabeth. "Matti, are you sure this is who you want to marry?" Elizabeth asked quietly.

"Just because he would not offer for one of you, Lizzy, does not mean I should not be his choice," Matilda said with some asperity.

"Did he tell you that, Matti?" Jane asked quietly and Matilda nodded. "He wanted to offer for me, but our father barred him from offering for any of us."

Matilda knew both Jane and Elizabeth well enough to know they were not lying to her. "Then I suppose I must be grateful to your father, as he gave me the opportunity to become betrothed when I had given up hope of it ever happening," Matilda stated.

"In that case, you need to thank Charlotte as well, Matti," Elizabeth revealed.

"He did not," Matilda was shocked.

"She refused him this morning," Jane confirmed.

Matilda had heard Collins tell her father about his patroness and her order to marry, but she had thought mayhap he was jesting. It seemed he was not. Miss Dudley rationalised that without his offer she would have died a spinster, so, as much as she disliked his misrepresentation of the facts and the humiliation of being his third choice, she wanted to be married and have a home of her own, she would not break off the betrothal.

Collins was sitting in a chair and sulking again, but at least his odour was bearable. He heard his cousins reveal his humiliation to his betrothed, and so far, it did not seem as if she was moving to withdraw. He was deeply relieved, as he did not want to return to his parsonage without being able to inform Lady Catherine he was married or betrothed.

"Dudley, will you attend me in my study? There is something I need to discuss with you," Bennet requested. Mr. Dudley stood and Collins made to stand as well. "Only Mr. Dudley, thank you."

Bennet stationed Hill outside his study door before he joined his friend within. "Given your daughter's news this day, what I need to ask you may be awkward, and before I do ask, I need to ask your complete confidence as a member of the clergy," Bennet stated.

"I will reveal nothing of our conversation to anyone save my Lord and Master," Dudley vowed.

"After the Netherfield Ball, once your future son-in-law has departed, I will be marrying. Miss Lucas has agreed to be my wife," Bennet revealed.

"Now I understand your need for secrecy. It puts me in a difficult position as it affects my daughter's future prospects," Dudley steepled his fingers.

"Possible prospects. We have tried to point out to Collins on several occasions there are some possible factors that may preclude his inheriting the estate. Regardless, he talks and behaves as if the estate is his by wrote and I am already in the ground, his impertinence at inviting you to a house not his being merely one example." Bennet poured two glasses of port and offered one to the vicar.

Dudley decided he would not counsel Matti to withdraw. Even without Longbourn, Collins had a good income and livings were for life. He would support her in whatever decision she made. "Besides notifying me, I assume you want me to perform the marriage rites?" Dudley surmised.

"After I speak to Sir William on the morrow, I will need a common licence. If this puts you in an awkward position, I will go see Hinkley at St. Alfred's in Meryton," Bennet offered.

"I am Matti's father and I know nothing is being done with an eye to harming her, so, as your pastor, it will be my pleasure to conduct the ceremony and issue a licence when you require it." Bennet expected nothing less from Dudley. He was a jovial man, but one who took his pastoral duties extremely seriously. "You should know, I issued a common licence today. Collins will marry Matti, if it still her choice, on Friday before they depart for his home."

Bennet said nothing; he had heard something of this from Collins but took it with a grain of salt until his friend confirmed the news. He knew that, unlike Collins, Dudley would never repeat anything told to him in confidence by a parishioner. Bennet would not go into Collins' deficits unless and until Dudley asked him a direct question on the subject. Thankfully, his friend asked nothing.

Not long after, the two men returned to the drawing room, the Dudleys departed, thankfully taking Collins with them. "Should we not warn the Dudleys?" Elizabeth asked.

"No, Lizzy. I decided that unless asked direct questions about Collins, we will not interfere," Bennet stated unequivocally.

"Understood, Papa," Elizabeth returned as her sisters nodded. Bennet would make sure his two youngest were informed that no further comments were to be made about their cousin.

CHAPTER 7

Bennet arrived at Lucas Lodge at ten in the morning, two days before the ball. It was a bright day, and warm considering it was the second to last day of October. At his knock, the door was answered by none other than his betrothed.

"Good morning, Miss Lucas," Bennet bowed.

"Mr. Bennet," Charlotte curtsied. "My father is in his study," Charlotte informed Bennet at his questioning look.

"Come!" Sir William's welcoming voice boomed after the knock on his study door. Bennet hoped the voice would still be warm once he stated his purpose for being there.

"Sit Bennet," Sir William indicated a chair, then he noticed his daughter Charlotte had entered the room with his friend and had closed the door. "Charlotte?"

"What Mr. Bennet needs to discuss with you affects me, Papa, and I want to make sure there are no misunderstandings," Charlotte stated evenly.

Sir William could not imagine what his friend wanted to discuss which somehow involved his eldest daughter. "Lucas, Sir William, I have asked for Charlotte's hand in marriage, and she has done me the great honour of accepting me," Bennet stated in as matter-of-factly as he was able to. "We are here seeking your blessing."

"Charlotte, are you out of your senses accepting a man who is just a few years younger than myself?" Sir William demanded. Then he remembered it was his friend who was standing opposite him. "No disrespect meant, Bennet."

"None taken," Bennet assured Sir William.

"Papa, do you have any other objection, other than my betrothed's age?" Charlotte asked.

"No, I do not. We all know Bennet is a man of impeccable character and honour, so if he is truly your choice, I will not stand in your way. However, let me urge you to think on this. Are you doing this only because you see yourself as a burden to me? Is it because you do not believe you have any other chance at marriage, my daughter?" Sir William asked seriously, the jovial side of Sir William not in evidence.

"No, Papa, it is not that. He is my *choice*. It is not one made of desperation or my worry of being a burden to you and Frank in the future. It is my firm belief we are more than compatible, and the additional bonus is if I bear a son, I will be securing the future of the estate for Bennets for generations to come. It is a choice I made to help the Bennets, both with discipline of the youngest two and hopefully for the estate's future," Charlotte stated emphatically.

"Help?" Sir William questioned.

"That despicable toad of a parson has engaged himself to Matilda Dudley. After his insulting proposal to me, he hied to the parsonage at Longbourn, and she *accepted* him. You remember I relayed to all of you what the vindictive clergyman said he would do as soon as he inherited?" Charlotte reminded her father. Sir William nodded.

"Charlotte," Sir William did not react to his friend using his daughter's familiar name, "came to see me after she had been proposed to and told me all—what the sycophant ranted about—which she overheard, and his words to her. But it is not just for the possibility of an heir that I proposed to your daughter, Lucas.

"As she correctly stated, we are well matched in intelligence and interests. I spoke to my three oldest daughters. Charlotte was present and she will affirm for you that, Jane, Lizzy, and Mary all gave their blessing and quickly realised we would be good for one another. If children come of this union, and one is a son, so much the better. We do not love one another, but we do respect and honour each other," Bennet relayed to Sir

William.

"If that be the case, and this is truly what you want, Charlotte," Charlotte nodded, "then Bennet deserves you. I could not have let you go to one less worthy, my Charlotte. Welcome to the family *Son*," Sir William jested with his soon-to-be son-in-law.

"Do not expect me to call you Father, my friend," Bennet returned the jest as the two men shook hands. "Phillips will have a settlement to you for signing later today."

"When will you two marry?" Sir William asked.

"On Saturday," Charlotte informed her father.

"I will receive a common licence from Dudley today, now that we have your blessing, Lucas," Bennet told Sir William.

"Come; we need to inform your mother, brothers, and sister," Sir William started towards the door.

"We will not announce this publicly until Friday, after Collins marries and departs," Bennet explained. "We do not want a scene at the ball, making the evening about us. Further, we both agree the man does not know how to regulate his mouth." Bennet saw the quizzical looks from Sir William and his daughter. "If I understood Dudley properly this morning, his daughter and Collins want to be married as soon as may be, so he will issue a licence and they will marry Friday morning after the ball, and then depart directly for their home at Hunsford in Westerham, Kent."

Sir William nodded his understanding, and the three left the study to join his wife, his two older sons, and Mariah in the sitting room. Nick, the only Lucas not present, was away at Oxford and would receive the news by letter.

"Our Charlotte will become Mrs. Thomas Bennet on Saturday," Sir William announced.

For a full minute there was shocked silence. Then the questions started, initially by Franklin. A half hour later, the betrothed couple had accepted good wishes for their future felicity from all present. The rest of the Lucases well understood the need for silence on the subject until the objectionable man departed the area, even Mariah, who found it amusing she would be her friends' aunt.

"Mariah, you understand you may not tell Lydia and Kitty, do you not?" Charlotte verified.

"I do. I do not believe I will see them before the ball at any rate," Mariah opined.

"If all is settled, I will return to Longbourn." Bennet started to stand, but Charlotte stayed him with a hand on his arm.

"There is another issue we need to discuss: Lieutenant George Wickham," Charlotte stated.

"What about Wickham?" Sir William asked.

"From my observations, he seems to have opened accounts with most of the merchants in Meryton. From the information I have gleaned, his debts with two or three merchants will be more than a junior militia officer will earn in a few years. Papa, you were a merchant, so you know the damage even a ten-pound unpaid debt can cause. What will happen to our friends and neighbours if the man's debts are many multiples of that amount?" Charlotte postulated.

"But his countenance is so pleasant! I see no duplicity in him," Lady Lucas stated, "I am sure you are mistaken, Charlotte."

Charlotte proceeded to relay her misgivings about the man's character and informed her parents how Mr. Wickham had told Eliza his tale of woe on their first meeting, noting how many times the man contradicted himself in the space of one recitation. Bennet added his opinion, which concurred with his betrothed's.

"What I suggest, Papa, is that you and Thomas quietly visit each merchant; mayhap Frank and John should help in case the officer sees the same men visiting every merchant. I am sure he is the type who will run as soon as things become uncomfortable for him. Once we have a tally of his debts, we will know how to act. We all care about this town too much to allow one profligate man to ruin many of our merchants.

"If it is as I suspect, the next step would be for Papa and Thomas to meet with Colonel Forster. I would wager the Lieutenant has many debts of honour with his fellow officers," Charlotte opined.

It was decided the men would gather information on *all* the officer's debts, that way there would be no mention of Mr. Wickham specifically.

~~~~~~~/~~~~~~~

"Bingley, I have a note from my Cousin Richard, who is in Town and has liberty. Would you be willing to extend him an invitation to the ball? If we send it express, he will be able to arrive this evening," Darcy requested.

"Go ahead and send the express; you know how much I enjoy the Colonel's company. Have him invite his brother, the Viscount. Mayhap having him here will give you some relief from my sister's attentions," Bingley grinned as Darcy scowled.

"I will include Andrew in the invitation as well," Darcy returned.

Not long after, Darcy sealed the missive and wrote the direction. He summoned one of his couriers, and the man was soon heading to Matlock House in London. "Do you think they will both decide to come?" Bingley asked after the courier left his study.

"I am confident Richard will; I am less sure of Andrew. It will depend on his social calendar," Darcy surmised. "Your sister would be wise to behave more properly in their presence; neither of them will be as patient as I am with her."

"In two days, I will open the ball with my angel, Miss Jane Bennet. She is the most beautiful lady," Bingley said wistfully.

This was not the first time Darcy had heard his friend extoll a young lady with whom he was currently in love. As it had been in the past, Darcy expected as soon as the next angel presented herself, Bingley would forget about Miss Bennet and move on, so he said nothing to discourage his friend.

"Darce, why did you not ask them to bring Miss Darcy with them?" Bingley asked.

As much as he hated to tell an untruth, for he abhorred deception, Darcy knew he had to. Even to Bingley he would not reveal Gigi's near ruin. "My sister has too many studies and sessions with her music master to leave London at this time. In the future, we will see." Darcy would not chance his sister being exposed to the rake again.

~~~~~~~/~~~~~~~

Just over three hours later, Colonel Richard Fitzwilliam entered the family sitting room at Matlock House on Grosvenor Square. "Andy, you and I are invited to a ball," Richard drawled.

"By whom and where?" Andrew Fitzwilliam, Viscount Hilldale, asked.

"Bingley and his leased estate just over twenty miles from Town in the wilds of Hertfordshire," Richard informed his brother.

"Bingley? Oh, you mean Darcy's friend. Is our reserved and taciturn cousin not there teaching his friend estate management?" Andrew remembered.

"Correct. In fact, it is our reserved taciturn cousin who penned the note," Richard responded. Before his brother asked why the host did not pen the note, the Colonel pre-empted him. "If you ever had the displeasure of trying to read Bingley's atrocious script, you would know why William performed the office."

"Bingley," Lord Reginald Fitzwilliam, the Earl of Matlock, intoned, "is he not the puppy Darcy leads around by his nose?"

"The same. Very affable and jovial, but no backbone and hates confrontation," Richard confirmed." He turned to his brother. "Well Andy, are you joining me, or should I depart in an hour on my own?"

"I will join you. Let us see what Hertfordshire has to offer. Wait, Rich! Will not that awful Miss Bingley be there?" Andrew asked with distaste.

Georgiana Darcy, who had been sitting quietly during the exchange, giggled. "She thinks we all are enamoured with her,"

Georgiana said softly.

"Then she is delusional, Gigi," Lady Elaine, Countess of Matlock, stated firmly.

"D-did W-William not invite me?" Georgiana asked timidly.

"I am afraid not, Gigi. Allow us to arrive and get the lay of the land. I am sure William wants to protect you from Miss Bingley's false friendship," Richard assured his ward. He shared guardianship with his cousin and was pleased to see Gigi perk up as she accepted his logic.

The Colonel was certain before he gave her his supposition, she assumed her brother did not want to be in her company because of Ramsgate. How he would like to get his hands on one George Wickham's scrawny neck!

Within the hour, the brothers were on their way to Netherfield Park.

~~~~~~~/~~~~~~~

After the four men canvassed the town's merchants and tradesmen, they met at Mr. Phillips's office to tally the totals. As each came in, they handed their notes to Charlotte, who quickly tallied them. When she was done, she gasped. "How did they allow one man to amass close to four hundred pounds in debts?" Then she examined some of the notes again. "It seems like the good Lieutenant also enjoys seducing young girls half his age."

"*How much?*" Phillips was flabbergasted. Charlotte showed him the list and total, and all Phillips could do was shake his head. He was disgusted when he saw the names of the tradesmen's daughters with whom he had dallied.

"Mr. Phillips, could you send your clerk to Colonel Forster's office and request the Colonel attend you urgently?" Charlotte suggested.

Within minutes, the young man was on his way to the regimental offices. Less than a half hour later, Colonel Forster returned with him. "Gentlemen and Miss Lucas," he said in greeting, "how may I be of assistance to you?"

"We are hoping we may be of assistance to you, Colonel," Sir William began. "The militia had always been welcomed in Meryton, but we have discovered a situation which could sour the relationship between your unit and the town irrevocably."

"This must be grave; I will do all I am able to rectify the situation, as we would hate to lose our welcome here," Colonel Forster stated with all seriousness. "Please give me the details so that I may correct the problems."

"Problem, Colonel Forster, *problem*," Bennet emphasised. "You seem to have one rather bad apple in the barrel who, if unchecked, will ensure the militia will never be welcomed in our town again."

"One man has caused such a problem as to threaten our welcome here?" the Colonel asked. He was visibly shaken there might be such a man under his command. "Who is it?"

"Lieutenant Wickham," Sir William informed the Colonel.

"*Lieutenant Wickham*?" the Colonel repeated. "He is one of my better officers. He warned me Mr. Darcy might spread lies about him; is that man the source of your intelligence?" The Colonel bristled, as he had assumed the proud man from Derbyshire was blackening his officer's good name.

"Mr. Darcy has never mentioned the Lieutenant's name to any of us. No, the problems we now know of were discovered because the Lieutenant told my second daughter a tale full of contradictions, which we now believe to be falsehoods spun around a kernel of truth," Bennet explained. "My betrothed, Miss Lucas, noticed some behaviour of the man which made him suspect. On her suggestion, Sir William, his sons, and I canvassed all the merchants and tradesmen in Meryton." Bennet paused and then asked a direct question. "How much does a Lieutenant earn on an annual basis, Colonel?"

"Four and twenty pounds per annum," Colonel Forster shared. He had a sinking feeling in the pit of his stomach that he had been played by his new Lieutenant.

"Then how do you suppose Mr. Wickham will pay the

debts he has accumulated so far, Colonel?" Sir William handed over the list his daughter had tabulated, which listed the merchants by name and amount owed to each. Thankfully, like the tailor, it was the cost of an order not yet collected, and for the most part not made; after the advice he had received today, nothing further was being sewn.

The Colonel felt defeated; he was usually such a good judge of character. How had this man slipped passed him? "Three hundred, four and seventy pounds! How is a fraction of that debt to be paid?"

Charlotte spoke up for the first time, "Luckily, about half is for orders he placed, which the cobbler, blacksmith, and tailor have stopped. Thankfully, none of them had expended much for materials yet. His single largest debt, over fifty pounds, is to the inn where he drinks and eats. It is also where he seems to host a few with his fellow officers to get on their good side."

Having been the recipient of the Lieutenant's largess more than once at the Red Rooster Inn in Meryton, the Colonel could see how the man had incurred such a debt in a short time. "He told me he had a legacy from his late godfather when I asked how he could afford to keep paying for others to drink and eat," the slumping Colonel revealed.

"I would wager, Colonel, if you had your men check, you would find out the man has large debts of honour as well as money he has borrowed from his fellow officers," Charlotte suggested. "According to what we already know and my estimation of the man, I would not be surprised if some of your officers found items of theirs were missing, as it seems to me your Lieutenant is a man who believes it is his due for others to pay his way, whether they agree or not!"

"How do you suggest we proceed?" the Colonel asked. He was determined to deal with the scourge in the midst of his militia unit.

"Before we address that, there is more, I am afraid," Bennet informed the shocked man.

"More, as if his debts and possible thefts are not bad enough?" the Colonel exclaimed.

"He has been seducing *young* daughters of the same merchants to whom he owes so much money!" Sir William related. "From what we were told, he uses the line that if they love him, they will not make him wait for the wedding, and then once he has what he wants, he threatens them with ruin if they tell anyone. The man is not just a wastrel and profligate, he is a black-hearted libertine!" The Sir William who was mayor and protector of his town and friends was fully evident, and Charlotte smiled, grateful her father took even his ceremonial title to heart.

"Colonel, I believe we should reconvene at Longbourn in a few hours. I will invite Mr. Darcy to join us, as I am sure he has information which we could use," Bennet suggested.

"Thomas, may I suggest Eliza be included in this meeting?" Charlotte recommended.

Bennet saw the sense in his betrothed's suggestion, as his daughter still was not of a mind she was wholly wrong. "In the meanwhile, I will have my adjutant, Captain Carter, tally of all of Wickham's debts within the unit," the Colonel stated.

"Colonel, if I may, I would suggest you have the man watched. From everything we have seen and taking the massive orders for clothing and footwear into account, I am sure he is preparing to escape his obligations. He will try to desert if he catches a whiff that the truth of his character is known. Lieutenant Wickham does not seem like the type of man who would be willing to face the consequences of his actions," Charlotte proposed.

Colonel Forster agreed it would be so and the group set a meeting at Longbourn three hours hence.

~~~~~~~/~~~~~~~

"Richard and Andrew, Welcome! I was not sure Andy would accompany you, Rich." Darcy was fairly ebullient; he was more than pleased to see his cousins with whom he was so close, and he gave each of them a back slapping bearhug. Due to their closeness in age, Richard was more brother than cousin.

"I second your cousin's welcome," Bingley stated affably.

"Where are you off to, Darce?" Richard enquired.

"I am to the neighbouring estate, Longbourn. Rich, I should have told you, Wickham is here." Seeing his cousin was about to blurt out his displeasure, Darcy shook his head and directed his eyes to Bingley. "Evidently, *dear* Georgie boy is the subject of a meeting to which I have been invited."

"I *am* joining you, William!" Richard stated. It was not a request.

"Me too!" Andrew insisted.

So it was the carriage departing Netherfield Park held one Darcy and two Fitzwilliams. Miss Bingley was most put out her highborn guests departed without a word of greeting to her.

CHAPTER 8

About an hour before the scheduled meeting at Longbourn, Kitty and Lydia returned from Lucas Lodge to a peaceful Collins-less Longbourn; it was not hard to see the youngest Bennet was in high dudgeon. "You will not believe what Mariah told me!" Lydia screeched. Charlotte was about to take Eliza aside to inform her of the upcoming meeting so she would not be taken by surprise, but Lydia's commanded everyone's attention before Charlotte could do so. "*My* Wickham is betrothed to Mary King! How dare that freckled thing steal *my love!*"

As his youngest screeched, Bennet realised how close they had come to ruin. It seemed Wickham's seductions were not restricted to merchants' and tradesmen's daughters. Bennet looked at Charlotte, who nodded, making him understand her expectation. He needed to invite Miss King's uncle to at least part of their meeting. Bennet went to his study to write a note and send a footman to deliver the missive directly into the hands of Miss King's guardian.

"So what if she inherited ten thousand pounds! I am still prettier and livelier than any of the girls in Meryton. Mama used to tell me I could catch any man I want, and *I want my Wickham!*" Lydia announced loudly enough to inform the whole county as she stamped her foot petulantly.

Charlotte looked at her friend Eliza and was gratified to see disgust in her mien. She was sure she was finally, and rapidly, re-evaluating her belief in Mr. Wickham's honour.

"Lydia, calm yourself," Jane attempted to quiet youngest sister.

"*I WILL NOT! I WANT MY WICKY…*" Whatever Lydia was

about to scream next would never be known, as Charlotte stood and slapped Lydia's face.

The four seated Bennet daughters were caught unawares, and Lydia stood, holding her cheek with her mouth gaping—but at least no sound was emanating from it. "I thank you, Miss Lucas, for ending that childish display," Bennet stated calmly, as he entered the drawing room. He turned to his youngest, who was still in shock as this was the first time anyone had ever stopped her from making a scene. "As of this moment you, Lydia, are back in the nursery."

"Noooooooo Papa! I hate you..." Lydia started but halted when Bennet raised his hand as he would when he wanted silence and would not stand for any more whining. Lydia's jaw snapped shut. "Not only are you not mature enough to be out, but you are certainly not ready to be around men! Based on your conversation before Miss Lucas stopped your tantrum, I would surmise you have had far more unchaperoned time with the officers than I suspected. I want to know all *now*, Kitty, or you will join your sister in the nursery!"

Lydia shot her father a defiant and mutinous look. "Often times when we say we are going to visit Aunt Phillips, we meet the officers," Kitty related with her head down.

"*KITTY!*" Lydia screamed, "How could you betray me in this fashion?"

"One more word, Lydia, and I will request Miss Lucas to discipline you in truth," Bennet threatened. He did not believe in corporal punishment for a male, let alone a female, but right now the threat seemed to have the required effect. Lydia closed her mouth again and sat down on a chair, her arms crossed and angry tears of flowing down her cheeks.

"Lydia, I am sorry, but I will not return to the nursery because I was not honest with Papa." Kitty turned back to her father; her head raised slightly. "We never allowed the officers more than a kiss or two. Mr. Wickham wanted more, but I was able to convince Lydia it was not a good idea, although just before Mariah told us about Mary King, my sister agreed to sneak out at night and give Mr. Wickham anything he desired." Kitty burned red with embarrassment as she related this before her father, sisters, and Miss Lucas. Lydia was red as well, but with fury at having been found out.

"Mr. Hill!" Bennet called. "Miss Lydia is to be removed to the nursery. She is not to leave it for *any* reason. Have Edward nail the windows shut as a precaution; I do not want this stupid child falling to her death. Once done, Edward and the other two footmen will take turns on duty outside her door at all times." Hill nodded his understanding and left to have the footman bring a hammer and nails to secure the window before moving Miss Lydia into the nursery.

Elizabeth was reeling. Every word Charlotte ever said about Mr. Wickham replayed in her mind, and she could not but admit the fact the man was nothing but a scoundrel, possibly even worse. "I have been a prejudiced fool, have I not?" She asked no one in particular. "I thought I was so intelligent and could sketch characters to perfection, yet my pride did not allow me to see the facts in front of my face! Charlotte, you were completely correct," Elizabeth acknowledged openly.

"Even I did not suspect how truly evil the man is, Eliza," Charlotte soothed.

Lydia was about to try and defend her erstwhile lover when Hill and the footman Edward returned. At Mr. Bennet's nod, they lifted the defiant girl and carried her, kicking and screaming, up the three flights of stairs to the nursery. Once they reached the third floor the noise of Lydia's tantrum lessened for those in the drawing room, and once the door slammed shut, peace once more reigned.

"I was going to include only Elizabeth in a meeting which will be held here in less than an hour, but I think it would behove all of you to be present," Bennet decided after Charlotte said something quietly in his ear. "Keeping salient information from you is no way to protect you. I also promise, starting now, not just after I marry, that I will be more aware of what happens any of my family. Kitty, are you mature enough to not repeat anything you hear in the meeting to anyone but those present?"

"You have my word of honour, Papa. But who are you marrying?" Kitty squeaked out the last taking her completely by surprise.

Bennet realised his *faux pas*, but as he thought about it, mayhap it was for the best and fit his new determination not to hide pertinent information from his daughters. Bennet stood, walked over to Charlotte, and took her hand. "Miss Lucas. Charlotte and I will marry on Saturday coming."

"Mariah will be my sister?" Kitty asked in confusion.

"No, Kitty, as I will be your stepmother, Mariah will be your aunt, technically," Charlotte explained.

After wishing her father and Charlotte happy, Kitty agreed not to say a word to their Cousin Collins, fully understanding why Lydia would not be told until after the ball.

~~~~~~~/~~~~~~~

Mr. King joined Bennet, his four older daughters, and Charlotte, along with Mr. Phillips, Sir William Lucas, and Colonel Forster, in the Bennet drawing room. He asked why he had been summoned and was asked to be patient for a few minutes when a carriage drew to a halt in the drive.

Mr. Darcy had been expected, but it was a surprise to them all when Hill announced Andrew Fitzwilliam, Viscount Hilldale, and the Honourable Colonel Richard Fitzwilliam. "I hope I was not presumptuous," Darcy apologised. "My cousins arrived as I was preparing to depart Netherfield Park, and upon hearing the subject of the meeting, asked to join us."

"Why is that man here?" Mr. King pointed at Darcy. "My niece's betrothed told us how Mr. Darcy is jealous of him and hates him! I know it all; you will attempt to blacken his name, so I will not remain here and hear you try," Mr. King stated, starting to stand.

"Yes, Mr. King, I was fed the same lies by my Lieutenant," Colonel Forster stated.

"Forster! What are you doing here?" Richard recognised

his friend, who he had not noticed before the man spoke. He had been distracted by the pretty faces he saw, especially the one with glasses who tried to hide her light in a corner and observe without being seen.

"Good to see you, Fitzwilliam. I am in command of the contingent of the Derbyshire Militia encamped in the environs of Meryton." The two Colonels shook hands.

"So you have the *pleasure* of having that libertine Wickham under your command," Richard shook his head that such a man would be allowed to sully the uniform.

"What is it I do not know about Mr. Wickham?" Mr. King asked. All his former bravado dissipated as he watched high-ranking men who obviously knew and respected one another commiserate over a man he had just met.

"Let me guess, Sir. You were told I denied him a living my father designated for him at Kympton near my estate in Derbyshire?" Mr. King nodded. Elizabeth nodded as well, although Darcy did not see it, as others in the room did. "It is true, I did in fact deny him the living—when he applied for it *after* first refusing to take orders and accepting three thousand pounds in return for relinquishing all claim to said living. He signed a document relinquishing that claim, which is in the hands of my legal counsel, Norman and James. If you wish to see it, I will have a copy delivered for your perusal. He left with that three thousand and an additional thousand pounds my father gifted him in his last will and testament. In less than two years, all that money was gone; that is when he insisted he was ready to take orders. I hope you will understand why I denied his request, as he is the last man on earth who should be a clergyman.

"Let me guess that your ward recently inherited a substantial sum of money, and then Wickham began to pay her attention. Before that, did he pay her no heed?" Darcy asked, already knowing the answer. "If you are all here then he must have meddled with some young girls in the town or run up debts he cannot hope to pay, or perhaps both?" Miss Lucas and the men other than Mr. King all nodded.

"I can only apologise for believing what that blackguard told me about you, Mr. Darcy. I should have known to not believe him at face value. What a foolish old man I was to be taken in by one such as he," Mr. King lamented.

"You are not the first to have the wool pulled over your eyes by that wastrel, Mr. King," Andrew informed the man. "In fact, you are one of many."

"You have my heartfelt thanks for helping me to protect my Mary; she is all I have left of my family now. We will depart for Manchester at first light, and not return until we know the man is no longer a danger to my niece." Mr. King stood, bowed to the room, and took his leave.

When looking at the Bennet daughters, one would have had a hard time deciding whether Elizabeth or Kitty were paler. "Before we continue, I must apologise to Mr. Darcy for believing any poison Mr. Wickham poured in my ears about him. Even though my stepmother-to-be . . ." Elizabeth stopped, realising she just announced her father's betrothal to all in the room.

"It is well, Eliza. Other than Mr. Darcy and his cousins, there is no one in the room not aware that I am marrying your father on Saturday," Charlotte relieved Elizabeth's concern.

"On behalf of my brother and cousin, I wish you both happy," Andrew stated.

"To continue, after the insult you delivered to me at the assembly, I was looking for anything which would lower you in my estimation, so Mr. Wickham found a willing and foolish reception to his lies," Elizbeth owned contritely.

"William! You insulted a gentlewoman?" Richard asked, deeply aghast.

"The assembly was the day I arrived. Miss Bingley had been grating on my nerves, along with Ramsgate, and Bingley would not leave me alone, insisting I should dance. The truth was, Miss Elizabeth, I hardly saw you; my aim was to get Bingley to return to his partner and leave me in peace. When I looked at you, truly looked at you, I saw an extremely hand-some woman and hoped against hope you did not hear me. Please accept my heartfelt apologies," Darcy beseeched.

"I will grant you my pardon as long as you do the same for me, for allowing my good sense to be overruled and believing Mr. Wickham's lies," Elizabeth said.

"Easily done, Miss Elizabeth," Darcy agreed.

"What did my cousin say to you, Miss Elizabeth?" Andrew asked. "I am sure my parents would love to hear how their nephew behaves when he is abroad."

Elizabeth looked at Darcy with an arched eyebrow, and he lifted his hands in surrender. "He said I was tolerable, but not handsome enough to tempt him and he would not give consequence to young ladies slighted by other men," Elizabeth reported.

"William! Could you think of no better way to make Bing-ley subside?" Andrew asked.

"As ungentlemanly as it was, it was the only thing I thought of at that moment. I apologise again, Miss Elizabeth," Darcy averred.

"It is I who made the greater error; I allowed my vanity to overrule my good sense," Elizabeth insisted.

"Let us not argue who owns the larger part of the fault. May we start again, Miss Elizabeth and try and move past the errors I made?" Elizabeth nodded. "I need to share some infor-mation with you, and I ask it does not leave this room," Darcy scanned everyone present. Everyone vowed not to repeat it while his cousins looked at him questioningly. "I need to share this so they will understand the depths of his depravity," Darcy explained to his cousins.

"I do not think we are unaware of how depraved the man is, Mr. Darcy," Charlotte spoke. "Let us decide what needs to be done to protect our town from the wolf in sheep's clothing."

"I find I need to make another apology, Miss Lucas. I could have warned the residents of the area, but I chose not to. I did not want my private concerns known in order to protect my sister. Wickham attempted to harm her as well. It was a failure on my part she was ever in the situation she was." Darcy lowered his head, the shame of almost failing his sister again overwhelming.

"William, if it were not for you, Gigi's life would have been ruined! But for the chance of your deciding to visit her two days earlier than planned, she would have been lost to us forever!" Richard insisted. It was one of his cousin's few failings, that he always tried to take what was not his fault onto his own shoulders.

For the first time, Andrew Fitzwilliam looked around the room and then he saw her—Miss Jane Bennet was a vision. But all the beauty in the world would mean nothing if she was vapid and did not have a good character. Like his cousin and brother, he had looked among the ladies of the *ton*, but was yet to find one who had garnered his attention. This was not the time, but he intended to dance with her at the ball and discover if there was more than external beauty to the lady.

Charlotte explained what had roused her suspicions about Mr. Wickham, and what they had learned of his debts and the young girls with whom he had meddled in Meryton. "Colonel Forster, do you have an estimate of how much Wickham owes in debts of honour?" Charlotte asked after she finished explaining what they knew of the profligate's debts and seductions.

"I do, Miss Lucas. With debts of honour plus loans from his fellow officers, he owes close to one thousand pounds," Colonel Forster reported angrily. "I suppose with his debts in Meryton, plus the vowels he had signed to my officers, we could have him sent to Marshalsea for a time."

"We can send him away for life!" Darcy exclaimed. "I have over three thousand pounds' worth of his vowels."

"William, why did you not send him away after he attempted to elope with Gigi?" Richard demanded. Noticing the confused expression of the lady in the corner, he added that that "Gigi" was Darcy's sister Georgiana's preferred nickname.

"I always felt I would somehow dishonour my father if I took action against his godson, so I kept buying up his debts. I will do so again here, including his debts of honour, Colonel Forster," Darcy pledged.

"You take too much on yourself Sir," Charlotte opined. "If you ask me, after what that man attempted with your sister, your late father would have been at the front of the queue to send the man away. Do you think he would have allowed Mr. Wickham to not pay for whatever it was he attempted with your sister?"

While he had been observing, Colonel Fitzwilliam did not miss the surreptitious looks William had directed at Miss Elizabeth Bennet. Never had Richard seen his cousin look at a woman twice, never mind multiple times in a single meeting.

"No, Miss Lucas, I believe you are correct," Mr. Darcy replied at length. "It is time to allow the man to feel the consequences of his actions. I will send an express to Sir Randolph Norman, requesting he send all of Wickham's vowels he holds for me as soon as he is able." Darcy looked around, seeing only four Bennet sisters. "Where is Miss Lydia?" Darcy asked.

"She is no longer out, and is back in the nursery," Bennet responded, "My betrothed and I agree it is the best course with her."

"Your betrothed?" Darcy asked with raised eyebrows. Then he remembered the reference Miss Elizabeth had made to that subject.

"Did I not mention Miss Lucas has agreed to be my wife? We marry on Saturday." Just as Bennet finished speaking, the door was pushed open and Mr. William Collins sauntered into the drawing room, his pompous attitude as much on display as Lydia's anger had been.

"You did not inform me you were to have guests, Cousin," Collins stated as he puffed himself up with self-importance.

"Since when do I need to notify a *guest* in *my* house about what I do or do not do, Mr. Collins?" Bennet asked acerbically.

"Collins, you are a pastor are you not?" Darcy asked.

"I am, but I was not addressing you, sir," Collins turned back towards his cousin.

"As I believe you are the rector in Hunsford, which is under the gift of my *aunt* Lady Catherine, I am sure she will enjoy hearing how you spoke to one of her nephews," Darcy replied nonchalantly.

"Mr. Bennet, will you introduce this man to us?" Andrew asked, as he was the highest-ranking person in the room. Collins was too flustered to note the request as he was trying to figure out how to introduce himself to someone of such venerated status as the nephew of his patroness.

"Viscount Hilldale, Colonel Fitzwilliam, and Mr. Darcy, this is my distant cousin, Mr. William Collins, heir *presumptive* to my estate..." Before he completed the introductions Collins was close to an apoplexy.

He had just slighted Mr. Darcy, not only her ladyship's favourite nephew, but he was Miss Anne de Bourgh's, who was the rose of Kent, betrothed! If his actions got back to his patroness, his life would become a living hell. Not only that, but the Earl's sons were present.

Mr. Collins fainted.

CHAPTER 9

Before Colonel Forster departed Longbourn, he agreed to Colonel Fitzwilliam accompanying him to the encampment, and to his request to be present when Wickham was brought to his office. Wickham being summoned to see the Colonel was not unusual, so his suspicions would not be raised. On their way to the encampment, Colonel Fitzwilliam suggested that while Wickham was with them, his quarters be thoroughly searched.

Wickham was not sure why he had been summoned to the Colonel's office. He hoped it was not because of his flirtation with his commander's young wife. Harriet Forster was very much like Lydia Bennet in intelligence, but she was a woman he would not dare touch until the day he was to make his escape. Wickham calculated that would be in a fortnight, mayhap three weeks, after his new clothing and boots would be ready.

When he arrived at the outer office, Captain Carter indicated that the Lieutenant should proceed directly into the Colonel's office, as the door was ajar. Wickham ambled into his commander's office with his usual swagger and gave the Colonel a jaunty salute. When Wickham heard the door close behind him, he thought nothing of it.

His fear became overwhelming when, from behind and close enough to feel the heat of the man's exhale, he heard the voice of the only man who he knew would never show him mercy. "Does not give a very good salute, does he, Forster?" Wickham prayed he was wrong, but as he turned his head, he saw Richard Fitzwilliam standing at his left, which meant that Richard's fighting hand was in the middle of his back, and the man was giving him the most malevolent look he had ever seen. Not even women ruined and laughed away had affected such malice.

"W-Why a-are," Wickham cleared his now dry throat, "Why a-are you h-here, Fitzwilliam?" Wickham stammered.

"That is *Colonel* Fitzwilliam to you, Lieutenant," Richard growled, purposefully remaining between the quivering man and the door.

"Lieutenant, would you like to repeat the tale you told me about Mr. Darcy cheating you?" Colonel Forster asked.

"Ahem, errrr, I am not sure of what you speak, Colonel," Wickham was sweating profusely now, unable to see a way forward which would keep him in good standing and not get him run through. He could see the man he was petrified of in his peripheral vision and was well aware his only avenue of escape was cut off. The last thing he wanted to do was give Darcy's cousin a reason to unsheathe the sabre hanging at his side.

"You really need to polish up your lying skills, Georgie boy. Not only did you tell your pack of lies to both your commander and Mr. King—by the way, your betrothal is no more —and to Miss Elizabeth Bennet, but now you try to make your Colonel a fool in front of me?" Richard growled.

"H-he did deny me the living," Wickham managed.

"Except, Lieutenant, you left out the part of your *refusal* of the living and the receipt of three thousand pounds when you signed away all rights to it!" Colonel Forster thundered. He had no time for dishonourable men.

There was a smart knock on the door. On receipt of a command to enter, Captain Carter entered with Lieutenants Sanderson and Denny. Each Lieutenant was holding items in his hand, and both were glaring at Wickham whose pallor changed to a sickly white when he what they held.

"The items being held by the two Lieutenants were discovered secreted in Wickham's mattress," the Adjutant reported. There were watches, rings, and similar items, plus one or two purses, now almost empty.

"Captain, do you think the value of the pilfered items is above twenty pounds?" Richard asked, ignoring that Wickham was looking from one of them to the other, now ashen with fear.

"Yes, Colonel, well over that amount, in fact," Captain Carter replied.

"There you have it, gentlemen; we all know this is a hanging offence," Richard stated nonchalantly. Colonel Forster dismissed his three men with instructions to return all items to their rightful owners. "Here are your choices, Wickham. You will be arrested, tried, and hung, or you will be arrested and transported with twenty years hard labour in Van Diemen's Land. You will never be allowed to return to this island, *ever*. If you do, you will be hung with no delay!" Richard enumerated the man's choices, one of which was horrible, but the other was death.

"If Darcy does not help me, I will make sure everyone knows about his sister–," Wickham tried, earning a fist in his stomach from Colonel Fitzwilliam before he was finished speaking. Wickham dropped to all fours as he gasped for breath.

"Mention one word about *Miss Darcy*, and your *only* option will be hanging!" Richard informed the man menacingly.

It was at this moment Wickham realised no one would be coming to assist him this time, and he mumbled something to the floor.

"What was that, Mr. Wickham?" His former commander demanded. The change in how he was addressed reminded him that the instant he had been caught committing an honours violation, he was no longer a member of the militia.

"Transportation," he managed.

"So be it. Captain Carter," Colonel Forster called. "Do you have the men ready to escort this sorry excuse to Newgate where he is to be held until his transport ship departs?"

"Yessir," the Captain replied. With a nod from his commander, the captain had two soldiers drag the disgraced ex-officer to the stockade, after cutting his rank insignia off his epaulettes.

~~~~~~~/~~~~~~~

"I must apologise to my patroness' nephews," Collins insisted once he was revived by the leftover salts the late Mrs. Bennet used almost daily.

"They returned to Netherfield, Mr. Collins," Elizabeth informed him.

"I must travel thither and make my apologies. If my beneficent patroness becomes angry with me, it will be a disaster," Collins looked from one to another fearfully.

"Mr. Collins, the gentlemen will be at the ball. You may see them there. Until then, they have requested to be left in peace. I advise leaving it until then unless you would like to anger their aunt by ignoring their wishes?" Bennet played his trump card.

"Sage advice, Mr. Bennet. No, I will address them there," Collins decided.

"As a clergyman, is a ball something you should be attending?" Elizabeth asked.

"A ball such as the one we will attend tomorrow can have no evil attached to it. Not only is it given by an honourable gentleman, but my patroness' nephews will attend; for these reasons, it will be above reproach. I will retire to rest and then return to see my dear Matilda. We are of one mind; it is as we were formed for one another," Collins pontificated.

Elizabeth was in a daze. It was not just finding out each of her preconceived notions about both Mr. Wickham and Mr. Darcy were completely wrong, she still could not believe Mr. Darcy had requested the opening *and* supper sets from her before he and his cousin departed for Netherfield. She had had no reason to refuse, and if she were honest with herself, she did not want to refuse.

Before he departed with Colonel Forster, much to the middle Bennet sister's dismay, Richard Fitzwilliam requested Mary's first and supper sets, Elizabeth's second set, and Jane's third set. The Viscount asked for Jane's first set but settled for her second and supper sets; he claimed Mary's third set and Elizabeth's fourth set.

Even more surprising than asking Elizabeth to dance, Mr Darcy requested Mary's second, Jane's fourth, and the one after supper from Kitty. The Viscount asked Kitty to open the ball with him, and the Colonel claimed her fourth set.

Luckily, none of this had happened in front of Mr. Collins who was passed out at the time. He surely would have objected strenuously on behalf of his patroness with some nonsense about preserving the distinction of rank. He also might go on about how Mr. Darcy was betrothed to Lady Catherine's daughter, something the man himself had warned them the sycophant might spew.

Even rarer—Bennet was to dance. He and Charlotte would pair for the opening and supper sets. When her father had expressed reservation due to Collins's possible reaction, Charlotte had simply pointed out there was nothing the man could do which would affect them. She opined that if he found out they were to marry, so be it. She was happy with their choices and would not allow such a man to put a damper on their future.

~~~~~~~/~~~~~~~

If Miss Bingley had been put out when the three men had departed earlier, she was near apoplectic when she found out they had been with the Bennets. "We are all from the first circles; how can you bear to spend time with ones so low as the Bennets?" Miss Bingley asked, certain that at least the Viscount would agree with her.

"Excuse me, Miss Bingley. Since when have you, the daughter of a tradesman, been part of the first circles?" Andrew asked calmly.

Miss Bingley went from pink to scarlet in seconds, and her mouth opened and closed but emitted no sound. She looked to someone to rescue her, but no one offered, even Louisa pointedly avoided her gaze by playing with her bracelets.

No one jumped in to assist her.

"I tried to warn you, Caroline," Mr. Hurst stated through a grin. "You choose never to listen."

Andrew decided it was time to put paid to the awful woman's pretentions, "Also, please elucidate for us, Miss Bingley, how it is you think yourself above a gentlewoman whose father owns land and has done so for generations?"

Again no one came to Miss Bingley's aid. She exercised the only option available to her; she ran out of the room. A few minutes later, the sound of a door slamming reverberated throughout the house.

"I apologise, Bingley, but I cannot countenance blatant pretention like that. Did they not teach social order at your sister's seminary?" Andrew asked pointedly.

Before her brother answered, Mrs. Hurst excused herself and followed her sister to her bedchamber. As he always did, Bingley looked uncomfortable with confrontation. "We have tried to tell her," Bingley stated weakly.

"That is brown, Brother," Hurst stated with a single bark of laughter. "I told her; Darcy told her; but you refused to say anything!"

Bingley had no answer; he only looked embarrassed and avoided the gaze of all those in the room. "By the way, Bingley and Hurst, Mr. Bennet is remarrying. He will marry Miss Lucas on Saturday and we are invited," Darcy informed his host.

"Did you hear dear old Georgie's troubles started because the soon-to-be Mrs. Bennet was not taken by his lies and then noticed his shopping habits, all on credit?" Richard relayed to the men.

"Richard has the right of it. I already noticed one positive consequence of her influence. Mr. Bennet used to sit back and laugh at his youngest daughter's bad behaviour, but no more," Darcy stated. "The youngest, Miss Lydia, who is younger than Gigi, is both brash and an incorrigible flirt. Evidently, she was ready to physically attack Miss King for 'stealing her Wicky' from her. At least he was apprehended before he ruined her as well."

"Who did he ruin?" Bingley asked in horror.

"Recently? Some merchants' daughters here in Meryton," Richard supplied. He and Andrew knew Bingley had no knowledge of the Ramsgate affair, and Darcy preferred to keep it that way.

"I suppose I should be thankful the man did not get near Caroline. Did you not say he is a fortune hunter, Darce?" Bingley asked.

"He is, but as he was arrested and will be transported, he will not trouble us again," Darcy closed the discussion of Wickham.

"I envy you, as you were with Miss Bennet today. Is she not an angel? I have never seen beauty such as hers before," Bingley stated.

Andrew raised his eyebrows but remained silent. Bingley was certainly shallow if all he saw was Miss Bennet's looks. Unlike himself, Mr. Bingley had known the lady for some time now. No one mentioned to Bingley his angel's supper set was no longer available.

~~~~~~~/~~~~~~~

The next morning, Darcy was riding Zeus across the fields when he spied Miss Elizabeth walking at a brisk pace. Her bonnet was loosened and hanging behind her neck, allowing her chestnut curls to blow in the wind. He drew close and jumped down from his horse, allowing him to graze freely.

"Good morning, Miss Elizabeth," Darcy greeted her.

"Good morning," Elizabeth returned. "Will that big beast not wander off?" Elizabeth asked as she watched the horse warily. She had never recovered from her fear of horses since she was eight, when she took a bad fall and broke her arm. Since then, the closest she had gotten to a horse was sitting in a carriage.

"Zeus is well trained; as I walk, he will follow. Do you object if I join you, Miss Elizabeth? Darcy asked.

"I do not object, Mr. Darcy, as long as you do not ask me to sit upon that huge horse of yours." Elizabeth eyed the stallion with fear, but he paid her no attention as he munched a clump of grass.

Darcy offered his arm, gratified when Elizabeth placed her dainty hand lightly upon his forearm. "How is your sister, Mr. Darcy? If I understood the little you and your cousins did say yesterday, Wickham almost ruined her."

"Gigi, that is Georgiana, is much recovered since the summer, but is still far more withdrawn than she was. She was always shy, but now it is far worse," Darcy related. "May I tell you the full story?"

"If you choose to I will listen, Mr. Darcy. Before us, you see Oakham Mount," Elizabeth pointed to the hill about two hundred yards ahead of them. "There is a big rock under the old oak tree on the summit; it is a good place to talk. What about your horse?"

"Zeus, his name is Zeus. He will wait for me. I see a stream, so he will be at his leisure to eat and drink until we return from the top." With that Darcy made a show of telling his horse to wait for him, and, as if the stallion understood, he ambled slowly toward the stream and began to drink.

"This is very pretty, Miss Elizabeth," Darcy said once the gained the flattened summit.

"It has been my sanctuary since I was a little girl. I should not speak ill of the dead, but my mother and I did not see eye-to-eye, so this was where I often escaped to," Elizabeth shared. It warmed Darcy's heart she was willing to tell him something so personal.

"You are correct, Miss Elizabeth; the rock under the tree is the perfect place to sit and talk. I thank you for being willing to listen to me," Darcy stated will all sincerity. The more he was with this woman, the more he was seeing she would be his ideal match, his family's expectations be damned.

When he thought about it honestly, his Aunt and Uncle Fitzwilliam would accept anyone he chose, if she loved him and not his position and wealth. The only one who would take umbrage would be his Aunt Catherine and, after all, what did he care for her opinion? "Wickham and I used to be friends, until his vicious propensities came to the fore. As he grew older, he became more envious and coveted what I was to inherit. All he saw was the wealth, not the responsibility that comes with it.

"My sister had good memories of him, and I made the mistake your father did not when he allowed all of you to hear the truth about Wickham. I thought I was protecting my father and sister by not telling them the truth about Wickham," Darcy looked to the heavens where his parents were, "I should have told you, Father."

"I am sure your father understands." Elizabeth told Darcy before he was overcome by melancholy.

"Earlier this year, Richard and I hired a companion for Gigi. In hindsight I know we did not exercise due diligence in checking the woman's characters. Her name is Mrs. Younge. The references were glowing, and what we did not realise was they were too perfect. When Mrs. Younge suggested it would be good for my sister to spend some time at Ramsgate, I agreed immediately. We have a cottage there and I sent word to have it opened."

"I travelled with them, and after a sennight I returned to London. I had business which would keep me busy for three weeks, but they both knew I intended to return three weeks hence. What Richard and I did not know was that Mrs. Younge was, in fact, one of Wickham's paramours. Once he received word about the journey from his accomplice, thither Wickham went also." Darcy was getting angrier as he related the tale, which Elizabeth understood.

"If it is too hard for you, there is no need for you to continue telling me, Mr. Darcy," Elizabeth soothed. Her words broke his tension and he relaxed.

"Mrs. Younge made sure her paramour knew where Gigi would be. At first, he would *run into* them by *chance*. After a while, he came calling and Mrs. Younge and Wickham encouraged my naïve sister to believe herself in love. She eventually agreed to an elopement, which was to take place the day before my expected return. I arrived unexpectedly two days before the elopement, having concluded my business early.

"When I knocked, Mrs. Younge answered and almost swooned at seeing me, which put me on alert. I found my sister on a settee, sitting next to that libertine. She happily told me she was engaged; she was but fifteen," Darcy remembered.

"Lydia's age," Elizabeth stated quietly.

"When she saw my visage, she understood I was deeply angry. I succinctly conveyed the restrictions on my sister's fortune of thirty thousand pounds, which was the rake's object along with revenging himself on me. Had he succeeded, his revenge would have been complete indeed. Once he understood he would not see a penny of her dowry even had they eloped, he made some derogatory comments about her and myself and left the place." Darcy hung his head, drained by the retelling.

"I just remembered another lie he told me. At the time, I thought you proud and disagreeable, he told me your sister was like that as well, only worse," Elizabeth recounted. "It would be good to meet, Miss Darcy."

"Now, with no possibility she will encounter Wickham, I will leave before sunup on the morrow and return with her before the ball," Darcy related. Implied in his response was his desire for Elizabeth to meet his sister.

Elizabeth recalled Charlotte's telling her this man did not disdain her; he instead saw her as an object of affection. She was beginning to believe Charlotte was correct. *Oh Lord, that would mean Miss Bingley was a wit!* Elizabeth smiled at the thought.

Darcy thought she had never looked prettier than she did the very moment she smiled. Not long after, the two returned to where Zeus had been grazing, waiting patiently for his master.

~~~~~~~/~~~~~~~

Collins was walking to the parsonage to visit his betrothed when he saw Mr. Darcy walk his Cousin Elizabeth to the back wall behind the kitchen garden and lift her hand to bestow a kiss on it. He scurried to the parsonage as fast as his legs would carry him and requested quill, ink, and parchment. He needed to write to his esteemed patroness about his impertinent cousin using her feminine whiles on Miss de Bourgh's betrothed.

He excused himself and hurried back to Longbourn to place the missive in the salver. His intent was to have his cousin pay the postage forgetting it would be his patroness who paid for the postage when she received the letter. After he had completed his mission, he returned to his betrothed.

Charlotte was touring her soon-to-be home with the housekeeper. She had been looking over the mistress's bedchamber with Mrs. Hill when she looked out of the window and saw Collins staring at something with disgust. When she followed his line of sight, she could see he was staring at Eliza and Mr. Darcy, and that Darcy was kissing her friend's hand. Charlotte made as if she had much to look at in the bedchamber and did not miss Collins lumbering back to the house with a missive in hand some minutes later.

Once she heard the front door close a second time, she descended the stairs and saw a letter to Lady Catherine de Bourgh in the salver. Charlotte picked up the missive, and as she passed the fire in the drawing room, she consigned it to the flames.

When Collins returned to Longbourn later in the afternoon, he made a point of asking Mr. Hill if all the day's letters had been posted. Mr. Bennet's manservant confirmed that all letters in the salver had been posted, and Collins felt very pleased with himself, knowing that his patroness would be grateful for the information.

CHAPTER 10

E lizabeth was starting to see another side of Mr. Darcy—one she appreciated. He must think well of her to lay his sister's history bare before her as he did. One thing she was sure of was that Mr. Darcy was a reserved man, and careful about whom he shared himself. As she entered the house, she noticed Charlotte looking at her knowingly.

"Charlotte!" Elizabeth coloured. "Why are you looking at me so?"

"So we allowed Mr. Darcy to kiss our hand, did we?" Charlotte stated, causing Elizabeth to turn bright scarlet.

"It is *possible* you were correct about the man and I incorrect," Elizabeth owned.

"Mama always knows best," Charlotte teased.

"You do not hold the office *yet*!" Elizabeth jested in return.

"I would recommend you two be more circumspect until Mr. Collins leaves the area. Have you not heard his drivel about his patroness claiming a betrothal between Mr. Darcy and his cousin Miss de Bourgh? I believe Wickham alluded to it as well," Charlotte reminded her friend.

"It seems our delusional cousin has a patroness who is herself delusional. I have learnt my lesson and I know Mr. Darcy to be honest to a fault, so when he stated there was never a betrothal between his cousin and himself, I did not doubt him," Elizabeth allowed.

"We have we come a long way, have we not? I take it he is no longer the proud, hateful man you thought him?" Charlotte asked with raised eyebrows.

"Do not remind me of my wrongheaded words then. In

cases such as these a good memory is unpardonable," Elizabeth decried.

"Is it still your opinion he looks at you to find fault?" Charlotte pressed.

"No, Charlotte, it is not," Elizabeth acknowledged, and the admission caused her to blush all over again.

"I have been watching Jane and Mr. Bingley. He is rich to be sure, but I do not think he is a good match for Jane," Charlotte opined.

"Why is that?" Elizabeth asked. She knew Jane was infatuated with Mr. Bingley, but Jane had not yet shared with her that she felt any tender feelings for the man.

The two sat in the drawing room. "Each time I have heard Mr. Bingley extol Jane; it has only been for her looks. Not once have we been in company with him where he has complimented her character. I believe him to be both capricious and weak-willed, as he has proven with his sister." Charlotte looked at her friend, awaiting her answer.

Elizabeth's first inclination was to defend Mr. Bingley, but then she sat back and thought before voicing the first thing that entered her head. The more she considered Charlotte's words, the more they rang true. "When Jane was ill at Netherfield Park, I remember how he told us if he decided to leave the area, it would be the work of a moment." Charlotte nodded her head, as she and Eliza had discussed the sisters' sojourn at Netherfield Park in detail. "He is led by his sisters, and they believe we are below them even though they are a tradesman's daughters. They—especially Miss Bingley—will never allow him to offer for Jane, and he will not have the gumption to go against their wishes." Elizabeth realised Charlotte's perspicacity was keener than her own; she had relied only on her own judgements previously, believing them infallible. This was one more example of her friend's slower, deliberative process being superior to her own quick judgements.

"You have made my point for me," Charlotte stated. There was no gloating about her being correct, just satisfaction she had helped her friend look at the situation after a deeper examination of the facts. If she could help Eliza realise her suppositions were not a substitute for facts, it would be well for all, especially Eliza herself.

"Do not expect me to call Miss Bingley a wit just because it seems you might have been correct about Mr. Darcy admiring me," Elizabeth smiled.

"When have I ever asked you to lie, Eliza?" Charlotte smiled. "We can add her to the delusional group. I had not known her for long when I realised she was the last woman in the world Mr. Darcy would ever marry, yet she is blind to all the subtle and overt indications she is given by the poor man."

"Yes, she is rather pathetic. She chases after him like a hound chases after a bitch in heat, does she not? I am sure with two sons of an earl in residence—one of them a viscount —Miss Bingley may be expanding her marriage targets." Elizabeth shook her head at Miss Bingley's blindness.

"Speaking of the Viscount, did you notice the way *he* was looking at our Jane?" Charlotte asked passively.

"I did. I am not *that* blind," Elizabeth stated with mock affront.

"Then you noticed at whom his brother the Colonel was looking?" Charlotte asked conspiratorially.

"I cannot say I did. Who, as it only leaves Mary?" Elizabeth asked.

"He seemed to be looking at Mary quite frequently," Charlotte revealed. "Their looking at your sisters means nothing at this point. However, unlike Mr. Bingley and rather like Mr. Darcy, I surmise those two are not men who are led around by the nose by anyone!"

"I dare say you are entirely correct, Charlotte," Elizabeth allowed.

Her tour complete, Charlotte made for the study to meet her father and her betrothed to go over the settlement.

~~~~~~~~/~~~~~~~~

Jane and Elizabeth were sitting in the drawing room

when Matilda was announced. "Welcome, Matilda," Jane stated for both sisters as the three curtsied to one another.

"It is good to see you, Jane and Lizzy, I apologise. I have been caught up in the planning of my wedding and have not had time to see both of you as much as I would like," Matilda owned.

"Is your betrothed not with you today?" Jane asked.

"Your family does not like him much because, according to him, he is to inherit your home," Matilda opined.

"That is not it at all, my friend. As it would be impolitic to speak negatively of the man in your presence, we will leave it at that," Elizabeth returned, with no little emotion in her voice.

"I know you well enough to know that neither you nor Jane would prevaricate, so I will leave it there," Matilda stated. The truth of the matter was she did not want to know. She believed happiness in matrimony was a matter of chance, and not knowing too much about one's betrothed before the wedding was preferable to her.

Both Jane and Elizabeth felt sorry for their friend. They had seen the bully emerge in Mr. Collins and had no doubt he had a vindictive side to him. Just then Charlotte joined them. She, her father, and her betrothed had just signed the marriage settlement, and she was looking for her friends before she returned to Lucas Lodge.

"Hello, Matti," Charlotte greeted Matilda after she had done the same with the two Bennet sisters present in the room.

"My, you seem to be visiting our friends even more than usual lately, Charlotte," Matilda observed.

"Sometimes I see them more than others. This morning my father had business with Mr. Bennet, and I walked with him," Charlotte related. Nothing she said was untrue.

"Be that as it may. It is fortuitous you three are here together, for it will save me the walk. I would like to invite you to visit me in my new home in March of next year and remain for Easter," Matilda proffered.

Seeing Jane and Lizzy were uncomfortable, as neither

would enjoy telling Matilda they would not want to be in Mr. Collins's house under his so-called protection and power. "Jane and Eliza, you did not forget you will be spending Easter with me and the family?" Charlotte asked.

Matilda did not notice it, but both Jane and Elizabeth visibly relaxed. Again, Charlotte had not lied, although her wording led Matilda to believe the sisters would be her guests at Lucas Lodge; no one corrected her misapprehension.

"We thank you for your kind invitation, Matti, but Charlotte has the right of it. I am sure Papa will not countenance a change of plans at this point. But we will see you when you visit your father," Elizabeth stated.

Although Matilda was not as intelligent as the three other ladies in the drawing room, she understood enough to grasp that her friends would not accept an invitation to reside under her future husband's roof for their own reasons—even for a short time. For the first time, serious doubt about her decision to marry Mr. Collins began to take root.

"I need to speak to Papa." Matilda stood abruptly and swept out of the room as fast as her legs would allow. The three friends looked to one another, each one having a good idea what was bothering their friend.

~~~~~~~/~~~~~~~

Darcy decided to leave the same day to collect Gigi and return in the morning rather than follow through with the plans he had shared with Miss Elizabeth. Neither Andrew nor Richard wanted to remain in the house with the cloying Miss Bingley, so they joined their reserved cousin in his carriage for the overnight trip to London.

"William, if I did not know better, I would say you are a man in love," Richard said after watching the emotions play over his cousin's face for the first half hour of the journey.

"I am," Darcy said simply.

Richard was not sure what to say, and neither did Andrew, as they had not expected William to admit to it so openly. "Who?" Andrew asked carefully, hoping that their stoic cousin would for once be open with them. "It is Miss Elizabeth, is it not? I should have known when you asked for the opening set and the supper set. You *never* dance the first. I was blinded by the vision of a serene, blond lady," Andrew owned.

"Andrew, you did not tell me that. When did this occur?" Richard asked incredulously.

"After you left to have your fun with Colonel Forster," Darcy averred. "That scoundrel is at Newgate, is he not?"

"He is," Richard confirmed. "The Governor has been paid to make sure he is in the most secure cell, and no one is allowed to visit him. His ship departs within a sennight," Richard reported with satisfaction. The only thing which would have given Richard more pleasure was if the blackguard had given him half a reason to run him through. "Let us not change the subject. What changed since your infamous insult of the delectable Miss Elizabeth? And you, Andy, taken with Bingley's angel, are you?"

"You heard my request for us to begin again at the meeting, did you not?" Both cousins nodded. Darcy waved off the asking of when things had changed. "I chanced upon her this morning, and she allowed me to accompany her on a walk to Oakham Mount, which is a sanctuary of sorts to her. We spoke at length, and it seems she is warming to me. As for my feelings, I believe they started the same night I insulted her, after which I truly looked at her for the first time. I admitted to myself that I love her when she walked to Netherfield Park to nurse Miss Bennet, and the way she parries Miss Bingley's barbs is masterful! The harpy has no idea she was being set down, and Miss Elizabeth never employs spite to do so."

"Well, well, Darce, I hope you win her, for she would be the making of you. As for your question to me, Rich, as far as I can tell, Miss Bennet is *not* Bingley's angel. She needs a man, not an immature boy," Andrew countered. "I am attracted to her, but I do not know the lady well enough to claim any feelings beyond an initial attraction to her. I hope to find out more about her character at the ball, which was the impetus of my requesting the supper set from the lady. Unlike Bingley, I desire more than a pretty face, but it is true she is one of the most beautiful women I have ever beheld."

"She is a classic beauty, but I much prefer my Elizabeth," Darcy replied, not realising he used her familiar name.

"I did not know *Miss* Elizabeth had granted you permission to address her so familiarly," Richard ribbed his cousin.

"A slip of the tongue," Darcy replied quickly. "What about your attention to Miss Mary, the middle sister? I have heard some call her plain."

"She is anything but plain! I do not know yet, but mayhap she has felt lost in the middle of her more outgoing sisters, and she hides her light. I believe she may be the most interesting of the sisters we have met," Richard opined.

"You are a lucky man that the youngest is back in the nursery, Rich. Anyone in a scarlet coat is good enough for her, and at fifteen she is the most flirtatious girl I have had the displeasure to meet. I laud Mr. Bennet and his betrothed for taking her in hand. Doing so has made the second youngest, Miss Kitty, far more likeable. Without the brash one around, I am sure Gigi will be very comfortable with the other four Bennet sisters and the soon-to-be Mrs. Bennet," Darcy informed his cousins.

Not long after, the men dropped off to sleep, one by one.

~~~~~~~/~~~~~~~

"Papa, I need an honest answer from you," Matilda beseeched her father. "Am I making a big mistake? Before you answer, tell me the unvarnished truth, not what you think I want to hear. I am aware you agree with anything I want as you are the best of fathers, but I need the honest vicar now, not my overly-protective father."

Dudley suspected he might be asked to have this particular conversation with Matilda. "Why now, Matti?" he asked carefully.

Matilda related her doubts to her father, ones she had been able to put aside until the reaction of Charlotte, Jane, and Lizzy to her invitation to Mr. Collins's home. "None of them have ever said anything other than relating the truth of Mr. Collins's rejections before he came to me. But to be fair, I have not asked," Matilda admitted.

"Truth be told, I was not overjoyed at your accepting him, but as you correctly stated, I will do anything to support you, Matti. I could have asked Bennet for the truth about your betrothed, but I chose not to. If it is what you want, you may join me on my weekly meeting with him on the morrow. If you change your mind and withdraw from the betrothal, I will support you as I always have, and always will." Dudley hugged his daughter to him.

"Please Papa, I do not want to be blind. It is possible I was wrong about not wanting too much information about my future mate before the wedding. There are too many signs for me to ignore, so yes, I will join you on the morrow." Matilda rested her head on her father's shoulder as he placed a comforting arm around her and kissed the top of his daughter's head.

She was a full-grown woman, but she would always be his little girl.

~~~~~~~/~~~~~~~

"William! Andrew! Richard!" Georgiana welcomed the three to Matlock House enthusiastically. "Why are you back? Is the ball not to be held on the morrow?"

"It is, Gigi. We are to return in the morning and wanted to know if you would like to accompany us." Darcy asked.

"Truly William, you want me with you?" she asked tremulously.

"Never doubt that I will *always* want you with me, Gigi. If I have ever given you any other idea, then I must beg your pardon." Darcy enfolded his sister into his arms. "Yes, I, we all, want you to join us."

"But Richard said you wanted to protect me from Miss Bingley?" Georgiana questioned.

"Although it was part of the reason, it was not the main reason. I have seen from the example of others that hiding the truth from you fails to protect you. I am so sorry I never told you the truth about that scoundrel. You would have been able to make better decisions had I done so," Darcy stated contritely.

"William, I knew better, but let us move forward. Nothing will change what was. What was the true reason for not wanting me in Hertfordshire?" Georgiana pressed forward to learn what she wanted to know.

"George Wickham was a member of the Derbyshire Militia stationed there. Again, in a misguided desire to protect you, I decided you would not be able to face him. I should have asked you, Gigi. I am sorry, sister dearest," Darcy explained.

"He did not hurt others, did he?" Georgiana asked with concern.

"The libertine meddled with some merchants' daughters and tried with a gentleman's daughter, but he was stopped when a very intelligent lady saw through his façade. He now sits in Newgate and will be transported, never to return, in the matter of a few days," Richard informed his ward.

"Will you introduce me to Miss Elizabeth Bennet, William?" Darcy started in surprise at his sister knowing Miss Elizabeth's name.

"Yes, William," Lady Elaine said as he entered the room, "I, too, want to hear about this paragon you mentioned in each letter you wrote to your sister, mentioning her name more than once in some. She is not a fortune hunter, is she?"

"**NO**!" All three men chorused emphatically.

"I want to hear this," Lady Elaine commanded as she seated herself in a comfortable wingback chair.

Darcy explained his history with the Bennets, not skipping any embarrassing facts. Then her sons added their impressions of the Bennets.

"I am looking forward to meeting the Miss Bennets!" Georgiana said enthusiastically, once all three were done with their recitations.

"Gigi, if you are comfortable with them, would you like me to ask if the Bennets will host you? That will keep you far from Miss Bingley's false friendship and fawning," Darcy offered.

"Do you think they will like me, William?" Georgiana asked shyly.

"No, Gigi, I think they will *love* you!" Darcy opined.

The Countess spoke not a word, but she could tell by the way they talked that William was not the only one taken by a Bennet daughter. "William, do you think your friend, Mr. Bingley, has room at the Nether House for your Uncle and me?" she asked casually.

"It is Netherfield Park, Aunt Elaine, and yes, the house has more than enough room. Is Uncle Reggie free to join us?" Darcy asked.

"He will be," the Countess stated, and everyone smiled, well aware they should not doubt her word.

Darcy sent an express to his friend to request chambers be made ready for the Earl and Countess of Matlock. He hoped Bingley would warn his younger sister, as his aunt and uncle would have even less patience with the harridan than Andrew had shown his first night at Bingley's estate.

CHAPTER 11

"Good morning Bennet, Miss Lucas," Dudley greeted the couple as he was shown into the study with his daughter. The pastor had sent a note to Bennet telling him what he and his daughter needed to discuss, and Bennet had asked Charlotte to join him.

"Good morning, Charlotte, Mr. Bennet," Matilda greeted, very much confused as to why her friend was present.

Once Bennet made sure his man was watching for any eavesdroppers as Mr. Collins was up and breaking his fast, he turned to Miss Dudley. "I know this will come as a surprise to you Miss Dudley, but I am marrying Charlotte on Saturday," Bennet explained, amused at her shock as he sat down. As it wore off, Matilda started to understand why Charlotte had been at Longbourn so much lately.

"I wish you happy," Matilda said softly. "Is this why you refused Mr. Collins, Charlotte?"

"Do you want the truth Matti? I will relate all if you want to hear it, but I must be sure it is what you want," Charlotte confirmed.

"It is the reason we are here. After I left yesterday, I went to my Papa and asked him his true feelings about my betrothed, not what he felt I wanted to hear. His reply and my growing concern are the reason we are here today, I must know before I tie my life to the man irrevocably," Matilda clarified.

"If you are sure." Matilda nodded. "No Matti, it is not why I refused his proposals, though it was later the same day Mr. Bennet proposed to me. Until Mr. Collins spewed his vile words to me, both about what he intended to do to the Bennets and about me, I had never thought about being the new Mrs. Bennet. It all started..."

Charlotte retold all, from hearing the rant to his abominable proposal, to her refusal. Then once he finally accepted she was refusing him, his words to her, then his attempt to intimidate her.

As Charlotte spoke, Matilda felt chagrined. Mr. Collins had told her his plans for the Bennets, and she had been too wrapped up in her own selfish concerns to think about his words. She felt like the worst kind of person. Here was Charlotte, who heard those same words, and her reaction had been to take steps to help. There was no selfishness in what her friend had done.

"He mentioned his plans for your family, Mr. Bennet, and to my shame, I did not pay attention as I should have; I never questioned his unchristian plans," Matilda hung her head.

"Matti, why did you not tell me?" Mr. Dudley asked gently. "Had I known that, regardless of wanting to please you, I would never have given my consent or blessing."

"Deep down I think I knew that Papa. I so wanted to get married I ignored things I should not have. Once he agreed to bathe daily, I thought it would be enough to have a somewhat felicitous marriage. Mr. Bennet, do you have more to add to what Charlotte shared with us?" Matilda asked, dreading that he might. Oh, how wilfully blind she had been!   "I think Charlotte covered most of what I would have told your father. I will add he seems to have a vicious steak with those he thinks weaker or inferior to himself. On the one hand, he venerates his patroness as a god who walks among us mere mortals on earth and shows a pomposity and a belief his being a clergyman places him above the rules which govern the rest of us, other than his patroness." Bennet sat back in his chair.

"I will add if it were not for my brothers coming to my aid when I refused him, I believe the man would have struck me. If he had, we would not be having this conversation as my brothers would have torn him apart," Charlotte related seriously.

"What am I to do, Papa?" Matilda asked plaintively.

"Matti, you know there is only one decision to be made. I would never rest easy if I gave my only daughter away to such a man," Dudley replied gently.

"I cannot marry him, can I?" Matilda asked rhetorically. She knew the answer, but she had so wanted to be married and have a home of her own, but the price of being married to such a man was far too steep.

"How would you like to proceed, Matti?" Dudley asked his daughter. "Would you like me to tell Collins the betrothal is no more?"

"No, Papa, I must be present and tell him myself, but will you be with me?" Matilda asked.

"Of course I will, Matti. When?" her father inquired.

"The sooner, the better. There is no point dragging this out," Matilda stated the obvious.

"If Thomas agrees, I suggest we invite Mr. Collins to the study. If you like, we will remain with you and your father. As soon as he enters the study, Mr. Hill and a footman should pack his trunk, and there should be one or two footmen in the hall in case he must be removed physically. I think we should tell him of our upcoming marriage as well," Charlotte advised.

"You make eminent sense, Charlotte," Bennet agreed.

"Matti, can I tell you a secret?" Charlotte asked. Matilda nodded. "Franklin will be most relieved that you are breaking your betrothal. I warned him he had hidden his feelings too well." Charlotte smiled and Matilda beamed.

Mr. Hill was asked to enter the study and was given his instructions. He confirmed that Collins was still in the dining parlour. He and a footman headed directly to the corpulent parson's bedchamber to pack, while another told Mr. Collins he was required in the study.

Collins took the time to down a few more sausages, then headed to the master's study with grease dripping down his chin. When he entered, he was taken aback to find not only his Cousin Bennet, but three others as well.

SHANA GRANDERSON A LADY

Before he had a chance to speak, his betrothed spoke. "Mr. Collins, I am sorry if this grieves you, but I am withdrawing from our betrothal, I cannot and will not marry you, Sir," Matilda said with as much calmness as she could muster.

"Are you out of your senses? No other will offer for you!" Collins blustered.

"Is that not what you told me, Mr. Collins?" Charlotte asked evenly.

"It is, and I stand by my words to you that day," the furious man sneered.

"That is strange, Mr. Collins, for in two days I will be Mrs. Bennet," Charlotte informed the man in a matter-of-fact manner.

It took Collins a minute to absorb what Miss Lucas told him. "You cannot marry! I will not allow it! You are not allowed to have a son! You will not steal my estate from me!" Collins shouted at no one in particular, spraying spittle and pieces of sausage in all directions.

"Mr. Collins, may I remind you that you have absolutely no say in whom I marry and whether or not I beget a son? How many times have you been warned you are only the heir *presumptive*, not the heir? You, Sir, are no longer welcome at my estate, and from this day forward, until and unless you have inherited, if you set foot on *my* land, I will have you arrested for trespassing! Do I make myself clear?" Bennet thundered at the ridiculous man.

"My patroness will…" Collins started to screech.

"Do nothing," Charlotte interjected, "unless she wants to be made to look as ridiculous as you!"

"It was you who filled my betrothed's head with lies about me," Collins advanced on Charlotte, his hand up and ready to strike. He stopped dead in his tracks when he felt the tip of a foil against his neck. The foil had been lifted from the stand on which it hung behind Bennet's desk, pulled with the intent to defend for the first time.

"We told Miss Dudley the truth, but only after *she* asked

us!" Bennet informed the quaking man as he held his foil to Collins's neck. "If you make a move towards my betrothed, you will be the one to end your life, Collins. It is up to you," Bennet growled.

"You are a disgrace of a clergyman! It is the likes of you who give our profession a bad name. I will be sending a full report to the Bishop of Kent and to the Archbishop. If you are not defrocked, I will be surprised," Dudley stated with disgust.

"Edward!" Bennet called. The footman entered while a second stood in the doorway. "I am going to remove my weapon from your throat, Collins, but I dare you to give me reason to run you through." Bennet looked at his footman. "Is this man's trunk packed?" Edward nodded. "Good, show this disgusting excuse for a man off my property. Have Hill see him to the post. He is to be watched, and if he does not take the first stage heading to London, have someone notify Franklin and John Lucas that Mr. Collins attempted to strike their sister again."

Collins would have collapsed had the two footmen not taken hold of his arms. Having lost the ability walk for the moment, he was dragged out to the cart in the drive and dumped in the bed next to his trunk. William Collins departed Longbourn in disgrace.

~~~~~~~/~~~~~~~

The Darcy carriage led the Matlock conveyances toward Longbourn as they passed a cart heading in the opposite direction, containing a crying man in the bed next to a trunk. The man seemed vaguely familiar, but Darcy did not give the matter a second thought. As his coach came to a halt, Mr. Bennet, Miss Lucas, and the four oldest Bennet daughters exited the front door.

"Mr. Darcy, you seem to have returned from Town with more people than you had on your departure," Bennet noted dryly. "Let us enter the house, for it is easier to proceed with introductions indoors."

Everyone entered the drawing room. Elizabeth immediately identified the young lady partially hidden behind her brother and Colonel Fitzwilliam as Miss Darcy. "You must be Miss Darcy," Elizabeth stated in a welcoming tone. "I am Elizabeth Bennet; I have been looking forward to meeting you."

"Y-you h-have?" Georgians stammered, in a *sotto voce*.

"Most certainly." Elizabeth smiled at the younger girl and received a half smile in return. Darcy knew how it would be; he was sure Elizabeth Bennet was the key to helping his sister regain her confidence. The warm way Miss Elizabeth approached Gigi only bolstered his belief.

"William, will you introduce us please?" Lord Matlock requested.

"Uncle Reggie, Aunt Elaine, these are Mr. Thomas Bennet, Master of Longbourn; Miss Lucas, his betrothed; Miss Jane Bennet, Miss Elizabeth Bennet, Miss Mary Bennet, and Miss Catherine Bennet, who is known as Miss Kitty." The Bennets and Charlotte bowed and curtsied as each was introduced. None of them missed the raised eyebrows when Mr. Darcy used Kitty's given name. "Mr. Bennet, Miss Lucas, Misses Bennet; Lord Reginald Fitzwilliam, Earl of Matlock; Lady Elaine Fitzwilliam, Countess of Matlock; and last but certainly not least," Darcy gave his sister a reassuring smile, "Miss Georgiana Darcy, who we all call Gigi, my beloved sister."

"It is not every day we have a peer of the realm in our modest home," Bennet drawled. "To what do we owe this honour?"

"When my sons returned and told us not only had they met some good and honourable people, but your betrothed saw through that scoundrel's façade, which initiated the events leading to his residence in Newgate, we knew we had to make your acquaintance," Lady Elaine stated. "Also, there was not much of note going on in London's social scene, so we decided tonight's ball should not be missed."

"Is your cousin not here, Mr. Bennet?" Darcy asked. "If he lost his control of his senses when introduced to my cousins and me, what will his reaction be when he meets an earl and countess?"

"William, did you not note the cart leaving Longbourn as we arrived?" Richard asked with a big grin. Darcy nodded. "Am I mistaken, or was the distraught man in the bed of the cart Aunt Catherine's venerable parson?"

"You are correct, Colonel," Charlotte replied. "He has been removed until the day he inherits, if there is no other heir born first."

"I thought he was to marry before he departed," Andrew asked in confusion. Seeing the look his father was giving him, he turned toward the Earl. "Yes father, he was a toady sycophant. Your sister outdid herself this time."

"He is no longer betrothed to Miss Dudley, and Lady Catherine will have to look for a new clergyman..." Charlotte then enumerated the parson's behaviour, and how Longbourn's rector was writing to both the Archbishop and the Bishop of Kent.

"This was the second time he was about to strike you, Miss Lucas?" Lord Matlock asked with a look of disgust.

"It was, your Lordship," Charlotte confirmed.

"My name was Manner-Sutton before Reggie married me," Lady Elaine informed everyone, "Charles, the current Archbishop, is my late uncle's son. I think I should write to my cousin about this man; one such as he should not represent the Church of England."

"In addition to his other offences, your Ladyship, I suggest adding that he discloses information shared in confidence by his parishioners to his patroness, and is proud of the fact," Mary spoke up. Anything she could add to help in the defrocking of the last man who should have ever been a clergyman, she was happy to do.

"I believe my cousin is visiting his old parish in Norwich. An express will be on its way today," Lady Elaine stated with purpose.

Charlotte rang for tea, and soon Mrs. Hill and two maids delivered the service. After Charlotte poured, the rest of the party sat and talked quietly in smaller groups. Miss Darcy sat with Miss Elizabeth and Miss Kitty. "I would be happy if you call me Elizabeth or Lizzy, as most everyone does, except Charlotte and her family who call me Eliza," Elizabeth told Miss Darcy.

"And you must call me Kitty. Papa only uses Catherine if he is angry with me," Kitty added, her smile bright and welcoming.

"In that case, please call me Georgiana, or Gigi, as my family and friends do. Is it true you put Miss Bingley in her place without her being aware of it, Lizzy?" Georgiana asked.

"I have been known to do so. I find I have no patience for one with her airs, graces, and pretentions," Elizabeth admitted. The admission elicited the first smile from Georgiana that reached her eyes.

"I do not like her very much. Mrs. Hurst is a little better, but only when not with Miss Bingley," Georgiana admitted quietly.

"Jane and I saw as much when we were hosted at Netherfield when she fell ill," Elizabeth agreed.

"My brother wrote to me and mentioned you were there to nurse Miss Bennet," Georgiana shared.

"Your brother mentioned me in a letter?" Elizabeth asked with genuine surprise.

"In each of his letters," Georgiana owned shyly. "It is why I was so keen to meet you."

Elizabeth was astounded. Not only had Mr. Darcy written about her to his sister, but often and in a most positive way. How many more examples of Charlotte's perspicacity would she be presented with?

The more she thought about the enigmatic Mr. Darcy, the more Elizabeth realised she had never been indifferent to him, which explained her reaction to his slight. Had she not wanted his good opinion, it would have rolled off her like water off a duck's back.

The Earl and Countess were talking to Bennet and Charlotte and were impressed with the intelligence of both. The

Fitzwilliam brothers were sitting with Miss Bennet and Miss Mary. As they talked about many subjects including the neighbourhood, their tenants, and the charities Miss Bennet was involved in, Andrew began to understand Miss Bennet was much more than a pretty face, which pleased him.

~~~~~~~/~~~~~~~

"Charles, you cannot be serious about Miss Bennet! Oh, she is a sweet girl, but look at her connections, her lack of fortune, and that family. The two youngest are wild and will ruin themselves. Is that what you want our name associated with?" Miss Bingley ranted.

"Caroline is correct, Charles. Aligning yourself with that family will do nothing to raise us—er, I mean you in society," Mrs. Hurst said in support of her sister.

"But she is so beautiful! She is an angel, and I want her to be *my* angel," Bingley responded weakly.

"She does not love you, brother," Miss Bingley reported with false empathy, attempting to make her brother believe she felt for him.

"Of course she loves me," Bingley returned, but without confidence. His sisters had been working on him for some hours already, and he was ready to give in to them just to reclaim some peace.

"Charles, a woman knows. She smiles at you no differently than any other man. She will accept you for your fortune alone if you offer for her," Miss Bingley drove in the final nail.

"What am I to do? I have asked her for the opening set tonight," asked a distraught man.

"Have you asked for any other sets?" Mrs. Hurst asked with concern. Bingley shook his head. "Then do not ask her for another set tonight."

"It is a pity Mr. Darcy had to travel to Town with his cousins," Miss Bingley stated. "I am sure he would have asked to open the ball with me, and then take my supper and final sets." Miss Bingley thought for a minute. "We should leave tomorrow morning for Town. I am sure Mr. Darcy, the Viscount, and Colonel will all agree with us. I will have the servants begin to pack our bags." Miss Bingley sailed out of the room as if what she wanted was a *fait accompli*.

Miss Bingley was unaware Miss Darcy was in the area, as her brother had omitted that fact per Gigi's request. Instead, he was worrying about putting on a good show for his neighbours later that night. Bingley decided a trip to Town would be just the thing and was sure he would be back once Caroline and Louisa cooled off. He would request his sister write to his angel on the morrow before their departure.

~~~~~~~/~~~~~~~

Collins would have preferred to stay in Meryton and take care of those who had cost him his betrothal; this idea was rejected almost as fast as it formed when he had a vision of the two Lucas men coming after him. So, here he was on the stage to London in cramped quarters, with none of the comfort he believed was his due.

He was sure his fellow clergyman would not write the letters he threatened! Dudley only said that so he would not sue for breach of contract. The fact a woman could withdraw from an engagement with no repercussions was one of the inconvenient facts Collins ignored.

Even if Dudley did write, Collins was certain his patroness would put a stop to any action against him—after all, he was trying to obey her edict to marry. Lady Catherine had told him many times she could order things the way she desired, so he had nothing to worry about.

All would be well on the morrow, for he would arrive home in Hunsford, go to see her Ladyship, and she would put all to rights. Besides, she would be happy with him for informing her of the scandalous way his Cousin Elizabeth was practising her feminine arts and allurements on Mr. Darcy.

CHAPTER 12

Darcy and Richard requested a word with Miss Bennet, Miss Elizabeth, and Miss Lucas. The two men followed the three ladies to a small parlour. "We have a favour to of ask you. Would it be too much of an imposition to request you host Gigi here?" Darcy inquired. "It would be Gigi only, for I granted her companion's request for time off to be with her daughter during the lady's first confinement."

"I assume you do not want her to be in Miss Bingley's company," Charlotte surmised.

"Correct, Miss Lucas. That lady believes if she fawns over our Gigi, it will somehow translate into William offering for her," Richard explained.

"From the time I spent at Netherfield when Jane was ill, it seems to me Miss Bingley only hears that which fits her preconceived notions," Elizabeth opined.

"I could not have described the woman any better myself, Miss Elizabeth," Darcy averred.

"Hearing this, I understand; Charlotte and Elizabeth were correct when they warned me Miss Bingley is a false friend," Jane realised.

"It was perceptive of Miss Lucas and Miss Elizabeth to tell you such, Miss Bennet. Miss Bingley cares for no one other than herself. In private, and sometimes in public, she displays a selfish disdain for the feelings of others," Darcy informed Jane.

"Mr. Darcy, I know you are his friend, but is Mr. Bingley very biddable and somewhat capricious?" Jane blushed, knowing her question was most forward.

"May I ask to what this question tends, Miss Bennet?"

Darcy asked.

"Initially, I felt an attraction to Mr. Bingley. Charlotte opined he may not have much resolve and is easily led, which would not bode well for a long-term relationship. As I have been in company with Mr. Bingley since I was ill, I have observed your friend, and I think I agree with Charlotte. You are under no obligation to answer, but I am seeking confirmation, as I might be in error." Darcy had never heard so long a speech from Miss Bennet before and wanted to fully understand her intentions before he answered.

"Given his wealth, would you not accept him even with these flaws?" he asked, realizing his mistake as soon as he saw the anger and outrage evident on both Bennet's and Miss Lucas's countenances.

"Neither Jane nor I will marry for anything but the deepest love! It says more about you than us that you would ask such a question!" Elizabeth hissed and started to rise.

"Miss Elizabeth, I do not believe you or your sister to be fortune hunters. I am sorry, I asked a question I should not have," Darcy tried to recover.

"Then why ask the question if you do not believe Jane or Elizabeth to be fortune hunters, Mr. Darcy?" Charlotte demanded.

"When Miss Bennet asked about Bingley, I wanted to test my theory she was not of that ilk, and I did it in a bad way. It was not meant to offend. I proffer my deepest apology to both of you." Darcy held his breath as the sisters looked at one another to communicate silently, Miss Elizabeth waiting until Miss Bennet gave her a slight nod.

"We forgive you, Mr. Darcy, but we suggest you think about what you want to say *before* you open your mouth in future," Elizabeth admonished him.

"My cousin here is not always the most articulate man when he speaks; however, in writing, I find few who match him," Richard stated in support of his cousin who was trying to extricate his Hessian from his mouth.

"I suggest he practice," Miss Lucas stated succinctly.

"Excuse me, practice?" Darcy looked confused.

"I am not the most proficient harpist, but I have always blamed it on my lack of inclination to practice. So I suggest you practice, Mr. Darcy," Charlotte clarified.

Darcy bowed his head to Miss Lucas. "In answer to your question, Miss Bennet, and as much as it pains me to admit it, both Miss Lucas's and your observations are on point." Darcy turned towards Elizabeth. "I assume you remember his statement at Netherfield about Town and the country, Miss Elizabeth?"

"I do, though I did not think about it when Charlotte advised Jane, but I did disclose it to her later when we discussed my stay at Netherfield." Elizabeth related to Richard and Jane how Mr. Bingley had spoken about how quickly he would decide to leave a place and the way he excused his bad handwriting by stating there were too many ideas jumping in and out of his head. "Now that I think on what he said in hindsight, it seems he is unable to order his thoughts and has not chosen to improve his writing," Elizabeth suggested.

"In that case, I am glad my heart was not engaged. It may have been by now had Charlotte not given me reason to be cautious. If he requests a second set tonight, I will refuse him," Jane stated evenly. "I do not want to give rise to expectations which will never be met."

Richard's positive opinion of the Bennet sisters and their soon-to-be stepmother only grew, and he had not been sorry to witness his reserved cousin being called out for his badly phrased words. It was not every day someone called the master of Pemberley to account for anything; there were times everyone needed it.

Elizabeth's thoughts returned to their original subject. "We never gave you an answer about Gigi." Darcy was most pleased the lady he loved, and had just deeply offended, was on a first name basis with his sister. "I will confirm with my father, but for our part," Elizabeth indicated her sister and friend, "we would welcome Gigi with open arms."

"I think I can say without contradiction that your father will have no objection, Eliza," Charlotte opined.

"In that case, yes, she may stay as long as she desires," Jane stated.

~~~~~~~/~~~~~~~

Fitzwilliam Darcy had gone from 'intensely disliked' to 'folk hero' in the space of a few days' time. Once the truth about both men became known, Darcy was acquitted of all the lies Wickham had spread. After the money was received, money that for some tradesmen meant the difference between solvency and ruin, he became the most popular man in the region.

There was a similar reaction at the militia encampment, as everything Wickham owed was paid to rightful recipients, including debts of honour, as Mr. Darcy had pledged to do. The morale in the camp had never been higher. Mr. Darcy was owed a debt of gratitude by Colonel Forster for repairing the damage to the unit's reputation in Meryton and making his men whole, which led to an extremely positive change among his officers and men.

~~~~~~~/~~~~~~~

On the group of five's return to the drawing room, Charlotte whispered in her betrothed's ear, and he nodded vigorously. Miss Lucas had been correct about Gigi remaining at Longbourn. Said young lady was engrossed in a discussion with Mary, both having an abiding love of music.

Darcy instructed his footmen to bring in his sister's trunk. As there was a vacant spot in Kitty's room, Gigi would share with her. Kitty was most pleased her new roommate came with her own lady's maid who could assist Kitty in dressing and with her coiffures.

Once they saw Gigi was well settled, Andrew retrieved his father from the study, where he and Bennet had retired and were locked in a battle of chess. It was agreed among those traveling to Netherfield Park that no one would mention Gigi's presence in the neighbourhood to the shrew who was mistress of Netherfield.

When they arrived, Bingley, Miss Bingley, and Mr. and Mrs. Hurst stood outside to welcome the arriving party. "Welcome to Netherfield Park, your Lordship and Ladyship," Miss Bingley said, attempting to display her superior abilities as a hostess.

All she achieved was pointing out her lack of manners by cutting her brother off before he, as host, was able to welcome the arrivals. Once they all gained the drawing room, the Earl requested introductions. Darcy performed the office, although the Earl was certain he could have forgone one to the red-haired harpy attempting to act like the highest of sticklers, thinking it proved her position in society. He and his Countess had seen it time and again, and not once had it been someone worth spending any time with.

"Darce, I thought you were to depart London this morning? How come you only arrived now, and did you not bring your sister? I forgot you had said you might bring her until now, when I see she is not among you," Bingley asked, forgetting his friend had requested he not mention Darcy's sister's presence to Miss Bingley.

"Where is dear Georgiana? How I miss her," Miss Bingley interjected insincerely.

"Miss Bingley, when did my sister allow you to address her so informally?" Darcy asked pointedly. The days of his allowing the woman's pretentions regarding him or his sister were over. Miss Bingley got a pinched look, and after a glance at the Earl and Countess, who seemed to resent the disrespect shown to their niece, she receded. "I was about to tell you before I was interrupted that my sister is being hosted by a family who will not offer her false friendship in an attempt to gain my notice." Darcy, who abhorred deceit, was happy he said nothing untrue.

"As to your question, Mr. Bingley, we did leave London at the time we planned, but we stopped to visit friends in the neighbourhood before we came here," Andrew related.

"You know people in this backwater town?" Miss Bingley asked, aghast, her hand covering her heart as she stared at them all in surprise.

"Yes," Lady Elaine averred, "I think you may know them, the Bennets of Longbourn."

For some seconds Miss Bingley looked like a fish out of water as her mouth opened and closed but made no sound. She was furious *her* guests should have stopped to visit those people first. It was supposed to be her triumph to welcome them to the neighbourhood! As has been often noted, angry people are seldom wise.

"How could you deign to visit those so far below us?" Miss Bingley spat out. Seeing the outraged looks on the Fitz-williams' faces as well as Darcy's, her brother and sister knew immediately that Caroline had made a major *faux pas.* Hurst just grinned as Caroline was once again providing him with an inordinate amount of entertainment.

"Miss Bingley! How dare you, the daughter of a trades-man, equate yourself to us?" Lady Matlock asked with asperity. "You attended that obviously useless seminary in Town, did you not?" Miss Bingley blanched but nodded, for it was the seminary and her wealth she drew on for her feeling of self-worth. "Is the school so bad they taught you a tradesman is above a landed gentleman, one whose family has been on his land for generations?"

"It is entailed, and they have no wealth! I have a twenty-thousand-pound dowry; they have merely a thousand!" Miss Bingley tried to recover.

"You are by far the most vulgar hussy I have ever had the displeasure to meet! It is *birth* not *money* which determines social order! Well I never! To boast about your dowry openly in polite society is unconscionable!" The countess turned to a white Bingley. "If you do not take this in hand," Lady Elaine gestured toward Miss Bingley, "she will ruin herself and you with her."

"I think we should rest and prepare for the ball, Mother,"

Andrew suggested easily. Mrs. Hurst summoned the house-keeper to show their guests to their rooms, as her sister stood frozen.

After the guests had departed the drawing room, Mrs. Hurst returned. "Caroline, have you learnt nothing? The Viscount set you down for the same thing not two days ago! Are you insensible? Lady Matlock is a good friend of Lady Jersey. You will never gain admittance to Almack's now!" Mrs. Hurst berated her sister.

"All will be well when we leave this backwater on the morrow!" Miss Bingley insisted as she started to recover her colour.

"You will write a note to Miss Bennet to inform her of our departure and send it before we leave, will you not?" Bingley asked his sister as he sat, his knees feeling decidedly weak. "I am not sure about pursuing her yet, but I do not want her to think we are abandoning her."

"I said I will write, and I will," Miss Bingley stated with a straight face. "I will rest now. With this unnecessary unpleasantness, Mr. Darcy did not have time to request the opening set from me, but he will." With that, Miss Bingley swept out of the room.

"If I did not know better, I would say your sister is more than slightly delusional," Hurst told his brother and wife.

~~~~~~~/~~~~~~~

"You are being so kind to me, Lizzy. If you knew about my shame you would not want to know me," Georgiana lamented. The two were sitting in a corner away from the rest in the drawing room.

"You mean if I knew about Ramsgate and Wickham?" Elizabeth averred softly.

"Y-you know?" Georgiana stammered.

"I do, and not only does it not change how I feel about you, but I lay the blame on him and his paramour. While you should not have agreed to the elopement, you were but a girl of fifteen manipulated by a man almost twice your age who was skilled in the art. He did this with the assistance of your companion, who was charged with your protection. That woman violated the trust your brother placed in her in the worst possible way!" Elizabeth stated as she looked right at the young girl so her new friend could see the truth of her words.

"I have felt so guilty; what you say helps me very much," Georgiana said as she threw her arms around Elizabeth. "Are you the only one who knows?"

"No Gigi, everyone knows the basics, except my sister Lydia, who came very close to being seduced by Mr. Wickham like some others were in Meryton. Your brother gave me a detailed account. As you can see, there is not one in this house who judges you for your error," Elizabeth assured Georgiana.

"I thank you, Lizzy. I wish I had your wit then I would not have been taken in by that blackguard," Georgiana insisted.

"But I *was* taken in by him. Not in the same way as you..." Elizabeth explained all to her new friend.

As much as she hated that Wickham had seduced some girls in Meryton, it made Georgiana feel better about herself to know that someone as intelligent as Elizabeth Bennet could be taken in by Wickham's lies. It was a turning point for Georgiana Darcy; it was the last day she blamed herself and started to move forward.

~~~~~~~/~~~~~~~

William Collins was not happy. He had not budgeted for a stay at an inn on the way home, and he did not enjoy spending his money. His father had drummed, and sometimes beaten, the need for austerity into him from a young age. He reluctantly handed over the coin at the coaching inn.

Pursuant to his inquiry, the landlord informed Collins there would be a stage departing in the morning which would take him as far as Bromley. If he was lucky, a conveyance from Rosings Park would be there, but if not, he would have no choice but to hire a gig.

His greatest problem was determining how to explain to his patroness why he was returning to Hunsford with no wife, or even a fiancée. Disappointing Lady Catherine was something he abhorred. He would have to think long and hard to come up with a plausible excuse for failing to satisfy her charge to him.

He was sure she would be thankful of the letter he had sent her about her nephew, which should be in her hand by the time return to his parsonage.

<center>~~~~~~~/~~~~~~~</center>

Charlotte waited at Lucas Lodge until she received conformation Collins had departed before informing her family what the coward had attempted to do once Matilda withdrew from the betrothal. Franklin and John wanted to make sure he was gone, hoping he was not as they desired to beat him within an inch of his life, or mayhap beyond.

"I assure you, Brothers, that he is gone. One of my betrothed's grooms followed the stage for five miles and he did not alight, so he is on the way back to the bosom of his patroness," Charlotte calmed her brothers.

"I wonder what pack of lies he will tell her," Sir William surmised.

"It will make no difference..." Charlotte told her family who the Countess' cousin was and about the express on the way to the Archbishop of Canterbury. "No matter what he tells her, he has mere days left as a clergyman. Given the viciousness we have seen bubble to the surface, I think we all need to be vigilant. A wounded animal can be a dangerous one."

There was no disagreement expressed. As the family dispersed to rest before preparing for the ball, Charlotte made a mental note to recommend the same to her betrothed when she saw him.

CHAPTER 13

The residents of Netherfield Park were assembled in the drawing room having sherry and port, except for Miss Caroline Bingley. For some reason, she thought everyone would be waiting at the base of the stairs to watch her as she descended. She was dressed in what she believed was the finest, most fashionable colour. Her gown was a burnt orange, as was her turban. She had had three oversized ostrich feathers dyed the same colour, which protruded almost two feet above her turban.

Miss Bingley was dripping in jewels. When her maid attempted to point out most of the jewellery did not match her outfit, it earned her a slap from her mistress. She was determined to set herself apart from the country misses who would attend, especially that chit Miss Eliza.

In her mind's eye, Mr. Darcy would beg for the three significant sets as soon as he saw her superiority when he watched her descend the stairs. She reached the top of the stairs and held her head high but heard no reaction from below, so she looked down, flummoxed when she saw not a single person was waiting to applaud her triumph.

By the time she entered the drawing room with now-broken feathers as there was insufficient clearance between the monstrosity on her head and the doorframe, Miss Bingley was primed to explode. She regulated herself, although it was not easy. No one looked her way, except Louisa who was looking at the bent and broken feathers.

Her expectation that Mr. Darcy would fall at her feet and beg for dances was never realised. She sidled up next to him and tried to take his arm, but he placed his hands firmly behind his back, ignoring her, so she decided the man merely required a hint. "I know you do not normally dance the first, Mr. Darcy," she cooed, "Mayhap tonight you will?" Miss Bingley batted her eyelids at Mr. Darcy in a coquettish manner.

Darcy wondered if the lady had embers in her eyes the way they were blinking. "I *am* dancing the first tonight, Miss Bingley." Darcy did not miss the way the woman looked at him so expectantly. "I have already been granted the sets I intend to dance by my partners. Excuse me, Miss Bingley." Darcy joined his cousins, aunt, and uncle.

Behind him, Miss Bingley did not know which way to turn. Not only had he not requested the first from her, but he also did not ask for *any* sets! He told her in an unambiguous way he had already requested all the sets he intended to dance that night! If there were not so many members of the first circles present, one a peer, Miss Bingley would have had a tantrum and thrown the closest object to her with all she had.

Mrs. Hurst walked over to her sister. "Caroline, what is it? Calm yourself, for you are making a spectacle!" Mrs. Hurst whispered in her sister's ear.

"Mr. Darcy is dancing the first with someone else, and not me. If it is that Eliza, I will scratch her eyes out!" Miss Bingley hissed.

"Unless you want to ruin yourself and us along with you, you will do no such thing. Do not forget who is present tonight. One word from the Countess of Matlock, and there will not be any who receive you," Mrs, Hurst told her sister softly as she held onto her arm stopping her sister from accosting Mr. Darcy about dancing with her. "Leave it be before you make a bigger fool of yourself than you already have!"

Although she was seething, Miss Bingley regulated herself. What her sister said was true. She would just have to compromise the man after the ball. If he would not realise she was the perfect woman to be mistress of Pemberley and Darcy House, then she would have to *make him* give her what she wanted!

As it was time, the receiving line, comprised of Mr. and Miss Bingley and Mrs. Hurst, formed just as the first guests arrived. Mr. Hurst had begged off and was examining the refreshments. Standing next to her brother, Miss Bingley pasted on her best false smile on her face.

~~~~~~~/~~~~~~~

As Georgiana was not out and desired to keep the fact she was in the area from Miss Bingley, she would remain at Longbourn. Kitty Bennet, in a display of maturity her father was proud of, volunteered to remain at home with her new friend.

Before the Bennets were ready to depart, the Lucas conveyance arrived at Longbourn. Charlotte, after receiving a note from Eliza telling her Kitty had chosen to remain at home with Gigi, suggested the same to Mariah, who agreed right away. Mariah had confided in Charlotte she preferred Kitty and did not always feel comfortable with the way Lydia behaved.

The three girls remaining at Longbourn would have a full complement of servants with them, and before they departed, Kitty asked her older sisters to apologise to her partners for her. Charlotte, Jane, and Lizzy assured Kitty they would understand. Given how much Kitty loved to dance, her family was impressed by the selfless way she decided to remain at home with their guest.

It was easy to see how the separation from Lydia was having a positive impact on Kitty's behaviour and character. She was starting to bloom now she was out of Lydia's shadow. Charlotte had opined Gigi and Kitty would be good for each other. Kitty would draw Gigi out of her shell, while Kitty would learn how to behave like a true lady.

Before they departed, Charlotte called the three girls to her side. "Gigi, if you are up to it, it may benefit Lydia to hear from one her own age who has experienced Wickham's perfidy first-hand. If it is too hard for you, do not attempt it." Charlotte had a good feeling Gigi would be able to succeed in reaching Lydia where all others had failed.

Not long after the carriages departed for Netherfield,

the three girls were admiring some of Kitty's drawings and sketches she kept hidden away because Lydia would mock her for *wasting* time on pursuits not connected to flirting with officers.

"Lydia, who is obsessed with officers, always made me feel bad about my art," Kitty admitted to Georgiana. "I should not have allowed her that power over me."

"She always made me feel badly about myself as well, Kitty," Mariah shared. "Mayhap she saw us as competition for the officers' attentions."

"What is your younger sister like?" Georgiana asked, not having met the youngest Bennet yet.

"She is very outgoing and thinks nothing of flirting, especially with one officer before he was taken to gaol," Kitty revealed.

"Do you mean George Wickham?" Georgiana asked, trying to keep her disgust from showing but failing.

"Yes. Oh my, I remember from the meeting when your brother spoke about him almost ruining you. I am sorry to bring him up if it is painful for you," Kitty stated contritely. Kitty clamped her hand over her mouth, realising Mariah Lucas was with them.

"Do not feel uncomfortable, Kitty, I think it will be good for Mariah to hear this as it may help her in the future," the newly confident Georgiana assured her friend. "It used to, but I no longer feel pain when I hear his name—only disgust at what he has become." Georgiana proceeded to tell Kitty and Mariah the full story of her past with George Wickham.

As they spoke, the girls were not aware the subject of their conversation was chained in the hold of a transport ship on its way to Australia. The scourge that was George Wickham had departed English shores for the final time in his miserable and wasted life.

"Lydia has been told all about her favourite's crimes here in Meryton, yet she refuses to believe anything bad about her 'Wicky,' claiming he will return for her as he loves her." Kitty shared once her new friend completed her recitation.

"May we go visit Lydia as Charlotte suggested? I have not met her yet." Georgiana asked with purpose.

"We may. Just be ready for an extremely mulish and belligerent girl," Kitty warned.

"I will remain here," Mariah stated. "I have a feeling Lydia will not be as open with me in the nursery, as she always feels we are in competition, something I do not feel."

"Please unlock the door, Edward," Kitty requested when she and Georgiana reached the nursery. "But do be ready in case she tries to bolt again," Kitty looked to Georgiana, who gave her a questioning look. "She has attempted escape a few times already."

The footman opened the door carefully. Thankfully the woman-child did not attempt to escape. When Kitty and Georgiana entered, Lydia was lying on the bed. "Have you come to gloat again, *Catherine*," Lydia spat out, then she noticed a girl in elegant clothing she had never seen before. "Who are you, and why are you here?"

"My name is Georgiana Darcy," Georgiana started to say.

"The proud, arrogant one George told me about!" Lydia returned petulantly.

"I do not know about proud and arrogant, but we do have one thing in common," Georgiana remained calm in the face of Lydia's rudeness.

"What could I have in common with one such as you?" Lydia demanded.

"George Wickham. Do you think you are the only, or even the first, he has plied his lies with?" Georgiana asked pointedly.

"Wicky never lied to me. He told me he loved me and if…" Georgiana cut the stubborn girl off.

"If you loved him, you would give him your virtue before the wedding!" Georgiana completed Wickham's well-worn manipulative line." Seeing Lydia shock at her repeating his words verbatim, Georgiana drove her point home. "As I said, you are not the first he has attempted to seduce. Unfortunately, too many have fallen for his lies, including four in your town!" Once the truth of George Wickham was well known, a fourth girl had admitted the truth to her family. "You and I are two of the lucky ones he did not succeed in ruining!"

Lydia, normally so certain she was right about anything she believed, experienced doubt, a new experience she did not enjoy. As she looked at the girl opposite her, she saw only sincerity in her mien. Lydia looked at her older sister. "Everything I was told about George was the truth, was it not?" she asked softly. It was hard for Lydia to look at her own actions critically, but it seemed she had no choice.

"Yes, Lyddie, every word of it. As we speak, Wickham is either in Newgate Prison or on his way to Van Diemen's land where he has twenty years of hard labour waiting for him. He was caught with stolen property from his fellow officers, and it was a choice between hanging and Australia. He chose the latter," Kitty informed her sister gently.

"There is only one person in the known world George Wickham loves," Georgiana stated.

"Himself," Lydia realised, wincing as both Kitty and Miss Darcy nodded. "I have been a big ninny, have I not, Miss Darcy?"

"Please call me Georgiana or Gigi as my family and *friends* do. You are in good company; both Lizzy and I were almost taken in by his lies." Georgiana revealed all to Lydia.

"If your brother had not arrived in Ramsgate early, you would have eloped with him?" an incredulous Lydia asked at the end of the telling. "And Lizzy, our witty Lizzy, fell for his lies?"

"She did before Charlotte saw through him and started making Lizzy question her beliefs about both men. As you know, Wickham blackened Mr. Darcy's name to Lizzy," Kitty added.

"None of it was true, was it?" Lydia realised.

"William," seeing Lydia's confused look Georgiana explained, "that is the name by which we all call my brother. William *did* refuse the living, the *second* time the scoundrel tried to claim it. That was after he gave up rights to it and received three thousand pounds in return!" Seeing the look on Lydia's face, Georgiana clarified further. "It is the way he manipulated people. He would take a shred of truth and build a story around it full of prevarication."

"You were educated in the ways of being a lady as I have not been, and you still agreed to an elopement?" Lydia wanted to know.

"I agreed despite my education. I knew it was wrong, but I was in love with being in love, so I ignored my lessons. It did not help that Mrs. Younge, who was supposed to protect me, and Wickham were both manipulating me," Georgiana elucidated.

Lydia started crying, not crocodile tears, but tears born of genuine anguish. It finally hit her that all the talk of her ruining herself and her sisters was the truth, not jealousy, which was the way she had tried to rationalise it. "I have much to make amends for, do I not?" Lydia asked once her tears subsided. Kitty and Georgiana nodded.

"Will you remain with me and keep me company until you go to bed?" Lydia requested almost timidly.

"Mariah is here as well. If you can be pleasant to her, we will; otherwise, we will join her below stairs," Kitty stated firmly.

"I have much for which to beg Mariah's pardon, so please ask her to join us," Lydia stated with sincerity.

Kitty asked Edward to summon Miss Mariah and have their supper sent up with Lydia's.

~~~~~~~/~~~~~~~

The Bennet and Lucas carriages pulled up to Netherfield Park. The house was glowing with the light of hundreds of candles and the drive had been illuminated with torches. Bennet helped his three eldest daughters out and then walked to the Lucas conveyance to perform the office for his betrothed.

Together, the two families entered the receiving line. Miss Bingley was already upset at Mr. Darcy not requesting her to dance with him at all, and now, after she had loudly predicted the Bennets would be the first to arrive and last to leave, they arrived right in the middle of the arriving guests.

"My Eliza, where did you find such a plain dress for a ball?" Miss Bingley asked rudely.

"Caroline!" Both her siblings admonished.

"Why, Caro, wherever did you find broken feathers in that colour? What sort of bird did they come from? Not even a peacock has so hideous a colour in its splendour." Elizabeth knew she was not being polite, but she had enough of the witless woman's snide comments.

Miss Bingley spluttered and was unable to rebuff the statement before the hated Eliza moved on. Charlotte considered adding to Eliza's remarks but decided the woman had been put in her place sufficiently.

"Well, I never! Who is that country mushroom to speak to me thusly?" Miss Bingley hissed.

"You deserved it, Caroline. It is the height of rudeness to insult a guest the way you did," Mrs. Hurst stated. Bingley remained silent, and his lack of reaction was noted by Jane Bennet as she watched one of his sisters insulting one of hers.

Darcy had been standing with his relations when the Bennets and Lucases entered the ballroom. Seeing Miss Elizabeth took his breath away. She was wearing a simple yellow ball gown with very little embellishment, but, in his opinion, it needed none. She was a vision of beauty. How he loved this woman!

He reminded himself they had just begun again after their initial misunderstandings, so he had to take things slowly. He was sure he was looking at the only woman in the realm who would refuse him if he did not first engage her affections. He prayed he would be able to control his thoughts and not put his foot in his mouth, or worse, insult her and her family when he finally proposed to her.

~~~~~~~/~~~~~~~

Collins arrived home after sundown. As much as he

wanted to see his patroness as soon as he arrived at the parsonage, he knew she would not countenance his arriving at Rosings at this time of the night without a specific invitation.

He had crafted what he believed to be a plausible story to explain his return without a bride or fiancée. It was one he was sure would only increase the righteous indignation she would feel against the Bennets after reading his letter.

He had arrived at Bromley in the mid-afternoon. Rather than hire a gig he had waited, hoping in vain that a Rosings vehicle would stop at the coaching inn and allow him to ride to his home without further expense. In the end, as the sun was approaching the western horizon, he had broken down and rented a gig.

His servants were not expecting him, as he had not thought it worthwhile to write to ones so far below him, so no food had been prepared. After berating his cook for not knowing he would be home, he made do with some stale bread and hard cheese.

He retired as soon as he could, trying to ignore the fact he should have been at a ball dancing with his betrothed had she not withdrawn from the betrothal. The Bennets and Miss Lucas had much for which to answer!

~~~~~~~/~~~~~~~

As the receiving line wound down, Mrs. Hurst left to find her husband. Miss Bingley kept on inventing reasons for her brother to remain with her waiting for, in her words, the last few guests. Although she never cared for any in the neighbourhood before, she suddenly seemed worried their guests would think them rude if they were not present to greet them all.

The truth was Caroline Bingley knew full well all the guests had arrived. She was delaying her brother until she was sure the first set had begun. If she was not to dance the first with Mr. Darcy, she felt she was punishing Eliza by proxy by having her dearest sister miss dancing the first.

Elizabeth had relayed Kitty's apologies to the three men. None of them were upset but lauded her unselfish decision to remain with Gigi. The same sentiments were expressed to the Lucases about Mariah.

As the first set was called, Darcy led Miss Elizabeth out. He was followed by his aunt and uncle, Richard and Miss Mary, and Miss Lucas and Bennet. The Viscount could not dance the first with Miss Kitty, as she was unable to attend, but he saw Miss Bennet was looking around for her partner, who was nowhere to be seen.

"Miss Bennet, are you bereft of a partner?" he asked hopefully.

"It seems Mr. Bingley has been held up by his hosting duties. I will sit this set out," Jane stated. Both had a strong suspicion of what, or more likely who, was delaying Mr Bingley.

"As I have no partner for the first, may I have the honour?" Andrew requested. He held out his hand to Miss Bennet as the first few bars were played. She hesitated for only a second, then took the proffered hand and allowed the debonaire Viscount to lead her to the floor.

Once Miss Bingley was sure the first set was well underway, she turned to her brother. "I am sorry, Charles; it seems the last people have decided not to join us." With no further explanation, Miss Bingley flounced into the ballroom.

She felt her bile rise at scene which greeted her. Not only was the hated Eliza dancing the first with *her* Mr. Darcy, but rather than sitting on the side like a wallflower, Miss Bennet was dancing with Viscount Hilldale! Even the plain Bennet daughter was dancing with Colonel Fitzwilliam while she, sophisticated and educated Caroline Bingley, was the wallflower! It was not to be borne!

At the end of the first set, Bingley approached Miss Bennet and apologised for missing the set he reserved. She excused him and offered him the second, as her partner for that set had danced the first with her. When Bingley asked for another set, ignoring his sisters' wishes as they were not near him, Miss Bennet informed him her dance card was full.

The residents of the area were beyond shocked when they

saw Mr. Bennet take to the floor for the first, with none other than Miss Charlotte Lucas. Speculation was rife as to what this could mean.

Miss Bingley was stalking around the edges of the dance floor. This was supposed to be her triumph, to prove what a good match she would be for Mr. Darcy, yet she had not a single request to dance, and Mr. Darcy had not so much as looked at her to compliment her fashionable outfit. She reminded herself it mattered not; for she would have her heart's desire after the ball tonight.

CHAPTER 14

"Come, Mr. Darcy, we must have some conversation," Elizabeth teased as they danced the supper set.

"I am at your disposal, Madam; we may discuss any subject you please," Darcy returned with a grin.

Elizabeth had very much enjoyed their first set as Mr. Darcy, while claiming not to enjoy the activity, was one of the best dancers she had ever had the pleasure to partner. "I suppose I could remark on the number of dancers and you on the size and decoration of the ballroom," Elizabeth suggested in jest. The more time she spent with the true Mr. Darcy, the more attracted she became to the man.

Neither had missed the daggers sent Elizabeth's way by Miss Bingley as they danced the first, but that was nothing to the looks she was throwing Elizabeth's way as soon as the hoyden saw Mr. Darcy lead her enemy to the dance floor for the second set that night. Not only had he danced the first with the chit, but now the supper set! Her intention to compromise the man became ever more urgent. Her future was in jeopardy!

What Miss Bingley did not know was she had been ranting about her plans during the second set within earshot of Miss Lucas. Miss Bingley had not realised she was speaking aloud, and Charlotte knew she and Thomas would be seated at supper with his daughters and their partners, as well as the Matlocks, so she was satisfied she would have a chance to mention what she had heard to Mr. Darcy.

"We could discuss books, Miss Elizabeth, as the written word is a passion for both of us," Darcy offered as the dance brought them back together.

"No Sir! Books in a ballroom? Never! We could discuss fashion and lace," Elizabeth stated with a mischievous look.

"Given all the trips I have made to the modiste with Gigi, I am willing to discuss that subject." Darcy called her bluff, knowing Miss Elizabeth would not desire a subject so inane. His gambit won him a tinkling laugh from his partner.

"Eliza seems to have changed her opinion of Mr. Darcy," Charlotte commented to her betrothed on hearing her soon-to-be stepdaughter's mirth.

"So it seems," Bennet stated. "Is Mr. Bingley no longer in favour with Jane?" he asked as he noted his eldest daughter dancing her second set with Andrew Fitzwilliam.

"Jane has begun to see the lack of substantial character in Mr. Bingley. In my opinion, he is far too immature, and relies too heavily on the judgements of others rather than his own," Charlotte informed her betrothed.

"I sense some wise Charlotte-counsel in Jane's new awareness. I agree with you, by the way. Regardless of his wealth, I would never approve of a man ruled by his sister as Bingley is. In my opinion, marriage would not change that," Bennet opined.

"I agree, Thomas, except I believe she will do everything in her power to separate her brother from Jane, as she would not see an alliance to your family as an acceptable connection in her quest to reach the first circles," Charlotte surmised.

"Based on what you overheard, it seems she plans a more direct route to satisfy her ambitions," Bennet agreed.

"Have you noticed your Mary is dancing a second set with a Fitzwilliam brother?" Charlotte pointed out.

"I have. It seems that Miss Bingley's machinations to stop her brother dancing with my Jane for the first did not go quite as she planned," Bennet said with amusement.

"Thomas, have you noted the pinched look on the lady's face? Miss Bingley looks as though she has been sucking on the sourest lemon in the kingdom!" Charlotte had a quiet melodic laugh at the imagery she conjured in her own mind.

Andrew Fitzwilliam was happy with his dance partner. The more he was around her, the more he could see she was so much more than a pretty face. She did not have the sharp wit either her future stepmother or her next youngest sister possessed, but she was in no way deficient in intelligence.

She was kind and considerate to a fault, and after Richard related Darcy's gaffe he was sure that none of the Bennet sisters were fortune hunters. Miss Bennet did not fawn over him, which he greatly appreciated, and when she disagreed with him, she stood her ground. She did not debate as her sister did with his cousin, but she knew how to communicate her thoughts clearly.

From the conversations he had with his parents, they had offered no objections were he to decide to get to know her better, or even request a formal courtship in the future if they reached that point. Richard had relayed to their parents how poor William had put his foot in his mouth when he asked about wealth as a deciding factor.

Both Bennet sisters had been ready to excoriate his poor tongue-tied cousin, but he had had the good sense to explain himself and apologise. However, the fact that only the deepest love would tempt the older Bennet daughters into matrimony was another point in Miss Bennet's favour.

Colonel Fitzwilliam was enjoying his second dance with his Bennet sister. For the first half of their first set, she had been quiet, even shy. He had guessed correctly she was not used to being the object of a man's interest, and he had worked to put her at ease. By the second dance of the first set, Richard had succeeded.

During the supper set, Mary allowed her natural reserve to drop and allowed the Colonel to experience her wit and dry sense of humour. She was not quite as well read as Elizabeth, but she was getting there.

As Miss Bingley looked around, ripping her eyes away from the sight of Eliza dancing with her Mr. Darcy a second time, she gave a long look toward the other two Bennet sisters, each dancing with a Fitzwilliam brother.

Miss Bingley had written her letter to Miss Bennet already, and it would be delivered in the morning when she, her brother, and the Hursts were on their way to London. She had made certain any expectations the fortune hunter had would be killed by her letter. She was also sure Mr. Darcy and his relations would leave on the morrow, for she would be betrothed to Mr. Darcy and there would be no reason for him to remain in this backwater swamp.

As she had been on the opposite side of the ballroom when the supper set ended, by the time Miss Bingley entered the room where supper was being served, the table Mr. Darcy and his highborn relations sat at was full. It grated on her that the Bennets and that plain Miss Lucas were at the same table, but after tonight it would not matter.

After Mr. Bingley sat down for dinner, nowhere near his angel to his chagrin, Sir William approached him and requested permission to make an announcement during the meal, and Bingley gave his permission freely.

Lady Lucas had suggested her husband talk to Mr. Bennet and Charlotte. Sir William had done so during the brief break between the first and second dances of the supper set, after the talk rose to a fever pitch when Mr. Bennet led Charlotte onto the dance floor for a second significant set. Neither member of the betrothed couple objected to the official announcement being made.

So it was that when he noticed most had completed their meal, Sir William stood and cleared his throat to garner the attention of the diners. "It is my great pleasure to announce," he began as soon as there was quiet in the room, "that my eldest daughter Charlotte is betrothed to my friend and neighbour, Mr. Thomas Bennet of Longbourn. Lady Lucas, my sons, and Mariah all wish the couple felicitations."

No sooner had Sir William completed his announcement and raised his glass so all could toast the betrothed couple, the 'I told you so's' began. As had been expected, the couple were mobbed by their friends and neighbours.

As none of the Netherfield party who were aware had bothered to tell her the news, Miss Bingley was taken completely unawares. She realised if the new Mrs. Bennet bore a son, there would be no more entail and she would lose one of the things she had used repeatedly to denigrate the Bennets.

When most of the guests stood and started to make their way back to the ballroom where the pianoforte waited for ladies to exhibit, Charlotte asked those at her table to remain seated.

Once no one else was within earshot, Charlotte shared what she had heard Miss Bingley ranting about. "Even if she succeeded in compromising me, I would not marry her!" Darcy stated emphatically.

"If you did, I would personally truss you up and deliver you to Bedlam," Richard threatened in jest.

"I will have Carstens," he saw questioning looks from the Bennets, "my valet," he clarified, "sleep on a cot in front of my door. As added security tonight I will have two of my footmen hidden in the corridor. After we enter the bedchamber, we will transfer to an empty chamber as soon as we know the corridor is empty. Carstens will be with me, and the doors will be barricaded, so Miss Bingley could compromise naught but an empty bed!" Darcy decided.

"It is a sound plan, William. You know I will ruin her after this and it will trickle down to the family," Lady Elaine stated.

"Whatever happens will be by her own hand. I always felt sympathy for Bingley, but that has ended, as he refuses to take charge of his own household," Darcy said with regret at the probable loss of a friendship which had lasted many years.

With that, they all stood and joined the rest in the ballroom. Miss Bingley had exhibited first, thinking she would show up anyone who chose to follow her. She also wanted to highlight her superior skill on the instrument to Mr. Darcy, but, to her disappointment, the man and his party entered the ballroom just as she competed her piece. As the next young lady was waiting her turn, Miss Bingley had no choice but to cede her place at the pianoforte to the next in line.

Darcy was well pleased they returned after Miss Bingley's performance. Her playing was technically proficient, but she played with the feeling of a cold fish. After the lady who replaced Miss Bingley completed her piece, to applause far more enthusiastic than what Miss Bingley received, Mary took her turn.

Miss Bingley sneered most unattractively, certain that she was about to watch a disaster for the Bennets. To her growing annoyance, when Mary Bennet ended her performance, she garnered the biggest round of applause of all three. Miss Bingley was even angrier and more discomposed than she had been before.

~~~~~~~/~~~~~~~

The rest of the ball passed without incident, and Bennet and Charlotte were inundated with well-wishers. All their friends who had known the late Fanny Bennet could not but agree about the compatibility of Bennet and Miss Lucas, regardless of the age difference. Any who had had the displeasure of meeting Mr. Collins decided to add a prayer for the Bennets to be blessed with a son after their marriage.

Miss Bingley was proved wrong again when it came time for the guests to depart at the end of the night, for the Bennet and the Lucas families were among the first to depart. As far as she was concerned it was one of the worst nights of her life, having had every expectation thwarted, from not being waited upon at the staircase to when guests were leaving. The only thing keeping her from an epic tantrum was the knowledge she would soon compromise Mr. Darcy and finally get her wish of becoming the mistress of Pemberley and Darcy House. She would be a member of the first circles at last, as was her due.

There had been a small adjustment to the plan for Darcy's evacuation of his chambers. As an extra level of precaution, Darcy would join Richard in his chambers. They would not only have Carstens with them, but also Richard's batman, an irascible ex-sergeant who took nonsense from no one and was fiercely loyal to his colonel.

Darcy went up to his chambers and locked the door, as he always did. Miss Bingley felt in her pocket for the spare key to Mr. Darcy's room, which she had taken from the housekeeper's office. Once she saw Mr. Darcy enter his chambers, she went to her own. To be safe and to make sure everyone would be asleep, Miss Bingley planned to wait two hours before making her way to Mr. Darcy's chambers.

As soon as the two Darcy footmen posted out of sight in the corridor signalled the coast was clear, Darcy and his valet left his bedchamber, locked the door, and joined Richard and Sergeant Barlow in his cousin's chambers.

~~~~~~~/~~~~~~~

When Bennet and his three older daughters arrived home, there was no sign of Kitty, Mariah, or Gigi. Before he allowed any of the women to panic, Bennet summoned Hill and asked him where the girls were.

Hill was clearly amused as he asked the master and his daughters to follow him. They arrived at the nursery, and when Bennet opened the door, he was met by a sight he had never expected to see. The four girls were asleep on the floor, one next to the other.

They had removed the mattresses from the beds and placed them together on the floor and made themselves a comfortable pallet. The four looked at one another in question as they closed the door softly. It was then they realised that the door had not been locked, yet Lydia was asleep with the rest of the girls.

When the footman on duty was interviewed, he reported Miss Lydia had not attempted to escape, even when there were times when the door remained open, not just unlocked.

"There is a story to be told about this," Bennet surmised, "but it will keep until the morning. Good night, girls."

His daughters each kissed him on the cheek and took themselves to their chambers to prepare for bed. All three were happy and had enjoyed themselves at the ball, but Elizabeth prayed especially that her Mr. Darcy would be safe from the harridan this night.

~~~~~~~/~~~~~~~

Matilda Dudley had enjoyed herself at the ball more than she had for a long time. Part of the reason was Mr. Franklin Lucas. He had asked her to open the ball with him and had danced the final set with her as well. She had always had a tendre for Mr. Lucas but had believed he saw her as naught but his sister's friend. Thank goodness Charlotte had prodded both of them.

He had told her that night how happy he was she had withdrawn from the betrothal with Mr. Collins. It was the only time she heard him mention that man's name, as she knew her former betrothed was disliked heartily by all the Lucas men. She knew the Lucas ladies felt the same way.

"You seemed to enjoy yourself, Matti," Her father observed just after they entered the parsonage.

"I did, Papa, very much indeed. To think I was about to marry that man on the morrow!" Matilda shuddered as she considered what a mistake she would have made just because she wanted to marry more than she wanted to look at the man she was marrying.

"The important thing is you are not. I must beg your forgiveness; I should have refused my consent, Matti. Sometimes a parent must cause some short-term pain for long term happiness. I forgot that axiom," Dudley stated with conviction.

"Let us adopt Lizzy's saying about the past and move forward. I will not think about the man anymore if you will not, Papa," Matilda vowed.

"As I will do, though I may have to talk about him if I am contacted by the Bishop's or the Archbishop's offices. The content of the conversations is wholly different and will make that promise easy to keep." Dudley pointed out.

Matilda agreed that was an acceptable exception to their vow to move forward.

~~~~~~~/~~~~~~~

Just short of two hours after entering her bedchamber, Miss Bingley, dressed in the most transparent of nightgowns, left her chambers and crept down the darkened hallway towards Mr. Darcy's bedchamber, key in hand.

The two Darcy footmen hidden in alcoves in the hallway did their best not to laugh at the lack of womanly assets Miss Bingley displayed. They watched as she advanced to their master's empty bedchamber door.

Miss Bingley slowly tried the door handle; finding that it was locked as she had suspected. She placed the key in the keyhole and slowly turned it until she heard a click as the lock released. Worried the noise might have woken her prey, Miss Bingley waited for a few moments with her ear to the door, but when she heard nothing, she entered the chambers.

It was dark and she could barely make out the shape of the bed. "I have come as you summoned me, Fitzwilliam," she cooed as she walked to the bed. She lifted the coverlet and slid under the covers. "I am yours, Fitzwilliam, take me as you desire," Miss Bingley cooed.

It was then she realised she could not feel anyone in the bed with her. She climbed out of it, searching for, and finding a candle and flint on the bedside table. Once she managed to light the candle, she looked around to discover that the chamber was empty except for herself! Where was her Mr. Darcy? He could not have known about her plan, could he?

No amount of searching the room produced her quarry. After almost an hour of waiting after her pointless search, she gave up and returned to her chambers. If only he had been in his chambers! She would have to plan the best way forward now, as in a few hours they were departing Netherfield Park at long last.

The two footmen secreted in the corridor grinned at one another; they would have an amusing story to tell their friends and family for many years to come.

CHAPTER 15

Later that morning, Darcy and the Fitzwilliams were breaking their fasts when Bingley, Miss Bingley, and the Hursts entered the breakfast parlour in travelling clothes. Even when travelling, Miss Bingley looked like an orange monstrosity.

"I did not know you intended to depart today, Bingley," Darcy stated.

"My sisters prefer to go to Town," Bingley replied, not able to look his friend in the eye.

"Let me see if I understand you correctly, Mr. Bingley," Lady Matlock declared. "You invited my nephew to be your guest to teach you estate management, then you invited my sons, and then very graciously included my husband and me, and now with no prior notice to your guests you are ready to leave on a whim?"

"It is not a *whim*!" Miss Bingley replied with asperity, forgetting who she was addressing. "We can no longer abide the lowborn fortune hunters in this neighbourhood!"

"Then if that be the case, you should leave with alacrity, as I am sure, Mr. Bingley, the neighbourhood will be relieved to hear you have removed this lowborn fortune hunter," Lady Matlock gestured at Caroline Bingley so there would be no confusion as to whom she referred.

"Me? I am a wealthy and well-educated lady!" Miss Bingley screeched.

"Wealthy, possibly. Well educated, absolutely not! A lady most certainly not! You are the farthest thing from a lady I have ever beheld," Lord Matlock announced as he stared down the shaking woman.

"I have never been insulted so in my life!" Miss Bingley was flabbergasted.

"Do you know your sister attempted to compromise me after the ball, Bingley? How many times have I told you *even* if she succeeded, I would not offer for her?" Darcy retorted angrily.

Miss Bingley was shaken to her core. He had to be guessing as he had not been there, so she decided to bluster. "What a vile lie! Do you take me for one of those Bennets that I would sink so low?"

"Miss Bingley, any of the Bennet daughters have more class and gentility in one of their fingers than you have! First, you were seen as I had footmen on duty in the hallway outside my chambers." When Mr. Darcy mentioned the footmen, Miss Bingley almost cast up her accounts. "But you were heard planning it at the ball. You ranted about your intentions in the hearing of someone who warned me. Why do you think I was not in my bed when you climbed into it?" Darcy asked.

"How did you know..." Miss Bingley clamped her jaw shut, realising she had just made an admission.

"Because, as I said, I had two footmen stationed as added protection. They were singularly unimpressed by what they *saw*," Darcy twisted the knife.

Miss Bingley collapsed into a chair, finally starting to see her dreams turn to dust. When she looked around the room, there was no mistaking the disdain clearly written on the countenances of the Fitzwilliams and Mr. Darcy.

"Mr. Bingley, William tells me you have family in Scarborough, and I believe your estate, Winsdale, is in Yorkshire, Mr. Hurst?" the Countess asked. Both men allowed it was so. "Town will not be an option for some years for anyone named Bingley, as expresses are on their way to Lady Jersey and the other patronesses regarding Miss Bingley's despicable behaviour, and your apparent inability or lack of desire to check her, Mr. Bingley. That being said, I cannot tell you where to go, but I would strongly recommend Scarborough.

"Mrs. Hurst, you have the advantage of no longer carrying the Bingley name. I do, however, recommend you remain in Yorkshire for this season." As the Countess finished speaking, a footman entered the dining room with a note for Mr. Darcy.

When he opened it, to her horror, Caroline recognised her own writing. "That is mine, Mr. Darcy! I do not give you permission to read my private correspondence," Miss Bingley attempted to lie.

"Are you out of your senses, Madam!" Darcy thundered.

"William, is that from Longbourn? Is Gigi well?" Richard asked out of concern. It was then Miss Bingley realised where Miss Darcy was, and her pallor took on a sickly cream colour.

"No, Gigi is well, but her reputation would have been damaged had the pack of lies this harridan wrote to Miss Bennet ever been known!" Darcy looked at Miss Bingley with something akin to hatred.

Bingley was silent as he did not know what to say or do. It was bad enough his sister had sunk so low as to try and compromise his friend, but now she had sent a note to Miss Bennet full of lies that somehow involved Miss Darcy. "What did you do?" Bingley asked when he found his voice.

"Read this drivel," Darcy commanded as he passed the note to a footman to hand to Bingley.

As Bingley read his face went from white to red with anger. "Caroline, how could you write this? You told me you would tell Miss Bennet we would be returning and wished to keep the connection. Instead, you tell her I have designs on Darcy's sister. A girl of fifteen I have always seen as a younger sister and nothing more!"

Mrs Hurst let out a gasp as she read the disgusting missive. She finally realised the price of always appeasing their younger sister was a cost none of them could afford to pay. "Caroline, how could you have fallen so far? I cannot support you any longer; you are on your own in all of this," Mrs. Hurst stated with sadness.

"We will depart for Scarborough today. What about the lease on Netherfield?" Bingley asked.

"I will write a statement that you are giving up the lease and have you sign it. I will take the lease until the end of the year term so you will not be penalised," Darcy offered.

Bingley and Darcy hied to the study while Mrs. Hurst led a catatonic Miss Bingley to their coach. When Darcy returned, he had the signed document in hand. "Bingley, I hope you finally take your sister in hand. I like you, but I will never permit Miss Bingley in my company or that of my sister again. If you are unable or unwilling to separate yourself from her, then I am afraid we are at the end of our friendship. The choice is yours." Darcy offered his friend his hand and they shook, neither knowing if they would see one another again.

"Now what, William?" Andrew asked.

"I will take this document to Mr. Phillips, the local solicitor you met at the ball and uncle to the Miss Bennets, who is the leasing agent for this estate and transfer the lease to my name. Then I will be off to Longbourn," Darcy informed his family.

Richard and Andrew volunteered to join their cousin on his errands and their parents said they would call on Longbourn in an hour. Lord Matlock wanted to test Mr. Bennet's chess prowess again. He had to gain his revenge; few could beat him, but Bennet had.

~~~~~~~/~~~~~~~

After Collins consumed his breakfast at his normal fast pace, he made for Rosings Park to see his patroness, walking just as quickly as he was able. Rosings' butler showed the profusely sweating parson into Lady Catherine's preferred drawing room, where she was seated on her raised throne-like chair.

It was the only comfortable chair in the room by design. Lady Catherine did not want her guests feeling too comfortable. She made sure she was higher and could look down on them, and they had to look up at her.

Mr. Collins genuflected as one would for the King. "Mr.

Collins, what is the meaning of your presence here? Were you not to return on the morrow with the new Mrs. Collins? What is the meaning of you lying to me?" Lady Catherine demanded.

Already sweating profusely, he was suddenly bathed in it as his revered patroness berated him. "My sincerest, most contrite apology, your beneficence," Collins bowed and scraped again, and would have been gratified to kiss the great lady's feet were he allowed such an honour.

Lady Catherine preened at his deference, which she knew was naught but her due. "Explain why you are early and why you are not here with your wife! When will I meet her?"

"You remember I wrote to you telling you that after my cousins disrespected you, I could never take one of them as my wife. Therefore, I offered for the daughter of the local parson who would have been the ideal clergyman's wife." Collins replied.

"Yes, what about it?" the imperious lady demanded.

"The same dastardly cousins, after pleading with me to take one of them as my bride, in their jealousy told my betrothed all manner of lies. As her father, Mr. Dudley, is beholden to my cousin who owns Longbourn until I claim my inheritance, he withdrew his consent for me to marry his sweet daughter, because Mr. Bennet demanded it. She was devastated, but her negligent father cared not for her wishes. My cousin then evicted me from my future estate," Collins told his patroness.

He cared little that nothing in his story was fact, as long as Lady Catherine acquitted him of disobeying her. "In that case, I will go thither and make sure this cousin of yours is put in his place," Lady Catherine decided.

Mr. Collins turned a sickly colour of puce. If Lady Catherine went to Longbourn, she would discover the truth and he could not have that now. It would cost him much more than a possible bride. "A-as much a-as I appreciate your condescension and willingness to reverse the wrongs perpetrated against me, your Ladyship, I beg you do nothing for now. My betrothed, who worships the ground I walk on as if we were formed for one another, requested time to work on her father. If she fails, I will inform you forthwith, and then bow to your way of dealing with my cousin."

Lady Catherine considered her clergyman's words. It cost her nothing to wait, so she agreed and dismissed the relieved man with a wave of her wrist. Remembering Lady Catherine had not mentioned his letter, the senseless parson said "Before I leave . . ."

"What is it, Mr. Collins, as you know I am a very busy woman!" Lady Catherine returned impatiently.

"The letter I posted to you three days ago had some distressing news about your nephew, Miss de Bourgh's betrothed. I wanted to ask if you had any concerns I might be able to assist with in this matter, your Ladyship," Collins offered; certain she would be gratified at his solicitousness.

"What of my nephew Darcy? Why did you not mention this before your inane nonsense?" Lady Catherine barked.

"B-but y-your L-Ladyship, I told all in my letter." Collins was fearful, for his venerated patroness was obviously angry and upset.

"I received no letter from you that mentioned my nephew! Now out with it man!" the great lady demanded. Her patience wearing thin with him this day.

"My wanton cousin has been distracting your future son-in-law with her arts and allurements, distracting him from your daughter, the very rose of Kent..." Collins was cut off by a blow from his patroness' cane.

"**WHAT IS THIS**? You fool! And you are only telling me about this now? You are coming with me! We leave for Hertfordshire within the hour! Mrs. Jenkinson," Lady Catherine called. After a few minutes, Miss de Bourgh's companion curtsied before her mistress. "Have my daughter ready to travel. We are going to Hertfordshire to order my nephew to do his duty to me!"

As Mr. Collins scurried off to the parsonage to prepare, he

realised he had just caused the opposite of what he wanted. His patroness was to travel to Longbourn, and there was naught he could do to stop it.

~~~~~~~/~~~~~~~

Bennet sent a note to ask Charlotte to join them at Longbourn as soon as it was convenient for her that morning. When Charlotte arrived, she saw all *five* Bennet sisters present, in addition to Gigi and Mariah.

"Charlotte, did you give our guest, Georgiana, some advice before we departed for the ball last night?" Bennet asked with a straight face.

"I did? To what does your question tend?" Charlotte asked, somewhat confused.

"It seems Georgiana followed your advice, and the Lydia who you see before you no longer need be locked in the nursery," Bennet shared, while his four older daughters looked at the youngest Bennet with pride.

"Charlotte, it seems I need to welcome you to the family," Lydia spoke in a calm, regulated manner, for perhaps the first time in years.

"Thank you, Lydia, I welcome your good wishes. Do you want to share what the epiphany was you had which caused us to gain the company of a ladylike young girl today?" Charlotte asked.

"Gigi and Kitty came to visit me in the nursery last night. As you know, no matter what any of you told me, I did not believe it to be the truth. I now know it was the truth you spoke about that seducer and thief with whom I thought myself in love, and I apologise for not listening as I should have." Lydia had the decency to look embarrassed as she disclosed the next. "I am aware now had I gifted that man my virtue as I had intended, he would have deserted me as soon as he received what he wanted. He has done thusly to many before me." Lydia hung her head.

"We all err, Lydia. We should acknowledge our errors and not blame others for our choices. How we learn from our mistakes and even from those others commit is that which will define us as people," Charlotte encouraged the youngest Bennet.

"Once Gigi told me about Ramsgate and the self-same words he used on her in an attempt to manipulate me, my eyes began to open. A little after Gigi's revelation, Mariah joined us. We made our bed on the floor for the four of us and talked until we fell asleep. I realise Mama loved us, but she spoilt me, and as she never corrected or educated me, I learnt the wrong ways to behave around men. It will take me time to learn, and I have told Papa I feel I need to go to school as I have a lot to catch up on to be the type of young lady I need to be. The change may be slow and painful, and I may relapse into my former behaviour, but I desire to be better. It is quite clear to me I need to be in school, as maturation is needed before I can be out," Lydia stated with purpose.

"I could not be prouder of you were you my own daughter," Charlotte praised as she enfolded Lydia in a hug.

With Bennet's permission, Kitty, Georgiana, and Lydia would walk Mariah back to Lucas Lodge and then return, so long as they were accompanied by a footman and a maid.

~~~~~~~/~~~~~~~

The transfer of the lease to Mr. Darcy was the work of half an hour and the three men arrived at Longbourn before the Earl and Countess arrived. They were shown into the drawing room where, for the first time, the Fitzwilliam brothers met the youngest Bennet. On hearing Richard was a colonel, everyone else waited for her to start fawning over him, but Lydia surprised them all by merely asking about his regiment and where they had travelled.

Gigi was well pleased to see her brother and cousins. She hugged all three then returned to her friends, sitting between Kitty and Lydia on a sofa and talking with them about their interests. The three men looked at each other and then back at Gigi, struck with wonder as the girl they saw before them was the version before Ramsgate, mayhap even less shy than she had been then.

The Fitzwilliam parents arrived, and there was another round of welcomes. It did not take long for Bennet and Lord Matlock, who had told Bennet to call him Matlock, to excuse themselves to play chess. Lady Matlock, who asked to be called Lady Elaine, joined Charlotte to chat, and the three older Bennet sisters suggested a walk. Darcy and his two cousins agreed a walk would be welcome, while the three younger girls demurred so they could stay and talk inside or pursue their hobbies.

As there were three couples, it was decided no additional chaperone was needed. "Should we walk to Oakham Mount? It is a warm day for November." Elizabeth suggested.

"Out of the five of us, you Lizzy, are the only great walker. Could we not take turns around the park?" Jane proposed an alternative, which was accepted by all. They could walk separately in the park while still being visible to one another at all times.

Richard and Mary ended up sitting on the bench under the big willow where a swing was suspended from a branch. Jane and Andrew sat on the bench under a stand of poplars, while Elizabeth and Darcy walked circuits in the park.

"It must be something in the air at Longbourn, Miss Elizabeth." Elizabeth looked at her walking partner with a question in her eyes. "Gigi is back to, if not beyond, where she was before —well you know before what. I am tired of mentioning the libertine's name," Darcy clarified.

"It seems her helping Lydia was cathartic for your sister. She is such a sweet girl," Elizabeth stated.

"I find I must agree with you, but then I am biased as Gigi is my sister," Darcy gave Elizabeth his first dimple-revealing smile, and the recipient of the smile had never seen him look so handsome. Her heartbeat sped up significantly and caused her knees to weaken, so it was fortuitous that he offered her his arm.

"I see a massive coach coming down the drive," Elizabeth

pointed.

"There is need to apologise in advance, Miss Elizabeth," Darcy let out a groan. "You are about to meet the badly-behaved member of my family, Lady Catherine de Bourgh." Darcy winced.

The other two couples having noted the carriage as well, they all headed back towards the house, to the inevitable looming confrontation.

CHAPTER 16

"Where is that harlot Miss Elizabeth Bennet?" Lady Catherine screamed, resembling a harridan more than the widow of a baronet.

Collins followed behind his patroness looking smug, at least until he was knocked flat on his back and the footman Edward held him down with his booted foot. "Your Ladyship," Collins squeaked, but his cry was ignored as his patroness lumbered forward screaming like a banshee.

"Johnson, bring Sir William. We have a trespasser." The footman nodded and rushed away to Lucas Lodge. "Did my master not inform you what would happen to you if you set foot on Bennet land again?"

"Let me up! I am here in the company of Lady Catherine de Bourgh! As she brought me, I am here by her authority," Collins blustered from the flat of his back.

"Edward, have Smithers help you to lock *that* in the coal cellar," Hill instructed, then followed the trail of invectives coming from the woman who had barged into the house while the two footmen dragged the protesting parson away.

Lady Catherine heard voices within a room and slammed open the door as she made her way into the drawing room. "Where is that slut who is using her arts and allurements to entrap my daughter's betrothed?"

"Do you think everyone sinks as low as you did, Catherine, when you compromised poor Sir Lewis after no one offered for you in your fifth season?" Lady Elaine stated calmly, amused at the surprise on her sister-in-law's face when what she had said claimed the lady's attention. Lady Catherine froze, for the last thing she expected to see was the Countess of Matlock seated in the drawing room talking to a younger woman.

"Lady Elaine, is this Mr. Collins' exalted patroness who he worships like God Almighty?" Charlotte asked pleasantly and Lady Elaine nodded, her smile unchecked. Unnoticed so far, the three younger girls stared in slack-jawed surprise at the uncouth display from an elderly woman, a Lady, and Lord Matlock's sister at that. "You three go upstairs, for there is no reason for you to have to witness such behaviour, not even if such were performed in public by actors. Even the lower classes of our society have better manners."

The three girls exited with all speed before Lady Catherine could react. "Who are you to talk to me thusly? Do you know who I am?" Lady Catherine tried to recover, and addressed Charlotte, choosing to ignore her sister-in-law's words.

"Your relatives have informed me about you, so I know exactly who you are, Lady Catherine de Bourgh. You are a woman with no sense, only bluster. You are ignorant and without accomplishments and believe that being the widow of a baronet and daughter of an earl somehow makes you above the rules of decorum and decency in society. You have proven you have less manners than a worker at the docks, as you entered a home uninvited, and did not have the decency to knock," Charlotte replied calmly, her eyes unwavering and keeping Lady Catherine focused on herself.

"I have never been thusly insulted in the whole of my life!" Lady Catherine was shaking with anger.

"Oh do shut up, Catty!" Lady Catherine heard the voice belonging to the one person in the world she was afraid of, as he was executor of her husband's will.

"R-Reggie, what are you doing here?" Lady Catherine asked carefully as she turned around to find her brother, accompanied by a man who was unknown to her. Both were obviously angry, and it was only then she noticed her parson had deserted her.

~~~~~~~/~~~~~~~

When the six walkers neared the coach, they heard a series of sneezes from within. Darcy opened the door to reveal his cousin Anne, shivering from the cold while Mrs. Jenkinson sat by doing nothing but waiting.

"Anne, let me help you out. Mrs. Jenkinson, why was my cousin left outside in the cold?" Darcy demanded.

"Her ladyship ordered we wait in the carriage and gave me no further instruction," Mrs. Jenkinson replied.

"Are you senseless, or do you only care what my aunt says when you can see my cousin suffers?" Andrew was angry. The lady, obviously another sycophant employed by his aunt, blanched at the Viscount's rebuke.

Andrew and Darcy helped their shivering cousin from the conveyance. "Jane and I will help her up to our bed chamber. There is a blazing fire already lit to warm the room and blankets as well," Elizabeth stated. She and Jane each took one of Miss de Bourgh's arms and escorted her upstairs.

"T-thank y-you s-so m-much," Anne managed between shivers.

"My father is here, Mrs. Jenkinson; and he *will* hear of your neglect. If I were you, I would be ready to seek a new position without a character!" Richard growled with anger as he slammed the carriage door closed, leaving the frightened woman sitting within.

As the group was about to enter, Mr. Collins was dragged out of the front door by two bulky footmen. "Edward, did that man dare to enter our home after my father warned him away?" Jane asked.

"'E did, Miss Jane," the footman answered. "Johnson 'as gone ta' call Sir William. Mr. 'ill told us ta' lock this in the coal cellar."

Once the two footmen passed, dragging the snivelling Collins behind them, the three Bennet sisters assisted Miss de Bourgh up the stairs and into the warmth of Jane's and Elizabeth's shared bedchamber.

~~~~~~~/~~~~~~~

"The better question is why are *you* here, Catty?" Lord Matlock used the appellation he knew most galled his sister, since she considered it too undignified for her station in life. Before his furious sister could answer, his sons and nephew entered the drawing room.

Hoping to divert her brother, Lady Catherine blustered, "There you are, Fitzwilliam! You will do your duty and marry Anne today as your mother and her mother planned when you were in your cradles! I know it all! How that whore Miss Elizabeth..." Lady Catherine got no further.

"*THAT IS ENOUGH!*" Bennet was the first to react. "You foul-mouthed termagant! How dare you push your way into my house, uninvited, and then dare to denigrate my daughter. If you were a man, I would call you out," he announced, and his words caused her to take notice of all who had seen her so humiliated. She began to see the thunderous visages of everyone in the room, all directed at her rather than at the whore, who had not yet been produced as she had demanded.

"As would I, Mr. Bennet," Darcy agreed. "I am beyond tired of that well-worn lie you tell, Lady Catherine. After you came to Pemberley to exert your will while my father was ill, he wrote a letter to me and to Uncle Reggie, wherein he expressly delineates the lies you attempted to tell after my honoured mother passed away. Did you think everyone had a marriage like yours where the man you compromised wanted as little to do with you as possible?" Darcy advanced toward the officious woman, who shrank back in fear of his knowing so much. Luckily for Lady Catherine, Darcy would never lift a hand to a female, although for the first time in his life, he came close to it.

"William speaks the truth, unlike you, *Catty*. Not only did Robert write to me, but he also refutes your lies in his will," Lord Matlock backed up his nephew's words.

"If you cared for your daughter, you would know neither I nor Anne wish to marry one another. Even if Anne were healthy enough to bear a child, which she is not, it would not alter our wishes. Instead, all you care about is finding a way to hold onto Rosings Park. It does not belong to you; it never has, even though you have been its mistress these last twenty years. Neither she nor I have any inclination toward a relationship beyond that of cousins," Darcy declared, allowing his aunt to feel his palpable anger towards her as she cowered.

"Where is my parson? He told me all about Miss Elizabeth!" Lady Catherine tried to salvage some of her dignity.

"If Mr. Hill has done his duty, which I believe he has," Charlotte related, "then that man is about to be arrested. I am sure he did not share with you he was enjoined from setting foot on my betrothed's lands again, did he? I am also certain he did not tell you of his despicable actions, which he claimed were by your authority. Those actions led to letters being dispatched to the Bishop of Kent and the Archbishop of Canterbury. I would be surprised if he is not defrocked before he is released from the Meryton gaol."

For once in her life Lady Catherine de Bourgh was speechless. "I have written to Cousin Charles in order to verify the veracity of the charges against your so-called parson," Lady Matlock told her sister-in-law. Lady Matlock allowed her disdain for her sister-in-law free rein.

"Do you realise that two weeks ago, when Anne turned five and twenty, she became the mistress of Rosings Park?" Lord Matlock pointed out. "I was waiting to hear from Anne, though I am sure you had her post intercepted by that lackey you employ as her companion." Lady Catherine had the decency to look away as her brother hit the nail on the head.

"Father, Anne's situation is something we wanted to discuss with you," Andrew cut in as the perfect moment had presented itself. He related how they had discovered Anne in the freezing carriage with no blankets or warming bricks.

"Where is my niece now?" the Earl thundered as his sister cringed.

"The three Bennet sisters took her to a bedchamber with

a fire to try and warm her as quickly as possible.

"Does your avarice know no bounds?" The Earl rounded on his sister. "Were you attempting to make your daughter sicker so she would not be able to claim her inheritance?" Lord Matlock thundered.

Just then Mary entered the drawing room. "Your Lordship, Miss de Bourgh is requesting the services of a solicitor," Mary informed the Earl.

"We can have Mr. Phillips summoned," Charlotte informed the Earl. "He is Thomas' brother-in-law and the local solicitor."

"Charlotte has the right of it," Bennet agreed, stepping out to instruct a groom to ride to Meryton to request his brother's presence in all haste.

"Are there no limit to the depravity you will sink to in an attempt to get what you want?" Lord Matlock asked his sister, rhetorically. It was sad, as it seemed his older sister was without a scrap of motherly instinct. Lady Matlock and Charlotte went to join the Bennet sisters taking care of Anne.

Lord Matlock felt guilt as he realized he had failed his niece by believing her mother's lies. Catherine had said Anne was well cared for. He berated himself as he realised he should have taken a more active role in Anne's life, or even better, he should have taken her into his household.

Just after the two left the drawing room, Sir William arrived, accompanied by his older sons. "I understand you have a trespasser who needs to be moved to the gaol," Sir William observed.

"Yes, the vermin is in the coal cellar," Bennet informed his father-in-law-to-be.

"We are here to help Father transport him," John stated with a malevolent glint in his eyes.

"Yes," Franklin added, "it is time for us to have a little *chat* with *Mr.* Collins."

The three Lucas men departed to take charge of the trespasser and to make sure he was never in the proximity of their sisters and friends again.

~~~~~~~/~~~~~~~

"Anne, I am so sorry we did not remove you from your mother's care right after your father passed away," Lady Matlock said as she held her niece's frail hand, disgusted at what she was seeing; the poor girl's skin was almost translucent. "We mistakenly believed your mother when she swore she had your best interests at heart."

"As this last birthday approached, things got worse. I am sure she or Jenky intercepted my letters to you," Anne managed before she had a coughing fit.

"I think we should call for Mr. Jones," Charlotte suggested. "He is the local physician and apothecary in one. He is trusted by all in the neighbourhood," Charlotte explained, and Lady Matlock nodded her agreement. Mary went to convey the message to a maid, who would pass it onto Mr. Hill.

"We will nurse you back to good health, Anne," Lady Matlock promised, though even she doubted her words as they passed her lips.

"As much as I appreciate the sentiment, Aunt Elaine, I am a realist. I believe I am not long for this world, and that is the very reason I require a solicitor," Anne related between coughs.

No one wanted to lie to Anne, so they said nothing. Not too long after, there was a knock on the door. Mr. Phillips was shown in, along with the Earl, his sons, and his nephew. The three Bennets and Charlotte departed the chamber, knowing it was a family matter.

Once the introductions were made, Anne got straight to the point. "I am unsure how much time I have left; I need a last will and testament drawn up," Anne rasped.

"It is my understanding you are a wealthy heiress; it will be a complicated document," Phillips averred.

"No, it will be simple, I wish to leave all of my worldly possessions to my cousin, the Honourable Colonel Richard Fitzwilliam," Anne insisted.

"It is too much, Anne, it should go to another," Richard

asserted. "I would much rather you save your energy and live with me there so I can assist you as you need."

"William has Pemberley and more, so he and his family are secure," Anne stated, pausing to cough. She offered a small smile when Darcy nodded his agreement. "Andy has Hilldale and will one day have Snowhaven and the Matlock holdings, so that leaves you, Rich."

No one could argue with Anne's logic. Lady Matlock offered up a silent prayer of thanks as her son would be able to resign from the army and sell his commission. She had long dreaded Richard going back to the front lines. He had resisted their attempts to help him in the past, but this was different.

"Anne, I thank you from the bottom of my heart," Richard was humbled by the freedom his cousin was gifting him.

"I want a clause making Richard the owner of Rosings Park from this day forward," Anne took a sip of water to help quell her coughing. "All I ask is to live out my days in comfort in my suite."

It took Mr. Phillips but a few minutes per copy; in the end, he had made five of them. Anne signed, followed by her uncle and cousins Hilldale and Darcy as witnesses. Phillips would hold one copy; another would be sent to Norman and James in London who would file a copy with the Court of Chancery. The remaining three would remain with Lord Matlock, Mr. Darcy, and Colonel Fitzwilliam himself.

"If God calls me home, I can rest peacefully now, knowing my mother's dastardly plans have come to naught," Anne stated between coughs.

"Where will Lady Catherine live when I move into Rosings Park?" Richard asked quietly.

"That Son, is entirely up to you. Sir Lewis's will left it up to Anne when she inherits, or whoever the master or mistress is, to make that decision," Lord Matlock explained.

"So, I will not have to have her in the main house, or even the dower house if I so choose? How would she live?" Richard enquired.

"She will receive a three hundred pound per annum allowance for the rest of her days. She is allowed to remove any of her jewellery she brought with her when she married Sir Lewis, but none of the de Bourgh jewels or property are hers. Sir Lewis never forgave her for compromising him, hence the size of her settlement," Lord Matlock informed his son.

"How do we proceed and deal with Lady Catherine?" Darcy asked, wanting to know how to help Richard in these next hours and days.

"The deeds to Rosings Park and the de Bourgh house are held by Norman and James in London. When Anne is well enough to travel, we will have the deeds made over in Richard's name." Lord Matlock turned to his younger son. "Now you are a landed gentleman of considerable wealth, is there not something you need to do?"

"I will depart for the Dragoons' headquarters in London to see General Atherton, resign from the army and sell my commission. If you excuse me, I will go request writing materials from Mr. Bennet and send an express to the General so he may begin the process and knows when to expect me." Richard exited the bedchamber to go write his letter.

"Anne, you do not know the gift you have given a mother. Each time Richard has gone into battle, I have prayed he would return home to us, while dreading every visitor and letter in case it was to deliver the news I feared." Lady Elaine hugged her niece delicately and kissed her on both cheeks.

"I was most fearful when Richard would go to war as well, Aunt Elaine and Uncle Reggie; it is the principal reason he is my heir; my decision was made easier knowing my other cousins do not need any more." Anne looked tired, so the family withdrew from the bedchamber to allow her to rest; they were replaced by Gigi's maid, who offered to sit with Miss de Bourgh.

~~~~~~~/~~~~~~~

When the three Bennet daughters and Miss Lucas returned to the drawing room, a belligerent Lady Catherine wanted to know which was Miss Elizabeth Bennet. She felt she could harangue the young lady into giving her satisfaction, as her family was not present for the moment.

"That would be me, Lady Catherine. How may I be of service?" Elizabeth owned.

"Remember my betrothed's warning about issuing of further insults, or crass language, before you continue talking to Miss Elizabeth," Charlotte warned the woman, just as the imperious woman opened her mouth to state her expectations.

Lady Catherine's head swivelled until she realized Mr. Bennet was listening and saw the thunderous look on his visage. She closed her mouth but lifted her head higher to show her superiority, but all she achieved was looking more ridiculous.

Richard entered just then and spoke quietly to Bennet who nodded as he offered a quiet response. Richard thanked him and headed to the study. A few minutes later the rest of his family returned to the drawing room.

"As of some minutes ago, *Catty*, you are no longer the mistress of either Rosings Park or de Bourgh House," Lord Matlock stated, his voice cold and emotionless.

"What nonsense, Reggie. Anne knows not how to run an estate," Lady Catherine replied dismissively.

"Only because you refused to educate her," Lady Matlock returned.

"She is also too ill to perform the duties," Lady Catherine claimed.

"You may be correct, Lady Catherine, but as Anne has gifted me with all of her holdings, the point is moot," Richard stated, returning to the drawing room to find the conversation he intended to start was already in progress. He was grateful for whoever had opened the topic.

"Impossible! I will not allow it!" Lady Catherine blustered.

"You have no say in the matter, Catty," Lord Matlock pointed out. "As of two weeks past, when Anne became five and twenty, all of Sir Lewis's former property became your daughter's. As you like to boast, there is no entail on any of it, which allowed Anne the freedom to do as she wished. She wished to gift everything to Richard. She exercised the free will you denied her for so long."

"No, it is **MINE!**" Lady Catherine screamed.

"As you well know, it was *never* yours. I failed as executor because I believed you when you said would teach Anne what she needed to take her rightful position. All you have ever done is in service to further your own delusional claims. I think I need to have you examined by a doctor to see if he recommends a long stay at an institution for the mentally unbalanced," Lord Matlock challenged.

Lady Catherine realised at that moment all her plans and schemes to retain Rosings and access to Pemberley's coffers had failed. "What is to happen to me?" the defeated woman asked.

"You do not deserve to live in the dower house. I will offer you a pensioner's cottage at Rosings Park rent free on the condition you do not interfere in the lives of any servants, tenants, or others. If that is not acceptable to you, you are free to take the five and seventy pounds you will receive each quarter and make your own way in the world," Richard laid out for the lady.

Knowing she had no other option; Lady Catherine chose the cottage. Lady Catherine was escorted to Netherfield, along with a note to Mrs. Nichols to assign the broken lady a room on the guest floor.

~~~~~~~/~~~~~~~

When the coal cellar door opened, Collins thought his patroness was there to put things to rights. Instead, he saw Sir William and his two sons glowering at him. He was dragged out and handed directly over to Franklin and John Lucas.

Collins had never been so frightened in his life. By the time they reached the Meryton gaol, Collins was decidedly the worse for wear. "You will be held for a month for the crime of trespassing. You should be defrocked by then."

"Dudley will never write to anyone," Collins scoffed.

"He has already done so, but your greater concern should be the countess of Matlock, who is the Archbishop's first cousin and the Bennets' friend. She wrote to her cousin as well, informing him *why* you should be defrocked as soon as may be." Sir William grinned as he shared the information with the man he hoped would get his just deserts.

Only then did Collins realise that his patroness had not come to his aid, and he might have overestimated the strength of the cards he held in his hand.

CHAPTER 17

The wedding of Thomas Bennet and Charlotte Lucas took place in a church filled to capacity Saturday morning, the third day of November. Mr. Dudley conducted this particular wedding ceremony with particular pleasure; both he and his daughter added their voices to those praying the new Mrs. Bennet would present her husband with an heir.

Charlotte had wanted Eliza to stand up with her but decided as she was about to become the Bennet daughters' stepmother, it might be strange if one of them stood up or signed as a witness. After they signed the register, with Gardiner and Mariah as witnesses, Bennet kissed his new bride tenderly.

The two walked to the house and were met with a rousing cheer when Hill announced Mr. and Mrs. Thomas Bennet. The neighbourhood understood the wedding breakfast would be an intimate affair, so there were no hurt feelings among those not invited. To allow the newly married couple some privacy, the Bennet sisters' trunks had been moved to Netherfield, where they would reside for a fortnight before returning home again. The Gardiners would also be hosted at Netherfield for two nights before returning to London on Monday morning.

Lady Lucas had given Charlotte *the talk* the night before, which had been short and to the point. As with most things she considered as part of the natural order of life, Charlotte was not worried about the marriage bed. What would be, would be.

After an hour or so, the guests started to depart. The Bennet sisters hugged their father and new stepmother and wished them well, then were assisted into one of the two coaches departing for Netherfield Park.

"I assume Lady Catherine is under watch and will not try any of her nonsense with our daughters before she departs Monday morning?" Bennet asked.

"Thomas, you know your daughters will be as well protected there as they would be here. Now I think it is time to go see our chambers," Charlotte stated forwardly, with a becoming blush.

Bennet had no objection to her suggestion. They decided they would share a bed as they hoped to share all of their lives with one another. As Bennet watched his wife undress, he wondered who the fool was who had ever called his Charlotte plain. She was anything but.

Thomas Bennet found immense pleasure in making his very sensible bride lose her sensibilities when in their bed, and Charlotte found she liked marital congress very well and when their eyes met as they were fully joined, one would be unable to profess this was never to be a love match.

~~~~~~~/~~~~~~~

As Mr. Collins sat in a squalid gaol cell, he could not imagine how he had ended up in these straits, especially as he had obeyed his patroness's edict. How could he, a venerated man of the cloth, be treated like a common criminal? Try as he might, he could not reconcile this reality to his certainty of his own consequence.

What confused him most of all was why his patroness had not come to rescue him so they could return Kent. Had she not told him things always occurred as she wished? The only explanation he could think of was that she had been incapacitated somehow, as he could not envision a scenario where she would leave him, her faithful servant, to rot in a cell for a month complete. Would she? For the first time since he had been granted the Hunsford living by Lady Catherine, Collins began to experience doubt regarding the limit of his patroness's power and influence.

If what those Lucas brutes, who abused him so abominably, said was correct and Lady Matlock was a cousin to the Lord Archbishop of Canterbury, and if she had been turned against him by those artful Bennets, Dudleys, and Lucases, would Lady Catherine be able to save him, or would he be defrocked as they predicted? This introspection was the first time Collins acknowledged the fact he might, in fact, soon be defrocked.

~~~~~~~/~~~~~~~

The subject of her loyal sycophant's musing was herself trying to divine how her well-thought-out plans had failed her. Not only was she unable to access Pemberley's coffers, but she had lost Rosings Park and the de Bourgh fortune.

She was to live in a cottage, like one of her tenants. No, not her tenants anymore but her ungrateful nephew's tenants. She attributed this to her error in bringing Anne with her. If she had left her at home with Mrs. Jenkinson, Anne would not have seen the family nor given Rosings Park away to her undeserving nephew.

And Fitzwilliam! She was sure the more she repeated the story the more sway she would have over him as he revered his parents and would never do anything to dishonour their wishes. How was she to know her late brother-in-law had put his wishes in writing. It had long vexed Lady Catherine that her sister would not agree to a betrothal between their children, regardless of how much she attempted to browbeat her. Anne had always been biddable, yet all her efforts resulted only in being sent away from Pemberley and told never to return unless specifically invited—an invitation which had never been forthcoming.

Yes, she compromised her husband and forced him into marriage. How could he have held that against her for so many years, even after his death? He had left her residence at Rosings Park dependent on the master or mistress, and with a pittance of three hundred pounds per annum. She had spent more than that amount in a month all these years as mistress of Rosings!

Lady Catherine was sure Richard would not know how

to run the estate and soon enough would beg her to return as mistress; *then* she would make him pay!

~~~~~~~/~~~~~~~

On Monday morning, two carriages departed Netherfield Park for London. One contained Miss de Bourgh, three Fitzwilliam men, and one Darcy. The second carried Lady Catherine and Mrs. Jenkinson. The latter would be Lady Catherine's companion, her salary to be paid from Lady Catherine's allowance.

They were farewelled by the ladies who remained behind under the watchful eyes of Lady Elaine. That lady had taken notice of the connection between her nephew and the second Bennet daughter since they arrived, and was confident Darcy would ask for a courtship, perhaps even a betrothal, soon. She expected it would not be long after the men, minus Richard, returned on Wednesday or Thursday.

Colonel Richard Fitzwilliam was on his way to meet with his general to finalise his resignation from the army and to sell his commission. Then he would travel to inspect Rosings Park, intending to remain there until a fortnight before Christmastide.

"Lizzy, may I ask you something personal?" Georgiana asked as the two were sitting in the music room listening to Mary's playing.

"You may ask, but I may choose not to answer," Elizabeth averred.

"Do you like William?" Georgiana asked shyly.

"We are friends; why do you ask?"

"I hoped you would be more than friends."

"Gigi, it would be impolitic of me to discuss my feelings for your brother with his younger sister if, in fact, I have them," Elizabeth explained gently so her friend knew she was not upset at the question.

"I understand, Lizzy," Georgiana returned quietly, "I have never seen William so relaxed around any woman who is not a member of the family before."

What Gigi said made Elizabeth experience butterflies in

her belly. She had long suspected Mr. Darcy thought of her as more than a friend, as she did him, but hearing it framed by his sister made her realise that she was falling in love with Fitz-william Darcy. She had a dreamy look in her eyes and seemed to be far away, as she wondered if others saw the truth of her feelings. Elizabeth asked herself if her heart was trying to trick her, but she realised it was not; her feelings were true. Elizabeth was so lost in her own thoughts Gigi had to nudge her; even then Elizabeth did not respond until the third time she tried to get her attention.

"I'm sorry, Gigi, I am not sure where I went just then," Elizabeth claimed.

"It is fine, Lizzy; we all get lost in our thoughts at times," Georgiana gave Elizabeth a knowing look that produced a corresponding blush.

Mary completed the piece she had been playing, and Elizabeth suggested Georgiana play a duet with Mary while she went to seek out Jane.

~~~~~~~/~~~~~~~

On Tuesday morning, a solicitor from Norman and James presented himself at Matlock House with the deeds and other paperwork necessary to transfer all de Bourgh assets to Richard.

A much-fatigued Anne signed a few documents, after which she was free to rest. An hour later, all paperwork was completed, and Richard was officially the new owner of all de Bourgh assets, including the estate and townhouse. All that was left to do was to file the papers with the Court of Chancery, a mere formality. When it was revealed to Richard there were liquid assets in excess of two hundred thousand pounds, he was flabbergasted. In addition to that, he was informed that Anne had transferred her dowry of forty thousand pounds to him.

When Richard asked how it was Lady Catherine had never been able to access the funds, he was shown a copy of Sir Lewis's will, which had made most of the Rosings Park and de Bourgh funds inaccessible to his wife. The open question became how Lady Catherine had paid for her lavish spending, which included the needlessly gaudy furnishings and baubles found at Rosings Park and de Bourgh House.

When they examined the estate's profits before and after Sir Lewis's death, it told the story. There was a drop in income between one and two thousand pounds per annum. It was assumed previously that this was due to Lady Catherine's mismanagement, when her spending habits were coupled with her available income, a different answer presented itself.

Lady Catherine went from shocked to sullen. When she was called into her brother's study, she intended to make her displeasure known until she saw the looks on the men's faces. She decided not to say anything until she heard what they wanted to talk about.

"Lady Catherine, are you able to explain the drop in estate income after Sir Lewis died?" Richard asked directly. None missed how the lady blanched at the direct question. "I will caution you, lie and you will no longer have even a cottage. Thanks to a clause in Sir Lewis's will, your thefts from the estate invalidate your allowance."

"Catherine, you have one, and only one, chance to tell all; it will mean the difference between having a place for your future or not," Lord Matlock impressed on his sister.

"Because my late husband blocked my access to the de Bourgh accounts, I had no choice but to withhold part of each year's profits," Lady Catherine admitted.

"The steward must have helped you." Darcy asserted.

"He did. As far as he knew it was all my money, and he never questioned why I was diverting some money to a personal account," Lady Catherine revealed. "I made sure he was not aware of the terms of my late husband's will."

"How much money is in that account now, Catherine?" Lord Matlock asked.

"A few hundred pounds; I am not sure." She saw the question in her brother's eyes. "You know my spending habits,

Reggie. The bulk of the money is residing inside the manor and town houses, in things I acquired," she confirmed.

"I will decide what to do about the steward. However, unless I find out you were dishonest in your disclosure now, I will not change your living arrangements or allowance. I will verify the amount in the bank. If it is you say, a few hundred pounds, it will remain yours. I have more than enough," Richard allowed magnanimously.

"You will allow me to keep the funds?" Lady Catherine asked in amazement. This kind of kindness was foreign to her —certainly, it was nothing she would do for any other.

"I do not like your way of getting a spouse, but I believe Sir Lewis has punished you enough over the years. *If* I see you are not interfering in the running of the estate in *any* way or being unpleasant to any of your neighbours, I will consider moving you to the dower house and increasing your allowance. It will depend completely on your behaviour," Richard offered. "Make no mistake," Richard added, "I abhor the way you treated Anne over the years, and you have many amends to make."

"Thank you, Richard," Lady Catherine offered and then remained quiet. She was coming to terms, slowly, with the fact that the way she tried to achieve her aims was mayhap not the best way.

"Be ready. We depart for Rosing Park at sunrise on the morrow," Richard instructed. "This afternoon I will finalise my resignation from the army and sell my commission."

Once Lady Catherine departed, the men discussed issues Richard might face. As much as Darcy and Andrew preferred returning to Meryton, they volunteered to accompany Richard to the estate in order to assist him with interviewing the steward and inspecting Rosings' ledgers, including the hidden set Lady Catherine had disclosed to them.

Both wrote a letter to Lady Elaine, asking her to give their regrets for not being able to return when planned, and that they would return to Netherfield Park once Richard no longer needed them. The Earl agreed to take the letters for them when he returned to his wife at Netherfield Park on the morrow.

~~~~~~~/~~~~~~~

Elizabeth and Jane understood why both Mr. Darcy and the Viscount had decided to assist Richard, but the three oldest Bennet sisters missed the men. About ten days later, when a convoy of carriages arrived at Netherfield Park, it excited their anticipation, until they realised these equipages were not known to them—and as far as they knew, the men did not travel with an escort of soldiers.

The men who exited from the lead coach were revealed to be clergymen. "Cousin Charles!" Lady Elaine exclaimed in welcome, then directed the group to the drawing room.

"Cousins Elaine and Reggie, may I introduce you to Sir Paul McCartney, the Bishop of Kent? Sir Paul, my cousins, Lord Reginald and Lady Elaine Fitzwilliam, the Earl and Countess of Matlock," the Archbishop made the introductions once they reached the drawing room. "And who are these young ladies, Elaine? You do not have daughters yet, do you?"

"I do not—yet. Cousin Charles and Sir Paul, Miss Jane Bennet of Longbourn, Miss Elizabeth, Miss Mary, Miss Catherine, Miss Lydia and lastly my niece, Miss Georgiana Darcy. Ladies, my cousin Charles Manners-Sutton, The Most Reverend Willowmere, by Divine Providence Lord Archbishop of Canterbury, and The Right Reverend Sir Paul McCartney, Bishop of Kent." The young ladies made deep curtsies as each of their names was mentioned by the Countess.

"Your Grace, what brings you to visit us, although I must own I have a good idea," Lord Matlock asked.

"Matlock, I have requested you address me as Cousin Charles," the Archbishop pointed out, "and yes, based on the fact one of the letters I received was from my Cousin Elaine, I decided to come in person rather than send Sir Paul here to represent me. The allegations in both your letter and that of Reverend Dudley are serious, as is defrocking a clergyman. Once we have interviewed all parties with knowledge of his behaviour here, we will travel to Kent and speak to the man himself."

"If I may, Your Grace and Bishop," Jane Bennet addressed the two clergymen, "you need not travel to Kent; Mr. Collins is but a mile from this very house."

"That is convenient," Sir Paul stated. "Is he visiting friends?"

"Not exactly, Bishop McCartney," Jane averred, "I am afraid he is not here by choice. He is in gaol for another twenty days or so."

The surprise shown by both men was enormous. If nothing else would have sealed Collins' fate, being arrested and thrown into gaol would have done it. "Will you have Mr. and Miss Dudley summoned? Once they are present, we will hear all about this man," the Archbishop requested.

"If I may, Your Grace, I would suggest you invite Sir William, the magistrate, as well as our father and stepmother. They will be able to provide you first-hand testimony on this subject," Elizabeth suggested. "If you request it of Sir William, he will have Mr. Collins brought here as well."

The Archbishop turned to his private secretary, "*Let it be so.*"

Within two hours, all of those invited were present. Collins almost cast up his accounts when he was led into the drawing room at Netherfield in irons. He first noticed his Bishop, Sir Paul, but then he saw the spiritual head of the Church of England sitting next to his Bishop.

The Archbishop addressed him first. "Mr. Collins, based on your arrest and sentence for trespassing, I already have reason to defrock you."

"But Your Grace, it is my..." Collins attempted to defend himself.

"Be silent, Mr. Collins; you will talk when I tell you it is your time, and not before then. Do I make myself clear? If you are unable to regulate yourself until it is your turn to talk, I will have one of my soldiers gag you." The look the Archbishop gave

Collins was one of pure disdain.

Mr. Bennet spoke first, followed by Charlotte, Matilda, Sir William, and Mr. Dudley. As each successive speaker had their say, the looks of disgust directed at Mr. Collins from the two senior clergymen became unmistakable and grew with each new revelation.

"Mr. Collins," Sir Paul addressed him, "Do you believe it reflects well on a clergyman when he attempts to strike a woman, on at least two occasions we know of?"

"She was rude to me, and she deserved it," came the petulant reply from Collins.

"And by what right did you reveal communications made by your parishioners in confidence to you?" Sir Paul asked.

"Lady Catherine needed to know the nearest concerns of her tenants and neighbours; as she is a peer, I complied with her wishes," Collins reported, sure the men would understand how he had no choice but to obey the great lady.

"We could address each of your offences, and there are many. However, it is my ruling that you shall be stripped of your ordination and defrocked forthwith, based on your two main offences alone—breaking the confidence of your parishioners and committing the crime of trespassing. I do not know how you were allowed to take orders, as you seem to have no grasp of basic canon law," the Archbishop pronounced his judgement. "In addition, if you are an example of the clergymen Lady Catherine de Bourgh appoints, I will remove the Hunsford living from her gift."

"That will not be necessary, Cousin Charles," Lord Matlock reported. "My sister is no longer mistress of Rosings Park; it is now the property of my son Richard. It is he who will gift the living."

"Knowing the good sense my young cousin possesses, I see I have no need to remove the living from the purview of Rosings Park. Mr. and Mrs. Bennet, Sir Paul and I apologise. We understand you are celebrating your honeymoon and we disturbed you," the Archbishop addressed the couple.

"No need, Your Grace. My husband and I were ready to see some different faces," Charlotte smiled.

"They only married to beget a son and steal my estate from me," Collins spat out. Sir William nodded to two men standing behind Collins who clamped their hands on his arms and half walked, half dragged him out of the room.

"I never liked the man, but until Mr. Dudley's letter, I never suspected him to be vicious," Sir Paul shared.

The two clergymen accepted an invitation to spend the night at Netherfield Park, gratefully delaying their journeys to their dioceses until the morning. Mr. Dudley spent a few hours talking to the most senior clergyman in the church as well as to Sir Paul. The two gratefully accepted an invitation to dinner with Mr. Dudley and Matilda.

All five Bennet sisters were more than pleased to see how happy their father and Charlotte were together. There was a spring in their father's step they had not seen for many a year; the youngest Bennet owned that she did not remember ever seeing it.

CHAPTER 18

T hings progressed apace at Rosings Park. The three cousins had a long and detailed interview with Mr. George Harrison, the steward. It was clear to them he had never done anything dishonest intentionally, nor had he enriched himself while following Lady Catherine's orders. Mr. Harrison was to keep his position.

Richard met with all his tenants who were overjoyed when the new master agreed to forgo two quarters' rents to make up for unreasonably high rents the former mistress charged; thereafter, rents would be lowered by thirty percent.

When Richard authorised all needed repairs to his tenants' dwellings, he earned their undying loyalty. Lady Catherine had always loathed spending money on such things.

Next, the three met with the parishioners of Hunsford to introduce the new master of Rosings Park and to inform them Mr. Collins would never again darken the door of the Hunsford Church. The parishioners expressed their joy almost unanimously; not only had Collins been a bad pastor, but they also knew anything told to him in confidence was relayed to Lady Catherine.

When asked how well the curate was liked, a Mr. John Lennon, that response was uniform as well—he was loved and respected by the members of Hunsford Parish. When the three cousins talked to Mr. Lennon and discovered Collins only paid him but two pounds per month, they were disgusted anew.

As soon as Richard received word that Collins had been defrocked, he offered the living to Mr. Lennon, who accepted it gratefully. The former curate was appreciative, as he was betrothed to a Miss Cynthia Powell from the village and had been unable to marry on the pittance he received from Mr. Collins.

The new parson achieving his heart's desire caused Darcy to feel pangs and longings due being separated from Elizabeth. He had never experienced such strong feelings in his life, but he was experiencing both while he assisted Richard. After three weeks he and Andrew were feeling confident they would be able to depart for Hertfordshire within the next few days.

It was time to grab the bull by the horns. Although he was not completely certain she had tender feelings for him, Darcy suspected Miss Elizabeth, Elizabeth, did have such feelings. He hoped he was correct. She had been "Elizabeth" in his thoughts for some time now. Rather than being timid, the time had come for him to declare himself. He would offer her the option of a courtship or betrothal. He prayed she would accept the latter, but even if it were the former, he would be overjoyed that she accepted either offer.

Andrew was no less keen to return to see his Bennet sister. He was developing tender feelings for Jane Bennet and hoped she thought of him favourably. He suspected she did, and when he and Darcy returned to the environs of Meryton, he intended to offer the lady a courtship, if she would accept it.

"Rich, do you see any reason why William and I cannot depart on the morrow?" Andrew asked after the three returned home from services at Hunsford. There had been no open pews as there often were—many—when Mr. Collins held services, and some were obliged to stand in back. Mr. Lennon was a dynamic speaker, and his singing voice was a pleasure to hear.

"I see no reason, and I plan to follow you two in a sennight or so. Lady Catherine has been quiet, and Anne is comfortable; I have a good idea what is going on around here. It will be good for me to be master on my own without you two to prop me up. I have learnt much from both of you and know you will return if I need you again," Richard averred.

"Will Anne be well on her own here?" Darcy asked.

"Yes, the new doctor we hired, Mr. Richard Starkey, does not bleed her or ply her with the draughts the quack who used to attend her would. She will not be with us for as long as we would hope, but with Mr. Starkey's care, I am confident it will be longer than it otherwise might have been. Speaking of Mr. Starkey, did you know he, Mr. Harrison, and Mr. Lennon were all born in the Liverpool area? They never met before they came to Rosings Park, but it is a coincidence none the less. Even stranger, Mr. Lennon tells me that Sir Paul McCartney, the Bishop of Kent, is from there as well." Richard paused and then quipped, "It is an infestation of Liverpudlians."

The next Monday, the twenty-sixth of November, Andrew and Darcy farewelled Richard as they departed for London. They would overnight at Darcy House and depart for Netherfield Park at first light. Darcy planned to retrieve a ring from the safe in his study at Darcy House.

~~~~~~~/~~~~~~~

"Aunt Elaine told me Andrew and my brother will be returning today," Georgiana reported as she sat with Mrs. Bennet, the Bennet sisters, and their *Aunt* Mariah in Longbourn's drawing room.

"What news is there of the Colonel, I mean *Mr.* Fitzwilliam," Mary asked hopefully.

"According to my last letter from William, Richard will be leaving his estate within a fortnight, and he shared good news. Anne's new doctor has helped her a great deal, and William reports she looks far healthier than when we saw her here," Georgiana shared.

"How is Anne's new companion, Mrs. Katheryn-Elizabeth Hudson?" Elizabeth asked.

"From what Lady Elaine told me, Anne's companion is responsive to her and caters to her needs, unlike her predecessor," Charlotte responded.

The four younger girls excused themselves to walk in the park, accompanied by Mrs. Annesley who arrived a few days earlier, after her daughter had delivered and both mother and daughter were doing well.

"Eliza, I saw the way you lit up when Gigi mentioned her

brother. If I did not know better, I would say you are looking forward to that gentleman's return," Charlotte opined.

"I will not deny that I have missed him," Elizabeth owned.

"A lot," Jane added.

"You are a good one to talk, Miss Jane Bennet! I did not miss your looks when Viscount Hilldale was mentioned. I can read you, Jane, but there are many of those we know who find you inscrutable; I would wager most of them do. My recommendation to you is if you feel any inclination towards the Viscount, then allow him to see it. If your heart is not touched that is one thing, but I think that is not the case." Charlotte looked at Jane and waited for her to cogitate.

"He is everything a *man* should be," Jane acknowledged. "Unlike Mr. Bingley, he sees all of me and not only my looks. You are correct, Charlotte; I am not indifferent to him."

"Mama always knows best," Charlotte repeated the quip she had previously used on Eliza. It had the desired effect, as all three sisters smiled widely. "And you, Miss Mary?"

"What of me?" If Mary had thought she might escape any discussion of her feelings toward a certain gentleman, it was not to be.

"Mary! You know Charlotte is referring to Mr. Richard Fitzwilliam," Elizbeth prompted.

"I would be lying if I tried to claim I was not interested in him, but why would he be interested in the plainest Bennet daughter? He is a wealthy estate owner now; he can have his pick of ladies from the *Ton*." Mary looked down and away from everyone else. Mary could still hear the words of derision spoken by her dead mother echoing in her head.

"Mary Eloise Bennet! You detest lying, do you not?" Charlotte asked sternly.

"I do," Mary confirmed.

"Then why did you lie just now? You are anything but plain. You choose to wear spectacles you do not need; your hair is always in the most severe style you can make it; your dresses are drab. I *know* what your late mother used to tell you." Mary looked at her feet. "Look at me Mary, and you know if either Jane or Eliza disagrees with me, they will say so, do you not?" Mary lifted her head and nodded, for she knew Jane and Lizzy were always honest, sometimes to a fault.

"Mary, please listen to Charlotte. We have tried to tell you the same; mayhap you will listen this time," Jane implored her middle sister.

"Please take off the spectacles, Mary." Charlotte reached her hand out and Mary tentatively deposited the eyewear in her opened hand. "Now, try and tell me you need these," Charlotte challenged.

"I do not," Mary admitted softly, barely audible to the other three in the drawing room.

"Next, you will allow Sarah to start styling your hair; this is to begin as soon as we have completed our conversation." Mary had no doubt it was the first, but not the last, order her new stepmother would be issuing to her. "Although you try to hide it, you have a figure similar to Jane's and are only a bit shorter. Jane will help you select one or two dresses to wear until we have some more made for you." Charlotte turned to Jane. "Given Mary's hair is Eliza's colour, some lighter dresses will work, do you not think?"

"I do," Jane responded excitedly. "Mary, you have no idea how long, I, we," Jane indicated Elizabeth, "have wanted to help you do this. You will allow us to help, will you not?"

Mary realised the days of hiding behind the persona she created to defend herself against the unkind words her mother used to direct at her were over. It was time for the real Mary to emerge, and she hoped the man she was falling in love with would like her as she was, not as she had pretended to be. "Yes, I would be very happy to accept your help."

The three older sisters left the drawing room as excited as little children unleased on a confectionary for the first time. Charlotte smiled. She had a feeling even Mary would not recognise herself once her sisters and Sarah were done with her.

~~~~~~~/~~~~~~~

"Where are you two going?" Lady Elaine asked, although she was sure she knew. Andrew and William had arrived barely an hour ago on horseback ahead of the carriage, sprinted upstairs to bathe, and after a perfunctory greeting to her and her husband, they were calling for their horses again.

"Do not tease the boys, Elaine; you know full well where they are off to and why," Lord Reggie grinned at his son and nephew. "If your purpose is to secure a Bennet daughter, then you have our hearty approval and all I can say is it's about time."

Without another word, the two made for the entrance, and were soon riding toward Longbourn. After the ride from London, they did not push their horses. Soon enough, they were handing their reins to a Longbourn groom.

"Viscount Hilldale and Mr. Darcy," Hill announced. Although it was good to see Gigi, the two were disappointed the three older Bennet sisters were absent, especially the eldest two.

After he greeted Mr. and Mrs. Bennet, Andrew was about to ask where the other sisters were when the youngest Bennet exclaimed, "MARY!" When the two men turned, to their delight, they spied the two sisters they desired to see, but they were astounded, for between them was Miss Mary Bennet.

She was not wearing spectacles. her hair was styled in a becoming coiffure, and she wore a yellow day dress. "Mary, you look so much like Jane, but with dark hair like Lizzy. You are beautiful!" Kitty said in wonder. She had heard Charlotte's words; she had not believed it would be so, but her eyes could not lie to her.

The two men were speechless, as though they had watched a butterfly emerge from its cocoon. "I think I know why my Mary hid herself from the world, and I must beg your forgiveness, my beautiful daughter. I will not speak ill of the dead, but you know to what I refer. Rather than protect you. I laughed. Please forgive me, Mary," Bennet beseeched his middle daughter.

190

"Of course, I forgive you, Papa," Mary granted gently, feeling like a princess, and relieved she would never need to hide herself away again.

"It was my fault, Mary," Lydia said softly, head down.

"Of what do you speak, Lyddie?" Mary asked as she walked further into the room.

"You know how Mama used to dote on me?" Mary and the other girls all nodded. "When I was about five, I was jealous as you were so pretty, so I started making comments to Mama. It was not long after that she started to call you plain and denigrate your looks. I am so sorry, Mary," Lydia admitted.

"I remember now, I was eight or nine when Mama started to say those things to me," Mary recalled.

"It was not your fault, Lydia," Charlotte stated. "No matter what you said, you were but a small child who reacted as a small child would. You did not make your late mother do or say anything. She was the adult, and she made her decisions, not you. You have heard the saying: *you can lead a horse to water, but you cannot make him drink?*"

"I have," Lydia sniffled, as the weight of her perceived guilt had caused her to cry.

"What does it mean, Lydia?" Charlotte pressed.

"It means..." Lydia went silent as Charlotte's meaning hit her. "I should not have said what I did, but it was Mama's choice to say what she did."

"Charlotte is correct, Lydia," Bennet told his daughter as he pulled her into a hug. "If each of us had to apologise for every silly thing we did when we were young children, we would never do anything but apologise.

"I agree with Papa and Charlotte; Lyddie, I forgive you, and I do not hold you responsible for Mama's actions. She said those things to me until she left this world, and no one besides herself was forcing her to do so," Mary relieved Lydia's guilty feeling.

"Once our neighbours see you, Mary, they will not know who you are; they will think Jane suddenly has a twin sister with darker hair," Mariah observed. "What a proud *aunt* I am," she jested.

"I have an idea," Elizabeth said, "the December assembly will be the first Friday of the month; that is where most of our neighbours can see Mary looking as she always could have, for the first time."

"I will make sure Richard will arrive before the assembly," Andrew said quietly to Darcy. "He liked her as she was before, but I want to see his face when he sees Miss Mary now." Darcy nodded in agreement.

Just then Hill announced the Earl and Countess of Matlock. "Hello everyone..." Lady Elaine stopped midsentence as her eyes rested on Mary. "Mary, is that you?" Mary nodded, her smile spreading as she saw the approval of her efforts in Lady Matlock's eyes. "Richard said you were hiding your light, but my goodness, you are gorgeous, Mary!"

It made Mary warm all over to think that Richard Fitzwilliam had seen past the severe façade she presented to the world and detected that there was more to her. "Bennet, before any other surprises reveal themselves, may I speak to Miss Bennet in private?" Andrew requested.

"And may I have a private interview with Miss Elizabeth?" Darcy managed; his eyes riveted to Elizabeth.

Charlotte gave both named Bennet sisters an 'I told you so' look, and both looked anywhere but at their sometimes-too-perceptive stepmother.

CHAPTER 19

"Jane, take the Viscount to my study; the door will remain partially open, and you have ten minutes. Lizzy, same rules. You may use the small parlour, that is, if you both wish to grant these interviews," Bennet stated. He had an idea it would not be long until he would lose his three oldest daughters to matrimony. Having Charlotte as a companion became even more gratifying with the prospect of his daughters leaving home.

"I am more than happy to hear whatever Mr. Darcy has to say," Elizabeth allowed. No one missed Georgiana's little squeal of joy she attempted to contain under her hand.

"Same for me, Papa. I have no objection to hearing what the Viscount has to say," Jane confirmed. Jane led Andrew to the study while Darcy followed Elizabeth to the parlour, his heart racing as he hoped Elizabeth's was racing too.

Once she closed the door halfway, Jane turned to face the Viscount. Remembering what Charlotte had told her, she gifted Andrew with a beatific smile that conveyed the warmth she felt for him.

Andrew did not misinterpret her smile and the signal it sent him, for it was proof that the lady was open to his suit. "Miss Bennet, may I call you Jane?" Jane nodded her acquiescence. "Jane, when we first met, I was taken by your beauty," he saw her face fall somewhat and understood she felt like an object, thinking men like Bingley only saw her outer appearance. "But, for me, outer beauty is not the most important factor, not even close to it." Andrew was gratified to see her relax. "You, Jane, are generous, compassionate, and charitable, a lady in the best sense of the word. You are kind to one and all, and I have noted how you try and see the best in life, while not being blind to the evils of the world. Anyone who thinks you are biddable and that you do not think for yourself, is dead wrong.

"I enjoyed our discussions and appreciated the fact you would not change your position to agree with mine. You never fawned over me; you see me, not my title or my family's wealth." Andrew paused for breath.

"I know you want to marry for the deepest love, and so do I. I will not tell you I have feelings I do not *yet* possess, but I will tell you I have tender feelings for you. I would like to request a formal courtship, to see if our feelings will grow and we might recognise we want to spend the rest of our lives together." Andrew waited while Jane considered her answer.

"It pleases me more than I am able to articulate that you see all of me, and not just my superficial looks. You are correct, I will not marry for title or fortune, only for love. I do not object to the former if the latter is present before I accept a proposal of marriage. I do not love you—*yet*. I would not accept a courtship unless I had tender feelings for you—and I do." Jane gave him another heart-warming smile. "So, if I may call you Andrew...," he nodded rigorously, "then if that be the case, Andrew, I would be most pleased to enter into a formal courtship with you."

Andrew took both of Jane's hands, kissed the top of each and then turned them over and placed a lingering kiss on each of her wrists.

~~~~~~~/~~~~~~~

Elizabeth partially closed the parlour door, then turned to face Mr. Darcy. "May I call you Elizabeth?" he requested, and she nodded once to indicate assent. "In that case, please call me William," Darcy offered.

"Why, William?" Elizabeth asked.

"You know my first name is Fitzwilliam," he confirmed, and she nodded. "I ask to be called William because of Gigi. When she was young, she had a hard time pronouncing my full name, Fitzwilliam, so she called me William and it stuck.

I prefer it because it reduces confusion when I am with my cousins. My family has had the tradition of naming the first-born son by the mother's maiden name for generations. I suppose I am lucky my mother's family was not named Snodgrass."

"I dare say you are correct. I imagine if your mother's maiden name had been Titts-Bottom it would have been even more problematic," Elizabeth smiled at the thought.

"As amusing as the naming conventions of the Darcys are, I have a particular reason for my request to speak to you today." Darcy approached Elizabeth and stood as close to her as he dared without an understanding between them.

"Did you want to talk about the reason you mentioned my name in every letter you wrote to Gigi, even the one when Miss Bingley would not leave you in peace for more than a minute at a time?" Elizabeth asked with an arched eyebrow.

"It is, Elizabeth. Seconds after my ill-advised slight of you at the assembly, I truly looked at you for the first time, and what I saw was the opposite of what I claimed. You know now what was perturbing me that night, but that does not excuse my words.

"As much as my pride and head fought against it, I started to fall in love with you after the night at Lucas Lodge. Your refusing to dance with me only increased my ardour. The day you walked to Netherfield Park to nurse Miss Bennet, I was lost to you. It was then I realised how specious were the arguments my head was using to counter the arguments of my heart. I had thought myself above you, but as we are both born of landed gentlemen farmers, we are equal. Next, my head tried to tell my heart my family would not accept you; that was wrong, for the only one who would object was Lady Catherine. We know she would have objected to a princess if I were not marrying her daughter as she demanded." Darcy paused as he looked deeply into the fine eyes which were a window to Elizabeth's soul. What he saw reflected back was—love!

"You have my stepmother to thank for my reconsideration of my wrongheaded prejudices against you. Once I began to see clearly, my pride let go of the prejudices I held and I was able to see you for who you are—one of the best men of my acquaintance," Elizabeth informed Darcy as both their hearts sped up, neither knowing they were beating in time with one another.

"I came here today willing to ask one of two questions. The one I will ask depends on you, Elizabeth. I must tell you I ardently love and respect you. If your feelings are not at that point yet, as I know only true love will tempt you into matrimony, I would request a courtship. If, however, your feelings tend toward love, I would ask the question I long to ask." Darcy held his breath when Elizabeth cocked her head to one side, making a show of cogitating.

"The truth is, I was never indifferent to you. I believed, no, I tried to convince myself I hated you. If I did not care about you and your thoughts, what you said at the assembly would not have affected me to the extent it did. Once I allowed myself to know the real you, my feelings progressed from acquaintance to friend, and from friendship to tenderness. I am not sure when it happened because I was in the middle before I realised I had begun, but I love you too, William. Most ardently." Elizabeth said the words Darcy dreamed of hearing.

Darcy dropped onto one knee while still holding her left hand, retrieving the ring from his pocket. "Elizabeth Bennet, I love and respect you. I want to debate with you for the rest of my life; you are the *only* woman in the world I could ever marry. Will you grant me my heart's desire and be my wife, my partner in life?"

"It seems there is no choice William," Elizabeth said saucily. "You are the only man I would agree to marry, so yes, William, yes I will absolutely marry you."

On receiving the answer he had dreamed of; Darcy slid his Grandmother Darcy's ring onto the ring finger of her left hand. The ring held a cluster of four emeralds perfectly matching the colour of her eyes, which were surrounded by a ring of small, brilliant diamonds.

"William, it is a perfect ring, but should your mother's ring not go to Gigi?" Elizabeth asked as Darcy rose to stand.

"My mother's ring *is* Gigi's. All my mother's personal jewellery was bequeathed to Gigi. The Darcy jewels will belong to my wife, and unless your father refuses us, that will be you. This was my Grandmother Darcy's ring. Like you, she had green eyes, which I believe was the impetus for my grandfather presenting her with this ring." The look Darcy gave his betrothed told her the last thing he wanted to do was talk about jewellery at this moment.

Elizabeth moved toward him until their bodies were as close as possible and lifted her head expectantly. Her betrothed did not disappoint her as he brushed her lips with his own. As he did, Elizabeth drank in his masculine scent of sandalwood and spice.

He deepened the next kiss, captured her lips, and proceeded to demonstrate his passion for her. Even though it was Elizabeth's first kiss she pressed into him and sighed with pleasure when his lips captured hers. The following kisses were slow and deep, soft, and stirringly thorough. His hands explored the tresses of her hair, knocking out some pins. He had long dreamed of being allowed to touch her hair. They would have lost all sense of propriety, time, and place had they not heard the clearing of a throat in the hallway.

They jumped apart and tried their best to put themselves to rights. There was a light knock on the door and Charlotte entered. "If my estimation is correct, I think you need to wait to talk to my husband after your cousin," Charlotte stated as she looked from one blushing person to the other.

"Yes, Mrs. Bennet," Darcy bowed his head and after one last longing look at his betrothed, made a quick exit from the parlour.

"If that ring is anything to go by, you are betrothed, Eliza. He is a good and honourable man who is worthy of your love. I know he loves you, and I assume you reciprocate the feeling?"

Charlotte asked.

"I am so happy, Charlotte. Why cannot everyone be as happy as me?" Elizabeth gushed as she held her left hand up for Charlotte to inspect.

"As far as I know, Jane is not far from that feeling; she has accepted a courtship with Viscount Hilldale. I believe it will not be long before they too are betrothed. I expect our Mary will not be far behind. Richard Fitzwilliam was well on his way to being in love with her when she hid her true self away. He already recognised she was more than she showed as she held herself back. I have the feeling when he sees her, someone will have to help him raise his jaw from the floor," Charlotte opined. "As much as her looks, or perceived lack thereof, have never been a factor, they will not hurt."

After Charlotte wished Eliza happy, the two returned to the drawing room.

~~~~~~~/~~~~~~~

William Collins had five days left before his release from gaol. His resentment towards all those who he felt had wronged him reached the boiling point. How could the spiritual head of the Church of England have done what he did? He had believed all the lies the Bennets, Miss Lucas, and the Dudleys had told about him!

On one hand he dreamed about revenge, but then it hit him that unless and until his cousin was sent to hell without a male child, he was homeless. He admitted to himself his cousin looked hale and hearty and would not be going anywhere anytime soon, so what was he to do?

His self-worth had been tied both to his position as a pastor and his association with Lady Catherine de Bourgh. Now both were gone. His cousin had come to see him a few days ago and had informed him how the former Colonel Fitzwilliam was now master of Rosings Park, and that his former curate had been given the living at Hunsford.

At the same time, Cousin Bennet made him an offer. Join in breaking the entail and he would receive five thousand pounds and a first-class ticket on a Dennington Lines ship to the Canadas with a promise never to return.

His gut reaction was to reject the offer out of hand. But after his cousin departed the gaol, Collins had cogitated on his situation and realised it was his only option. He had no more than fifty pounds to his name, as he had not been in his position for more than three months and he had no prospect of earning more.

As much as it irked him to do anything which would benefit his cousin, the money and a fresh start would allow him to be free. Collins asked the guard to have someone take a message to Mr. Bennet at Longbourn to inform him that his terms were acceptable.

~~~~~~~/~~~~~~~

Bennet was about to accompany Andrew to the drawing room so that he could announce his courtship of Jane when Darcy knocked on his door. "Come in Darcy; let me see what my second announcement will be." Bennet saw the look of pleasure on the man's face, so he was sure Darcy's question had been met with a positive response.

"I requested Elizabeth's hand in marriage, and she has accepted me," Darcy said as soon as the study door was closed.

"Sit," Bennet indicated the chair in front of his desk. "It would have been my preference to make sport of your inauspicious beginning with my daughter at this moment, but I will spare you. I know you apologised to Lizzy for your ill-advised slight at the assembly, and once she saw past Wickham's lies, she began to enjoy your company," Bennet stated.

"I count myself a most fortunate man as she finds me *tolerable enough to tempt her*," Darcy averred self-deprecatingly.

Bennet was heartened to see the man who could be dour at times was able to make sport of himself. He was also secure in his understanding of Lizzy. She would not have accepted Darcy unless she loved him. Before Charlotte, it would have been much harder to say goodbye to his daughters and watch another man replace him as their protector. Having Charlotte had changed all of that. Bennet would still miss his daughters, but he had a partner and helpmeet now, one he liked and respected, who was his intellectual equal.

"You have my consent and my blessing," Bennet related as he stood and offered his hand to his future son-in-law. Darcy stood and clasped Bennet's hand firmly.

"It will be my most important duty to make your daughter happy always," Darcy promised.

"You had better," Bennet ribbed. "You do know I was a champion fencer at Cambridge, do you not?" Bennet asked as his head indicated the foils hanging on the wall behind him.

"You are *the* Tommy Bennet!" Darcy exclaimed. "When you come to Town or visit Pemberley, we must fence. As an incentive to visit us, have you heard about the library at Pemberley?"

"I once heard Miss Bingley waxing eloquently about it, but I thought it was hyperbole. Is it true?"

"If anything, that lady understated the library's collection and size," Darcy smirked when Bennet lit up at the confirmation.

"Then I suppose Charlotte and I will have to check on my daughter often," Bennet stated.

"You will all be welcome anytime, Bennet, with or without notice," Darcy offered.

"Be careful what you ask for, Son!" Bennet jested as the two men headed for the drawing room.

Elizabeth had been keeping her left hand out of everyone's sightline as she did not want to pre-empt her father's announcement. When Bennet and Darcy returned to the drawing room, the latter went to stand behind his betrothed. Darcy gave a slight nod as he entered the room which caused Elizabeth to beam—not that she doubted the outcome.

"It is my pleasure to inform you that Jane has accepted Andrew's offer of a courtship. Words of congratulations flowed until Bennet held up his hand. "It is also my pleasure to tell you that William asked a question of Lizzy," he did not miss the smiles on the betrothed couple's faces. "Sorry, belay that. Not just *a* question, *the* question! He asked for her hand in marriage, and she accepted him..." If Bennet was about to say more, but no one knew, as a blond streak launched herself at her brother just then.

"I take it you approve, Gigi?" Darcy asked.

"Yes, William, I most certainly do! At last I will have a sister. Five sisters!" Georgiana spied the ring when she reached for Elizabeth's hand. "Lizzy, Grandma Darcy's ring is perfect for you."

Anything else anyone wanted to say was lost in the melee as each sister needed to see the ring, hug Elizabeth and Darcy, and express their joy at gaining a brother. Jane and Andrew were not forgotten as they received their fair share of the well wishes.

"My sister would have loved your Lizzy," Lord Matlock said gruffly to his nephew.

"I know, Uncle Reggie. Both she and Father would have loved her had they the chance to meet her," Darcy stated with confidence.

Mary hugged both sisters and congratulated them, though Jane noticed her wistful look when she returned to her seat next to her. "He will be here soon, Mary," Jane promised quietly, patting Mary's hand, understanding well what was ailing their sister.

Last to hug and well wish the sisters had been Charlotte, who graciously omitted any 'I told you so's' as she expressed her joy. "Do you have a wedding date in mind, Eliza?" Charlotte asked.

"We have not discussed it yet. I know I do not want a long betrothal, and I feel certain enough of my William to say he feels the same," Elizabeth surmised.

By the time the betrothed and courting couples fell into their beds that night, they felt well pleased by the events of the day.

CHAPTER 20

The day after the excitement at Longbourn, Bennet, Phillips, and Sir William met with Collins at the gaol. "Mr. Collins, are you doing this of your own free will or has someone coerced you into breaking the entail on Longbourn?" Sir William asked as he held a document to that effect in his hand and passed it to Collins.

"Why is this needed?" Collins asked belligerently.

"You are in gaol, so if you ever change your mind and claim you were forced to break the entail on Longbourn, we will have this document," Phillips elucidated for Collins.

"If it is your choice, Mr. Collins, you may sign all of the documents and receive the sum I agreed to pay you, or you may return to your cell and pray my *young* wife never delivers a son. I must caution you, if that is your choice, the next time you set foot on my land while I am alive, I will take it as a threat against my family and act accordingly," Bennet explained.

Collins could still feel the foil pressed against his neck, even though that fateful day in his cousin's study had been weeks ago. He had no doubt his cousin was not making an idle threat. "I will sign everything," Collins opted.

Once three copies of each document were signed, Phillips summoned his courier to ride to London and have one copy filed with the Court of Chancery. Once that was done, the entail on Longbourn would be no more, ensuring the continuity of the Bennet line at the estate. "Once we receive the proof of filing and the cancelled entailment documents on the morrow, you will be free. My two younger brothers will escort you to London and you will board your ship. Once the ship has sailed four days out from Liverpool, the captain will present you with your funds; you will be able to verify he holds the funds when you board. He will present the amount we agreed upon, along with the fifty pounds Mr. Lennon found hidden in the Hunsford Parsonage study." Bennet explained all so Collins would be fully aware. "Do you have any questions?"

The sullen man shook his head and was locked back in his cell. "That was fairly painless," Phillips opined as he gathered the remaining paperwork. "Bennet, you should institute a new entail on Longbourn, not restricting which gender may inherit, but ensuring some future descendant cannot sell off pieces or the whole to satisfy a gamester's lifestyle," Phillips suggested. After this, the gentlemen walked to Phillips' office, only a few doors down from the gaol, for glasses of celebratory port.

"That sounds like a good idea. I will talk to Charlotte and canvas her opinion," Bennet replied. "Did you see Collins' face when I mentioned who would accompany him to London? He has not met Nick yet, but he is the strongest of my three new brothers. If he gives any trouble, either John or Nick would take pleasure in punishing him."

"Hattie told me she heard from Lady Lucas that Franklin is courting Matilda Dudley. They are well suited, and unlike that defrocked fraud of a parson, he will place her needs above his own, and he has no patroness to worship," Phillips opined.

"Charlotte informed me, as did Dudley during our weekly meeting," Bennet answered. "I am for home; thank you for your assistance and port, Brother."

~~~~~~~/~~~~~~~

Darcy and Elizabeth were walking in the park. The three younger girls, two Bennets and one Darcy, were pushing each other on the swing under the oak tree, as the day was unseasonably warm.

"Have you thought about when you would like to marry, Elizabeth?" Darcy asked. "I am sure I mentioned I would prefer a short betrothal. I assume you would like to marry from Longbourn?"

"As to the second part of your question, yes, I want to marry in the church where I have worshiped all of my life and where I was christened. Like you, I do not require a long betrothal; if it is all the same to you, I prefer a small wedding attended by our closest family and friends," Elizabeth responded.

"What say you after Twelfth Night?" Darcy asked.

"That would be perfect, William," Elizabeth replied. "That is close to six weeks from now so no one will be able to say we rushed to the altar."

"As it will be winter, I suggest we go south for our wedding trip. I own a house on a bluff near Brighton, overlooking the sea. It is called Seaview Cottage, but it is not a cottage; it is about the size of Longbourn's manor house," Darcy revealed.

"That sounds perfect, William. I have always wanted to try sea bathing, but I suppose January is not ideal for the exercise." Elizabeth looked at her betrothed with warmth.

"You have the right of it. I believe it will be too cold, unless there is a day with unseasonable warmth, far greater than today. We will visit Seaview in June before we return to Pemberley after the season, then you and I will bathe in the sea. There is a private beach in a protected cove which is not visible from the sea." Darcy waggled his eyebrows and Elizabeth blushed scarlet. She had to own, to herself, she could not wait for the weather to be warm enough to explore the beach.

~~~~~~~~/~~~~~~~~

"It is done," Bennet reported to his wife as they were sitting in the study after he returned home. "Everything was done and done for the best. The last piece is to wait for the confirmation from the Court of Chancery, which I expect to receive in two days. For all intents and purposes, there is no longer an entail on our estate."

"Did Collins behave?" Charlotte asked.

"Like a child whose favourite toy had been lost," Bennet related. "I am very glad you suggested I make him that offer. What made you think he would accept?"

"Once he was defrocked and then discovered his patroness had no power to arrange things as she desired, I surmised he would rather have something than nothing," Charlotte explained.

Bennett pulled his wife into his lap and kissed her soundly. "You said you wanted to talk to me, Charlotte," Bennet remembered when they came up for air.

"I did, though your kisses are almost powerful enough to make me forget. You gave our brother Gardiner your late wife's dowry to invest just after she passed, did you not?" Charlotte checked.

"I did," Bennet confirmed.

"Have the funds grown?"

"Very nicely. Gardiner used the initial investment to purchase a large load of textiles, mostly ones never seen in England. He doubled the investment. When I pointed out it was rather risky to invest all on one venture, he pointed out had I listened to him twenty plus years before, there would have been a very respectable sum saved up for the girls' future. To my shame, he was correct," Bennet owned.

"And now?" Charlotte asked.

"After two years, and having paid Collins, there is over fifteen thousand pounds in the fund. After the initial investment, our brother used less risk in his investing," Bennet revealed.

"Have you been adding excess profits from the estate to the fund?" Charlotte asked.

"No. Gardiner wanted me to, but I have omitted doing so," Bennet admitted.

"An omission you will repair, will you not?" Charlotte suggested with raised eyebrows.

"Yes dear," Bennet answered.

"I have started to economise in the running of the house, and as the estate's profit approaches three thousand per annum, we should be able to give Edward over one thousand each year to add to the portfolio. It is not just the girls we must plan for, but any potential siblings as well," Charlotte explained.

"Did we find a school for Lydia yet?" Bennet enquired.

"I believe we have," Charlotte responded. "Lady Elaine recommends the Wrightfield School for Young Ladies in Wiltshire. It is a school with a rigid structure, which can only be beneficial to Lydia. Ever since Gigi's revelations to Lydia, she has been like a different girl. In my opinion school, which you remember she wants, will help her become the young gentlewoman she wants to be."

"Kitty should be encouraged in her endeavours in art," Bennet opined.

"Agreed, although I do not believe Kitty needs such instruction at a school; we can hire an art master for her. She no longer follows Lydia around, and ever since Gigi has been here, Kitty has come into her own," Charlotte suggested.

"There are two things I would like to ask your opinion on, Charlotte..." Bennet explained Phillips's suggestion regarding a new entail.

"His suggestion is sensible. What was the second issue?" Charlotte asked.

"It just came to my notice Purvis Lodge will be offered for sale soon. Old Mrs. Purvis would like to retire to Bath and has no family, and no heir. She offered her estate to me first," Bennet said.

"Would we be able to purchase it without taking a mortgage?" She inquired.

"If Gardiner agrees to invest with me, then yes," Bennet averred. "It is worthwhile. The additional land and tenants will add about one thousand two hundred pounds per annum, and as we apply better farming methods, eventually the combined profit could reach five thousand pounds. In my opinion, if we purchase the estate, the house should be turned into Longbourn's dower house."

"If Gardiner agrees to invest, then I think it is a worthwhile purchase," Charlotte opined.

There was a knock on the study door, but before Bennet responded, Charlotte climbed off his lap and took a seat on one of the chairs in front of the desk after straightening her skirts.

Once bade to do so, Darcy and Elizabeth entered the study and informed Bennet and Charlotte of their proposed marriage date. There was no disagreement, so after consulting the calendar, they chose Tuesday, the eighth day of January 1811.

~~~~~~~/~~~~~~~

It was the first day of December, a Saturday, when Richard Fitzwilliam arrived at Netherfield Park after leaving Rosings Park before sunrise. The longer Richard had been away from the neighbourhood, the more he missed the middle Bennet daughter. He decided that he would refresh himself immediately and then he would hie to Longbourn in order to see her and ease the ache he hoped she, too, was feeling.

Richard Fitzwilliam was taken by her intelligence and the dry wit that she allowed others to see from time to time. In his discussions with her, it had not taken him long to discern her intelligence was almost as sharp as her next oldest sister, even though Miss Mary tried her best to hide that fact. He did not care if she was plain, but as an officer trained in the art of deception, it was but short work for him to determine she was more than she allowed the world to see in character and, he suspected, in looks. He hoped he would be the one to show her she had no need to hide her true self from the world any longer.

"No need to go tearing over the countryside on that charger of yours, Richard," his mother waylaid him. "The Bennet, Lucas, and Phillips families will be here in about an hour for dinner. I think you will be *surprised* to see them," Lady Elaine stated cryptically. Knowing all the mentioned family members, Richard could not fathom why his mother had emphasised the word *surprised*.

An hour later the guests' carriages arrived at Netherfield Park. Richard joined his brother and William as they strode towards the Bennet equipage to assist the ladies. Bennet was first to emerge; he handed out his wife, Kitty, Gigi, and Lydia. He then stood back and allowed Darcy to hand out his betrothed, followed by Andrew, who performed the office for Jane.

Richard offered his hand to Miss Mary, and when she stood before him, his breath was taken away from him as he beheld the vision of beauty she was. "Our Mary is a vision, is she not?" Bennet quipped, which broke the spell.

"Miss Mary, it is so very good to see you again," Richard managed when he could again draw breath.

"And you, Mr. Fitzwilliam," Mary returned with a smile.

"Do you not think we should enter the house?" Lady Elaine suggested as she watched her son's reaction with pleasure.

As they all moved indoors, Richard did not miss the smiles and grins on the faces around him. It seemed no one had shared that Miss Mary was no longer hiding her light. While he was longing for the companionship of Miss Mary before, now it was a deeper ache. That he pined for and needed her was both pleasure and torture. The confidence he felt radiating from Miss Mary only enhanced the attraction he felt for her.

As they walked into the house, Richard was in awe of the woman he was walking next to. He had suspected Miss Mary did not allow herself to be seen as she actually was, and held back her true character, the true depths of her intelligence, and her wit. He had never suspected the extent of her beauty. He would have asked the question he was about to even if she looked the way she had presented herself previously. "Miss Mary, would you grant me a private interview?" Richard asked as soon as they arrived in the drawing room.

"If my father grants it, then yes sir, I do," Mary replied softly.

"As Mary has agreed, I have no objection," Bennet allowed.

"The study is open," Darcy informed his cousin.

"Mary, you know my restriction about the door, do you not?" Bennet reminded his third daughter, who nodded. "You have ten minutes."

"Miss Mary," Richard began as soon as the door was partially closed, "I have desired to ask you this question for all the weeks of our separation as I learnt about running my estate. I tell you this, as I want you to know that my feelings for you were never tied to your external beauty, which I always suspected you had."

"Your being shallow never entered my thoughts, Mr. Fitzwilliam," Mary granted.

"Richard, if you please, Miss Mary," Richard requested.

"In that case, Mary."

"Mary, I find I have fallen in love with you. I was not looking for love when I came to join William for Bingley's ball, but as soon as I saw you, I knew you were special. I was certain that, for your own reasons, you were hiding your true self from the world. I was never fooled by the façade you presented. I saw you, Mary, the real you. I knew there was so much more to you, and I do not refer to your looks. I know you have much more to offer the world than you were willing to show, and I pray that you are confident enough to reveal yourself to the world and allow all to see you are second to none," Richard saw tears form in her eyes, and reached out to brush them dry with his finger.

"These are tears of joy, Richard. I allowed my late mother's voice to hold sway over me. That you saw me as I am, before I allowed any to see how I truly am, tells me how pure your love for me is. I do not love you—yet, but I am well on my way to being in that state. I am grateful I have earned your love and regard," Mary stated with feeling.

"Do not forget respect, Mary; I have the highest respect for you. Mary Bennet, will you honour me by granting me a courtship? Hopefully, you will come to love this old soldier as he loves you. I could not see anyone, but you navigate the vagaries of life with me," Richard stated.

"It is with the greatest of pleasure I accept your courtship, Richard," Mary's heart sang, for she had won the love of a good and honourable man.

Richard leaned forward and brushed his lips lightly on Mary's. He did not deepen the kiss, but neither missed the electricity the brief touch of their lips produced. "Mary, will you ask your father to join me so I may request his consent and blessing?" Richard asked.

Mary smiled and left to pass Richard's request forward. Five minutes later, before the families were called to dinner, Bennet announced his blessing for Richard's and Mary's courtship. The announcement did not come as a surprise, and congratulations flowed. Once the room calmed, Bennet announced the date for the wedding of his second daughter and William Darcy.

~~~~~~~~/~~~~~~~~

It was bitterly cold in Scarborough—almost as cold as Miss Caroline Bingley's heart. No matter how many letters she had written to her *friends* in Town, she had received only one reply. The short missive was from Miss Hawthorne-Smythe, who told her not to have the temerity to contact her again as word of Miss Bingley's actions were known throughout London society. She was ruined and Mr. Darcy was lauded for escaping her attempted compromise.

Bingley and his younger sister were residing with their Aunt and Uncle Bingley, their father's younger brother. The London papers, delayed due to the weather, were delivered one morning while they were sitting together in the parlour, during the worst snowstorm Scarborough had experienced in recent memory. As was her wont, Caroline searched the gossip and social columns. All was peaceful until she screeched: "**NOOOOOO!**"

"Caroline, what is wrong?" Bingley asked with concern.

"We must go to Mr. Darcy and save him. He has proposed to that country mushroom Eliza Bennet, I must…" whatever the harpy was about to spout was cut off.

"*Shut up*, Caroline!" Bingley growled. "Your delusions ruined you in society and I have more than likely lost the friendship of my best friend, but you still ignore the facts. If you dare to approach Darcy or any of his family, they *will* give you the cut direct. Bingley turned to his uncle. "Uncle, we have all tried to talk sense into her and nothing has worked. Am I wrong thinking she needs to be committed to an institution for the mentally unbalanced?"

Before his uncle could answer, Miss Bingley sprang out of her chair and bolted out of the house into what could only be termed a blizzard, without a pelisse or coat. After wrapping themselves as well as they could, Bingley and his uncle tried to search for her, but there was almost no visibility. Even with the layers each was wearing, they were chilled to the bone after ten minutes and forced to return to the house without success.

The storm passed two days later, and as soon as they were able to make their way through the snow blocking the doorway, the two Bingley men and their footmen mounted a search. They found Caroline's frozen body not twenty feet from the house.

She had slipped and hit her heard on a fencepost. There was no way of knowing whether she had been killed by the blow to the head or by the sub-freezing temperatures. A few days later when the Hursts arrived, Caroline Bingley was laid to rest next to her parents.

"Did I drive her to do this?" Bingley asked his sister and brother-in-law.

"No, Charles, there was something inside of our sister which allowed her to hear and see only that which fit her beliefs and desires," Mrs. Hurst opined. "We tried everything, and you were left with but one option. Had she been sane, Caroline would not have bolted into the worst storm in the last fifty years. I pray she is finally at peace."

"I echo your prayer, Sister," Bingley stated.

CHAPTER 21

L ydia was looking forward to starting school after Elizabeth's wedding. When Charlotte and Bennet described the strictures and rules of the Wrightfield School for Young Ladies it did not concern her, because she was keen to learn. It was not only Kitty who benefited from Gigi's example of how to behave; Lydia had been absorbing lessons rapidly. Conversely, due to Lydia's lively and outgoing personality, Gigi had been drawn further out of her shell—to the point her brother and the Fitzwilliams hardly recognised the withdrawn girl who cried at the drop of a hat just a few months ago.

The Bennets were approaching two months of marriage; neither would say they were in love with the other at this time. However, against the expectations of both Charlotte and Bennet, each was developing tender feelings one for the other. Much to their mutual pleasure, they did not spend time together because they had to—they wanted to.

Bennet had thought the most difficult of mandates to live with would be Charlotte's condition that he no longer sequester himself in his bookroom to the exclusion of all else. However, as time passed, he found he did not have to force himself to leave his study; he preferred to. His whole world had been turned on its head and, far from objecting, Bennet found that he was much happier than ever before.

Charlotte's other condition, that he allow her to take the younger two in hand with drastic measures, ended up being a *not necessary*. Bennet no longer claimed his youngest two were the silliest girls in the Kingdom. He started to give them attention, as he had done with his three older daughter, which had borne fruit already.

"I have never looked forward to an assembly as I do to the one upcoming," Bennet shared with his wife as they lay in bed one night, the afterglow of marital relations evident in both. "It will be something to watch our neighbours when they see our Mary. If it were simply her looks it would be one thing, but it is her confidence and the fact she no longer hides her intelligence. When I started working with Mary after Fanny's death, I was able to see just how smart she is. She is not quite as quick as Lizzy, but she is close. I saw what Fanny was doing to Mary, and Lizzy to a lesser extent; to my shame I thought it would be too much effort to exert myself. Lizzy was older when it started, and she had me. Mary was on her own, and I allowed her to withdraw into herself," Bennet remonstrated with himself.

"That is more than enough self-indulgence, Thomas. There is naught you can do to change the past. You started making small changes after my predecessor passed, and now you are no longer the indolent man who used to hide in his study with his books and port. You are a good man, a man I am not sorry for marrying as I could not imagine myself with a man better suited to me," Charlotte avowed. She leaned toward her husband and kissed him languidly, and what followed was a pleasure most men at his age would not be able to indulge in a second time, but they did not have Charlotte, and he counted her as one of his principal blessings every day.

~~~~~~~/~~~~~~~

Franklin Lucas, Matilda, and her father visited Longbourn on Friday afternoon, the day of the December assembly. When Hill showed them into the drawing room, there was little doubt of the news about to be shared. No one was taken by surprise when Mr. Dudley announced the betrothal of Matilda and Franklin.

Genuine words of congratulation were shared, and although no one mentioned it to the bride to be, the difference between her current expression of pure joy and the tepid acceptance she showed about her previous betrothal was marked.

"I will not expect you to call me Aunt Matti after I marry your *uncle*," Matilda quipped with Jane and Elizabeth.

"Regardless of your expectation, it will not happen," Elizabeth stated.

"You realise Matti will be Papa's sister, do you not?" Jane pointed out.

"I stand by my previous statement," Elizabeth feigned being put out.

"When will you marry?" Jane asked.

"We discussed having the wedding around the end of January. My father will start calling the banns this Sunday, so once we pass the third calling, we can marry any time if we choose to advance the date," Matilda shared.

Just then Mary entered the drawing room. Matilda had not seen her since her metamorphosis. The woman looked familiar, but Matilda could not put her finger on who she was.

"Matti, I hear I need to wish you happy," Mary stated, her lips offering a slightly amused expression.

Matilda started at the recognition. She knew the voice but did not recognise the beauty before her. "M-M-Mary?" Matilda stammered.

"Matti, yes, it is Mary; not somebody who has stolen her voice," Elizabeth informed her gaping friend. The three sisters satisfied Matilda's curiosity and related all Matti was unaware of about Mary's past with her mother and her decision to stop hiding.

"Will Meryton see you for the first time at tonight's assembly? Matilda asked, and her friends nodded.

"The single men are safe," Mary replied to Matilda dryly, "I am being courted by Mr. Richard Fitzwilliam."

"You are betrothed, Lizzy, and both Jane and Mary are being courted—by brothers no less! Longbourn will be a lot emptier," Matilda opined.

"Not if Charlotte becomes with child," Mary replied.

"I supposed so," Matilda agreed thoughtfully.

Not much later the two Dudleys and Franklin Lucas departed to prepare for the assembly, leaving the Bennets to make their preparations as well.

~~~~~~~/~~~~~~~

Seeing Miss Bennet on the Viscount's arm and Miss Elizabeth on Mr. Darcy's was expected when the Longbourn and Netherfield Park parties arrived, shortly before the first dance was called.

Many mothers with daughters of marriageable age, having heard the former Colonel was master of a large and profitable estate, were looking forward to his arrival. At least they were until he walked in with a beauty on his arm. The unknown lady resembled Jane Bennet, but she had darker hair like the second and third Bennet daughters. The resemblance caused many to look from one to the other in surprise.

Speculation spread through the room quickly, but the truth was revealed only after Lady Lucas and Mrs. Phillips approached the couple, and Mrs. Phillips hugged the unknown lady.

"Congratulations on your courtship with Mr. Fitzwilliam, *Mary*; he is a very lucky man," Mrs. Phillips stated loudly, so those nearby could not fail to hear her.

"Thank you, Aunt Hattie." Mary kissed her aunt's cheek.

Those standing closest heard the lady reply to her aunt, realising only then that she was none other than their own Miss Mary Bennet. The news swept through the room; one and all found her transformation to the handsome and confident young lady before them nearly unfathomable.

The few exclamations of disbelief were put paid to very quickly by her family's continued use of her name. After the end of the first set, before Mary was collected by Andrew, she and Richard were inundated by well-wishers. Those who had had designs on the former Colonel were so pleased for Mary that their own desires were put aside.

Mary was relieved all of her sets had been taken before

she set foot into the assembly room. Richard, who claimed the first and last, her father, the Earl, William, Andrew, Sir William, and his sons claimed the rest. Many who had never looked at her twice in the past requested a set; all were as disappointed as she had been when they never asked when she acted the part of a wallflower.

Elizabeth and Darcy enjoyed the first set of the night together, much as they did anything they did in each other's company. If Aunt Elaine and Charlotte had not told them it was not done, the two would have danced every set together. Instead, Darcy surrendered his betrothed to Richard and sought out Jane for the second set.

The citizens of the area at the assembly were almost as astonished by Mr. Darcy's transformation but believed if anyone could draw out someone's better nature and help them smile it would be a Bennet daughter. Their Lizzy had been doing it for years. Mr. Darcy had never been seen as he was with Elizabeth; he appeared fairly ebullient, and he was dancing every set.

The three older Bennet sisters enjoyed the December assembly infinitely more than the first one the then-new Netherfield party had attended. The same was true for their father, who found he enjoyed dancing with his wife. It was remarked that Mr. and Mrs. Bennet enjoyed three sets with each other, for the first time in many a year.

~~~~~~~/~~~~~~~

As Mrs. Purvis required an answer before the Gardiners arrived for Christmas, Bennet was worried he might miss out on the chance to buy the property at such an unexpectedly low price. Charlotte suggested he approach his future son-in-law, not for a loan but with an investment opportunity. After some internal debate, rather than approach only Darcy, Bennet decided to ask for a meeting with Lord Matlock, his two sons, Darcy, and Mr. Phillips.

Bennet explained the purpose of the meeting, and the projected income which could be produced by this investment.

"It seems like a sound investment to me," Darcy stated.

"Andrew and I agree," Lord Matlock replied affably.

"And me," Richard granted.

"I have a little over forty percent available for the purchase," Bennet revealed.

"In that case, we will each invest twenty percent," Lord Matlock proposed.

Darcy and his two cousins put their heads together and seemed to come to a quick agreement. "In Elizabeth's marriage settlement, my stake will be given to her," Darcy informed the group.

"Richard and I agree," Andrew looked to his father who nodded, "if we eventually are granted the hands of Mary and Jane, they too will have our respective shares of the investment as theirs."

"This is not what I wanted; I was not looking for a way for you to gift your investment to me or my daughters. In fact, I am not comfortable with your doing so," Bennet returned.

"You would dictate to my sons and my nephew what they may or may not include in the settlements?" Lord Matlock challenged. "None of us thought for a moment it was what you were pushing for. If we did, we would never have made the offer. Do not let your pride spoil your future plans, Bennet."

"When you put it like that, Matlock, I find I have no logical argument against it. It is most generous of you. If this be the case, Phillips and I will visit Mrs. Purvis forthwith. I thank you for investing, gentlemen." Bennet inclined his head to the men.

Before he rode to Purvis Lodge, Bennet sought out his wife, for he wanted nothing hidden from his Charlotte. "Like you, I never expected them to gift their stakes to their future wives. It is a most generous offer," Charlotte opined. "Lord Matlock had the right of it, Thomas."

Bennet felt deep gratitude to his new family. He and Phillips rode the short distance to Purvis Lodge to close the purchase with Mrs. Purvis.

~~~~~~~/~~~~~~~

A week after the assembly, Jane admitted to Elizabeth she had fallen in love with Andrew Fitzwilliam, and not a day later Mary owned the same to her two older sisters about Richard.

"Richard told me he loved me when he requested the courtship; he is only waiting for me to let him know my feelings are engaged," Mary admitted.

"Then go to it," Elizabeth told Mary. "He is an ex-soldier and likes plain speaking. Some men might think a lady forward, but not Richard," Elizabeth turned to Jane, "or Andrew for that matter. Has Andrew indicated his feelings for you, Jane?"

"Not in so many words, but I believe my love is requited. He told me when we began our courtship that he knows I will only marry for love. As hard as it will be for me, I will have to give him an indication of my feelings," Jane shared with her sisters, blushing deeply just thinking about being so very forward.

"I think both of you should look to Charlotte for an example. If she had not taken charge of the situation and spoken to Papa, where would he be? And where might we be? So much good has come from that one act. If more women were like Charlotte, just think how many misunderstandings would be averted," Elizabeth opined.

"Lizzy speaks the truth, Jane. We need to take a page from Charlotte's book and at least let the brothers know how we feel. What they do with the knowledge is up to them," Mary concluded.

"I will think on the best way to do it," Jane allowed.

~~~~~~~/~~~~~~~

At Netherfield, Jane and Mary's affections were the subject of discussion in the cousins' private sitting room as all three were nursing snifters of brandy. "I envy you, William. You are betrothed, and you both have declared your love, one for the other," Andrew stated wistfully as he took a sip of the brown liquor.

"There is no reason you two cannot be in the same position as I am. I was under the impression your courtships were proceeding quite well. Am I wrong?" Darcy enquired.

"My courtship with Mary is proceeding as I expected. I suspect her feelings are engaged, but I have not asked her yet," Richard owned.

"Why not?" Darcy asked.

"What if she answers in the negative? I love Mary deeply. Right now all is perfect, but I am afraid to ask the question too soon and perhaps spoil things," Richard expressed his insecurities. "When you go into battle, you are forced to see how tenuous life really is and how it can be snatched from you in an instant. I suppose I was applying those thoughts to this situation."

"Rich, you have charged into battle on too many occasions to think about. Is it not better to know where you stand?" Andrew asked.

"That is brown, Andy," Richard returned, "what about you and Jane? Do you know where you stand?"

"*Touché*, little brother," Andrew allowed. "Jane is hard to read."

"You are both simpletons!" Darcy exclaimed. "Andy, Jane is *not* hard to read. The smiles and looks she gives you are unlike any she gives others. I used to watch her and Bingley and I detected a reticence on her part. With you she is open and warm. She is similar to me and does not allow others to see her feelings, except..." Andrew cut his cousin off.

"Except to those for whom she feels deeply." Suddenly Andrew had clarity. "I need to ask her about her feelings, do I not?" Both his brother and cousin nodded.

"You too, battle-hardened former Colonel. If I was able to detect a special partiality in Jane, what do you think I see in Mary, who is not nearly as reticent as her eldest sister?" Darcy looked at Richard, who slapped his hand against his forehead.

"I am worried without cause?" Richard asked rhetorically.

"Will you accompany us to Longbourn in the morning, William?" Andrew asked. "I think it is time to take Mrs. Bennet up on her open offer for us to join the family to break our fasts."

"Good idea, Andy," Richard slapped his brother on the back so hard he almost spilled the remainder of his brandy.

"Yes, I will join you two as well. I never pass up an opportunity to visit my Elizabeth," Darcy averred.

Andrew and Richard stopped at their parents' suite before going to bed to collect their maternal and paternal grandmothers' rings. Their mother handed them the ring boxes without a word, but her smiles for each of her sons spoke volumes.

~~~~~~~/~~~~~~~

"What think you, Charlotte?" Bennet asked his wife as they snuggled together that night, "I think it is merely days until we are invaded by a horde of Fitzwilliam brothers asking me to gift them two of my daughters."

"There is no reason for me to disagree with you; I agree it will be mere days, certainly less than a sennight. When I spoke to the three eldest before coming to our bedchamber, Jane and Mary acknowledged they have fallen in love with their respective gentleman. As soon as those two work up the courage to give Andrew and Richard a sign, if the brothers do not ask first, you will be applied to for their hands," Charlotte declared.

"Like Lizzy's William, I know they are honourable to a fault. I could not see myself denying them anything they deigned to ask, but giving them my blessing will be easy, notwithstanding the pain I will feel when three daughters leave this house under the protections of their husbands. It is the natural order, and I will never allow selfish urges to interfere in the happiness of any of my children," Bennet stated emphatically.

Charlotte understood her husband's melancholy and just hugged him to herself until they fell asleep in one another's arms.

CHAPTER 22

"Welcome, gentlemen," Longbourn's mistress greeted the three men. "You are just in time, so please join us in breaking our fasts."

"As long as it is no imposition, Mrs. Bennet, we would very much like to join you and your family," Andrew spoke for the group.

"I am a forthright woman, Andrew. I would not have extended the invitation if that were the case," Charlotte responded.

Jane and Mary blushed lightly as the brothers looked at them intently as they entered the dining parlour. Even while Andrew spoke to Charlotte, his eyes seldom strayed from Jane. Darcy sat down next to Elizabeth, and Andrew and Richard found seats next to their lady of choice.

Bennet would have had some sport with the men at the table had his wife not given him a cautioning look and shaken her head almost imperceptibly. Bennet found it almost disconcerting that his wife of but a few months seemed to understand his character so much better than his late wife, who he had been married to for over twenty years.

The meal passed with nothing of consequence being discussed. It was a cold January day, but Andrew asked if he and Jane might take a turn in the park. Remembering her previous night's resolution, Jane agreed she would like some fresh air, as did Mary and Richard. The younger girls demurred, choosing to remain indoors, but Elizabeth and William agreed to join the other four. As the only betrothed couple, they filled the office of chaperone, thus relieving Mrs. Annesley of the need to join them outside.

Mary and Richard walked to the left while Jane and Andrew walked to the right. Elizabeth and William walked directly to the bench under the oak. "William, am I wrong in assuming Andrew and Richard had a particular purpose today?"

"I am not at liberty to tell you that you are correct," Darcy averred with a dimple-revealing smile. "If I were a guessing man, I would say each of them needs to ascertain the level of feelings of his chosen lady. What proceeds from that point will depend on the facts gleaned."

"This should be interesting then," Elizabeth smiled widely, vastly joyful her sisters' hearts' desires would be answered within a day of their admissions. Elizabeth saw her betrothed's questioning look. "Mary certainly, and I suspect Jane as well, are looking for the best way to indicate their feelings without contravening propriety—too much," Elizabeth revealed to her love.

Darcy threw his head back and let out a deep rumbling belly laugh. Both couples stopped and looked back towards the source of the unexpected mirth. His cousins suspected they were the subject of his amusement.

"I have never seen my cousin more relaxed than he is with Miss Elizabeth," Andrew told Jane. "Miss Bennet, Jane, I have two questions for you, the second being predicated on the answer I receive to the first. I know you will only marry if you love your partner; my first question is..."

"Yes, Andrew, I love you!" Jane daringly pre-empted the remainder of Andrew's question. "I am vastly pleased you asked as I was trying to work up the courage to tell you without seeming grasping."

"How could I ever think that of you, Jane?" Andrew asked as he led her toward the house. "Do you agree to grant me a private interview?" Jane nodded vigorously. "Come, I need to request permission from your father for that purpose."

Mary and Richard watched as Jane and Andrew walked at speed toward the house. "Richard, I love you too," Mary blurted out.

"I was about to ask you, in as subtle a way as I could, that very question. Thank you for saving this old soldier from the possibility of placing his boot in his mouth," Richard stated with almost boy-like glee, hearing the very words from his Mary he had dreamed of even before his return from Kent.

"Jane and Andrew have the right idea. It is cold; let us return to the house. I believe you will need to request leave from my father for a private interview." Mary arched her eyebrow in the same way her next older sister was wont to do.

"I agree, Mary. Besides there is nowhere good to kneel out here," Richard grinned.

"We are not needed to chaperone any longer, William," Elizabeth observed as Mary and Richard disappeared around the front of the structure.

"So it seems, but does it follow we must return right away?" William waggled his eyebrows suggestively.

"No, I suppose it does not, but it is cold," Elizabeth responded as her betrothed lowered his head and captured her lips. All thoughts of the cold were forgotten as they shared some deep kisses.

Darcy pulled away reluctantly. "We need to return to the house before your father sends the other three girls to recover us." Darcy could imagine Mr. Bennet doing just that. When they entered the house to remove their outerwear, they met three relieved girls who would no longer need to seek them. The betrothed couple looked at one another, and Elizabeth's tinkling laugh was heard accompanied by Darcy's baritone guffaw.

The three looked on at the amused couple with quizzical looks. "It seems the cold has affected Lizzy's and William's good sense," Kitty opined as she led Gigi and Lydia back to the drawing room.

~~~~~~~/~~~~~~~

As they were the first to request a private interview, Jane and Andrew were granted use of Bennet's study. As soon as the door was partially closed, Andrew dropped to one knee and took Jane's hands in his own. "Jane Francine Bennet, I knew you were special almost from the first moment I met you, and it never had anything to do with your beauty. What attracts me to you is your inner beauty, which shines like a beacon in the night.

"When I requested a courtship, I was not in love with you, but I was teetering on the brink. It was not many days later when I acknowledged to myself that I was irrevocably in love with you, Jane." Andrew caressed Jane's hands with his fingers as he spoke causing a frisson of pleasure and warmth throughout Jane's body.

"Within a sennight of the beginning of our courtship I knew for certain you were the only man I would ever love," Jane admitted.

"If I had but asked sooner, we would have been betrothed already," Andrew berated himself.

"What are a few days in the scope of our lives, Andrew? As Lizzy says, only remember the past as that remembrance gives you pleasure." Jane squeezed his hands to emphasise her point.

"In that case Jane, all that remains is to declare my ever-lasting and undying love for you and ask you to make me the happiest of men and accept my hand in marriage." Andrew looked up at Jane expectantly from his position on one knee.

"Andrew, you are the man I was waiting for, and as I return your love in full measure, yes, I will marry you," Jane intoned the words Andrew most wanted to hear.

Andrew rose from his knee, withdrew a velvet bag from his pocket, and opened the drawstring. He took his paternal grandmother's ring, a gold band with a huge sapphire surrounded by two rings of diamond chips, and slowly slid it down Jane's ring finger.

Jane was looking up at her betrothed expectantly when he obliged her with a soft, chaste kiss, her first from a man not a relative. Jane let a sigh of pleasure escape as he deepened the kiss. After four or five kisses, Andrew stepped back and broke contact, much to Jane's chagrin.

"I know of your father's prowess with the foil, so I would rather not anger him," Andrew owned. "I think I need to speak to him."

"Wait here; I will request he join you," Jane kissed her betrothed on the cheek before exiting the room to ask her father to join Andrew in the study.

<center>~~~~~~~/~~~~~~~</center>

As soon as the door to the parlour was partially closed, Mary turned to her suitor. "Richard, you have no idea what a relief it was to be able to declare my love for you. I should have told you as soon as I knew, but I did not want to seem forward. How could I not love the man who saw me before I knew myself?" Mary asked.

Richard sank onto one knee. "I could see there was so much more to you than what you allowed others to see, Mary. It was my suspicion what you presented to the world was not the truth of the matter, but I loved you well before you revealed your beauty to all." Richard paused as he gathered his thoughts. "I know it is not my place to apologise for the inherent falsehoods your mother used to spout, but I am sorry that she made you feel less than you were."

"I allowed her words to affect me the way they did," Mary stated.

"They were words that were both untrue and should never have been spoken by a mother to a daughter. There is little point in arguing about your late mother's culpability as there is nothing, we, or anyone else, can do to change the past. The truth is that you, Mary Eloise Bennet, are perfect for me. You are strong, intelligent, kind, and compassionate, all in one person. I find you are the *only* one I want to walk life's paths with. Mary, please marry me," Richard beseeched.

"Yes, Richard, I will join my life with yours until death do us part." Mary averred. Richard stood and drew Mary into a hug. He lowered his head until their lips met and gifted Mary with her first kiss. For a battle-hardened ex-officer, his lips were surprisingly soft. Mary experienced the warmth of his lips on her own and a tingly feeling which travelled throughout her body.

"You have made me the luckiest and most grateful of men to secure your hand as my betrothed, Mary." Richard put his hand into his pocket and withdrew a ring box after they separated. "This was my maternal grandmother's ring," he stated as he opened the box, revealing a medium width gold band with a ruby in the centre and diamonds on both sides of it.

Richard lifted the ring from the box, took Mary's left hand, and slid it onto her ring finger. After replacing the box in his pocket, Richard captured his betrothed's head in his hands and lowered his head once more. His Mary responded as passionately as he had suspected she might; her emotions ran deep though they were hidden below the surface.

Both felt themselves slipping toward losing control as her hands roamed over his upper torso. When she raked her fingers across his chest, his groan brought them both back to awareness, both fighting for the breath their racing hearts would grant.

"I think I need to go to your father, my love," Richard stated once he had managed to calm enough not to betray his need of her.

"Yes, Richard, I believe you do," Mary agreed. After a kiss on each of his betrothed's cheeks, Richard took a step back and made sure his shirt was tucked in as it should be.

The two entered the drawing room at almost the same time as Jane, who also sought her father. Jane and Mary spied the rings on one another's fingers simultaneously and fell into each other's arms. As they were hugging, their soon to be parents-in-law were shown into the drawing room.

"It seems we are just in time, Reggie," Lady Elaine drawled, "I do love the rings Jane and Mary are wearing."

"Come, Richard, let us join your brother in the study; we may as well kill two birds with one stone," Bennet invited. He and Richard departed the drawing room.

"My sons have always considered you a brother, William," Lord Reggie told his nephew as they waited for Bennet to make the official announcement. "Now you will be brothers indeed."

It was not too many minutes later when Bennet returned with the Fitzwilliam brothers in tow, each sporting a huge grin. He motioned for Jane and Mary to join their betrotheds. "It is my great pleasure to announce the betrothal of Jane to Andrew and Mary to Richard." Bennet announced.

Although everyone had anticipated the news, it did not diminish the exclamations of joy and well wishes. The two newly betrothed couples had agreed on a joint wedding, to be celebrated on the eighth day of February 1811, the second Friday of the month, and one month after the date chosen by Elizabeth and William. Part of the consideration was to allow the then newlywed Darcys time to return from Seaview Cottage, where they planned to stay for three weeks after their nuptials.

It was quite late when the Netherfield party returned to that estate.

~~~~~~~/~~~~~~~

After they returned to Netherfield Park, Nichols handed the master a black edged letter in a script he did not recognise. Darcy broke the seal—the Bingley seal—in the drawing room; he hoped nothing had befallen his friend.

He read the note to all:

11 December 1810
Bingley Place
Scarborough, Yorkshire
Darcy:
Louisa is writing this for me so you will be able to read what is written.

Caroline is no longer in the land of the living. She went outside in intemperate weather and slipped, hitting her head. We only found her body two days later as there was no visibility on the day she went missing. Even though she was close to the house, we did not see her.

May God bless you,
Charles Bingley

"I will write and send our condolences," Darcy stated. He knew he should feel sorrow for Miss Bingley's passing, but he could not. He hoped she was finally at peace.

"As she is no longer with us, I will notify my friends to take no action regarding the Bingleys," Lady Elaine decided. She could not justify making the brother pay for the crimes of his later sister. Yes, he should have taken her in hand, but that was moot now.

"I think that is appropriate, Aunt. I only pray Bingley will grow up and start to take responsibility for his life," Darcy opined. "As much as I hate to speak ill of the dead, and as much as my friend will feel sorrow for losing his sister when she was so young, in some ways it will be a relief for him not to have to live with her constant dissatisfaction and manipulation. When enough time has passed, if I find out he has matured and taken responsibility for his own decisions, I will invite him to enter my circle of friends again."

Darcy's speech did not meet with any disagreement from his family members.

~~~~~~~/~~~~~~~

The next day when the three betrothed men arrived at Longbourn, they shared the sad news with its residents. Though Caroline Bingley was universally disliked, no one would have wished such a death on her. "I will send a note from all of us Bennets to Mr. Bingley, if you will provide me with his direction, William," Charlotte decided. With the information in hand, Charlotte sat at the escritoire to write the missive.

"Was she always the way we knew her?" Elizabeth asked after everyone had seated themselves in the drawing room.

"From the time I knew her, yes," Darcy replied after some

cogitation. "I do remember one day after she set her cap for me; Bingley explained to me her whole character had changed at the seminary. Being the youngest of the three siblings, she had always been indulged by her parents. During her first year at the school, they lost both parents in a carriage accident.

"From what Bingley told me, rather than learn how not to behave from the way she and Louisa were treated by daughters of the *Ton* at the seminary, Miss Bingley began to emulate them."

"That explains her pathological need to climb the rungs of society and believe herself above most others," Charlotte realised.

"You have the right of it, Mrs. Bennet," Andrew agreed. "I will not lionise her now that she had passed. I did not want this to happen to her, however. I was not sorry when she left Netherfield Park and I knew she would never be admitted to polite society again."

None of those in the drawing room wanted to dispute what Andrew had stated, as they all agreed with him. It was the final time any of them discussed Miss Caroline Bingley.

~~~~~~~/~~~~~~~

As the days and weeks passed, the time to celebrate Christmastide approached. In addition to the Gardiners and the Netherfield party, the whole of the Phillips, Lucas, and Dudley families would be present for the celebration at Longbourn. In a most pleasant surprise, Dr. Starkey had pronounced Anne de Bourgh improved enough to travel, so four days prior to Christmas Eve Andrew and Richard Fitzwilliam arrived at Rosings Park to collect their cousin. To make it easier for Anne, they would overnight at Hilldale House in London and depart for Hertfordshire in the morning.

CHAPTER 23

As Elizabeth's wedding gown was being made by the local dressmaker, it was not urgent for her to visit modistes and mantua makers in London, but in the end her betrothed convinced her of the need to do so. The Tuesday before Christmas, the large Darcy travelling carriage departed for London with Elizabeth and Mr. and Mrs. Bennet joining Darcy. As much as Elizabeth would have loved for Jane and Mary to accompany her, she understood their desire to remain with their betrotheds.

When the coach slowed to a halt in Grosvenor Square, Elizabeth was awed. She knew her betrothed was wealthy, but she did not expect the enormous home where they halted. "Welcome to Darcy House," Darcy intoned to his guests.

"William, your house is so large," Elizabeth exclaimed as they stood in the entrance hall.

"In less than two weeks this will be *our* house, Elizabeth," Darcy pointed out.

Elizabeth, her father, and her stepmother were introduced to Mr. and Mrs. Killion, Darcy House's butler and housekeeper. While Darcy led her father to the library, Elizabeth and Charlotte followed Mrs. Killion on a tour of the house. Elizabeth was impressed with the understated elegance of the public rooms, and could not help but compare Charlotte's quiet, appropriate comments with those her late mother would have made.

Elizabeth winced as she imagined her late mother's effusions about the cost of the furniture and how embarrassed she would have been at her vulgarity. Not for the first time, Elizabeth wondered if she and William would have come this far together if Fanny Bennet had still been alive. As they walked from the drawing room to a smaller parlour, Elizabeth tried to push thoughts of her late mother's probable behaviour out of her mind.

"I do not see anything you would need to change so far. What say you, Eliza?" Charlotte asked, snapping Elizabeth out of her reverie.

"You are correct, Charlotte. It is all so elegant. The furniture I have seen looks most comfortable; this a home for living in, not a house decorated to impress." Elizabeth opined as she looked around. The housekeeper showed them into the large ballroom. "Does this room get much use, Mrs. Killion?" Elizabeth enquired.

"The last time there was a ball at Darcy House was before my time, when Lady Anne Darcy was alive, which was before little miss Darcy's birth," the housekeeper explained.

"I will have to convince my betrothed balls are not to be eschewed. We will have one when Miss Darcy comes out, if not before" Elizabeth responded.

They toured three dining parlours after the ballroom, and then the three ladies climbed the grand marble staircase to the first floor—the family floor. The housekeeper pointed out the entrance to the library as well as the master and mistress studies, after which she directed them to the left towards the master suite.

As they toured, Mrs. Killion was becoming more and more impressed with her soon-to-be mistress. So many would want to put their stamp on their new home regardless of whether change was needed. The housekeeper had heard that, when compared to Pemberley, the master's betrothed was from a modest estate without a great deal of wealth, yet she was not planning to spend Mr. Darcy's funds just because she could.

She had promised Mrs. Reynolds, her counterpart at Pemberley, a letter with her impressions of Master William's betrothed after the tour. Mrs. Killion was discovering more positive aspects of Miss Bennet to put in her letter as they continued.

The housekeeper showed the two Bennet ladies into the mistress's chambers. There was a large bedchamber, a cavernous walk-in closet compared to hers at Longbourn, a dressing room, and a bathing room with a screen in one corner that hid the chamber pot.

The décor was not compatible with Elizabeth's tastes, for it was a pallet of pastels with light pink as the base. It was the only room in the house they had seen so far with ostentatious furniture, and when Elizabeth sat on the mattress, it was so soft she felt like she was sinking in quicksand.

Neither Charlotte nor Mrs. Killion missed the look of distaste on Elizabeth's mien. "I would be surprised if you did not want to make changes to this set of rooms, Miss Bennet," the housekeeper shared. "Lady Anne Darcy decorated the suite more than thirty years ago."

"I see nothing in here which would suit your tastes, Eliza," Charlotte encouraged her.

"Other than the mattress, which is far too soft for me, I can live with the rest. I am loathe to cause so much unnecessary expense," Elizabeth informed the ladies.

"Elizabeth," came the deep baritone voice of her betrothed from behind her, "as much as I appreciate you not wanting to spend money without a perceived need, these are *your* chambers and therefore must reflect your tastes, not my late mother's. I know you will not, but you could decorate the whole house over again multiple times and not put us in danger of insolvency. In this I must insist—I want you to have these chambers made over to your tastes. That includes the furniture," Darcy stated evenly.

Elizabeth was about to object, but one look at Charlotte who gave a slight shake of her head killed the words in her throat. "Thank you, William; that is most generous of you."

"It is my pleasure to do anything which will make you happy, Elizabeth." Darcy's voice was steady as he took his fiancée's hands in his own, almost forgetting they were not alone until Charlotte cleared her throat. "I will return to your father in the library," Darcy stated, and as he departed.

It did not take long for Elizabeth to articulate her tastes to the housekeeper, who took copious notes. New furniture would be ordered and be in place when Elizabeth returned for her wedding night, after which they were to travel to Seaview Cottage near Brighton. Elizabeth chose various shades of green accented with a little yellow for her chambers.

In the shared sitting room between the mistress and master chambers there was nothing Elizabeth wanted to change. After testing the sofa, loveseat, and two wingback chairs, she determined all were comfortable. In one corner next to the windows overlooking the back garden was a table with chairs and a sideboard. There were four bookcases, each one loaded with books.

Elizabeth could envision sharing meals with William at the table and spending many companionable hours with him in their shared sitting room. After a quick peek into William's chambers, where Elizabeth spied the biggest bed she had ever beheld, they joined the two men in the library.

Much to her father's delight, he would remain at Darcy House with Darcy while Charlotte and Elizabeth went shopping for more of Elizabeth's trousseau. Before they departed, Darcy asked for a word with Mrs. Bennet.

"I know Elizabeth is frugal by nature, but I am sure she does not realise all she will need as Mrs. Darcy, not to mention the cold of the north. The shops you are going to all have accounts in my name and have been instructed to charge all of Elizabeth's purchases to me. I am asking that you make sure she orders what is needed," Darcy requested once the two were away from his betrothed.

"I will leave you and my husband to deal with the finances, but I will do as you ask. I too am frugal, but you are right that as Mrs. Darcy she will have many demands," Charlotte agreed.

It was more than six hours later when Charlotte and Elizabeth returned to Darcy House. The next morning, just after sunrise, the Darcy coach returned to Meryton. Another trip would be undertaken the Thursday after Christmas for fittings and alterations, if needed.

~~~~~~~/~~~~~~~

The Gardiners would be hosted by the Bennets for Christmastide, as was their tradition. To make room at Longbourn, the three younger girls, two Bennet and one Darcy, moved to Netherfield Park the day before the guests from London were to arrive.

After arriving in London the previous afternoon, Richard contacted the Gardiners and was told they would depart for Longbourn the following morning, so they decided to travel in convoy. To make more room in the Gardiner carriage, Lilly, ten, and Eddy, eight, rode in the large Matlock coach with Richard, Andrew, and Anne de Bourgh.

The group from Town arrived at Longbourn a little before midday. The best surprise for those waiting to welcome the arriving family, was to discover that Anne looking healthier than they had seen her in years.

"Doctor Starkey does not bleed me or insist I drink the useless tinctures his predecessor used to insist I take while my mother blindly followed the quack's advice. I am better than I have been for many a year. Do not be fooled, however, for the underlying issues with my heart and lungs cannot be cured and I will keep getting weaker. The difference is now I can enjoy whatever time God allows me. I do not feel nearly as weak as I have in the past. It is still hard for me to exert myself, but I feel like I am living rather than simply existing," Anne related.

None of her relatives had heard her string more than a few words together before, and her uncle especially felt guilty for not intervening sooner. "Anne, I am so sorry I did not remove you from your mother's control years ago. I should never have believed her without talking to you."

"Uncle Reggie, the damage to my heart and lungs occurred after I contracted scarlet fever as a young child. Mr. Starkey thinks that, combined with some subsequent infections I had, it was what did the damage. I do not hold anything against you or any other members of the family. Recriminations are not what I need or want; I want to enjoy the time I have left." Anne turned to Richard. "Giving you Rosings Park was one of the best decisions I ever made. Your presence has made it a happy home. I no longer feel alone and am positive," Anne took one of Mary's hands, "that when you bring my new cousin back with you in February, it will be even more joyful than it is now."

"Mr. Gardiner, how goes the removal of Lady Catherine's items, those which reflected her poor decorating taste?" Richard asked.

"My clerk and his men catalogued it all, including the artwork you wanted removed. Everything noted was moved to my warehouse some ten days ago. I am pleased to inform you there are many other people with bad taste, for over sixty percent of the items have sold. Some of the items have been purchased at a higher cost than the original expenditure. Even after my commission, which you refused to allow me to reduce, you will have almost as much as Lady Catherine expended on all of the items. The rest should sell soon after Twelfth Night," Gardiner reported.

"Then we will be able to begin with the furniture." Richard turned to Bennet and asked, "Do I remember correctly that your family will be travelling to London after the wedding?"

"That is the current plan. Charlotte will take our two remaining betrothed daughters to help them shop for their trousseaus while I inspect the libraries of my future sons-in-law, the same as I did the Darcy House library last week," Bennet revealed. "I cannot wait to see the vaunted library at Pemberley I have heard so much about."

"In that case, with your and Mary's permission," Richard looked to his betrothed, "may I request we deviate from the plan and take the four-hour journey from Town to Rosings Park? It will kill two birds with one stone. Mary will be able to see our home and the uncomfortable furniture within."

"Richard is not exaggerating, Mary," Anne de Bourgh interjected. "My mother did not choose furniture for comfort but for show. The only comfortable chair in the house was her *throne;* the rest are anything but. I think she felt it gave her some advantage over her guests if they were uncomfortable."

"I would like to use all of the funds we have recouped from the items Gardiner has sold to purchase comfortable furniture. My hope is that after we view the items at Rosings Park, we will make a list of what is needed for each room, and then visit Chippendales to order everything we need. Gardiner," Richard turned to his uncle-to-be, "will your men be able to accompany us to catalogue all of the furniture?"

"Already done, Richard," Gardiner informed the master of Rosings Park. Seeing his confused look Gardiner explained. "When my men were noting all the artwork and other gaudy items you wanted removed, it did not take them long to see what would be next, so they made an extensive inventory of all of it. My clerk will accompany you to the estate with the lists, so all you will have to do is indicate which pieces you want removed and he will make a note of it. I assume you will do it in stages as new pieces arrive?"

"That is the most logical way, I believe," Richard averred, more than pleased Gardiner's men had the foresight to anticipate his intentions.

"I see no reason why we cannot make a detour to Kent. Do you Thomas?" Charlotte asked.

"Not at all. We will all accompany you so there will be no need for extra chaperonage," Bennet allowed.

"We plan to depart Hertfordshire for London the day after Eliza and William's wedding, so I suggest we depart for Kent after Jane and Mary have placed the orders for the clothing they need and have toured their betrotheds' town homes. That way, by the time we return from Rosings Park, it should be time for the first fittings of the new garments," Charlotte suggested.

"As usual, my wife is eminently sensible. Are there any objections to Charlotte's suggestion?" Bennet asked. There were none.

As planned, Elizabeth returned to London the Thursday after Christmas, this time accompanied by Charlotte, Jane, and Mary. Very few alterations were needed. The bulk of Elizabeth's new wardrobe would be sent to Darcy House and hung in Elizabeth's currently empty walk-in closet. Friday morning, the four Bennet ladies returned to Longbourn.

~~~~~~~/~~~~~~~

The evening before her wedding, Elizabeth had Charlotte and her Aunt Maddie talk to her about the wedding night. The talk Charlotte gave Elizabeth was vastly different from the one Lady Lucas had shared with her before she married Elizabeth's father. Rather than duty, which her mother had concentrated on, Charlotte reinforced the idea that pleasure would be discovered.

Even though receiving such a talk from one who had been just a friend before she married her father, Elizabeth appreciated Charlotte's words. Her initial belief was reinforced by her Aunt Maddie.

After the two left her, Elizabeth looked around her room, the one she had slept in from the time she had left the nursery. It was like saying goodbye to an old, familiar friend. Although she had not seen Pemberley yet, Elizabeth was most keen to do so. From the descriptions she had heard from the Darcys and Fitzwilliams, there was no doubt she would love her new home. She could already see herself taking long rambles in the vast forest she had heard about.

She was not nervous about marrying William. He was the best of men, and she was as sure as she could possibly be that he was her perfect match. They had decided they would share a bed every night. As much as she was in anticipation of never sleeping without William again, she was even more excited about the marriage bed.

When she thought about joining with her husband, the butterflies in her midsection took flight and she felt warm all over. Rather than apprehension, Elizabeth felt tranquillity and keenness when she thought about being one with her husband.

~~~~~~~/~~~~~~~

"Come now, William, surely you need some pointers from your *vastly* more experienced cousin," Richard ribbed as the cousins sat in Netherfield's library.

"I need no help from you. Just because I was more circumspect than you does not imply I am less experienced," Darcy returned.

"We do not need a cock fight before your wedding, William." Andrew turned to his younger brother. "Rich, we are supposed to be helping him relax, not the opposite!"

"William knows I am ribbing him, and, for your information, I too have been circumspect. I was as wary of contracting the French disease as you were, William," Richard informed his cousin. "Just because I am friendly, and flirt more than you does not make me less careful."

"In a month we will be brothers, William," Andrew observed. "If you had told me the three of us would marry three sisters even a few months ago I would have said you were insane. I did get the best Bennet sister though, as is my right as the eldest of the three of us."

"What hogwash! It is I who have the best Bennet sister," Richard insisted.

"Rather than argue the merits of each of our ladies, what say you we agree each of us has found the perfect lady for ourselves. Besides, my Elizabeth is superior in every way!" Darcy claimed with a huge grin.

He was rewarded by a sofa cushion being hurled at his head. Darcy ducked, but Richard had waited, anticipating his move, and his cushion found its spot. The three drained their glasses and headed for bed, but not before Darcy had Richard show him the rings to prove he had not lost them, as Richard was standing up for his cousin on the morrow.

~~~~~~~/~~~~~~~

Elizabeth woke with the sunrise, and as tempted as she was to make for Oakham Mount, she restrained herself. Sarah, the upstairs maid, helped Elizabeth bathe and wash her hair. Once her body was towelled off, Elizabeth sat with her back to the roaring fire as Sarah brushed out her hair, drying it with the fire's heat.

Jane and Mary knocked on the door and brought her a tray with some toast, jam, and tea. Charlotte had advised Elizabeth to have some sustenance in the morning as she did not want to swoon from hunger or thirst during the ceremony.

"It will be your turn in a month, sisters," Elizabeth stated.

"We know. I know I wish it were sooner," Jane replied wistfully.

"I do as well, Jane, but the month will pass quickly," Mary rationalised.

Both Jane and Mary kissed one of their sister's cheeks then they were replaced by the three younger girls. "I am so happy we will all be true sisters after today," Georgiana gushed.

"As are all of us, Gigi. I take it you are happy you will remain here until we return before Jane and Mary's wedding?" Elizabeth verified.

"Yes, I most certainly am. I will miss Lyddie though," Georgiana pointed out.

"I will be back for Jane and Mary's wedding and with all of you at Rosings Park at Easter," Lydia stated.

Elizabeth noticed the hour. "It is time for me to dress. I will see you below stairs soon." Jane, now wearing a pale pink dress, returned and helped Sarah slide the gown over Elizabeth's head.

CHAPTER 24

When Elizabeth descended the stairs to the entrance hall where her father and Jane were waiting for her, Bennet's breath caught. His daughter's dress was stunning in its simplicity. How well she looked in it! Charlotte, the rest of the Bennet sisters, and Georgiana had walked to the church a few minutes before.

"Elizabeth, I have never seen you look prettier. Your William is a very lucky man to become your husband today," Bennet said when he found his breath again.

"I'm the lucky one, Papa," Elizabeth insisted.

"You are both lucky, and perfect for one another," Jane settled the issue. "It is time for us to depart for the church."

Mr. and Mrs. Hill stood next to the front door and watched the girl they had known from the day she was born leave the house as a Bennet for the final time. Mrs. Hill wiped tears from her eyes as she watched her Miss Lizzy walk towards the church. The three Bennets passed the Darcy coach in the drive as it was being loaded with the last of Elizabeth's trunks.

When the three arrived in the vestibule, Charlotte was waiting for them. She and Jane made sure that Elizabeth's dress was in order, and then, before giving her friend and stepdaughter a squeeze of the hand, Charlotte lowered the gossamer veil into place and slipped into the church.

Darcy and Richard, standing with Mr. Dudley near the altar, noted Mrs. Bennet's entrance and her nod to the reverend indicating the bride was present. Richard was there for his cousin, but he had a hard time tearing his eyes away from the vision that was his fiancée, Mary, in a pale green dress which looked very well on her. Her hazel eyes were shining as she watched him, reflecting his love back to him.

The vestibule door opened, and Jane Bennet entered, making her way slowly up the aisle. As soon as Jane entered the church, her eyes found Andrew and their eyes locked. Luckily, Jane made it to her place opposite Richard without any of the unwanted effects of not looking where she was going.

Mr. Dudley gave the congregants the signal to stand just as the doors again opened. Father and daughter entered the church while the doors were closed behind them as Bennet slowly led his second daughter up the aisle. Darcy's breath hitched as soon as he saw his beautiful bride. Her dress was cream with no adornments, but with his Elizabeth filling it there was no need for anything else. She was wearing the string of pearls he had presented to her as a betrothal gift, along with the matching earbobs. Elizabeth was without the amber cross she always wore.

After a reminder nudge from a grinning Richard, Darcy walked to meet Elizabeth where she and her father had stopped. Bennet lifted the veil, kissed his daughter's cheek, and then after lowering the veil he placed Elizabeth's hand on Darcy's arm. Bennet took his place in the front pew next to his wife while the bride and groom took their places in front of Mr. Dudley.

Dudley gave the signal for the congregation to be seated and then opened the *Book of Common Prayer* to the service for weddings. "Dearly beloved..."

Before they knew it, the bride and groom had recited their vows and exchanged rings. The norm was for the groom to present the bride with a ring, but the two had decided they both wanted to give and receive a ring. It seemed like a dream, but Mr. Dudley was already reciting the final benediction, bringing the service to completion. All that remained was to sign the register.

The newlyweds signed their names, and Elizabeth paused for a moment as she realised it would be the final time she would sign the name Bennet. Jane and Richard signed as their witnesses, and it was done. Once the door closed and the Darcys were alone, they hugged one another as tightly as they could.

"Kiss me, husband," Elizabeth commanded. It was the easiest command Darcy had ever complied with. When their lips met, there was a mutual release of passion and tension as each explored the other's taste and the wonders which one could discover when restraint is forgotten. Before they passed the point of no return, and as if by mutual agreement, they drew back, remembering their family were awaiting them on the other side of the door.

Elizabeth did not realise her husband's hand had been exploring her tresses until she saw a pin or two on the floor. Following his wife's instruction, Darcy returned the pins to where they belonged as best he could, and once Elizabeth's hair was put to rights—or as close to it as possible—Darcy opened the vestry door and led his blushing bride into the church.

While Darcy was being congratulated by his new sisters, aunts, and uncles, Elizabeth was receiving them from her new aunt and uncle, sister, and cousins. Darcy shook his father-in-law's hand and Bennet welcomed him as a son. After the bride and groom changed places and received warm wishes from all, the family turned and started the short walk toward Longbourn. Elizabeth and Darcy remained outside for a moment while everyone else went in so that the Hills could announce them.

Once Hill had announced the new couple, Matilda was the first to reach Elizabeth. "I wish you and your husband every conceivable joy, Lizzy," Matilda imparted.

"You too, Matti. It is not too much longer before you will become Mrs. Franklin Lucas," Elizabeth returned her sentiments in kind.

"Do not forget I will be your step-aunt," Matilda teased, which earned her a roll of Elizbeth's eyes.

After about an hour of visiting guests in the drawing

room and parlour, the new husband and wife sat with their family in the dining parlour, who insisted they both have some food and drink. Neither realised how hungry and thirsty they were until they complied. Once they were revived, the newly-weds spent another hour or so socialising with those who had come to celebrate their nuptials.

Charlotte and Jane accompanied Elizabeth to her child-hood bedchamber, where she changed into traveling clothes while Sarah covered the wedding gown and placed it in a small trunk, which she handed to a waiting Darcy footman.

Her husband and family were waiting for her in the entrance hall. The family followed Mr. and Mrs. Darcy to the drive where, following more hugs and good wishes, the couple entered the conveyance. After final waves, Darcy struck the ceiling with his cane, and they were off. Soon after Longbourn disappeared from view, the couple fell asleep in one another's arms.

~~~~~~~/~~~~~~~

"If you think the house is quiet now," Charlotte told her husband, "can you see how it will be in a month when Jane and Mary leave us?" The two were sitting in the study after the guests had departed. It was especially quiet as the four remaining unmarried Bennet daughters and their new sister were visiting the residents of Netherfield Park.

"At least I have a one-day reprieve before I take Lydia to her school. I have secured reservations at an inn in Oxfordshire for both sides of the journey, so everything is in place," Bennet reported. "Yes, I am aware I have a month before Jane and Mary follow Lizzy and depart to their own homes. All I can say is thank God I have you, Charlotte. I will miss them, but I will not be alone."

"I never imagined we would have such a felicitous marriage. There was never a doubt about our compatibility, but nothing prepared me for the reality. It was something I was sure would never happen, but I believe I have developed tender feelings for you, Thomas," Charlotte reported.

"My expectations were the same as yours, Charlotte, yet you have caused this old fool to fall in love with you." Bennet informed his wife.

"Y-you love me, Thomas?" Charlotte was caught unawares.

"I do, Charlotte. You are the best thing that ever happened to me," Bennet related, reinforcing his point with languid kisses.

"I was afraid to admit it if you did not feel the same, but I have fallen in love with you too," Charlotte revealed when her husband ceased kissing her.

As married couples tend to do, the two expressed their avowed love in a physical way that night—as a matter of fact, several times.

~~~~~~~/~~~~~~~

When the coach pulled to stop at Darcy House, the passengers were awake, and had been since the stop to rest the horses more than halfway to London. Because it was bitterly cold, the servants were lined up to greet the master and new mistress in the large entrance hall inside the house, so no one was forced to stand in the cold.

Darcy handed his wife out of the conveyance, and the two quickly entered to escape the flurries which had just begun. Killion helped them remove their outerwear, then the new mistress addressed the waiting servants.

"My husband and I appreciate the warm welcome you have accorded us on this most special of days. It may take me more time than I would like, but I will learn all of your names, and until I do I ask you to remind me when you can tell I do not know it. Please continue with your duties." After the new mistress addressed them, the servants returned to their posts except for one.

"Mrs. Darcy, this is Miss *Éponine Thénardier*. She has been hired as your lady's maid," Mrs. Killion informed the mistress as her new maid gave her a deep curtsey.

"It is good to meet you, Thénardier. You will find out I am

not a demanding mistress; welcome to our service," Elizabeth stated. "Please have a bath prepared for me."

"Yes, Madame," the maid said in perfect but heavily accented English. She curtsied again and left to fulfil her mistress's charge.

"Is the redecoration of my wife's chambers complete, Mrs. Killion?" Darcy asked.

"Yes, sir, ready for Mrs. Darcy to view," Mrs. Killion related proudly.

"William, how can that be in two weeks?" Elizabeth asked in amazement.

"You never know what can be accomplished with an almost unlimited budget," Darcy replied. It was not a boast, but a simple statement of fact.

"Mrs. Killion, my husband and I will take our meal in our sitting room; please have our repast sent up at six unless you hear otherwise," Elizabeth instructed.

When they arrived at the mistress's suite, Darcy stood back so Elizabeth would see her newly decorated chambers first. "Oh William, it is perfect!" Elizabeth exclaimed excitedly.

"I agree," Her husband said, but he was looking at her, not the décor. "Your chambers look good as well," Darcy grinned, and his wife blushed. "How long do you need, Elizabeth?

"With my bath, an hour. Is that acceptable?" Elizabeth asked.

"Of course it is. Take as much time as you need, my love," Darcy averred and then left his wife to go have his own bath which Carstens would have ready for him.

~~~~~~~/~~~~~~~

After her bath, Elizabeth had her maid help her into a pale peach nightgown and matching robe. Together they did a credible job of covering her body, but the sheer nightgown left little to the imagination on its own. Almost to the very second that the one hour had elapsed, there was a knock on the door that led to their shared sitting room.

When she opened it, she found it hard to breathe at the

sight of her Adonis-like husband standing before her wearing only an opened lawn shirt and breeches. How long had she waited for this day to see him in such a state of undress? His muscular chest fairly rippled as she stared at him.

Darcy took her hand and led her to his bedchamber, using his foot to swing the door closed once they were both inside. "I want to see you Elizabeth, please," Darcy beseeched, his voice husky.

Elizabeth allowed the robe to fall and suddenly he could see all of her through the filmy haze of fabric. Her breasts were a nice size, and she was excited, cold, or both, as her nipples were pushing against the nightgown.

Silently they removed any remaining clothing and Elizabeth waited for him to close the distance between them, whispering, "Love me, William," when he was close enough to touch. Her husband lifted her as if she were a feather, then gently placed her on the huge bed and proceeded to obey that request and any others she asked of him.

After an early breakfast the next morning, the newlywed Darcys departed for Seaview Cottage near Brighton. Both were supremely happy as they had allowed their love and passion for each other free rein late into the night.

~~~~~~~/~~~~~~~

As planned, the Bennet and Fitzwilliam families departed Hertfordshire the day after the wedding. The Bennets were hosted at Darcy House by Georgiana. The Fitzwilliams were at Matlock House, just across Grosvenor Square from the Darcy townhouse.

"Lizzy is mistress of this mansion?" Kitty asked in awe as the Bennets were welcomed to the house by the housekeeper, who was happy to see how joyful and outgoing Miss Darcy had become since the last time she was at Darcy House. Mrs. Killion showed them into the drawing room, where refreshments were ready for the arriving party.

"This is small compared to Pemberley," Georgiana stated matter-of-factly.

"Kitty, it is but a house. It is the people who live in it who make it a home regardless of the size," Charlotte told her stepdaughter.

Lydia, who had so far been silent as she took in her surroundings, turned to Gigi. "How big is the park at Pemberley; is it larger than Longbourn's?" Lydia asked.

"It is ten miles around," Georgiana replied.

It was at that moment the youngest two Bennet sisters realised just how rich their new brother was. Rather than vulgar effusions, the two were quiet. "We will see Pemberley in the Summer," Charlotte shared. "Eliza and William have invited all of the family for at least six weeks. I understand your Uncle Gardiner intends to fish as much as he able."

"In my excitement of welcoming you to Darcy House, I almost forgot you would be with us for the Summer. Do you ride?" Georgiana asked Kitty and Lydia.

"I started to learn when I was ten and then gave it up," Kitty owned.

"It was lack of patience for me, and my late mother told me it was a useless accomplishment which would do nothing to assist me catching a husband," Lydia shared.

"Lydia, you know your late mother loved you and thought she was teaching you the right thing, do you not?" Charlotte asked and Lydia nodded. "You also know your mother was not brought up as a gentlewoman, so unfortunately her advice, no matter her intent, was not correct."

"It was a hard lesson to accept, but yes, I do know the truth of the matter now," Lydia agreed.

"Will you allow William to teach both of you to ride? He taught me, and I can attest that he is a good and patient teacher," Georgiana offered. Both Kitty and Lydia agreed.

"Lydia, I did not discuss it with you as I believed you had no interest, but Charlotte tells me they have a riding programme at the Wrightfield School. When we arrive, would you like me to inform the headmistress you hope to be included in their riding lessons?" Bennet asked and was surprised that

Lydia nodded enthusiastically. Seeing the disappointment on Kitty's face of having to wait until the summer, Bennet turned to his fourth daughter and said, "I will start teaching you at Longbourn, and we have grooms who are good teachers as well."

"Thank you, Papa," Kitty beamed with joy.

Charlotte assumed the duties of mistress and poured tea. Afterward the housekeeper showed the Bennets to their chambers.

~~~~~~~/~~~~~~~

The next morning, not long after Bennet departed with Lydia to take her to school, Charlotte and her stepdaughters, Gigi and Lady Matlock departed for Bond Street. They spent the majority of the day shopping for Jane's and Mary's trousseaus. Although Anne de Bourgh was invited to join them for the excursion, she demurred and remained at Matlock House with her uncle; she did not have the energy for a full day of shopping with the other ladies.

Dinner that night was at Matlock House. After the five ladies had rested, washed, and changed, they made the short walk across the square to the Fitzwilliam's house. While everyone was happy to be dining with friends, there was a debate as to whether Jane and Mary were more pleased to be in the company of their betrotheds again, or if the brothers were more pleased to be in the company of *their* betrotheds again.

"Mother tells us the stores on Bond Street will have to close for at least a fortnight to replenish their wares after your onslaught today," Richard jested.

"I said a few days, Son; do not exaggerate," Lady Elaine teased.

"There were one or two ladies who tried to snub us, presuming we were pretentious upstarts who trapped you and Richard," Jane related. "However, as soon as they saw Mother Elaine and her disdain for them, they scurried away."

"No one slights my daughters-to-be!" Lady Elaine stated emphatically.

"If you know their names, let me know. I will have a little *chat* with their fathers or husbands, and set them straight," Lord Reggie offered.

"Later, Reggie, if it proves necessary, but I believe I sent them running with fleas in their ears," his wife advised.

"Bennet will depart Wiltshire on Friday to return to Town on Saturday, will he not, Mrs. Bennet?" Andrew asked.

"That is his plan, Andrew. If he has to stay longer, he will spend the Sabbath at the inn and then come directly to Rosings Park on Monday," Charlotte informed the rest. "May I request you and Richard call me Charlotte as my stepdaughters do? My title is Mrs. Bennet, but in a matter of weeks you will be my stepsons-in-law, and I believe we are of about the same age."

"I will do so in future, Charlotte," Richard agreed.

"And I," Andrew bowed his head in agreement.

"Well done, you two," Mary smiled. "I see you can be taught, Richard, which bodes well for the future," Mary teased.

"Do not look at me, Son. You wanted a strong woman, and that is exactly what you, both of you, have been blessed with," said the Earl with a grin.

The Earl then proposed a toast was to his sons' fast-approaching nuptials and to the honeymooning Darcys.

CHAPTER 25

Bennet and Lydia left the inn in Oxfordshire before the sun came up on Friday morning and turned down the drive to the Wrightfield School for Young Ladies by midday. Upon arrival, they were conducted to Mrs. Olive Toppin, the headmistress, in her office. "Welcome to the Wrightfield School for Young Ladies, Miss Bennet. I understand from the reports I have received from your father and stepmother your behaviour and attitude have improved significantly. Are those reports accurate, young lady ?" Mrs. Toppin asked after the introductions, as she looked at Lydia intently over her spectacles.

"Yes Mrs. Toppin, they are. I was on a path which would have ruined not only myself but my sisters. Thankfully, my family loved me enough to make me see the truth even though I was stubborn and silly in the beginning. Now I want to learn as much as I can to be as accomplished a lady as Gigi," Lydia answered honestly.

"Miss Georgiana Darcy, Lydia's new sister. My second daughter is now Mrs. Fitzwilliam Darcy," Bennet filled in the information Mrs. Toppin did not have.

"I have been learning from Gigi, excuse me, Miss Darcy, how to behave more like a gentlewoman," Lydia informed the headmistress.

"From what I can see, I do not expect any behavioural issues from you Miss Bennet. If I am correct, and I seldom err in my assessment of a student, you will learn what you desire to here, and we will be happy to welcome you into the Wrightfield Family," Mrs. Toppin said as she rang a bell.

"Before I depart, there is one change I would like to make.

Lydia has indicated her interest in learning to ride, so I would like to enrol her in that programme if I may," Bennet added.

"Miss Bennet will be included with the beginners." There was a knock on the door and a young lady entered when summoned by the headmistress. "Miss Helen Jacobson of Janet's Well in Surrey, meet your new chamber mate, Miss Lydia Bennet of Longbourn in Hertfordshire. Helen is one year your senior, Miss Bennet, and is one of our best students. She will be able to show you around and answer any questions you may have. Please show Miss Bennet to your shared chambers, Miss Jacobson."

"With pleasure, Mrs. Toppin. Please follow me, Miss Bennet." Miss Jacobson stood back as Lydia hugged her father and then followed her out of the office.

"She will do well here, Mr. Bennet, of that I am certain," the headmistress stated with surety.

"As am I, Mrs. Toppin." Bennet bowed and returned to his carriage. After verifying Lydia's trunks had been unloaded, he was on his way back to the inn where he had spent the previous night.

~~~~~~~/~~~~~~~

On Friday morning, two carriages transported their occupant from Darcy and Matlock Houses to Portman Square, where both Hilldale and Fitzwilliam Houses were located. The Countess, Anne, and Jane were with Andrew, while Charlotte, Kitty, and Georgiana were in Richard's carriage accompanying Mary. The distance was less than a mile but took a full twenty minutes, as the drivers had to wait for other carriages to move out of the way on one of the narrower streets.

When they arrived outside Hilldale House, Andrew pointed out Fitzwilliam House diagonally across the small green from his home.

The brothers' townhouses on Portman Square were a little smaller than the Darcy and Matlock townhouses, but neither could be called small. After Jane was introduced to the butler and housekeeper, the tour commenced. The Countess and Jane accompanied her while Andrew kept Anne company in the drawing room.

After staying the night at Darcy House, Jane noticed the ballroom was about two thirds the size of the one at her sister's and brother's house, but she thought its capacity more than adequate. The furnishings in the public rooms were similar to what she had seen at both Darcy and Matlock Houses—understated elegance. Everything of the highest quality, but all designed for the comfort of its owners.

There had not been a Viscountess Hilldale since Lady Elaine had filled the office briefly before her father-in-law passed away within weeks of her wedding. Thus, the mistress's suite had not been redecorated in over sixty years.

"I did not have a chance to see Hilldale house before Reggie's father passed away and he became the Earl of Matlock, so you cannot blame me for the poor state of these chambers," Lady Elaine explained.

"We will be travelling north for our wedding trip, so we will not be back in Town until early March. There should be ample time to complete refurbishment of these chambers," Jane told the housekeeper, who took copious notes of what styles and colours would be used to decorate the soon-to-be mistress's chambers.

There was little to do in the rest of the house as the Countess had supervised the redecorating at her son's request some five years earlier, leaving the mistress's chambers to the future occupant of that space.

~~~~~~~/~~~~~~~

Richard's house had only a skeleton staff, as the housekeeper and butler had both retired in the last six months. Lady Catherine had not moved to replace them, or other servants who left her employ in London, because she had not used the former de Bourgh House in the last few years.

Charlotte had the perspicacity to suggest that Gardiner's man should meet them at Fitzwilliam House. Richard shared that he had never visited the London House, so Charlotte expected it would be decorated similarly to Rosings Park, given that it was done by, and in the taste of, Lady Catherine.

"This is what Rosings was like before you started making changes?" asked an amazed Mary. The house looked like someone with terrible taste had cast up her accounts all over the house.

"There is more of a concentration of gaudiness here than there was at Rosings Park," Richard bit out in disgust as he looked around. "Please excuse my oversight, Mary; I should have known it would be like this and changed it before you saw it."

"Do not be like William and try and take on that for which you have no culpability, Richard," Mary soothed. "Charlotte mentioned her suspicion to me, and I agreed that she request my uncle's clerk to join us."

"It has been some time since I was at Rosings Park; I forgot how absurd Aunt Catherine's taste was," Georgiana stated as the group walked from room to room.

"My goodness!" Richard exclaimed as they entered the primary drawing room, "I should have expected this."

The drawing room, other than in its dimensions, was a twin of the one at Rosings Park, from the throne-like raised chair to the room's uncomfortable seating. Thankfully, they had the foresight to bring notebooks, but Richard decided it would be premature to plan the redecorating. He turned to Gardiner's clerk, and said, "Please inventory everything, as it will all go. There is no need to move furniture out in stages as was done at the estate, for we will not be in residence here until it is completely redecorated. We have at least three options where we can be hosted if we are in Town before this house is ready for us."

"If I understand you, Mr. Fitzwilliam, you want everything catalogued and then removed for sale, leaving a bare shell of a house?" the clerk asked.

"Exactly. The sooner you can have it emptied, the sooner we can plan what we want to do in each room," Richard agreed.

"It is a capital idea, Richard," Charlotte complimented, "this way Fitzwilliam House will be exactly what you and Mary desire from the first day you occupy it."

"Thank you, Mrs. Benn—Charlotte. Sorry, I still have to get used to using your familiar name." Richard turned to the clerk and sent him on his way. "Mary, the next thing we need to do is staff the townhouse. We have two footmen and three maids remaining."

"As they have been loyal and remained when others left, are any of the maids capable of being promoted to house-keeper, and are any of the footmen capable of being promoted to butler?" Mary enquired.

"That is an excellent idea, Mary, let us summon the servants," Richard enthused.

After talking to the five remaining servants, it became clear neither of the footmen had the experience to become the butler, but one of them had sufficient experience to become an under-butler. There was better luck with the three maids. One, a Mrs. O'Rourke, had served in the house for more than ten years and had more than the prerequisite experience, so she was promoted on the spot, much to her delight.

The new housekeeper mentioned her husband was the butler at an estate in Surrey and how they lamented the sparsity of the time they were able to spend together. She was told to have her husband contact Mr. Fitzwilliam if he was interested, thereby doubling the new housekeeper's delight, and gaining her undying loyalty.

On her recommendation, one of the two remaining maids was promoted to assistant housekeeper, while the other would be an upstairs maid. As soon as a butler was hired, the staffing needs of the house would be addressed in consultation with the new mistress.

After Richard told his driver to swing around the square, he and the four ladies made the short walk across the small green to Hilldale House, leaving behind much invigorated servants whose salaries had more than doubled.

~~~~~~~/~~~~~~~

"William, this is delightful," Elizabeth gushed as she saw Seaview Cottage for the first time. "I am glad you told me the word 'cottage' in its name was not apropos to the size of the structure. To me it looks a little bigger than Longbourn."

"It is completely private, as we own all of the surrounding land that encompasses the secluded cove I told you about," Darcy waggled his eyebrows in anticipation of their return during the summer.

Darcy introduced his wife to the butler and housekeeper, a couple who had been in their positions at Seaview since his late father had purchased the house and land as a gift for Lady Anne more than twenty years past.

As they toured the house, Elizabeth was struck by the view from the windows in the sitting room and the master suite above it. Both looked out over the sea; Elizabeth would never tire of that view.

Once Carstens and Thénardier had unpacked and drawn baths for the master and mistress, they were dismissed. Dinner was ordered on trays that evening, and the Darcys did not emerge from their chambers until the morning—two days hence.

~~~~~~~/~~~~~~~

Charlotte was debating with herself on when to inform her husband of her suspicions. She had just missed her monthly courses for the second time, and she had always been able to set her clock by her cycles. Her next courses would be due around the time of the double wedding, so she decided to wait until then. She hoped that if she was with child she would be able to present her husband with a son. Even without the pressure of the entail no longer hanging over their heads, she knew her Thomas would be delighted by a son.

Luckily Charlotte did not feel any sickness in the morning—yet. She prayed she would be spared that particular malady as she remembered her mother suffered more than most during the first half of her time with child.

There would be another shopping expedition on the morrow, as the Countess wanted as many members of the *Ton* as possible to know she approved of her sons' betrothals. Part of her plan would be to take tea at Gunter's, where they would be met by Lady Jersey and two of her fellow patronesses. There would be no question of the Bennets' suitability after that.

There had been a smattering of talk, most of it driven by the bitter and jealous, that three unknown sisters had snapped up three of the most eligible bachelors in society. It was conveniently forgotten by those same people that, until he was gifted Rosings Park, Richard Fitzwilliam would not have been considered good enough for any of their daughters.

Sunday would be a quiet day with a family dinner at Matlock House after church services, to which the Gardiners were also invited. Early Monday morning, everyone except the Gardiners would make for Rosings Park in Kent.

~~~~~~~/~~~~~~~

"Richard, your house is majestic," Mary noted as the carriages approached the house.

"Our house, Mary, our house," Richard corrected.

"Only when I sign the register," Mary countered playfully.

"As I feel married to you in my heart already, I assert that it is *our* home," Richard grinned at her blushingly silent concession.

"I am sure you will be happy here, Mary," Anne told her new cousin. "Since Richard took ownership and started to make changes, it was as though a dark veil has been lifted from the house and the estate," Anne opined.

"Will we see Lady Catherine while we are here?" Mary asked as the conveyance came to a halt under the portico.

"That is entirely up to you, Mary," Richard averred.

"Mayhap we should invite her for dinner tonight?" Mary suggested.

"I do not object," Anne replied when Richard looked to her.

"A footman will be sent with a note," Richard decided.

Bennet made for the library, where he found a large, well-stocked room, even if it seemed no one had updated it or added volumes for some years. Andrew confirmed that since his uncle's passing Lady Catherine had done nothing to the library. Bennet was joined by the Earl and Andrew, while the rest of the party joined Richard and Mary to tour the house. It did not take long before Lord Matlock and Bennet found a chess set and were playing in earnest.

Kitty and Gigi were acting as scribes for Mary and Richard. Mary was flabbergasted at the amount she believed would be laid out to refurnish the whole of the home as they moved through the family wing, but after she had tried out a few chairs and beds, she was convinced of the rectitude of the decision to replace all.

Perhaps, based on the information she had gleaned, Richard would not have to expend much additional money based on the amount from objects sold already and from the additional sales of unwanted furniture and objects. Like her two older sisters, Mary would never be one to spend money just because she could.

By mid-afternoon, they had made lists of furniture for about half of the rooms in the house; they intended to complete that task on the morrow. Mary was pleased to have Charlotte and Jane with her as she went from room to room. Mother Elaine had a very good eye for decorating, but she did not think about economy as Charlotte and Jane did.

The footman had returned with an acceptance from Lady Catherine. It would be the first time since being moved into a pensioner's cottage that the former mistress of the estate would set foot inside the house, and everyone was in anticipation to see how she would behave.

~~~~~~~/~~~~~~~

Lady Catherine de Bourgh had a lot of time to think since she and Mrs. Jenkinson had moved to the cottage. Initially, she had railed against everyone, especially those artful Bennets who had turned her family against her.

After a few days of self-indulgence, Lady Catherine became introspective. At first, it was hard for her to look at her life and decisions honestly, from her attitude towards others, to her compromise of Sir Lewis, and to the present day.

The more honest she was, the more she saw her own actions through the eyes of others, the more ashamed she became. By the time she was finished with her self-examination, she had accepted the fact that she had many amends to make. Her most difficult realization was how she had treated those around her, especially her daughter. She had come to accept the paucity of her knowledge and how much nonsensical advice she had dispensed.

She finally understood why her family felt it was a hardship to be in her company. Her greatest regret was lying about her sister's agreement for Fitzwilliam to marry Anne. Now that she was being honest with herself, she acknowledged the former Miss Elizabeth Bennet was probably the ideal woman for her nephew.

Thus, when a humble Lady Catherine arrived at Rosings Park and addressed her family with apologies spoken in complete sincerity, those who had known her for many years, thought they were hallucinating. But they were not, and there was no mistaking the genuine effort the lady was making and her absolute contrition.

The longest apology Lady Catherine made was to Anne. Lady Catherine then apologised to the Bennets for her indecorous behaviour when she invited herself to Longbourn and acknowledged that Mrs. Bennet had been accurate in the assessment of her character at that time. She informed them that if and when the Darcys were willing to hear her apology, she would make one to them, for her pushing the lie about the betrothal and for her disgusting words to the then Miss Elizabeth.

Then when the family sat for dinner, they experienced another shock, for rather than command the conversation as had been her wont, Lady Catherine only spoke when spoken to and did not once try to give advice about that of which she had no knowledge.

"What do you think of the changes to the house, Aunt Catherine?" Richard asked.

"Given how tastelessly I decorated, I may not be the best one to ask, Richard," Lady Catherine averred.

"Catherine, the change in you is both incredible and welcome. What occasioned such a change, Sister?" her brother asked.

"It is a simple answer, Reggie. I started to view myself and my behaviour through others' eyes—my family's eyes—and I did not like what I discovered. I had a choice; I could have denied the truth clearly before me or embrace it and begin to change. I chose the latter," Lady Catherine explained.

"It is my belief, Catherine, that it is better late than never," Lady Elaine opined.

"However it happened, whatever the reason, I am happy to have my sister back." Lord Reggie raised his goblet as did the rest of the diners and he offered a toast to his sister.

After dinner, Anne met with Richard, his parents, and Mary in the study. As Anne had fully forgiven her mother, she requested her mother be installed in a suite next to her with the clear understanding if Lady Catherine reverted to any of her old behaviours she would return to her cottage.

When the request was put to her, all were both alarmed and pleased to see the pleasure and relief Lady Catherine was overwhelmed by when she gratefully accepted her nephew's invitation to take the suite adjoining Anne's. The tears on her cheeks were proof that she was not ashamed to love them and to accept that they would love her in return. While the rest of the ladies made their lists in the balance of the rooms they did not get to the previous day, Lady Catherine was moved back into the manor house.

CHAPTER 26

In London, Richard and Mary, accompanied by Lady Matlock and Charlotte, made the manager at Chippendale's extremely pleased as the massive order to fabricate furniture in order to refurnish Rosing Park's manor house was placed. When the manager understood there would soon be another large order placed for Fitzwilliam House, he was doubly pleased.

As predicted, Mr. O'Rourke had expressed his interest in the position at Fitzwilliam House to be close to his wife and had been interviewed by Richard and Andrew. Like his wife, he was more than qualified and was available to start immediately, as his former employer had dismissed him without a character when he had been honest in telling him he planned to interview for a different position to be closer to his wife. The gentleman's snit benefited Richard, who gained a butler without the need to wait for him to join his staff.

The day before the planned return to Longbourn and Netherfield, Charlotte accompanied Mary and Richard to Fitzwilliam House. They were relieved to find it an empty shell. As the house was considerably smaller than the one at Rosings Park, it did not take many hours to note what furniture would be needed for each room.

After making their lists, Richard and the two Bennet ladies sat with the O'Rourkes. The housekeeper was effusive in her thanks for her husband's employment. After the recitation of the house's needs, Mary and Richard gave the two senior staff their instructions for redecorating the whole house. All of the dark wood panelling that made the house appear dreary and gloomy regardless of the time of day was to be replaced with light-coloured paper.

After they canvassed the redecorating, they moved on to staffing. Mary and Richard agreed to the numbers the housekeeper and butler proposed for their needs, adding a few additional maids and footmen to make sure there would be more than enough without overworking any servants.

The final subject they covered during this initial meeting was the servants' accommodation. As was expected, no refurbishment or repairs to the servants' quarters had been undertaken in many years. The couple authorised all needed work without delay. Until it was complete, the O'Rourkes suggested that they only hire four maids and the same number of footmen, and they would fill out the numbers previously decided on once the work was finished.

"You have an extremely loyal couple in the O'Rourkes," Charlotte opined on the carriage ride back to Darcy House after dropping the order for furniture at Chippendale's. "Promoting Mrs. O'Rourke to housekeeper ensured her loyalty; however, bringing her husband on as butler has them both determined to never disappoint and protect you at all costs."

"I would hate to be parted from Richard without true cause, and while I understand their circumstances, I was glad we could allow them this chance." Mary smiled at Charlotte when Richard literally sat up taller, her explanation proving again she loved him without even having to say the words.

The next morning, the carriages departed for Hertfordshire. The returning party were three less than when they came to Town because Lydia returned to school and the Earl and Countess remained in London. One letter had been received from Lydia, and in it she expressed her enthusiastic approval of the school, and most especially of her new friend who shared a bed chamber with her, Miss Helen Jacobson of Surrey.

~~~~~~~/~~~~~~~

Towards the end of January, Elizabeth and Darcy departed from Seaview Cottage after three bliss filled weeks. As the two sat on the forward-facing bench, comfortable in one another's arms, Darcy fell asleep within minutes of their departure. Elizabeth smiled, for she knew she would soon follow her husband's example as it had been well past midnight before they found asleep most nights, regardless of how early they had retired for the night. As she rested in the safety found only in the cocoon of his arms, she thought about how she had loved her stay in the area. Her last thought before sleep claimed her was of the private beach and all they might share when the weather turned warmer and should nothing delay their return the coming June.

~~~~~~~/~~~~~~~

Charlotte was fairly certain she was with child. In the last few days she had started feeling tired in the middle of the day, where before she had never needed to rest. Wanting to be sure, she had not said anything to her Thomas. If and when she missed her third set of courses, which were due in the next few days, she would let him know her suspicion, relieved there had been no sickness in the morning as of yet.

For his part, having seen his late wife with child five times, Bennet was well aware his wife was most probably in that state, but decided she would say something when she was ready, so he did not verbalise his thoughts. Bennet's thoughts drifted back to the previous night when they had finally admitted the truth of their feelings one for the other.

Bennet and Charlotte had finally climbed into bed close to eleven. When they were lying in one another's arms before succumbing to sleep, Charlotte had turned to look directly at him. "Thomas, I have known something for some time now, something I never expected, but it has happened, nevertheless. I find I have fallen deeply and irrevocably in love with you," Charlotte revealed.

"Hearing you say that makes me immeasurably happy, Charlotte. I too fell in love with you; and though it was wholly unanticipated, it is most welcome. I love you with all of my heart," Bennet had informed his wife, who beamed with pleasure at his matching disclosure.

"I have been sure for over a month, but as I am known as

being decidedly 'non-romantic', I was not sure how my disclosure would be received. Ours was a marriage formed from need, but it has become so much more," Charlotte opined.

"It has been over a month for me as well. When I understood what a gem of the first order I had gained in marriage, how could I not fall in love with you?" Bennet asked rhetorically. "You joined my family and took charge of a number of situations, and the results have been overwhelmingly positive."

"It is the happiest I can recall being, Thomas. As much as you say I helped you, being a member of this family has given me purpose that was missing from my life." Charlotte had averred.

"Let us not argue as to who has benefited the most and just accept the fact we love one another," Bennet had proposed.

"You will receive no arguments from me husband; now love me please," Charlotte had requested in a sultry voice.

Bennet felt a sense of pleasure as he remembered complying with his wife's wishes more than once that night.

~~~~~~~/~~~~~~~

After breaking their journey for a few days at Darcy House, Mr. and Mrs. Darcy approached Netherfield Park the Monday before the double wedding. The Darcy coach was followed closely by the Matlock conveyance.

"What will you about the lease goes once its term is complete?" Elizabeth asked her husband.

"It is fortuitous you ask that very question Elizabeth," Darcy replied as he hugged his wife close to his side. "I received notice from our Uncle Phillips that the owner would like to sell the estate. What say you we acquire it? It is close to London and would mean there would always be place for us and our extended family when we visit Hertfordshire."

"That is an excellent idea, William. I think it would be perfect. We would be able to stop here to and from Town each time we travel," Elizabeth agreed.

"Then it shall be done, my love. I will contact Phillips to start the process," Darcy told his beaming wife, capturing her lips before she could make further comment.

263

It was unsurprising to find neither Andrew nor Richard at Netherfield; Nichols informed the arriving family that the two were at Longbourn. The Darcys and the Matlocks agreed they would hie to Longbourn after washing and changing.

~~~~~~~/~~~~~~~

"William! Lizzy!" Georgiana squealed in her excitement when she spied her brother and new sister. Both smiled at her outburst as they were just as pleased to see her as she them. "Tell us all about your wedding trip," she insisted innocently.

"Gigi, Lizzy and William have just arrived. What say you we give them some time before we demand to know how their honeymoon was," Charlotte redirected the younger girl. She nodded, seeing the thankful look Eliza sent her way. "I am sure they will be happy to tell you about it when they have had a chance to relax."

"William, I hope you do not object, but there will be a pre-wedding ball on Wednesday," Richard informed his cousin.

"Of course we do not object," Elizabeth responded before her husband could. "Is that not so, William?" Elizabeth arched her eyebrow at her husband.

"We could not be happier," Darcy averred. The look on his face gave lie to his words. With Elizabeth's help, he was far more sociable than he had been in the past, but he still did not love large crowds of unknown people.

After Charlotte served tea and refreshments, Elizabeth was inundated with questions about Seaview Cottage and her impressions of the sea. Elizabeth told her sisters about the two times she and William had visited Brighton, and her impressions of the Regent's pavilion. The lack of a standard flying had indicated that his Highness was not in residence, but Elizabeth confessed what she could see from outside looked overly ostentatious and gaudy. Gigi was satisfied to have her desire for information sated.

Darcy had joined Bennet and the three Fitzwilliam men in the study. When they related the complete change in his Aunt Catherine to him, Darcy could scarcely credit what they were telling him. It took quite a bit of explaining for him to understand the truth of what they were saying.

It was not that he did not believe his uncle and cousins, for he had long believed them implicitly. He was having difficulty reconciling what he knew of his aunt to what the three were telling him, with Bennet's own voice as backup. Knowing how much his late mother would have liked to see such a change in her older sister, once his mind acknowledged the truth of Lady Catherine's change, Darcy was most pleased and looked forward to seeing her when they next went into Kent.

Lord Matlock informed the group he had received a letter from his sister earlier that day. Anne was somewhat weaker so Mr. Starkey had recommended she should not travel unless there was an improvement. Lady Catherine would remain at Rosings Park with Anne, so the de Bourgh ladies would miss the upcoming wedding.

~~~~~~~/~~~~~~~

The ball at Netherfield was a spectacular success. In the end, Darcy had enjoyed himself immensely. It did not hurt that he had danced all three significant sets with his wife. In addition, he danced almost every other set. Kitty, Gigi, Mariah, and Lydia—who was home for the wedding—were only allowed to dance with family or approved close family friends. They all had enough partners to dance practically every set as well.

Charlotte, who was suffering from fatigue, only danced the first and the supper set with her husband. She had informed Bennet that morning of her suspicion, having missed her third set of courses. It was no surprise to her that he had recognised the signs before she told him anything. What was surprising to both was there was already a slight bump they could see when she readied for bed. As Bennet remembered it, his late wife did not show until around the time she felt the quickening, which should be in about one month for Charlotte. Although her mother could tell already, Charlotte decided, with her husband's agreement, not to share the news with any others until she felt the babe move.

Many in the neighbourhood had expected the brash, flirtatious Lydia they had known in the past, so were truly and pleasantly surprised at the demure, well behaved young lady Lydia now was. In the past, some of the parents of young ladies in the area had decried their daughters spending time with the youngest Bennet. After seeing her behaviour at the ball, that became a thing of the past.

The two betrothed couples danced the same three sets as the Darcys. At dinner, they sat at a table with Elizabeth, Darcy, and Matilda and Franklin Lucas. "It will not be long before none of us seated at this table will be single," Matilda observed.

"As one who has been married to the man she loves this past month," Elizabeth stated as she smiled at her husband, "it is a state I highly recommend."

"To think I would have been married to..." Matilda started but her betrothed cut her off.

"Did we not discuss this Matti? You realised your error before it was too late, and as my *niece* likes to say..." Franklin grinned at Elizabeth, who gave him a mock scowl.

"Only remember the past as that remembrance gives you pleasure," everyone at the table besides Elizabeth recited in unison.

"It is the truth, Matti. Look how happy you and Franklin are; you will have a most felicitous marriage. You will be living close to your father, who we all know dotes on you," Elizabeth agreed. She turned to Franklin, "I will *never* call you uncle, Franklin."

"Thank you for the use of Seaview Cottage for our wedding trip, William," Andrew stated appreciatively.

"And for the use of the house in Ramsgate for ours," Richard added.

"When we were in London, Uncle Gardiner shared that everything from Rosings Park and Fitzwilliam House has sold. Has any of the new furniture been delivered yet?" Elizabeth asked.

"Most for Rosings has, Lizzy," Mary gushed. "I cannot

wait to see how well it looks. Both Anne and Aunt Catherine report a vast improvement. There are only a few guest suites left to be completed."

"Gardiner informed me of the good news. In the end most of the money our aunt diverted from Rosing Park's profits to pay for her baubles, artwork, and furniture has been recouped, and even after all we are doing to redecorate and refurnish both the estate and townhouse, there will be a little left over," Richard reported.

"Did you like Hilldale House, Jane?" Elizabeth asked.

"Very much so. As you discovered at Darcy House, I only needed to have the mistress's chambers redecorated. Thankfully, Mother Elaine redecorated the rest of the house at Andrew's behest a few years ago," Jane replied.

Mary shared how they had found Fitzwilliam House, and that the work on it would begin in earnest after Rosings Park's redecoration was completed. After dinner, the dancing recommenced, and it was a happy group of guests that departed in the early hours of the morning.

~~~~~~~/~~~~~~~

The next day Bennet asked Charlotte to join him in the study. "The purchase of Purvis Lodge has been finalised," Bennet informed his wife. "The land will be annexed to Longbourn, and Phillips will include it in the new entail."

"It has three tenants, does it not?" Charlotte asked, and Bennet nodded. "And none want to depart with the change in ownership?"

"None. They will have the same terms as they had under old Mrs. Purvis, so they are all happy. Added to the fact our tenants have told them they are most satisfied with us; it cemented their decisions not to move on. Within a year, our income should be over six thousand pounds per annum," Bennet reported.

"Were any of your girls moved from their positions regarding their stakes in the former Purvis Lodge?" Charlotte enquired.

"To my chagrin, no. I was never asking for a gift, and now it is what has occurred. Each of my daughters have signed their stake back to us. No matter how much I cajoled, they would not be gainsaid. It is my opinion the men knew exactly how it would be when they put their part of Purvis Lodge into the marriage contracts for their wives-to-be." Bennet shook his head. "At this point, after making my feelings known, it would be ungracious of me to continue to push them on the subject."

"Then it must be so." Charlotte kissed her husband before returning to the drawing room.

~~~~~~~/~~~~~~~

That night, Charlotte gave Jane and Mary a very similar talk to the one she had given Elizabeth before her wedding. Aunt Gardiner talked to them as well, and this time she was accompanied by Elizabeth. Without going into personal details between her and William, Elizabeth was able to confirm the validity of the advice Jane and Mary had received from Charlotte and Aunt Gardiner.

Already mortified enough with the subjects of the discussions, when asked if they had any questions, both demurred. After their aunt departed the bedchamber, the three eldest Bennet daughters talked late into the night before separating with the intention to get some sleep before the upcoming big day.

CHAPTER 27

Early in the morning before their double weddings, Jane and Mary sat and had a steaming cup of tea, toast, and jam with Charlotte and Elizabeth. The previous night Elizabeth and her husband had slept at Longbourn so she would be close to her sisters. "I am too excited to eat or drink," Mary admitted.

"It is highly recommended; ask Eliza," Charlotte pointed out. "If you do not eat and drink something now, it will be many hours before you do, and neither of you wish to faint from hunger during the ceremony or wedding breakfast, do you?" Both Jane and Mary began to eat and drink what had been sent up for them. It was not a large meal, but it would tide them over until the wedding breakfast. As this wedding had a larger crowd, including some from Town, the wedding breakfast would be held in Netherfield Park's ballroom.

"I cannot wait to be married to Andrew," Jane stated dreamily. "He is the ideal man for me."

"As is Richard for me," Mary claimed.

"And William for me," Elizabeth added.

"Your father is perfect for me," Charlotte admitted.

"We know you two do well together," Elizabeth smiled at her friend.

"It is more than that, remember when I used to claim I was not romantic?" Charlotte asked.

"You have fallen in love with Papa," Mary nodded, all of them had seen it happening over the months they had been under the same roof. "We are not blind, Charlotte, we have known for some time now."

"And if the way I have seen him look at you, I am sure

269

Papa has fallen in love with you as well, Charlotte," Jane added. "Why do you and Papa not renew your vows as now you will both mean *every single* part of them?"

Charlotte's blush of pleasure was all the three sisters needed to see Jane's suggestion was one that gave Charlotte pleasure. There would be another family wedding to plan soon enough, even if it were just to renew their vows. All three could not have been happier their father had found love in his marriage. His having done so would make their leaving Longbourn that much easier for him as well as them. It was a woman's lot, after all, to leave her childhood home to live with her husband when she married.

"Charlotte, you were the best thing that could have happened to our family," Jane told her stepmother on behalf of all of her sisters.

"Enough compliments, it is not my day. It is time for you two to get dressed. Come Eliza, you will return with Kitty to help the brides as needed after their baths." Charlotte and Elizabeth stood and left the bedchamber. Elizabeth was to stand up with Jane while Kitty would do the honours for Mary.

~~~~~~~/~~~~~~~

It was Richard's turn to make sure William had the rings safely in his pocket, as the latter would be standing up for him. Andrew had done the same with his good friend Lord Harry Smythe, the Earl of Granville, who would do the honours for him.

"It is so much more relaxing for me than when I was the groom," Darcy told his cousin Richard.

"I can now truly sympathise with you for the day you were married, William. I apologise for all the ribbing I visited on you in the days leading up to your wedding, and it speaks well of your character you did not feel the need to repay me in kind—too much," Richard slapped his cousin on the back. Darcy had returned from Longbourn to spend time with his cousins—soon to be brothers—before the wedding ceremony.

Just as had happened at Longbourn, the men at Netherfield Park had insisted the two grooms have some sustenance with tea and coffee so no one would be distracted from the ceremony by growling bellies.

"Granville, did I hear you have finally found a lady worthy of your attention?" Darcy asked.

"Yes Darcy, you did. I am betrothed to Lady Marie Rhys-Davies, the youngest daughter of the Duke and Duchess of Bedford. We will marry at the end of March at St. George's in Town; you will all receive your invitations in due course." Lord Harry Smythe was congratulated heartily by the men. "The announcement will appear in *The Times* in the next day or two. As her mother is cousin to the Queen, we needed their Royal Highness's approval before the notice was seen in the papers."

"Enough gossip," Lord Matlock interjected. "It is time, Sons. I could not be prouder of you two and your choice of brides. You have both selected jewels of the first order, as did William before you. I am sure you will both be extremely happy in your married lives."

"Thank you, Father," the Fitzwilliam brothers chorused.

"Let us depart; it would not do to be late to your own weddings," Darcy informed them as he stood and moved toward the door.

~~~~~~~/~~~~~~~

Mr. Dudley stood speaking to the two grooms and the men standing up with them as he waited for a signal the brides were present in the vestibule. "I assume the next wedding service you perform will be the most pleasurable for you," Darcy surmised.

"You are half-right, Mr. Darcy. I could not be happier for Matti to be marrying Franklin; however, as I will be the one giving the bride away, the curate from St. Alfred's will have the honour of performing the service," Dudley shared. "I will be forever grateful to your wife, Mrs. Bennet, and Miss Bennet, who assisted Matti in her reconsideration of her choice of a partner in life."

"It seems to me the Lucas heir is as grateful as you are,"

Richard observed. Just then, Charlotte entered the church and nodded to Mr. Dudley.

The men all took their positions, watching as Kitty Bennet walked up the aisle. When she was just past the halfway mark, Elizabeth Darcy started her walk towards the altar and Darcy was mesmerised. With the early morning sun streaming through the windows behind her, it seemed as if she had a halo surrounding her.

Once Kitty stood on Richard's side to the left of the altar and Elizabeth was next to Andrew on the right, the doors opened again, and the two brides entered on their father's arms as the congregation rose. Jane was on Bennet's right side, and Mary on his left.

Jane was a vision in a white satin dress with sleeves which ended above her elbows, and Mary's dress was in the same style, in cream. Jane wore a necklace Andrew had presented her which had a sapphire in the necklace's centre and matching earbobs. Richard had presented Mary with a similar piece with rubies, as she preferred.

Both Andrew and Richard were transfixed by the vision of his bride. Darcy was able to return the favour, subtly nudging Richard to get him moving toward his bride after her father kissed Mary's cheek. The Earl of Granville chucked to himself when he needed to employ the same tactic for Andrew.

The Earl and Countess, seated in the front pew across from the Bennets, beamed with happiness and pride for the love matches their sons had made, excited to gain the long-awaited daughters at last.

Once the two couples made their way to the place in front of the Reverend, Mr. Dudley commenced the marriage rituals. Andrew and Jane said their vows and exchanged rings first, Richard and Mary followed with theirs.

Each couple repeated their vows in strong clear voices, and when Mr. Dudley asked if any knew just cause why the couples should not marry, there was not a sound in response. The Reverend intoned: "Those whom God hath joined together let no man put asunder." Then the final prayer and benediction was given, and it was done.

The two sets of newlyweds, attended by those who stood up for them, followed Mr. Dudley to the vestry where they signed the register, witnessed by their attendants. The four witnesses withdrew, but rather than the usual delay for a moment of quiet, they were followed out almost immediately by the Jane and Andrew and Mary and Richard. There was, after all, a three-mile carriage ride to the wedding breakfast. Each couple would be alone in their own coach.

On returning from the vestry, the newlyweds were mobbed by their family and closest friends. The three Lucas sons offered their services to their new nephews in case they needed any sort of advice from the *older and wiser* uncles, but Mariah was much too intimidated by both grooms to jest with them.

"You will be very happy women," Bennet stated as he hugged Jane and then Mary in turn.

"I knew you two could not be such good girls for nothing," Charlotte wished them happy. "You have both married men who value and respect you. God has been very good to the Bennet family to gift you two and Lizzy with such honourable and good men."

"I had always intended to be the first to marry," Lydia admitted to her sisters and stepmother. "It was such a childish and petulant wish, and I would have thrown my life away for something I was truly not ready for," Lydia owned.

"It is a mark of your growing maturity that you are able to see that in yourself, Lyddie," Jane hugged her tightly, whispering that she was proud of her sister. Lydia moved on to wish her new brothers joy, and then it was Kitty's turn to hug her newly married sisters. "All I can hope is to find a man as good as the ones you both have married," she looked to Elizabeth, "and as you have married, Lizzy."

"When the time is right, I am sure you will find the perfect man for yourself, Kitty," Mary squeezed Kitty's hand.

"Are you ready to travel with William, Gigi, and me to Pemberley, Kitty?" Elizabeth asked.

"I am. I believe the footmen were loading my trunks just after we left for the church," Kitty confirmed.

"It is time to depart," Bennet pointed out.

The two brides and grooms gave their family and friends ten minutes' start before they boarded their coaches. On the way to Netherfield Park with blinds drawn, each couple took advantage of the privacy lacking in the vestry to revel in their happiness.

~~~~~~~/~~~~~~~

By the time the two carriages bearing the Viscount and his new Viscountess, and the Honourable Mr. & Mrs. Richard Fitzwilliam drew to a halt at Netherfield, both couples had put themselves to rights—insofar as they were able. When each couple stepped out, the sisters glanced at each other, needing all their self-control not to laugh, as both sported plump, red, well-kissed lips. Once in the entrance hall, Jane and Mary assisted each other to make sure all the pins for their hair were in the right places once they had handed off their outerwear.

After Mr. Nichols announced the two couples to the revellers assembled in the ballroom, they were welcomed with a rousing three cheers. As they walked around the room greeting friends and acquaintances, they fully appreciated the wisdom of the advice to take some sustenance before the church service.

When both Jane and Mary reached Matti, her father, and her betrothed, they wished them well for their upcoming nuptials, apologising for not being able to be there to witness the happy event. "Not for one minute would I have expected either of you to shorten your honeymoon to return for my wedding. Elizabeth and her husband will remain at Netherfield until we are wed, so she and Kitty will represent the Bennet sisters," Matilda assured the brides.

After about ninety minutes of circulating, both newly christened Fitzwilliam couples joined the family in sitting for a while. They succeeded in eating and drinking a little, regardless of how excited they felt, as the time to depart and to be alone with one another drew near.

"Mary and Richard, We will see you at Eastertime when we come to Kent," Lady Elaine smiled at her youngest son and his bride. "I look forward to seeing all the changes you have made to the manor house at Rosings Park by then."

"The house should be complete before you arrive, Mother Elaine," Mary informed her mother-in-law. "In fact, we believe it will be completed by the end of March. When the family starts to arrive the first week of April, the work on Fitzwilliam House will have begun, and it will be ready by the end of the season."

"It will be exciting for me to see Hilldale for the first time. We will leave for Staffordshire from Kent at the end of April," Jane shared.

"I anticipate Pemberley for the first time. We will leave the day after Matti's wedding. Both William and Gigi have told me so much about the estate. My feet are itching to start walking all the paths I will find there," Elizabeth enthused. "At least Jane will be less than a four-hour carriage ride from Pemberley. We will see you and Richard as often as we are able, Mary. After Easter, we all will be in Town together for part of the summer and Christmastide."

Charlotte sat back with Bennet watching his three married daughters. Then she looked to where Mariah, Gigi, Kitty, and Lydia were sitting and enjoying one another's company, the younger girls' behaviour just as it should be. "Yes Charlotte," Bennet leaned close to his wife's ear, "we have been blessed."

A few minutes later, both couples stood and circulated a while longer. Half an hour later, the two brides made their way to bedchambers which had been set aside for their use to change into travel attire.

Both couples would spend the night in London, Jane and Andrew at Hilldale House and Mary and Richard at Darcy

House. In the morning, they would leave in convoy until they reached Kent, where they would go their separate ways toward their honeymoon destinations.

Elizabeth and Kitty had each assisted the sister she had stood up with. Just before they exited the bedchamber, Jane and Elizabeth hugged one another tightly. "I missed you this past month, Lizzy, but now that I am married, even though I will still miss you, I have a feeling my thoughts will be consumed by my exceedingly handsome husband," Jane stated.

"As it should be," Elizabeth agreed. "I missed you for the last month, but not nearly as much as I would have if I had not been married to William. As Andrew is the perfect man for you, and Richard for Mary, William is the *only* man for me. He completes me, Jane."

"I feel the same about Andrew," Jane owned. "Also, now that it is confirmed Charlotte and father love one another, it has assuaged the guilt I may have felt leaving him at home with only Kitty and Lydia."

"You have the right of it; Charlotte is the perfect helpmeet for our father. He looks younger than he did before his marriage to her, and I love how engaged he is, especially how she evicted him from his study." Elizabeth smiled as she thought about the improvements in their lives since Charlotte's intervention.

"It is time, Lizzy," Jane leaned in and hugged her favourite sister one more time. By the time Jane and Elizabeth descended the stairs, Kitty, and Mary on Richard's arm, were already in the entrance hall. Andrew waited for his wife at the base of the stairs and offered his arm to her, which she happily accepted.

The Bennets, Darcys, and Fitzwilliams joined the two couples in front of the house where the two coaches stood ready in the drive. After many hugs, a few tears, and much well-wishing, the brothers each handed his wife into their conveyance. Richard and Mary's former de Bourgh carriage departed first, followed a minute later by the Hilldale carriage. The family waved them off until the second conveyance turned out of the drive and was no longer visible.

~~~~~~~/~~~~~~~

A little more than four hours later, the two coaches arrived at their destinations in London, one at Portman Square and the other at Grosvenor Square. Both couples elected to take trays in their rooms, as no one was hungry, thanks to the hampers of food each found in their carriage after leaving Netherfield Park. There was so much food and drink within, the uneaten—which was most of the food—was gifted to their servants when they arrived at the halfway rest stop.

Mary and Richard were in a large suite on the family floor at Darcy House. After a bath, it did not take long for husband and wife to be in each other's arms. As Richard had long suspected, once Mary's passion was unleashed there was no putting that genie back in its lamp—and neither desired for it to be, even had it been possible.

Less than a mile away, Jane and Andrew had not waited even so long as that. It had taken much will power from both of them, but, in the end, they did not want their first time together to be in a travelling coach. Agreeing that the delay was for this one reason only, they started to discuss some improvements to make their future travels more pleasurable. Once they gained Jane's newly decorated chambers, they dismissed their personal servants and their restrained passion burst forth like water escaping though a crack in a dam. Andrew had always believed that Jane's serene countenance hid depths of passion, and he was thrilled to discover he had been correct.

~~~~~~~/~~~~~~~

That evening after the feast at Netherfield Park, the four remaining Bennets and Georgiana had a light meal at Longbourn. After dinner, Gigi entertained them with some airs on the pianoforte, and all retired before nine o'clock due to the early start they had had that morning.

After loving his wife thoroughly, Bennet was lying with Charlotte in his arms. "The day you took charge of the situation and came to see me has turned out to be one of the most significant and best days in my life, my sweet." Bennet kissed his wife languidly.

"It was never my intention to take charge of anything, my love," Charlotte replied softly, revelling in the feeling of home she found in his arms. "I just knew after the offensive words I heard Collins speak in the park and then his disgusting speech to me, I had to do something. I almost lost my nerve to come see you that day, you know."

"I will forever be grateful you did come, but what convinced you of the rectitude of your actions?" Bennet asked.

"Thoughts of Collins and the viciousness just under the surface. I could not allow him to even attempt to inflict his plans on your daughters," Charlotte shared.

"Look where we are now; you are to gift me with another child in about six months," Bennet stated as he rubbed his wife's thickening belly.

"Will you be disappointed if I bear you another daughter, Thomas?" Charlotte asked softly.

"No! As long as you both are healthy, I will be content. With the estate no longer entailed away, it makes no difference, and even if it were I would not feel otherwise," Bennet replied emphatically. "You have become my world, Charlotte; so long as I have you by my side, I will be fine."

"When will you tell Eliza we are to travel with them to Pemberley after Matti and Franklin's wedding?" Charlotte asked with raised eyebrows.

"Are you a mind reader, Charlotte?" an astounded Bennet asked. "After we take Lydia back to school, it was my intention to surprise them; how you knew I will never know."

"Your thought processes are no longer so secret, Thomas," Charlotte relayed. "But I suggest informing them, so they are not caught wholly unprepared."

"I will talk to Lizzy and William on the morrow," Bennet conceded.

Not much later the couple fell asleep in each other's arms, and if one had been watching from the outside, they would have marvelled that even in repose, they both were still smiling contentedly.

EPILOGUE

"I am so excited you will be my sister on the morrow, Lydia! Helen Bingley, née Jacobson, enthused as she helped her best friend dress for her wedding. "How did you choose between Tommy and Will to act as your ring bearer?"

Six and a half years earlier, Charlotte had delivered twin boys, Thomas Junior, the heir to Longbourn, and William, named after his grandfather Lucas. They were known as Tommy and Will; thankfully they were not identical twins.

"The little tykes raced their ponies and Will won by a nose. He groused a little, but Tommy conceded he lost fair and square," Lydia explained. "I still cannot believe that I won Tim's hand. I fell in love with him the first time I visited your parents' estate. I always worried he saw me as naught but another sister."

Lydia had decided to wait until she felt ready to enter society, and it was not until she was twenty that she chose to come out again. After two years at the Wrightfield School and a year at a finishing school in London, Lydia emerged as an accomplished gentlewoman in every sense of the word.

She could have come out at eighteen, but it was her decision, which was fully supported by her father, Charlotte, and all of her sisters. The Lydia who made that particular decision was unrecognisable as being the same girl who had almost ruined herself and her family at fifteen.

Did you wonder what happened to the black-hearted libertine Wickham? After three years at Marshalsea, he angered the wrong person, who put an end to the wastrel's life. His death was investigated, but because no one came forward who witnessed the attack, the case had been closed. Over the years before his death, he had written to Darcy in an attempt to manipulate him into helping, but after the first insincere letter, any subsequent ones had been consigned to the fire unread. No one mourned his passing, not even Mrs. Younge.

Lydia had not been aware of it, but she caught Tim Jacobson's notice the first time she visited Janet's Well; his affections for her had grown with each subsequent meeting. As the two families became closer, he had the pleasure of spending more time with the object of his love. He had waited through her first season, but just after she turned one and twenty he requested a courtship, which led to a betrothal, and it progressed to this day when he and Lydia were to be married.

"Considering you will be his wife in two hours, I think not," Helen smiled at her sister of the heart and soon so be sister-in-law.

"Lydia, you are radiant," Charlotte said as she entered Lydia's bedchamber. Francine Sarah Bennet, called Fanny to honour the late Mrs. Bennet, now two, held her mother's hand tightly.

"Mama, Lyddie so pretty," the youngest Bennet exclaimed.

After her twin sons, Charlotte had become with child one more time, and Fanny would likely forever be the baby of the family. Her father was delighted that his youngest daughter seemed to be a copy of his second one in looks, intelligence, and character.

There was a knock on the door and Lady Catherine Rhys-Davies, Marchioness of Birchington, entered her sister's chambers. "Oh, Lyddie, that gown is perfect on you," Kitty gushed. Like her four sisters before her, Lydia had chosen a plain gown with few adornments. The one she was wearing was an ivory satin dress with empire waist, puffed shoulders, and a medium-length train.

Kitty had come out when she was nineteen, with her sister Gigi and her *Aunt* Mariah, who were both eighteen. None of the three had accepted any offers of courtship in that first season, though there had been more than a few who tried to approach them. Any men brave enough to make the attempt had to pass through the gauntlet of Darcy, the Fitzwilliam brothers, the Lucas brothers, Sir William, Bennet, and Lord Matlock.

In her second season, Kitty met Lord Sedgwick Rhys-Davies Junior, the Marquess of Birchington, who was six and twenty. There was an instant connection, and Lord Sed requested and was granted a courtship in the second month of that season. The two were married six months later from Longbourn, as Kitty was determined to marry from her home. The Duke and Duchess of Bedford, who approved of Kitty whole-heartedly, agreed without reservation to the location of the wedding.

Given that Lady Rose, the Duchess of Bedford, was a cousin to Queen Charlotte, Princess Elizabeth represented the crown at the wedding. Kitty had borne a son who was now almost two, and she suspected she was with child again.

Charles Bingley was waiting with most of the family not busy with helping the bride prepare in her chambers. He had mourned his sister Caroline for a full year and had matured during that time. He sent a letter to Darcy hoping all connection between them had not been severed and was delighted to receive a reply inviting him and the Hursts to spend Christmastide at Pemberley some five years ago.

The Jacobsons, who were now fast friends with the Bennets, thanks to the strong bonds of friendship between their respective daughters, were also present. That is when Charles Bingley met eighteen-year-old Helen Jacobson for the first time. She was to come out in February, and Bingley had been fascinated by her. She was not like any woman he had pursued before; her complexion was opposite that of his blond angels. After her come out he began to call on her; a few months later he requested a courtship; soon after that they were betrothed.

They had been married four years and had one daughter. Helen was with child again, though she had not yet felt the quickening. It was ironic to Bingley that by his marrying an inconsequential country squire's daughter, one his late sister Caroline would have decried as having no wealth or connections to speak of, he would gain connections all the way to the royals--once Lydia married his brother Tim. His late sister would have boasted of the connections far and wide. Louisa and Hurst had been blessed with only one child, a son who was six.

Lady Georgiana Carrington was sitting with her husband, sister Elizabeth, and her brother. She met Lord Brandon Carrington, the Earl of Harrington, around the same time Kitty met her husband. At first, she showed no marked interest in the Earl, but over the months of the season, she warmed to him and began to develop tender feelings. They married just before her twentieth birthday and so far had been blessed with a son and a daughter.

Mariah Jamison entered the drawing room with her husband. At the end of Mariah's second season she met Robert Jamison, the son and heir of the Jamisons of Oakmont in Bedfordshire, at an assembly in Meryton. They danced twice that night, both enjoying the other's company.

Robert requested, and Mariah had happily granted, permission to call on her. A month later, he was granted a formal courtship; within three months the two were married from Lucas Lodge. To date, Mariah and Robert had a daughter who was nearing three and, as was obvious to anyone with eyes, Mariah was with child again. She was in her fifth month of increasing.

In June of the year Bingley was invited for Christmastide, Elizabeth gifted her husband with a son and heir, Bennet Robert Darcy. Two years after Bennet, a second son, Alexander Edward, was born, followed by the baby, Annabeth Jane. The Darcys were more in love than the day they married, but that is not to say all was smooth sailing.

As might be expected of two strong-willed individuals who were stubborn, although each would accuse the other of being so while being unable to admit they themselves were, there were disagreements from time to time. However, the couple never allowed a day to end in anger and always enjoyed making up afterwards.

Pemberley once again rung with the voices of children, which added to the life the new mistress had brought with her. The annual harvest ball was reinstituted; a Twelfth Night Ball was held each year the Darcys were in residence at Pemberley for Christmastide; and the Darcys became among the most popular families in the neighbourhood as they regularly entertained and accepted invitations, something Darcy had eschewed since his father had passed away.

As her husband and other family members believed she would, Elizabeth Darcy—as did her sisters—became a force in the *Ton* helping to set fashion trends. Invitations to balls, dinners, and soirees at Darcy House were coveted. The fact the Darcys only spent part of the season in London increased rather than diminished their popularity among polite society. The only complete season they were in London was the first season their sisters came out together.

Jane and Andrew were seated with Mary and Richard, Lord and Lady Matlock, and Lady Catherine. Anne, under Mr. Starkey's care, had exceeded all expectations and lived two happy and full years after the double wedding in February 1811. Lady Catherine never reverted to the person she was before, cared for her daughter with much love, and held Anne's hand when she slipped from the mortal world.

Lady Catherine had been surrounded by a loving family who had helped her through the grief of her daughter's death. She had, in fact, been adopted as a surrogate grandmother by the growing number of children born to her nieces and nephews. In a strange twist of fate, Elizabeth Darcy became her favourite niece, so she spent at least three months a year with the Darcys. She never offered advice unless asked, and even then only if she was truly knowledgeable on the subject.

To date, both Fitzwilliam brothers' wives had gifted them with two children—a son and daughter for Jane and Andrew, and a daughter and a son for Mary and Richard. Lord and Lady Matlock, often times accompanied by Lady Catherine who lived with them at Snowhaven when she was not with the Darcys, spent a great deal of time with their children and grandchildren.

The complete redecorations of Fitzwilliam House had been completed by Christmas of 1811 and was a delight to see, for it was a comfortable and happy home. Everyone was complimentary of the end result, none more so than Lady Catherine.

As had been predicted, given the proximity of Hilldale and Pemberley, when both families were in residence there were almost-weekly visits in one direction or the other. After Kitty married, she was visited often, as Birchington was less than forty miles to the west of Pemberley in Nottinghamshire.

There was no paucity of visits with the rest of the family. Each time they travelled south, family members from the north stopped at Longbourn on the way to Town or Kent, with the same being true on their return home. Netherfield Park was utilised for a two month visit to the area each year and numerous shorter visits by many family members.

The Fitzwilliams of Rosings Park would always stay at Netherfield for the two months the Darcys and others were in residence each year, unless it was around the time of a final confinement, which had been the case when Mary's son had been born. Even with Mary and Richard being the farthest from their sisters and brothers in the north, they met a good number of times each year, just as had been predicted on the day Mary and Jane married the brothers.

Seaview Cottage had become a favourite destination for all members of the extended family. The Darcys returned in June of the first year of their marriage and explored the wonders of the secluded cove—many times. They were convinced

Bennet had been conceived there.

The *cottage* was used so much, it was a rare time when family was not in residence. In order to accommodate their growing families, Darcy had suggested to his wife they should extend the house; she agreed without reservation. The renovations had been completed four years previously and had almost doubled the size of the structure.

The extended family included the Lucases and Mr. Dudley. Franklin and Matilda Lucas had two sons and were as happy as could be. Charlotte's other brothers, John and Nick, each married a Long niece. The former and his wife had a daughter, while the latter and his wife had a son.

Mr. Dudley still ministered to his flock and saw his daughter and grandchildren—the lights of his life—two to three times a week, sometimes more. Two years previously, he hired a full-time curate, which allowed him more time to relax as he groomed the younger man to take over when he retired.

Other than Bennet, Charlotte, the bride, and her matron of honour, the rest of the family walked to the church to take their places. Elizabeth walked with little Fanny, holding her hand, while Tommy walked with his eldest sister. It had been decided the youngest Bennet was still too young to be a flower girl on her own, so her mother would walk her up the aisle carrying a basket with some petals in it for little Fanny to drop in the aisle.

When Lydia walked down the stairs with Helen holding her train, Bennet could see his late wife clearly in his second youngest daughter. Lydia was a mirror image of her mother in all but character.

Once Mr. Dudley had conducted the wedding for the fifth Bennet sister, everyone returned to Longbourn's enlarged ballroom, where a sumptuous wedding breakfast awaited them.

Charlotte and Bennet sat in a corner watching as Lydia and her husband made the rounds of the well-wishers in the room. The youngest Bennet had, until a few minutes ago, refused to move from her mother, but as she grew tired she agreed to allow Mrs. Hill, who was almost like a surrogate grandmother to her, carry her up to the nursery to nap.

"Charlotte, I find I love you more each day; you have given me so much. Who would have believed we would have eight such wonderful children? My late wife would have despaired at Lydia waiting until she was almost two and twenty to marry, but she would not have repined the matches her daughters have made," Bennet told his wife quietly.

"Thomas, I have received as much, if not more, than I have given. My heart is full with my love for you, and I believe things are just as they should be. It was ordained by the fates; I was simply the vessel," Charlotte replied as she gave her husband's hand a squeeze.

"You may try to minimize the effect you had on me and my family, my love, but it will not do. From that first fateful meeting in my study, you took charge, and have been quietly steering us ever since. You, my love, are a gift from God," Bennet insisted.

The reason for Charlotte's actions was never heard from again, a fact no one in the family repined. The family would never know, but Mr. Collins had met his end when he tried to assert his superiority in a small frontier town in the Canadas, and the man he insulted had shot him on the spot. The former parson was so unpopular in the town that no one cared about his demise; he was buried in an unmarked grave.

It was an oft repeated conversation they had over the years, though they both knew it was a pointless argument. Regardless of the reason, she, her husband, and family were all incandescently happy.

As the couple watched their twins being ushered to the nursery to rest along with their daughters' children, there was no denying how good their life was. It was the well acknowledged fact by many in the family that thanks to Charlotte's intervention, Longbourn would have a Bennet as master for many generations to come.

The End

COMING SOON

A Bennet of Royal Blood:

This story starts with one of King George III's sons marrying for love secretly. The woman is a daughter of an Earl. After about two years of marriage, all of the time with his beloved wife spent at her estate of Netherfield Park in Hertfordshire, the Prince reveals his marriage to his father thinking the elapsed time with protect them. It saddens the King to do so, but he forces a divorce. He was at least convinced by his son not to have the marriage annulled.

The reason was *NOT* that the lady was unsuitable, the opposite was true, but for political reasons, the King has promised his son's hand to a European princess to strengthen alliances for England.

In the meanwhile, the lady had become best friends with Mrs. Francine Bennet of Longbourn. They had met after Jane was born. When her devastated husband informs her of the forced divorce, his wife does not inform him she is with child. It so happened Fanny Bennet is also pregnant with her second child as well.

Due to the ignominy of divorce and worried about the social ramifications, the lady's family cut ties with her and the only one she feels she has left is Fanny Bennet. A few other friends write but the broken-hearted lady is not ready to accept their overtures yet. As both ladies near their confinements Thomas Bennet is called away—for what he tells his wife—is to assist his good friend from Cambridge the Earl of Holder in Staffordshire. He is actually investigating ways to break the entail on Longbourn.

Fanny moves into Netherfield to be with her best friend

during their confinements along with 2-year-old Jane. Before the final confinement, her brothers, Phillips the solicitor and Gardiner the man of business were summoned. Phillips draws up a will for the lady and Gardiner was given management of her fortune.

Just in case the worst happens, the lady writes a number of letters, among them one to her child, one to the Prince, one to Bennet, as she has a plan in the event of her death, and one to her parents.

The best friends go into labour within hours of each other. Fanny delivers a still born son and some hours later, her friend delivers a baby girl, who is the legitimate daughter of a Prince, making her a Princess of England. The friend has complications of birth and will not survive long. She implores her best friend—her sister of the heart—to take her daughter and raise her as her own and she will claim the dead baby son. Fanny cannot deny her friend her dying wish.

The Lady names her baby Elizabeth after her maternal grandmother. She charges Fanny with waiting until Elizabeth is 18 to reveal Elizabeth's birth right to her explaining her reasons for waiting. Her will bequeaths her child all of her worldly possessions, other than a few other small bequests to others, including an enormous fortune and Netherfield Park on reaching her majority.

When Bennet returns he is introduced to, and falls in love with, *his* second daughter. Jane and Lizzy are the favourites of their mother. As in canon, Fanny delivers three more girls, Mary, Kitty, and Lydia. The story looks at how the Bennets' lives are different with a much different Fanny than canon. Also how will Elizabeth and the world around her react to the news when she finds out her true heritage.

BOOKS BY THIS AUTHOR

A Change Of Fortunes

What if, unlike canon, the Bennets had sons? Could it be, if both father and mother prayed to God and begged for a son that their prayers would be answered? If the prayers were granted how would the parents be different and what kind of life would the family have? What will the consequences of their decisions be?

In many Pride and Prejudice variations the Bennet parents are portrayed as borderline neglectful with Mr. Bennet caring only about making fun of others, reading and drinking his port while shutting himself away in his study. Mrs. Bennet is often shown as flighty, unintelligent and a character to make sport of. The Bennet parent's marriage is often shown as a mistake where there is no love; could there be love there that has been stifled due to circumstances?

In this book, some of those traits are present, but we see what a different set of circumstances and decisions do to the parents and the family as a whole. Most of the characters from canon are here along with some new characters to help broaden the story. The normal villains are present with one added who is not normally a villain per se and I trust that you, my dear reader, will like the way that they are all 'rewarded' in my story.

We find a much stronger and more resolute Bingley. Jane Bennet is serene, but not without a steely resolve. I feel that both need to be portrayed with more strength of character for the purposes of this book. Sit back, relax and enjoy and my hope is that you will be suitably entertained.

The Hypocrite

The Hypocrite is a low angst, sweet and clean tale about the relationship dynamics between Fitzwilliam Darcy and Elizabeth Bennet after his disastrous and insult laden proposal at Hunsford. How does our heroine react to his proposal and the behaviour that she has witnessed from Darcy up to that point in the story?

The traditional villains from Pride and Prejudice that we all love to hate make an appearance in my story BUT they are not the focus. Other than Miss Bingley, whose character provides the small amount of angst in this tale, they play a small role and are dealt with quickly. If dear reader you are looking for an angst filled tale rife with dastardly attempts to disrupt ODC then I am sorry to say, you will not find that in my book.

This story is about the consequences of the decisions made by the characters portrayed within. Along with Darcy and Elizabeth, we examine the trajectory of the supporting character's lives around them. How are they affected by decisions taken by ODC coupled with the decisions that they make themselves? How do the decisions taken by members of the Bingley/Hurst family affect them and their lives?

The Bennets are assumed to be extremely wealthy for the purposes of my tale, the source of that wealth is explained during the telling of this story. The wealth, like so much in this story is a consequence of decisions made Thomas Bennet and Edward Gardiner.

If you like a sweet and clean, low angst story, then dear reader, sit back, pour yourself a glass of your favourite drink and read, because this book is for you.

The Duke's Daughter: Omnibus Edition

All three parts of the series are available individually.

Part 1: Lady Elizbeth Bennet is the Daughter of Lord Thomas and Lady Sarah Bennet, the Duke and Duchess of Hertfordshire. She is quick to judge and anger and very slow to forgive. Fitzwilliam Darcy has learnt to rely on his own judgement above all others. Once he believes that something is a certain way, he does not allow anyone to change his mind. He ignored his mother and the result was the Ramsgate debacle, but he had not learnt his lesson yet.
He mistakes information that her heard from his Aunt about her parson's relatives and with assumptions and his failure to listen to his friends the Bingleys, he makes a huge mistake and faces a very angry Lady Elizabeth Bennet.

Part 2: At the end of Part 1, William Darcy saved Lady Elizabeth Bennet's life, but at what cost? After a short look into the future, part 2 picks up from the point that Part 1 ended. We find out very soon what William's fate is. We also follow the villains as they plot their revenge and try to find new ways to get money that they do not deserve.
Elizabeth finally admitted that she loved William the morning that he was shot, is it too late or will love find a way? As there always are in life, there are highs and lows and this second part of three gives us a window into the ups and downs that affect our couple and their extended family.

Part 3: In part 2, the Duke's Daughter became a Duchess. We follow ODC as they continue their married life as they deal with the vagaries of life. We left the villains preparing to sail from Bundoran to execute their dastardly plan. We find out if they are successful or if they fail.

In this final part of the Duke's Daughter series, we get a good idea what the future holds for the characters that we have followed through the first two books in the series.

The Discarded Daughter - Omnibus Edition

All 4 books in the Discarded Daughter series are combined into a single book. They are available individually, in both Kindle and paperback format.

The story is about the life of Elizabeth Bennet who is kidnapped and discarded at an exceedingly early age. It tells the tale of her life with the family that takes her in and loved her as a true daughter.

We follow not only Elizbeth's life, her trials and tribulations, but that of the family that lost her and all of those around her, immediate and extended family, and the effect that she has on their lives. There is love, villains, hurt, and happiness as we watch Elizabeth grow into an exceptional young woman.

If you are looking for a story that only concentrates on our heroine, then this is not for you.

Surviving Thomas Bennet

Warning: This book contains violence, although not graphically portrayed.

There are Bennet twins born to James Bennet, his heir, James Junior and second born Thomas. They boys start out as the best of friends until Thomas starts to get resentful of his older brother's status as heir.

The younger Bennet turns to gambling, drink, and carousing. In order to protect Longbourn, unbeknownst to Thomas, James Bennet senior places and entail on the estate so none of his son's creditors are able to make demands against the family estate.

Thomas Bennet was given his legacy of thirty thousand pounds when he reached his majority. He marries Fanny the daughter of a local solicitor in Oxford where Thomas is teaching. He is fired for being drunk at work. He manages to gamble away all of his legacy while going into serious debt to a dangerous man in not too many years.

When James Senior dies, Thomas and Fanny Bennet arrive at Longbourn demanding an imagined inheritance. They find out there is no more for them and leave after abusing one an all roundly swearing revenge.

James Junior, the master of Longbourn, and his wife Priscilla have a son, Jamie, and daughters Jane, Elizabeth, and Mary. Thinking he can sell Longbourn if his brother and son are out of the way, Thomas Bennet murders them and James' wife by causing a carriage accident.

The story reveals how the three surviving daughters are protected by their friends and how they survive the man who murdered their beloved parents and brother. Netherfield belongs to the Darcy's second son, William. There are many of the characters that are both loved and hated from the canon in this story, some similar to canon, a good number of them hugely different, there are also some new characters not from canon.

Unknown Family Connections

This is a book of two volumes, but all in one book. It is a one off, standalone story.

Over 150 years in the past an Evil Duke plotted to separate his first and second sons. He was a man who had two interests: money and status. Lord Sedgewick Rhys-Davies, the 3rd Duke of Bedford sets off a chain of events that ultimately ends up doing the exact opposite of what his original evil intent was in the far future.

Mr. Thomas Bennet lives with his second wife and family on his estate Longbourn in Hertfordshire. As far as he knows, he is an indirect descendant of the last Earl of Meryton whose line died out with him over 150 years ago. The family has owned Longbourn and Netherfield Park for as long as anyone remembers. There is an entail on Longbourn, but not the one we are used to. As in the canon, this Bennet dislikes London, and the Ton and he and his family keep away from London society. His second wife is the daughter of an Earl but just goes as Mrs. Bennet.

The Bennet's new tenants at Netherfield Park are the Bingleys. One of the major deviations from canon in this tale, Jane Bennet has more than a little backbone while Bingley has little or none. How will Darcy behave, will he make assumptions and act on them? Will Elizabeth allow her prejudices to rule? When Wickham slithers onto the scene will he cause havoc?

The 7th Duke of Bedford is ill, and he will be the end of the line as there are no living relatives to inherit the dukedom and vast Bedford holdings. He removes an old letter from a safe in his study written by the 4th Duke. Witten on the outside of the letter is: 'Open ONLY if there are no more Rhys-Davies heirs.'

The Duke opens the letter and learns of the 3rd Duke's evil and there is in fact an heir, although a direct descendant, he is not a Rhys-Davies.

This is the story of different families and what happens when their lives intersect and are changed for ever. There is quite a bit about Lizzy & Darcy, but there are not always the main focus of the story as the title infers.

Cinder-Liza

No fairy godmother or magic in the story although there is some imagery we would expect to see in a Cinderella story – my apologies to those who thought there would be magic based on the title.

Mr. Thomas Bennet married the love of his life: Miss Fanny Gardiner. She gave him three children, Jane, Elizabeth and Tommy. 2 years after Tommy, Fanny was taken from her loving family birthing a second son, who was stillborn.

Another branch of the Bennet family, cousins to the Longbourn Bennets, are titled, the Earl and Countess of Holder, who live in Staffordshire with their 5 children. The two families are extremely close and after Fanny dies Bennet's cousins, at his request, keep and raise Tommy. In his grief Thomas Bennet doesn't think he can raise a 2-year-old at the same time as his two daughters. He also feels Tommy needs a mother figure in his life.

Martha Bingley is the widow of an honourable tradesman, Mr. Arthur Bingley, who had died of a heart attack. Bingley senior was a minor partner of Edward Gardiner in Gardiner and Associates. They had three children, Charles, Louisa, and Caroline. Unlike canon, the Bingleys are not very wealthy, and the girls have small dowries of £2,000 each.

Bennet is introduced to Martha at his brother-in-law's house. The Bingleys live in a leased house a few houses down from the Gardiners on Gracechurch street. Martha has always dreamed of climbing up the social ladder, raising her family above their roots in trade, so she compromises Bennet as he is a landed gentleman with an estate. Being an honourable man, and against advice of friends and family, he marries her.

Our 'prince' in the story is of course none other than His Grace Fitzwilliam Darcy, Duke of Derbyshire, Earl of Lambton. Like canon his parents have already passed away. Dear old Lady Catherine de Bourgh will do anything to make her sickly daughter with a nasty disposition a Duchess. At some point the Duke purchases Netherfield to be closer to London so his sister, Lady Georgiana, will have her preferred music master close by. Bennet never reveals the existence of his son or his relations, who are peers of the realm, to his new wife, who he dislikes intensely. The neighbours, none of whom like the new Mrs. Bennet or her children, keep the Bennet's secrets without question. Bennet allows his new wife to believe the entail on Longbourn is away from female line giving her the impression that on his death, she and her three spawn will be evicted from the estate by a distant unnamed cousin.

Sometime after sending Jane to live with his cousins, for reasons that will be revealed in the story, with Lizzy refusing to leave her father's side, Bennet has an accident which kills him. When no heir presents himself to throw her and her children, still at Longbourn, into the hedgerows, the stepmother feels more secure at the estate.

Several the usual suspects are present as well as some other characters. This is a story of hope and survival and the eventual triumph of good over evil.

Made in the USA
Monee, IL
16 June 2023

36000837R00171